More than three centuries after the Cataclysm, Krynn still bears scars from the wrath of the angry gods. In this land where fear prevails, magic is as mysterious and mighty as the legendary dragons. The Defenders of Magic trilogy is the story of powerful mages who daily defend their beloved Art against those who would corrupt it or see it abolished.

Bram—The new lord of Thonvil discovers that one of his parents is not his blood relative. His newfound magical heritage may be all that can stand against Lyim Rhistadt's obsession to destroy magic.

Kirah—Guerrand DiThon's sister has helped to restore Thonvil's prosperity, but she has never lost her longing for Lyim Rhistadt.

Lyim—The renegade mage is possessed by an ambition to destroy the magic he feels has betrayed him. Now he possesses an artifact that promises to bring that destruction about.

Saga

DEFENDERS
OF MAGIC

Night of the Eye
Volume One

The Medusa Plague
Volume Two

The Seventh Sentinel
Volume Three

DRAGONLANCE books by Mary Kirchoff

Kendermore

Flint, the King
(with Douglas Niles)

Wanderlust
(with Steve Winter)

The Black Wing

Saga

**Defenders of Magic
Volume Three**

The Seventh
Sentinel

Mary Kirchoff

DRAGONLANCE® Saga
Defenders of Magic
Volume Three

THE SEVENTH SENTINEL

Random House and its affiliate companies have worldwide distribution rights in the book trade for English language products of TSR, Inc.

Distributed to the book and hobby trade in the United Kingdom by TSR Ltd.

Distributed to the toy and hobby trade by regional distributors.

Cover art by Larry Elmore. Interior art by Valerie Valusek.

DRAGONLANCE is a registered trademark owned by TSR, Inc. The TSR logo is a trademark owned by TSR, Inc.

First Printing: August 1995
Printed in the United States of America.
Library of Congress Catalog Card Number: 94-68146

9 8 7 6 5 4 3 2 1

ISBN: 0-7869-0117-9

TSR, Inc.
201 Sheridan Springs Road
Lake Geneva, WI 53147
U.S.A.

TSR Ltd.
120 Church End, Cherry Hinton
Cambridge CB1 3LB
United Kingdom

**To Hayden and Alexander,
the two greatest kids this side of Krynn**

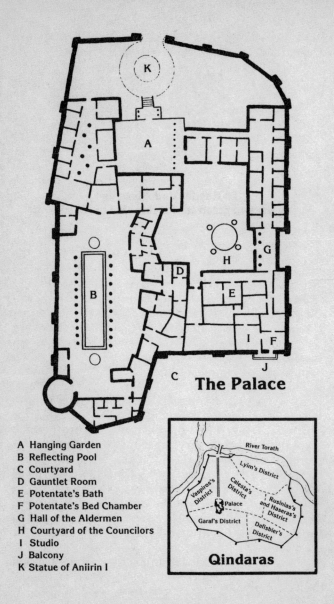

The Palace

A Hanging Garden
B Reflecting Pool
C Courtyard
D Gauntlet Room
E Potentate's Bath
F Potentate's Bed Chamber
G Hall of the Aldermen
H Courtyard of the Councilors
I Studio
J Balcony
K Statue of Aniirin I

Qindaras

River Torath
Lyim's District
Calesta's District
Vaspiros's District
Rusinias's and Haseras's District
Palace
Garaf's District
Dafsbier's District

Prologue

Bram's hand trembled as he held the burning torch to the kindling beneath his father's body. Custom dictated that the son who would inherit the dead man's estate light the pyre. He licked the sweat from his upper lip when the fire from the oil-soaked straw leaped to the dry timber. A gust of wind caught the small flame and sent sparks skyward with a loud crackle, forcing Bram back. With the back of his forearm, he shielded his eyes from the growing heat and the sight.

Cormac DiThon had died of a sudden heart attack six days before. A serving wench had found him slumped over his porridge. Now, the old cavalier's body, wrapped in his heavy military cloak, his shield laid across his barrel-shaped breast, was engulfed in yellow flames that jumped above a vivid sunset. Through the haze of smoke, Bram's mind escaped to the detached thought that the red sky boded well for the morrow.

When the old shaman began chanting, Bram snapped

back to the enormous fire that was consuming his father's body. The shaman recited the Ceremony to the Sky from an ancient scroll:

"Flame of life becomes flames of death;
Ashes of man and oak and pine
Mingle and soar in the painless night;
Follow the sun and find thy peace."

The old Ergothian custom of burning the dead instead of interring them had not been invoked around Thonvil for centuries, not since the Cataclysm had split Ergoth into two island nations. If the task was unsettling to Bram, it intrigued the small crowd of curious villagers. Even fewer of Cormac DiThon's subjects would have attended a typical serge-draped wake. Bram suspected his father had specified the unusual arrangements for just that reason. Cormac may have lost his wits, but never his pride in his full-blooded Ergothian heritage, nor his standing as a cavalier. His subjects' last thoughts of Lord Cormac DiThon would not be of his ineptitude and inebriation. They would remember that he went in a blaze of glory, a flash of fire in the night sky, as the ancient cavaliers had done.

Every aspect of the pyre was dictated by old Ergothian custom, remembered by few. In fact, a search of the whole fiefdom had turned up only one wise, long-lived elf who could still perform the ritual for the dead, established by the first barbarian tribes who settled the nation of Ergoth. The building of the pyre had begun two days before the Ceremony to the Sky. Only dried vallenwood was used, to symbolize the cavalier's stature. The old elf had instructed two of Bram's best workmen to layer the wood in alternating directions to a height of seventeen hands, upon which Cormac's body had been placed.

Watching through eyes stung by smoke, Bram recalled his mother's reaction to Cormac's wishes.

"It's barbaric!" Rietta DiThon had shrieked when Cormac's will had been read. "Even in death he spites me!"

"I doubt Father was thinking about you when he formalized his wishes," Bram had said, foolishly thinking to calm her.

"That's just my point!" She gave her son a look that would have withered the quills off a porcupine. "I'm the one who'll suffer the stares and pointed fingers of his thoughtless folly. I'll certainly not condone it by attending. Old Ergothian tradition, indeed. It's as delusional as the notion that cavaliers are the equivalent of true Knights of Solamnia. But then, Cormac was never anything but a peasant in his heart."

Bram had never appreciated or understood his mother's idea of propriety. Bram's sister had been notified in distant Solamnia of their father's death. Honora had dispatched the messenger with a hastily scrawled note, conveying the proper amount of sympathy but declining to attend. Though Rietta had been insulted, Honora's absence suited Bram just fine. His sister had too many of their mother's bad traits and not enough good ones to make her presence worth suffering.

Stiff-legged and dry-eyed, Bram stood alone by his father's pyre until dawn, long after the curious had lost interest. By then the flames had turned to glowing coals and the last ashes of Lord Cormac DiThon had flown into the purple sky of morning.

Though his heart wasn't in it, Bram walked alone to Castle DiThon and the joyous ceremony that awaited him.

Chapter One

Succession. The ceremony was about him, but not for him. It was a formality as far as he was concerned. Bram had been the lord of Castle DiThon in all but name for more than three years—ever since he'd accepted King Weador's challenge to restore Thonvil. He'd not accomplished that goal alone, though. Weador's faerie folk, the tuatha dundarael, had played a significant role in bringing prosperity and trade back to the region.

Trade needed roads that were reliable and safe, built and patrolled by able-bodied workers. Those workers needed food and clothing, but they couldn't work the land and spin the cloth while hauling stone to surface a road, even with magical help from Bram's uncle, Guerrand. That's where the tuatha came in.

Those diminutive folks' affinity for the land and for all living things amazed Bram. He believed they could coax crops to grow out of gravel, if they were inclined to. Their reward seemed to be nothing more than the hope that followed on the heels of prosperity.

Bram and Guerrand had agreed with Weador that it was wisest to keep the tuatha's presence in the village a secret. Though the villagers who'd benefitted from Guerrand's gifts had a new appreciation for magic, most humans were not open-minded enough to coexist with faerie folk, which suited the typically aloof tuatha just fine. Weador's legions worked under cover of darkness, tilling the ground and tending the crops. Because of them, Thonvil's fields were more productive, the livestock contented; everything flourished beyond reasonable expectations. Yet the tuatha's influence was so subtle, few of the townsfolk even suspected they were receiving special help from the faerie world.

But no one could miss the changes that had occurred in Thonvil. Surplus crops and new roads meant trade, and with the traders came craftsmen. Laws and peacekeepers were needed. The village established a central warehouse for grain in case of lean times. New homes were being constructed at the rate of three a week. Old homes had been repaired, gardens neatened. Even the castle was under renovation after years of neglect.

Bram believed that only a portion of the new prosperity could be credited to the tuatha. The faeries tended gardens and animals; they never touched brick or mortar, shingle or shutter. Most of the repair and construction had been done by the people of Thonvil themselves. They had regained their will to succeed and prosper, thanks to the tuatha's toils and Bram's leadership.

And Guerrand's magical guidance. Magic-wielder, spiritual advisor, Rand had been indispensable to Bram in his efforts to revive Thonvil's economy. Bram's initial exposure to magic had been witnessing his uncle's battles against a deranged wizard and his struggle to eradicate a deadly, magical affliction. The experience left him with tremendous respect for the power of sorcery, but the false impression that it had little practical application to the world of normal men and women. In the years since, Rand had demonstrated countless times that his magic could be applied to almost any problem.

Bram left most of the day-to-day particulars of running the estate to Kirah and Guerrand. In fact, Bram had relied on his uncle to find reasons to cancel his mother's less practical arrangements for the morning ceremony.

Bram blinked. Scores of people were waiting just for him. The realization hastened his steps as he crossed the inner courtyard, scarcely noticing the stands and banners there for the occasion. Bram pressed, unrecognized, through the unfamiliar throng of retainers and servants milling in the small foretower.

Rand's was the first familiar face he saw when he thrust himself into the entrance hall. Free from the prejudice once suffered in Castle DiThon, Guerrand wore his red mage's robe with ease. Today his garb was edged in gold in honor of the occasion of Bram's succession. Reassured by Rand's presence, Bram smiled for the first time in many days and crossed over to his uncle.

To Bram's surprise, concern pulled at the lines around Guerrand's eyes. "Are you well?" he asked, peering closely at his nephew. "I was worried when you didn't return last night."

Bram straightened his clothing self-consciously. "I'm fine, considering I just burned my father's body."

Guerrand frowned darkly. "I wish you had not forbidden Kirah and me to attend the funeral with you."

"There was no love lost between you two and my father. It would have been dishonest for you to feign grief, no different than those who gathered from the village out of curiosity."

"You know that's far from true," Guerrand said, eyes flashing hurt. "We would have grieved for you, with you."

"I needed to grieve alone." Bram's shoulders slumped. "Now it's done."

Guerrand said nothing, but laid a reassuring hand on his nephew's tight shoulder. Just then a serving woman rushed by with arms overflowing, jostling both men. In the woman's wake came Kirah, Bram's aunt, blowing back wisps of hair from her face.

"There you are!" she breathed. "We were getting worried about you, Bram."

No one could ever have guessed the horrors his aunt had bested just three short years before, when a plague had struck Thonvil. Kirah had suffered more than most, since she'd thought the villain who had inflicted the virus to be her friend. Snakes had once writhed where there were now shapely arms and legs. Her survival was only partly due to her stubborn streak. Kirah, as well as the other afflicted villagers, owed her life to Guerrand, who had discovered that the plague could be stopped by using his magic to turn the black moon, Nuitari, on its side.

With no lessening of her scrappy temperament, Kirah had grown since then into the mirror image of her mother, Zena, Bram's vaguely remembered step-grandmother. With her shining corn-silk-yellow hair, vivid blue eyes, and skin as pale and smooth as milk, Kirah glowed against the backdrop of tanned farmers and dark-skinned, full-blooded Northern Ergothians. She had taken on the office of seneschal rather than marry, as she had yet to meet a man worth the effort.

With an odd mix of sympathy and disapproval, her eyes ran over Bram's mourning togs. "Hadn't you better get dressed for the ceremony?" she asked. "I hear Mercadior arrived within the half-hour and is anxious to perform the ceremony so that he can return to Gwynned immediately."

"Yes," Rand cut in. "I nearly forgot! His chief counselor, a wizard I might add, was looking for you. When he couldn't find you, he informed me that the emperor

7

desires you to accompany him on a brief tour of Thonvil before he returns to Gwynned."

Bram rubbed his face wearily. "I can't fathom why my mother chose this opportunity to act the lady of the manor and request the presence of the emperor of Northern Ergoth. What's more, why would Mercadior Redic bother to attend a ceremony in such a minor holding?"

"Thonvil is no longer a minor holding, Bram," returned Kirah, arms crossed mannishly. "I'm certain the courtiers in Gwynned have wasted no time in apprising the emperor of that. He very likely wished to assess Thonvil and its new lord for himself."

"Whatever the reason for his presence, Mercadior's opinion of you won't be high if you keep the ruler of all Northern Ergoth waiting." Guerrand spun Bram around and pushed him toward the staircase that led to his chamber. "I'll send up Delby, the young squire, to help you."

With the manservant's aide, Bram dressed in his father's heavy, enameled breastplate. He refused the rest of the armor as it was offered by Delby, caring little how shocked the boy or anyone else might be by this departure from local tradition. Bram might be lord, but he was no cavalier; on him the armor was strictly ornamental. Even his father had worn it only once in Bram's memory. It was bulky and uncomfortable, especially for Bram, who had never trained much in arms, despite his mother's wish that he become a Knight of Solamnia. Fortunately for him, there had never been enough money for the training.

Bram returned to the entrance hall, thankfully empty now, in time to hear the swell of trumpets through the enormous double doorway. He moved through it on stiff legs and stopped just inside the inner courtyard. Past the hundreds of assembled guests, he could just make out the platform upon which he would officially become Lord DiThon.

Perhaps it isn't such a bad thing to have the emperor here, he thought. In addition to diverting unwanted attention from himself, the emperor's presence was a proud occasion, a formal recognition of the hard work that had gone into restoring Thonvil. The people deserved their moment in the sun.

And sun they would have. Though early, the sky was as bright blue and clear as the previous evening's red sunset had promised. Even his mother could not have hoped for better when she'd set the event outside. Because Bram cared nothing about pomp, he had allowed his mother to stage the event, heavily monitored by Guerrand.

Bram spotted Rietta seated on the raised platform at the far end of the courtyard. Even in a smile meant to encourage him, her thin lips were pinched, her arms crossed tightly over her small bosom.

Bram took a deep breath, walked through the parting crowd, and ascended the platform. His last thought before he became lord was that the breeze still carried the acrid scent of burning wood from the funeral pyre.

* * * * *

"I'm sorry to take you away from your feast," Mercadior declared, "but I've heard so much good about Thonvil during your stewardship. I desire greatly to see these things for myself."

Bram and Guerrand, responding to a request from Redic, had quietly excused themselves from the feasting that followed Bram's public oath of fealty to the emperor. Sounds of celebration drifted down from the castle to the dusty road at the edge of Thonvil. There, the newly installed Lord DiThon and his uncle met the hale emperor and an elderly but robust man who, judging from his red robe, was a wizard.

Redic had the naturally dark skin of an Ergothian blue blood. He was the fifth in a line of rulers stretching back to well before the Cataclysm, to the establishment of Ergoth as a nation. Beneath his gem-studded circlet, Redic's salt-and-pepper hair was cropped short at the nape of his neck, where a whisper-thin braid trailed down to his thick waist. His beard and mustache were full, surrounding perfect white teeth that flashed infrequently in a calculated smile.

Though once a cavalier of mighty repute, Mercadior's ascendance to the throne had put an abrupt end to that career. He was considered a good and just ruler by everyone Bram respected. The emperor was thick through the chest, shaped like a barrel, though nothing about him suggested a sedentary man's softness. His clothing was finely made, but of a simple pattern little different from what any commoner might wear: a long, dark red tunic, heavily embroidered with geometric patterns and heroic scenes, gathered at the waist by a sword belt stiffened with silver plates. Beneath were leggings wrapped with white leather and soft leather boots. Still, some undefinable quality about his bearing brought to mind words like "impressive," "composed," "commanding," "distinguished."

Bram's uncle found his voice first. "Guerrand DiThon, your humble servant," he said by way of introduction. "I am Lord DiThon's uncle, chief advisor, and wizard."

The emperor looked with great interest at Guerrand and granted him that uncommonly white-toothed smile. "We had heard that a mage of great ability was at work here restoring the holding."

"Did you study at the great guild hall in Gwynned?" asked Thalmus, the emperor's wizard.

Guerrand shook his head. "It was my desire to attend, having heard of its great reputation. But . . . *circumstances* did not allow me to seek application there. I was self-taught, until I traveled to the Tower of High Sorcery at Wayreth. There, I was fortunate that my skills were sufficient to catch the eye of the Master of the Red

Robes, Justarius, who took me as his apprentice."

Mercadior glanced back at the quiet, red-robed man who stood behind him. The wizard's eyes were wide with approval. "You must visit us in Gwynned, then. Thalmus would happily give you a tour."

Guerrand bobbed his head respectfully. "I would enjoy that, sire."

"Let us walk," Redic commanded, leading the way through the newly enlarged village gates. "Never could understand the trend since the Cataclysm to distrust the Art," the emperor remarked. "Such a useful skill, magic. I see it playing a significant role in rebuilding the glory of Northern Ergoth."

Emperor Mercadior Redic's life-goal was well known to most educated citizens of the island nation, who had learned the history of their people while in knee pants.

More than two thousand years before, a mighty chieftain named Ackal Ergot, Redic's ancestor, had united the tribes of Khalkist barbarians and founded the first nation of humans. He called it Ergoth. Ruled by sword and flame, Ergoth quickly became a dominant nation, with Ackal Ergot's primary goal expansion through war. But his heir, Ackal Dermount, had found war unprofitable. Dermount brought Ergoth into the mercantile age. He set aside Ergoth's swords and began trade with the Silvanesti elves and the dwarves of Thorbardin. For nearly six centuries, Ergoth was a vast and grand kingdom, the center of the civilized world.

But peace did not last, as always was the way between humans, elves, and dwarves. The worst of these battles was the Kinslayer War, which scarred the land for forty years. The war irreparably weakened Ergoth's dominance. Two thousand years passed, and still Ergoth did not recover. Then the Cataclysm struck, splitting Ergoth into two islands.

The great man paused, seemingly to study the wattle and daub houses that lined the road nearby. "Let it be understood it is my goal, my only goal, for our island nation to regain the former glory of Ergoth. I expect all my subjects to contribute to that end. For instance, our coffers are ever emptied by the need for castles, new ships, and strong armies. At the same time, there are many ruins of the former empire both on land and beneath the seas. I pay men to excavate these ruins and regain their riches, both in gold and knowledge, thereby helping to refill those coffers.

"What's more, in exchange for a state-sponsored education, mages who study at the great guild hall and pass the Test must return to us for a period of five years to research new magical arts.

"I'm pursuing diplomatic ties with the elves of Qualinesti, hoping to reestablish trade routes that would be beneficial to both nations."

Mercadior stopped speaking abruptly and began to walk. Then, just as abruptly, he continued: "Many believe Ergoth will never see a return to greatness. They would not say so if they could see what you have accomplished here in Thonvil—with the aid of magic."

"I have played but a small part," Guerrand interjected humbly. "The credit goes entirely to my nephew and his ability to inspire his people."

"The state of your village testifies to a miraculous recovery," observed the emperor. "Everywhere I look I see new houses, bountiful gardens, barns and stables filled with livestock. The surrounding fields are green and lush. My advisors had predicted a steady decline in this region, a failure of crop and citizenry."

Turning to Bram, he declared, "I have heard great things about you, young DiThon. I have also heard that a veritable army of faeries have aided you in the revitalization of the region."

"Is that so?" Startled by the abrupt revelation, Bram struggled to keep his face clear of any expression that might betray him.

"You realize, of course," Redic continued, "how useful such a force could be in our crusade to restore Ergoth to its former glory."

"I can see why you would think so, Sire," Bram said softly.

"One cannot help but ponder how far the servant who commanded such a skill would rise in my court, particularly a servant of the old Ergothian stock." The corners of Redic's bright eyes crinkled as he regarded the native dark skin and sharp angles of Bram's young face. "I am no bigot— I would take ability over blue blood on the worst of days—but I am always pleased when both reside in one body."

Mercadior scanned east, his keen eyes obviously noticing the thin trails of smoke streaming skyward from the funeral pyre. "I hear you cremated your father according to the ancient custom."

Bram colored, but he maintained his composure and dignity. "Yes, Sire. My father asked that his remains be treated in the manner of his grandfathers, and their fathers before them. I simply respected his wishes."

Redic nodded solemnly. "I confess, I had not heard the most favorable reports of Cormac DiThon. But it took great courage for him to break with recent fashion, and an even greater strength for you to comply. I don't know why we departed from the traditional pyre. All that black serge and weeping over a decaying body for days—what an ignominious departure. Far more impressive, I think, to go out in a blaze of glory." Redic turned to his wizard and flicked a ringed finger. "Make a note of that, Thalmus."

Mercadior sighed contentedly. "Ah, well, it is long past time for me to return to Gwynned, and for you to rejoin your citizens in celebration. I enjoyed the walk and the conversation. Bear my words in mind."

"I will," Bram vowed.

"Fare-thee-well, young DiThon. I will be looking forward to continued good reports of your progress."

Mercadior turned to Thalmus. "Let us return

straightaway to the palace. Important matters await."
Clearly the wizard had expected this request, for he
opened his palm to reveal a glass bead. With no ceremony whatsoever he hurled it to the ground between
himself and Redic. As the bead shattered, a vapor twined
out of it and seemed to devour the two men from the
floor upward. In only a moment they were gone.

Bram brushed off the dirt raised by the emperor's
magical departure and looked to the hill where the
pyre still smoldered. "Overall, I'd say it's been a full
day, wouldn't you?" he remarked with biting irony.
"Where do you suppose Redic got his information
about the tuatha?"

Guerrand shrugged. "Who knows? Redic's a smart
man. Perhaps he found the changes so remarkable, he
assumed magic was involved. With or without suspicions, he could have had Thalmus perform a divina-
tion to confirm it. The tuatha are masters of subtlety,
but even they can't hide their magical aura from a
determined searcher who has mastered the Art."

"I didn't like evading his pointed remarks," Bram
confessed sourly.

"Even if you did admit to their presence here, you
couldn't promise their aid to the emperor. It's not yours
to give. My guess is that Redic knows more than he let
on. He was merely trolling for confirmation, hoping he
had stumbled upon some new magical tool."

"So did I fail some loyalty test?"

Rand smiled without humor. "Not yet."

Bram pushed himself away from the fence where he
was leaning. "That's a problem for tomorrow. Right
now, I should join the citizens celebrating back at the
castle. They must be wondering where I am." Bram
took a listless step toward Castle DiThon. "Coming?"

Guerrand's hand on Bram's arm stayed him. "Yes,
but first I need to speak with you about something."

Bram looked back anxiously at his uncle. "Can't it
wait?"

"It could," conceded Guerrand, "but I think it's already waited too long." He waved his nephew back through the gates of the village. "Share a drink and a seat with me while we talk."

Bram's eyebrows raised. "I need to sit to hear this?" Still, he followed Guerrand past the bakery, into the tavern known as the Red Goose. "What you have to say must be very important—or very long-winded."

Rand led him to a hard-benched booth facing the street. "It may be the most important thing you'll ever hear." The mage signaled to the barkeep to bring two glasses and a pitcher. Guerrand wiped the dust from the mugs on his crimson robes, then filled both to the brim. Bram watched his uncle warily as Guerrand tossed back half a mug before handing the full one to him.

"To your father," Guerrand added hastily, seeing the look of surprise on Bram's face.

"To your brother," Bram replied. The new Lord DiThon took an obligatory sip of the strong, bitter drink and waited.

Guerrand regarded Bram over steepled fingers. "I have envisioned having this conversation many times, but my thoughts always stopped short of the words I would use. I had hoped, even until Cormac's death, that he would have saved me from this."

Bram shook his head. "What has my father to do with this?"

"Everything. Or perhaps nothing." It was Guerrand's turn to shake his head, irritated at himself. "I will tell you the story exactly as it was told to me." Guerrand took another small sip from the mug. "Three years ago, when Wilor the silversmith lay dying, he confessed something to me, something that has remained at the forefront of my mind ever since.

"Wilor told me, with great conviction, that my father and mother—your grandfather and step-grandmother— believed you to be a changeling."

15

Bram blinked. "A what?"

"A changeling. Descended from the tuatha, to be specific."

"I know what a changeling is!" snapped Bram. He closed his eyes to gather his thoughts and calm his tone. "What I meant was, what would a silversmith know of such things, particularly about me?"

"Despite class differences," Rand said, "Wilor was a long-time friend to the family. He recalled to me the night Rejik met him at this very inn. Apparently your grandfather arrived all sweaty-faced and edgy. After many tankards of ale, Rejik confessed to Wilor that he feared his grandson—you—were a changeling."

Bram swung away restlessly. "But what would make him think that?"

"My mother," Guerrand said levelly. "Apparently, she was very magically inclined. Rejik believed she was never wrong when it came to perceiving the magic in another."

"Let me get this right. You're asking me to believe the ravings of a pain-racked, dying man and your mother, whom many considered to be a bit *unusual* herself?"

"That was a slight worthy of your father," Guerrand said evenly. "I know you don't mean it. When you have a moment to consider this seriously, you'll recall that you yourself said you feel somehow magical. Have you never wondered why the tuatha approached you, but never Cormac? Why they thought you of high moral character?"

Bram met his uncle's gaze briefly, then looked away. He stood with his mug of ale, paced, drank, then peered out the window before pouring himself another mug with shaky hands. "Who else suspected this?" he asked at length.

"Rejik never said so, but Wilor believes that either Rejik told Cormac, or that Cormac guessed. Wilor thought it explained why your father kept a distance from you."

Bram was unable to deny the truth of that painful observation. "But why didn't my own father tell me if he thought it were possible?"

"Perhaps he believed he'd risk the wrath of the tuatha by exposing their deception. Or maybe he was afraid it would make it true if he said it aloud."

"Is it physically possible?" Bram asked, seeming to consider it for the first time.

"I think so, yes," conceded Rand. "From my readings I've discovered that changelings can be part human or entirely faerie, substituted for a human child at birth. I wouldn't suspect the latter, however, considering your human appearance."

Bram's eyes went wide. "You really believe it, don't you?"

"Having worked at your side for more than three years, I've had ample opportunity to observe you. I have consulted every written document I could find about changelings." Guerrand folded his hands in his lap. "To be honest, you exhibit enough of the outward signs of changelings for it to be possible."

Bram let out his breath, unaware that he'd been holding it during his uncle's answer. He reeled from the revelation. "All that time you were watching me—why didn't *you* tell me of your suspicions?"

Rand's eyes were downcast. "I felt that it was Cormac's responsibility—and his right. I was bitterly disappointed that he let the opportunity pass with him, but I was not very surprised."

Bram's mind jumped back to his last conversation with his father. Candles had just been lit in Cormac's bedchamber. The smell of the evening meal still filled the room, although once again the full tray had been sent away untouched. Bram had been seated, watching Cormac's still form in the huge bed and listening to his muttering. The new lord's heart skipped when he recalled one sentence that Cormac had spoken clearly: "I always loved you as my son." Bram had taken such heart from the words. It was the first time his father had ever expressed fondness for him. Now the words had a different meaning.

"I tell you all this now for a reason, Bram. If it's true, you may have inherited the aptitude for magic that you've always admired in others. You owe it to yourself to explore the possibility."

"I won't discount it outright," Bram conceded, "but it would mean that everything I ever believed myself to be is no longer true."

"I think we're getting ahead of ourselves," Rand cautioned. "First you need to verify your heritage. And there's only one being from whom we can request that answer."

"King Weador," lord and mage said in unison.

Chapter Two

Lyim rubbed his hands together in joyful anticipation of his favorite duty: tax collection. Today was Montigar, the third day of the week and traditional tax day. In addition to counting profits, it gave Lyim the opportunity to assess the mood of the citizens in his district. Did they still have that right combination of fear and adoration that made them loyal to the death? They were like infants who needed constant tending. But he would need them, the whole of this city in the desolate Plains of Dust, if he hoped to achieve his ultimate goal: the destruction of magic.

But first he had to stay alive. The amir strapped a broad-bladed punch dagger to the inside of his thigh. The weapon was unnoticeable under his baggy brown trousers, gathered at the ankle in the style favored in this city of thieves and cutthroats. Over his bone-white tunic, the short woolen jacket matched his trousers and announced him as a citizen of the highest rank, an amir of Qindaras. He had risen to the position quickly through hard work and determination.

After three years, he thought of the largest city in the Plains of Dust as the only real home he'd ever known. His decision to return to the lands of his childhood had nothing to do with sentiment, everything to do with survival.

As he waited to leave the town house, Lyim considered the events in his life, the tragedies that always harbingered triumphs. Coincidences? Lyim didn't think so. The gods seemed to strike him down, only to provide him with the means to raise himself again. He knew now it was no accident he'd been drawn into the plots of his master, Belize, who sought to gain ultimate power by opening a gate to the Lost Citadel. Belize's scheme had been thwarted by Guerrand DiThon, but not before Belize had crippled Lyim by thrusting his arm through an imperfectly formed gate between dimensions. In that brief moment of exposure, a nightmarish, snakelike creature from that other world had fused itself to Lyim's arm, depriving him of his right hand and turning him into a monster. The greatest mages of the Orders of Magic had been unable to free Lyim from the entity that had attached itself to him, or to restore his hand.

That regeneration became an obsession with Lyim. For a decade, he had researched every aspect of interplanar transit, spiritual and physical possession, biological rejuvenation, and other teachings too blasphemous to admit even now. His research eventually led him to the answer that ultimately restored his hand.

It also provided him with a solution to his current problem as a renegade mage. When Lyim had escaped the wreckage of Bastion, he'd returned to Palanthas, the city of mages, not knowing where else to go. Casting about for a secluded place to relocate, a historical note he'd previously turned up in the city's famed library came to mind.

More than three centuries before, in the years prior

to the Cataclysm, a powerful wizard named Aniirin had ruled a city in the Plains of Dust. This city, Qindaras, was situated at a fork in the river Torath, the main artery of commerce and travel through that desolate region. Somehow Aniirin and the Council of Three came into conflict, though the texts available to Lyim did not specify the nature of the dispute. Through an accident of good timing, Aniirin was able to hold the Council, distracted by events elsewhere, at bay.

The dispute had arisen just as the Kingpriest of Istar commenced his systematic persecution of the Orders of Magic. The Council, wanting to devote all their attention to that fateful confrontation, had opted to sign a treaty with Qindaras, at worst a minor irritation. In it they stipulated that the Council of Three would not interfere in any way with the internal workings or citizens of the city, provided that Aniirin and his successors did not try to extend their influence or affect matters beyond the immediate area.

Lyim had found the discovery interesting initially, but its recollection was potentially lifesaving. There was a place on Ansalon where a renegade mage could be safe—safe to plot the downfall of the magic he felt had betrayed him.

Lyim had already decided that the spell he cast to escape from Bastion would be his last. His final conversation with Guerrand DiThon had made him see his life clearly for the first time. It was not the canvas Lyim had intended to paint.

He'd always prided himself on the way he controlled his life. But Guerrand had forced him to see that he'd only been magic's pawn. Magic had its rules, and Lyim had been compelled to abide by them. Every waking moment had been spent learning the Art, acquiring it, trying to bend the forces of magic to his will.

Now he knew that the Art had conquered his mind, obsessed him like drink or the weed many degenerate elves in the theater district smoked. Spellcasting was not a skill, but a living, breathing creature that drained the life from any mortal fool enough to think himself its master.

Lyim had left for Qindaras that very day, taking nothing with him from his former life. He vowed never to wear a robe of any color again, lest it remind him of his days as a wielder of magic. No one would mistake him for a mage today. His amir's attire was nothing like his old garb.

"Assume standard positions," Lyim barked to his contingent of bodyguards.

Rofer and Lorenz, two burly humans who had proven themselves to be loyal, hustled into place to Lyim's right, one ahead and one behind. Four equally large gnolls took up parallel positions, forming a rectangle around the amir.

The gnolls resembled human-shaped hyenas and possessed the scruffy, vicious look typical of their race. Lyim didn't know their names. He found them difficult to tell apart under the best of circumstances and probably could not have pronounced the abominated syllables of their language anyway. Though intelligent enough to be trained, gnolls were too uncivilized to reside within the city. Lyim had recruited a handful of them from the small, barbaric clans that lived as nomads in the Plains of Dust. Their fierce appearance and evil reputation was enough to keep most people in line. When it wasn't enough, the brutes were always willing to live up to the stories told about them.

Lyim didn't need the bodyguards to protect him from the citizenry. The clumsy assassins sent, with the regularity of seasons turning, by the Council of Three made them necessary. Lyim hadn't been surprised when the first arrived; he was still considered a renegade by the Council for his presence at Bastion and entrance into the Lost Citadel. He was an outlaw to the magical society, a criminal and pariah to be hunted and killed. Neither was he surprised that the Council proved ignorant of the treaty drawn before their time. He would make them aware of it in due course, when he held a position of sufficient power to invoke its protective clauses. Until then, he had taken adequate precautions to fend off the Council's attacks.

Lyim snickered now, recalling their attempts to kill him. If they thought he was a threat before, he couldn't wait to see them reduced to less-than-ordinary mortals without their beloved magic. Then everyone would recognize the worthlessness of magical power.

Lyim was anxious to be off on his tax rounds, but he had learned patience. And stealth. And a whole host of survival techniques since the day he had emerged from the Lost Citadel with his hand intact. Looking for his assistant, Salimshad, Lyim's glance moved past his bodyguards to the black- and white-tiled foyer of the borrowed town house he would stay at through tonight. Lyim never resided in any one place for more than two days. Tomorrow the owner and his family would return from the streets, or wherever they had found shelter. It was Salim's job to secure the houses and displace the owners. Lyim gave no thought to them.

Where *was* Salimshad? Lyim looked to the door again. He was loathe to leave without his wily elf assistant to log the taxes. Salim had left the town house just after breakfast, headed for the potentate's palace to deliver last week's taxes to the royal treasurer— another of the day's traditional events. It was not like the elf to keep his master waiting.

Still, if Lyim didn't get on with the collection, he would be late for the least tolerable of the day's events: the afternoon soiree with Potentate Aniirin III and his amirs. He couldn't afford to offend Aniirin, which meant he couldn't wait for Salim. The elf would pay; he was just fortunate Lyim still had use for him.

Lyim peered between two guards to check himself in an oval of polished metal by the door. Gone was his trademark flamboyant clothing, in favor of the subtle amir attire. His once long, dark tresses were shaved weekly to shadowy stubble. His face was still smooth and unlined, which he ascribed to the fact that he no longer drank stimulants of any sort.

Satisfied, Lyim slipped his head through the strap of his cash pouch and signaled his retinue of guards to depart. "And this time," he admonished them, "exercise some restraint. I will not tolerate a repeat of last week's incident. No one is to be killed unless I order it."

"Yes, Amir!" Rofer and Lorenz swore in unison.

The gnolls bared their fangs and nodded. Lyim motioned to the door. Surrounded by his paid protectors, he walked into the side street beyond. Outside, they were joined by six more armed humans, who fell into step behind the others.

The thoroughfare was a small alley, just a single cart's width. The intersection at one end sported a recently restored public fountain. The crossing at the other end was home to a farmers market where conscientious shopkeepers, fearful of their amir's displeasure and his thugs' correction, swept the frontages twice daily.

Lyim had done much to improve the quality of life in the district. Chamber pots were no longer emptied from upper windows into the streets, at least not without severe fines. Neighborhoods were organized to fight fires and control crime.

When Lyim arrived in Qindaras three years past, the merchant district had been a den of corruption. The previous amir had taxed legitimate businesses so heavily that they could scarcely operate. Amir Bagus had encouraged gambling and prostitution, among other vices, but still the people of the district starved. When he was stabbed in an alley by a mob of overtaxed citizens, no one mourned—least of all Lyim, whose part in that event had gone far toward establishing his name in the district.

Lyim had nothing against vice, but he recognized

24

that it needed to be conducted in a safe and profitable manner. Among his first acts was to crack down on usury. He then established his own moneylenders to replace the violent mob he'd driven out. He designated vice-free blocks, where the gamblers and prostitutes who provided him with the greatest income could raise their families and where ordinary shops could operate.

In two short years, Lyim had turned his riverfront district from the most decrepit to the most profitable. Only one other district provided the potentate with more coin per week.

Patience, Lyim reminded himself, feeling his irritation at the other amir's success. Before very many more days passed, Rusinias would no longer be an amir and Lyim would have the most profitable district in Qindaras. Without an heir to his title, the potentate would surely recognize Lyim as the logical choice for succession. As basha of Qindaras he would be in a position to remind the Council of Three of the treaty, and he would be safe from their attacks.

Lyim's popularity in his district had been greatly aided by the fact that the current potentate of Qindaras was universally disliked. The direct grandson of the powerful wizard who established the city many centuries before, Aniirin III was the unfortunate result of a policy that forbade marriage outside the family line. All who knew Aniirin thought him decadent, foolish, and easily distracted by simple pleasures. Half of his day was spent in his nightclothes, fiddling with new toys or magical devices.

The rest of the potentate's time was spent deifying his paternal grandfather. Aniirin III was haunted by the image of his dead ancestor. He ascribed achievements to his beloved grandfather that no human could have accomplished. Lyim had been with the potentate when, after several goblets of wine, he'd spoken of his grandfather in the present tense. Lyim sometimes wondered if Aniirin didn't believe his ancestor still lived and was running the city, since he himself did little toward that end himself.

One accomplishment Potentate Aniirin III could have correctly attributed to his ancestors was their devotion to repairing the damage caused to Qindaras by the Cataclysm. Unfortunately, this had been corrupted into an official doctrine denying that a Cataclysm had ever occurred. Only preCataclysmic maps could be found in the city. Kender, whose stock-in-trade was selling obsolete maps, did no greater business than in Qindaras.

One of those top-knotted pilferers crossed Lyim's path as he entered a section of the city overhung by perilous balconies. Clothing draped to dry waved overhead like tired old flags. Scrappy dogs raced along in the gutter, followed by laughing children who called after them.

"Dogs must be leashed in this district!" Lyim shouted.

Even the dogs seemed to slow at the sound of his voice. The children stopped and turned. Spying Lyim, they bowed their heads in fright. "Right away, Amir!" they vowed, then scurried off, dragging their yelping hounds by the ears.

Lyim and his retinue rounded the corner and came to the main thoroughfare, River Avenue. Both sides of the street were lined with all variety of merchants: locksmiths, bakers, potters, cutlers. Between each building was an open stairway to the apartments above and a passage to the first-floor accommodations that lay behind the shops.

Lyim looked to the position of the sun and cursed openly. Damn that elf! There wasn't time to collect from every establishment today; now he would have to return on the morrow to some of the lesser shops. He hated for any of them to keep a single one of his coins for a moment longer than necessary.

Lyim mentally reviewed the shops along the route.

Which one would give him the greatest joy to relieve of its earnings? He sniffed the air, detecting the strong scent of hot sausages; it gave him his answer. Adjusting his tax pouch, Lyim directed the guards to lead the way into a narrow, two-story stucco building with a central belvedere overlooking the wide, colorful avenue.

Lyim frequently made the sausage merchant his first stop. Piepr made the best sausage in Qindaras. His business had done better than most under Lyim's predecessor, though not nearly as well as now. Considering that, Piepr was not obsequious enough to satisfy the new amir. Further, Lyim resented that Piepr's shop had an excellent view; the man had inherited it, not earned it. Lyim's goal was to fleece Piepr of enough money so he'd have to rent out the second story and its vista to someone else.

The air in the shop smelled strongly of garlic and sweat. Piepr stood behind the wooden chopping block that served also as a sales counter. The middle-aged man wore the usual short-sleeved workman's tunic. Two large hairs sprouted from a mole on his chin. He had the whimsical, slightly tired expression of a man who is brighter than his trade requires.

"Tax day again?" Piepr asked calmly. "Or have you come to buy my delicious sausages, Amir?"

Lyim slipped a stringed sausage off its drying rack and nibbled it without paying. "A particularly good batch, Piepr," he said, saluting the man with his half-eaten link.

Piepr bowed his head. He waved a young girl forward from behind the counter. Lyim knew Piepr's daughter, Yasmi. The sausage-maker was teaching the girl, his only child, the trade. Yasmi stepped up to Lyim and knelt as required. Still on her knees, face averted, the girl held a jingling cloth bag high over her head. Lyim took it, loosened the drawstring, and retrieved a handful of steel coins. They reeked of garlic, as did

Yasmi. Lyim nodded his approval of the amount, though his nose wrinkled in distaste at the smell. Yasmi skittered back behind the counter to her father's side.

Without a word, Lyim dropped the sack into his tax pouch. He was turning to leave with his retinue when Piepr's voice stopped him. "With all due respect, Amir, will our taxes be lessening anytime soon?"

"You are not doing well, Piepr?" Lyim asked with perfect pleasantness. "Perhaps you need to raise your prices."

Piepr looked at the sausage in Lyim's hand. "I am selling more sausages than ever, but have no more to show for my efforts."

"Perhaps you should consider renting out your second story to bring in extra income," Lyim suggested.

"I would not need to consider moving my family into the back room," said the sausage-maker, "if I could keep more of what I earn." Piepr looked uncomfortable, then plunged on. "I have spoken to my neighbors, Amir. The percentage of tax they are required to pay is significantly lower than mine." Behind him, the man's daughter gasped at his temerity.

"Your neighbors' businesses are not the same as yours," Lyim said, his tone unexpectedly reasonable. "You have safety hazards that many of them do not. For your tax money, you get excellent protection against fire, vandalism, theft, and harassment." Lighthearted music passed in the street outside the shop, a contrast to the serious conversation.

"Still," Lyim continued, "if you feel you are not getting your money's worth, I can ask a number of my associates—" he looked to his bodyguards "—to stay behind and discuss the matter privately." Lyim smiled.

Piepr bowed his head. "That will not be necessary, Amir. Thank you for your kindness."

"You must feel that you can come to me at any time with these concerns," Lyim said kindly, making a mental note to squeeze all of Piepr's neighbors, guilty and innocent, for having revealed the details of their arrangements. None of them would be so foolishly loose-lipped again.

Lyim nibbled the sausage as he strode down the avenue; passing citizens bowed when they recognized their amir. At smaller shops, Lyim sent two guards inside. After several moments, his guards would return with the requisite money, which Lyim would add to the pouch strapped across his chest. Licking the grease from his fingers, Lyim reflected there was little about tax collection that he didn't enjoy.

He waited outside the bakery, seated on the edge of a gurgling fountain. A sizable crowd had gathered, despite his bodyguards' best efforts. Most were respectful enough, stopping briefly to thank Lyim for the rebirth of the merchant district. Abruptly, a man with spindly arms and a wispy mustache ran up to the guards, begging to speak with the amir, but Lyim's thugs pushed the man back.

Lyim eyed the watching crowd and recognized an opportunity. "Let him speak," he commanded.

The man bowed and dropped to his knees, panting. "Bless you, beloved Amir! I have a modest shop on the eastern edge of your district, a small apothecary," he explained breathlessly.

The location told volumes; the east end included the blocks sanctioned for vice. "Ruffians have been vandalizing my business for months. Today they beat my son in the alley outside our shop!"

The man's business must have been small. Lyim didn't recognize him. "Do you pay your taxes, man?"

"Faithfully, Amir!"

"And your name is?"

"Ovanes."

Cursing Salimshad again for his absence, Lyim stumbled his way through the logbook for the previous week's payments. Sure enough, the man's taxes were up-to-date.

The amir reached into the pouch for a fistful of coins. He held them out to the wide-eyed citizen. "You paid for better protection. Take these coins for the damages you and your son have suffered. Can you identify those responsible?"

"I think so, yes."

"Two of my own guards—" Lyim waved Rofer and one of the gnolls toward the man "—will return with you to your shop. There they'll remain until you are able to point out the ruffians. Affairs can be set right. Rest assured that, henceforth, I will increase patrols in your area."

The man was so grateful he bowed his way out of Lyim's presence—just what the amir had hoped the crowd would witness. Lyim was absorbing the adoring stares and waiting for a duo of his guards to return from the basket-makers when Salimshad pushed his way through the guards clustered around Lyim.

"A little late, aren't you?" The amir fixed the slight elf with a glare.

Lyim and Salimshad had been together two years now. It had taken very little to persuade the elf to work for him: one moldy biscuit and an undisturbed night on the straw-covered stone floor of the room Lyim had first occupied in Qindaras. The Kagonesti elf had been near death from starvation and exposure.

Lyim had first noticed Salimshad in a dim and smoky inn in Qindaras's riverfront district. The slight, beggarly elf would have been indistinguishable to Lyim from the thousand others like him if not for his hand. Or rather, the lack of it.

Lyim noticed physical deformities like other people noted hair color. Savoring a tankard of his favorite purple Shalostian springwater, he spotted the elf working the crowd with a shell game. Salimshad was spinning the cups with lightning dexterity with his single hand. Lyim admired the elf's temerity and chuckled to himself with uncharacteristic good humor when the sharp promptly skunked the other patrons of their coin in a most expert manner. They'd all turned away, disgruntled but none the wiser. Apparently they didn't believe a one-handed man could cheat at the shell game.

Lyim had been in Qindaras for nearly a year on that night. He'd made less progress in that time than he'd hoped toward his short-term goal of securing amirship of the merchant district. It came to him in a flash, when Salimshad's dark, sly face, with its menacing tattoos, caught the firelight. Lyim knew in that instant what he'd overlooked in his efforts to take over the toughest and most beleaguered district in a city of poor districts.

"Well done," he'd called. His voice held a hint of knowing humor that made the elf pause long enough to bob his head in acknowledgment. But Salim did not meet Lyim's eyes or stop his press toward the inn's door.

"Very clever, but I don't imagine you can use the, um, technique, more than once in any district."

The elf stopped in his tracks. He turned his head so that his voice could barely be heard through the deep folds of his hood. "I won the coin fairly."

"I couldn't agree more," Lyim said. He leaned back in the wooden chair and crossed his arms. "I always consider it fair when fools are willingly parted from their money. How did you come to lose your hand?"

The elf was taken aback by the unexpected question. He looked briefly, unexplainably deflated. Then he faced Lyim squarely and dropped his hood to his shoulders. "It was chopped off by the Silvanesti, who sought to enslave me. Have they sent you to fetch me?"

It was Lyim's turn to be surprised. "So you're a hunted man, too." He nodded toward the severed arm. "Any good mage could fix that for you."

"I choose to keep it this way as a reminder. I will never allow myself to be enslaved again."

"We'll get on well, then. I mean to offer you a job. The pay is food and a place to sleep. In exchange I expect total and unfailing loyalty. Without question."

"I'll take it," the elf said promptly.

From that moment, Lyim's climb to the position of district amir had been swift. He'd needed a sewer rat, someone the people of the area would—but shouldn't—trust. Lyim would have always been the newcomer without the help of one such as Salimshad.

The elf did his best to remind his master of his importance from time to time—as now, under Lyim's cold scrutiny at the district fountain. "You wouldn't be looking at me that way if you knew what I've been doing on your behalf," Salimshad murmured.

"I thought you were at the palace, handing the district taxes over to the treasurer."

"Better," the elf said with clerkish contempt.

Lyim frowned. Salim knew he didn't like games, so the news must be juicy. "Tell me."

Salimshad looked slyly at the stony-faced guards. Reluctantly, Lyim ordered them to stand six paces away.

Salim leaned in, speaking from the depth of his hood. "Rusinias is having trouble making his tax payments."

"How is that possible?"

"The treasurer didn't say, despite my best efforts to squeeze the details from him. All he would reveal was that Rusinias has been suffering from terrible tooth pain, of all things. Perhaps he's been bedridden and has not been collecting as faithfully as usual." Salim glanced over his shoulder. "In any event, the treasurer is furious, which means that Aniirin is angry, too. Rusinias is definitely out of favor." The usually restrained elf was red with excitement. "This is a golden opportunity to remove him entirely!"

"I think you may be right," Lyim agreed. "But how?" The amir groomed a fingernail between perfect white teeth while he pondered.

"Poison?" suggested Salim in an undertone. "He's

already sick. Shall I make some arrangements in the palace kitchen before this afternoon's soiree?"

"No," Lyim said slowly. Still, the elf's question had given the former wizard a wealth of ideas with one word. "Tell me, is Rusinias too ill to attend today's soiree?"

Salimshad looked at him from that tattooed, cynical face. "You know that only death qualifies as 'too ill' to miss one of Aniirin's gatherings."

Lyim acknowledged the truth of that with a lift of his brows. Over the years he had considered endless convoluted plans to ensure his eventual rise to potentate, had discussed them at great length with Salimshad. Now one that was the soul of simplicity sprang to mind. Lyim felt certain it would work. Best of all, win or lose, there was little chance he could be caught at it.

"No," he repeated with greater surety, "say nothing to anyone. I have a better idea."

Salim's eyes sparkled with malicious delight. "Tell me!"

Lyim sprang from the edge of the fountain to his feet. Withdrawing his head through the strap of the tax pouch, he handed it to the elf. "Wait for the two inside the bakery. Then meet me back at the town house," Lyim instructed, his voice accelerating with excitement. "I'll tell you what I have in mind there, after I make a stop at the apothecary."

The elf knew better than to press his master further. Besides, he hadn't time. The amir had already disappeared from view on the busy River Avenue, sandwiched between two bodyguards.

* * * * *

The midafternoon bells rang all over Qindaras. In the time of the first potentate, they were meant to summon the faithful to daily worship. Few found reason to be faithful in the era of Aniirin III. Now, most citizens used the ringing of the bells as an excuse to break from the day's work and return home for a nap.

Aniirin himself used it as an opportunity for a major meal of sweets between the noon repast and dinner. Four bakers were occupied full-time in the palace kitchens, creating new concoctions daily for the potentate's insatiable sweet tooth. Once a week, on tax day, all seven of Qindaras's amirs were invited to join Aniirin in his orgy of confections. The word "invited" was a misnomer, as every amir, wise and foolish, soon learned.

Lyim stood in Aniirin's frilly, overstuffed parlor—far too feminine for any man to endure, he thought. His tiny, flower-shaped cup of hot bergamot water lolled indifferently at an angle, the weight of it in his hand merely comforting. Any moment now, the bakers would arrive bearing cart after cart of elaborate baked goods. In keeping with tradition, Aniirin would make a grand entrance immediately after.

All six of Lyim's peers were present with their tasters, another long-held tradition when dining at the palace. No one knew why the tradition continued, since no one had been poisoned there in any living person's memory. Lyim checked his own lackey, standing behind him with a look of greedy anticipation. Usually, Salim served, but today Lyim wanted the elf as far from this room as possible. Instead, he had randomly selected a pudgy, small-eyed youth from a crowd of toughs he had passed on his way to the palace. There was nothing complex about sampling a forkful of tart before a person of higher rank.

"Why must we come to this event every week?" moaned Vaspiros, amir of the garment district. He was a slight, nervous man who was prone to whining. Lyim thought it a travesty of fate that the stoop-shouldered, concave shadow of a man had the most opportunity to acquire quality clothing and the least suitable form to display it. "Aniirin doesn't care to see any of us, let alone hear our concerns about our districts," Vaspiros mewled.

"You know why we're here," snorted Garaf. The amir of the craft district was an older, cynical man who had seen much and been surprised by very little of it. Lyim thought he might have liked the compact, gray-haired man under other circumstances. "The first Ani-irin had these soirees. Our current potentate eats the same food, sleeps in the same bed, wears the same style undergarments as his ancestor," he finished in a humorous undertone.

"Besides," interjected boorish Dafisbier, overhearing their soft conversation, "like any trained animal, Ani-irin needs treats to perform!"

Most of the gathered amirs burst into self-conscious laughter, never quite sure if the potentate had some way of overhearing them. Lyim stayed out of their talk. Instead, he sought out Amir Rusinias, who sat in a ruffled, damask-covered chair next to a sideboard that would soon be lined with pastries. The forty-odd-year-old was slumped in his chair, his face the pale gray of dirty snow. A bald-headed, big-nosed man with a drooping right eye, he did not cut an impressive figure. Rusinias had the distinction of the longest reign as amir. It was largely the reason he was considered Ani-irin's favorite. Until recently, anyway.

"How's the tooth, Rusinias?" Lyim asked, sipping his tea.

The amir of the warehouse district cupped his cheek at the reminder. He looked up vaguely from his chair, not bothering to open his droopy eye when he saw who spoke. There was no love lost between the two men. "If you must know, it's killing me." He winced as his breath whistled over the sore tooth.

"Too bad," Lyim said pleasantly. "I could give you the name of a good barber in my district. He could remove it for you in a procedure as painless as sleep."

Rusinias looked askance at Lyim, who had not spoken a kind word to him in months. "Thanks," he said cautiously. "I may just need it."

Lyim nodded, then was forced to move back a step as the pastry chefs burst through the curtained archway. Each pushed a cart heaped with pastel confections.

The potentate followed. He was as eager-faced as Lyim's taster, who waited impatiently in the wings for the promised treats. All heads bowed according to custom. "Good! You're all here!" Aniirin III exclaimed, clapping his hands. "How I do love tax day!" He considered the carts with greedy eyes, but his manservant, Mavrus, whispered to him briefly.

With obvious reluctance, the potentate went on to greet his amirs with hasty handshakes. Aniirin came to Lyim second only after Rusinias.

Grinning up into Lyim's face, Aniirin pumped the mage's hand and lingered just long enough for his amir to get a good look at him. The potentate appeared to be possessed of fifty-odd human years, though Lyim knew he must be considerably older, at least according to his published birth year. His palm in Lyim's felt dry and paper-smooth, like an old man's. The flesh on the back of his bejeweled hands was dusted with age spots. The potentate had magical enhancement or a carefree life to thank for his relative youth.

For all his self-control, Lyim found it difficult not to stare at the potentate's face. His head was shaped like a gourd left too long on one side in the field; a lopsided and receding hairline aided the slightly bashed-in look. The indent was further marked by a kinked blue vein. At such close range, one could not help but notice it throbbed with every beat of the potentate's heart.

If his oddly shaped head weren't enough to attract attention, Aniirin had a feature that would have got him stoned by the superstitious if he were anything less than the potentate. One of his eyes was green, the other blue. To Lyim, at least, Aniirin resembled a badly painted picture, as if the artist could not draw a proper circle or even bother to decide which eye color to give his subject.

As the potentate departed to welcome the other amirs, Lyim noted that at least Aniirin's golden robe was expensive and well tailored. Unfortunately, it slipped off one sloping shoulder and so drooped over the hand of that arm. His belly was rounded from drink and the rest of him so lumpy his torso looked like potatoes poking through a homespun sack.

With the niceties out of the way, Aniirin wasted no time in snatching up the large plate of sweets intended for him. Ignoring the serving spoons, the potentate used his pudgy, ringed fingers to pluck sliced pastries from the silver trays, sucking the digits clean after each. To the watching chefs' silent dismay, Aniirin heaped one delight on top of the other as if he couldn't go back for seconds, until his plate was a hopeless pile of unidentifiable sugared pastry.

It was always the same.

Lyim waited to be last in line behind the fidgeting Vaspiros. As Lyim expected, Rusinias took nothing. Eating any of the items would have been agonizing to his tooth.

Better yet, everyone else had taken at least one of Aniirin's favorite delicacy: a chocolate- and cream-filled puffed pastry whose gooey center also concealed bits of candied pomegranate. The whole thing was smothered with powdered sugar and cinnamon. Lyim found them repulsive, but he took one of everything, careful to perch Aniirin's favorite on top.

Smiling pleasantly, Lyim sat and watched his compatriots. In his youth, he had traveled with a cruel magician, hoping to learn some real magic. His mentor had turned out to be a complete phony as far as wizardry was concerned, but Lyim did learn many sleight-of-hand techniques before finally running away. Lyim covertly passed his sleeve over the plate and shook it. A fine powder, indistinguishable from ground cinnamon, filtered down over the puffed confection.

Etiquette demanded that no one eat before Aniirin; it

had never been a problem. Today, however, Lyim watched the potentate closely. Aniirin's two-tined fork was raised and ready to descend.

"Wait!" Lyim's shout was so loud that even Aniirin, in his mesmerized state, gave pause. "Your taster has not sampled your food yet, Potentate," he pointed out, letting a desperate note creep into his voice.

Aniirin rolled his eyes in dismay. "I thought we might dispense with that; in all my years no one has ever been poisoned at a soiree. Am I not beloved by my amirs and my people?"

Lyim coughed uncomfortably, then cleared his throat. "*I* would hope that, Potentate. Yet I fear that today of all days may be the wrong time to depart from custom."

Aniirin's lop-sided head cocked suspiciously. "Speak."

Lyim adjusted his tone. "I wish it were not my duty to reveal that I have had word from a reliable source that someone means to poison you and all amirs who stand in his way." The other amirs gasped and looked aghast at their plates. Mavrus rose to the potentate's side, blocking his master with an arm, as if that could shield Aniirin from poisoned food.

"Who is this traitor?" demanded the potentate.

Lyim sent his gaze traveling to Rusinias, letting his eyes linger on the man only briefly. "If I knew that," he said, "the man would already be rotting in the dungeon."

"Yes, of course," Aniirin muttered. Even he had the sense to feel foolish at the question.

"How is it you came by this information?" asked Garaf.

"Like all of you, I have sources throughout the city," Lyim said. "I'm surprised you didn't hear of the plot, Garaf."

The man grumbled, but said nothing further. He'd already stuck his neck out farther than he'd intended.

"We can point fingers all day long," Lyim said. "Or we can put it to the test straight away. Let us see whose food has been poisoned, and whose has not."

He wagged a finger toward the pudgy youth he'd pegged as his tester. The boy's eyes were wide, his face pale and sweating. His fear was evident, but it was equally obvious he could think of no good way to run screaming from a room filled with the city's most influential citizens. At the very least, his flight would be taken as a sign of guilt. He might even be struck dead before he reached the curtained threshold.

Quaking visibly, the street thug stepped forward. Lyim handed him the plate of food he had collected. "I deliberately took a portion of each confection," Lyim explained. "Be sure to taste each."

The hand holding the fork shook. One after another it poised over a sweet, then plucked a morsel and carried it to the lad's fishy lips.

Many long, tense heartbeats passed. No one else ate. They scarcely breathed. Slowly, the youth smiled, the heavy folds of his face creasing and uncreasing. The entire room breathed a sigh of relief. Back by the curtains, the other tasters were the most relieved of all.

"I knew it! A hoax!" crowed Vaspiros.

Without warning, the pudgy thug grabbed his throat, gurgled once, and fell to the carpeted floor, dead.

The room exploded with shrieks and shattering china. Lyim called above the din. "Gentlemen, order! You are destroying the evidence!"

Slowly, the room quieted.

"Shall we continue with the tasting?" Lyim suggested.

But after the death of the frightened youth, no other amir would subject his tester to the same fate. Lyim had counted on their foolish sense of compassion.

"The death of your taster proves nothing," remarked Rusinias from his chair. "Maybe someone just wanted you dead, Amir Rhistadt."

"That is a possibility, though I can't imagine why anyone would want to poison only me," Lyim replied. "The position I hold is of no particular importance . . . unless one of us felt his own position weakening and was afraid I would usurp it."

Lyim's tone was innocent enough, but everyone present recognized the target of his barb. Obviously the news of Rusinias's tax problems had spread to all quarters.

None appreciated Lyim's poorly disguised accusation less than Rusinias. He sent Lyim a look that was as poisonous as arsenic. "Perhaps you staged this stunt yourself."

For an answer, Lyim arched a brow toward the amir's empty hands. "I notice you have taken nothing to eat from today's repast, Rusinias," he remarked pointedly. He could see that his remark had tickled the imaginations of all present.

"My tooth—how could I eat such sweets?" the amir protested, but Lyim cut him off.

"You have viciously questioned my loyalty to Aniirin, Rusinias," Lyim said, his voice as tight as a fist. "If you feel so strongly that this attack was directed only against me, I challenge you to taste our potentate's food as a demonstration of your conviction. I believe it is poisoned, as I have said. Yet I will taste it myself if that is what it takes to know the truth—and to keep our city's gracious sovereign safe. Are you willing to do the same?" For effect, Lyim snatched up a fork and crossed the room, headed for Aniirin's plate.

"Go ahead and taste it," Rusinias declared. "Poisoned or not, it proves nothing about me."

"That could be true," Lyim responded, turning to face the older amir, "but you are the only person here who has taken no food. Your toothache has struck at an unusually favorable time. I ask you again, Rusinias: Will you demonstrate your loyalty and taste this food with me?"

Like a cornered animal, Rusinias looked around the room. The other amirs were silent, glancing nervously from Lyim, to Rusinias, to the potentate, to the platter of delicacies before Aniirin. "It's only because of this tooth that I took none of the sweets," Rusinias protested again. "Everyone here knows how it plagues me."

Before Rusinias could utter another word, Lyim thrust his fork into the creamy pastry atop Aniirin's plate. As he did so, more of the finely powdered poison scattered down from his sleeve onto the remaining pastries. Tearing off a portion of the confection, Lyim raised the fork to his lips. In this supreme moment, his will was everything. He had studied these men since arriving in Qindaras and knew how they would react under strain. He was stronger than all of them. Glaring wildly at Rusinias, Lyim tipped the fork toward his open mouth.

"Enough!" cried Aniirin. Lyim turned to face the ruler of Qindaras. "Amir Lyim, you will give your fork to Amir Rusinias. *He* will taste my food first." All eyes followed Lyim as he strode obediently across the room to stand before Rusinias.

Rusinias winced and cupped his jaw with his left hand. But he rose and took the fork from Lyim. "I will taste it. I am not afraid." His eyes burned directly into Lyim's as he raised the fork to his lips.

No sound disturbed the harsh contest of nerve that raged between the two men. Lyim could see himself as a pillar of heated iron, wilting the fleshy thing before him. The morsel was nearly on Rusinias's tongue when Lyim saw the flash of understanding in the cornered man's eyes.

Rusinias hesitated. His face whitened, and a slight tremble in his hand betrayed his fear.

In that moment Aniirin was on his feet. A wave of his arm sent two guards scurrying to flank the elder amir. "You will eat it, Rusinias," cried the potentate, "by your own hand or be fed by a guard."

Rusinias, drained of color, stood frozen. "Yes, Sire." When a guard reached for the fork, Rusinias closed his eyes and thrust the pastry into his mouth. He inhaled sharply from the ache of his tooth, then chewed. After swallowing, he stood, swaying slightly, eyes still tightly closed.

The silence in the room was finally broken by the silver fork clattering to the floor as Rusinias doubled over, clutching his stomach. Then he collapsed. He lay kicking on the wood floor, unintelligible sounds gurgling up through his constricted throat.

"Get him out!" bellowed Aniirin. He scowled down at the man who had been the unstated heir to his throne. The guards grabbed Rusinias, still convulsing and moaning horribly, and dragged him roughly from the chamber.

Lyim hung back while the other amirs bustled out of the room in Rusinias's wake. Mavrus ordered the disposal of the taster's body and the sweets, much to Aniirin's dismay. Crestfallen, the potentate trailed behind the departing carts, whimpering about the spoiled soiree and untasted crullers.

Mavrus paused in the curtained archway and regarded Lyim with an appraising, slightly disapproving glance. "Aniirin is bereft now, but rest assured the proper punishment and credit will be doled out for this unfortunate episode." The manservant departed before Lyim could respond with the proper amount of humility.

Left alone in the frilly chamber, Lyim smiled.

The soul of simplicity.

Chapter Three

"I feel like a racehorse," Guerrand gasped, "and I'm beginning to sweat like one, too. Do you think we might slow down just a bit, Bram? I agreed to accompany you to Weador's court for moral support, but I don't recall agreeing to run a marathon."

Guerrand still held the elaborate faerie coin in his palm, all sweaty and warm. He and his nephew had been traveling at what he would call a run ever since they'd entered the realm of the tuatha dundarael.

Bram stumbled to a stop on the roughly paved road. "I'm sorry, Rand. I'm so preoccupied, I didn't notice how much I was pressing us." He glanced up at the odd trees above them. "I guess I'm not anxious to be on this faerie road any longer than necessary. It's not as benign as it might seem."

Nothing involving the tuatha dundarael was, including the system King Weador had established for contact between the mortal realm and his own. Bram had resisted the urge to call on the tuatha directly, for fear of drawing attention to their presence in Thonvil. If locals noticed a preponderance of lights in the night sky, they usually attributed them to fireflies. But Bram and Guerrand knew the truth; the lights were really fast-moving faeries at work.

Recalling King Weador's directions for seeking an audience, Bram and Guerrand had watched the gardens and fields around Thonvil for an excess of twinkling lights. When the two found a well-protected garden with the greatest amount of lights, they set out a plate of cookies, irresistible to most tuatha. To it they attached a note from Bram, addressed to King Weador and translated into the script of magic by Guerrand, in case some villager stumbled upon it.

The next morning, Bram awoke to find Thistledown, the first tuatha he'd met years ago on Stonecliff, sitting at the foot of his bed. Thistledown's bright blue eyes twinkled from beneath his bright blue cap. The tuatha handed Bram a small pouch containing two faerie coins and told him to speak aloud the destination he desired. The faerie road would then open for him. After reminding Bram of the dangers of leaving the path or relinquishing his coin, Thistledown informed him that they would be guided to Weador's court by the first centaur they met.

Two days later, after completing preparations to be gone from Castle DiThon for an indefinite period, Bram and Guerrand uttered the words "King Weador's Court" and entered the faerie realm.

Guerrand had seen many wondrous sights in his thirty-odd years, from foggy mirror worlds to the golden gates of the diamond-spired Lost Citadel. Yet he still had the capacity to marvel. A whole magical faerie kingdom, with all the detail of his own world, existed alongside the mortal realm, but invisible to it.

The road beneath their feet was crafted of interlocking blocks of worn stone. Above the road the green canopy was thick and close, making the path resemble a dark tunnel. The trees were most unusual, smooth-skinned as an elf's cheek, with broad, flat leaves variegated with whorls of white or entirely black-green. The underbrush was thick with thorny bushes and weeds. Slivers of bright blue limned the uppermost leaves, suggesting that somewhere above stretched a sky.

Strangely, it was a cheerful place for all its shadows. It seemed neither magical nor foreboding, just oddly silent. Guerrand could hear his heartbeat banging in his ears even after they had stopped walking. There was neither birdsong nor the sound of creatures shaking the underbrush as in most dense forests.

Guerrand watched the trees constantly. "I never presume that anything magical is benign," he said. "But I suspect we'll come to no harm if we abide by the rules and never step from the path or turn over our coin to anyone but Weador.

"I don't think our surroundings are what's bothering you, Bram," the mage continued. "You've been preoccupied and edgy since you decided to ask Weador about your heritage."

Bram snorted. "Wouldn't you be? To be honest, I've scarcely slept or thought of much else since the morning of the ceremony."

Guerrand eyed his nephew with concern. "I thought as much. A bad week in which to organize the smooth running of the estate in your absence."

"It wasn't that difficult," said Bram. "Kirah has managed the accounts for nearly two years. Rillard knows more about farming than anyone in the county, and Toal is the ablest lieutenant anyone could have. And even if I didn't trust them completely, Maladorigar is capable of helping however Kirah needs him to."

"As long as the gnome remembers to take the herbs to slow his speech so no one wants to throttle him," chuckled Guerrand.

"In an odd way," mused Bram, "now that Thonvil has been restored, I function as something of a figurehead anyway."

"That's just your dark mood speaking," Guerrand said, "and another indication that you should have had more rest before embarking on this trip. You'll need all your wits about you when you meet with Weador—"

"I'll be fine," Bram said more harshly than he had intended. "Besides, Weador is going to tell me Rejik and Zena were mistaken. I'll learn that I'm no tuatha, and we'll be back at Castle DiThon before midday meal."

"Is that what you want?"

"Wouldn't you, if you were me?"

Rand paused only briefly before answering. "In the short term, yes," he agreed. "It's the safe, fast answer that allows your life to remain unchanged. But if there's truth in what Wilor told me, your life has a whole new set of possibilities."

Bram shook his head vigorously. "I can't think that far ahead yet. I'll deal with it when—*if*—it comes. Until then, I need to cling to what I know."

Guerrand nodded in sympathy. "I've had years to consider something that affects your life much more profoundly than it does mine."

They walked in silence for a time, each lost in his thoughts. The wizard peered down the road. "How far did you say you traveled before you encountered the centaur last time you were here?"

Bram frowned, looking both ahead and behind them. "It's hard to say. Time is so distorted here, and we've not seen any of the creatures I met before." He scratched at his chin thoughtfully. "I don't even know if it will be the same centaur. I hope not, though. He was the most contrary cuss I've ever encountered, and not the brightest either."

The road cut through a copse of draping, willowlike trees. Though there was no breeze, the leaves shifted and wavered above them. Hearing a strange sound in the previously quiet woods, Guerrand stopped to listen. Whispering . . . He could swear someone was whispering. "Who's here?" Guerrand spun around, but there was no one else in sight.

"Can't you hear that?" he asked Bram.

Bram held a finger to his lips and pointed toward the copse of odd trees. The leaves were long, pink-tinged, and slightly humped in the middle. Though they vaguely resembled willow leaves, they were much more similar to delicate pairs of lips.

"*Leave the path,*" whispered the lips in an eerily apt pun. Guerrand could feel the message working at his mind; he shook his head, banishing the urge.

"The whispering threw me, too, when I first came through."

Guerrand shivered. "Let's get out of here." The two hastened down the road, and the whispering gradually receded.

"Unless I miss my guess," muttered Bram, "the birds are next."

"Birds?" repeated Rand, but the word was hardly out of his mouth when both men spotted a flock of flamingo-sized birds perched on a single, severely bowed branch to the right of the path. With bodies of pink feathers and heads of orange fur, they watched, five sets of yellow eyes glowing, as Bram and Guerrand passed.

They had walked only a short distance farther, to a fork in the road, when they heard a nasal voice above them: "Just where do you think *you're* going?"

Both men looked up. Reclining on a ledge cut into a towering boulder was the long-awaited centaur. His human face was propped up with a human-looking hand. His four legs were tucked under his body like those of a slumbering horse.

"I was beginning to think you'd been eaten by something," said the centaur churlishly. "You must either be very slow or very lazy to have taken so long getting here." He stood and stretched his limbs. "Weador must be loosening his standards, if he's giving coins to such riffraff as you."

Bram closed his eyes and muttered under his breath to Guerrand, "It *is* the same centaur."

With the aid of an elaborate staff, the sleek horseman slowly picked his way down the boulder. "I don't think I feel like guiding such stupid humans anywhere today," he announced. His hooves clattered like a mountain goat's against the stone. A shiny sword caught the light; he had it strapped between his shoulder blades.

"So don't," suggested Bram. "Just point us in the right direction. I'm sure we can find our way to Weador's court."

The centaur made it to the ground. "I doubt it." With a slow, evaluating gaze, he eyeballed Bram from the human's feet to his dark head. "Don't I know you?"

Bram bit his lip. "We might have met once before, yes."

The centaur looked smug. "You remember me, do you? Well, now that I've had a closer look, I realize I don't recall you at all. In fact, I've seen flies crawling on my flanks that have been more memorable."

"Yes, I suppose you have," said Bram. "Now, if you'll just tell us what you've been instructed to, we'll be on our way. Then you needn't give us another thought."

"Don't worry, I shan't," sniffed the centaur. "Very well. To reach King Weador's court, you must take the fork to the right."

Guerrand started to move in that direction, but the centaur's arm shot out and held him back. "Not so fast. You can't go that way."

"You just said that's the way to King Weador's court," Guerrand protested.

"Nevertheless, you may only go left," the centaur said.

Guerrand's eyes narrowed. "I thought that centaurs were polite."

"That's what you get for thinking."

48

"Yes, well, thank you very much for the directions," Bram called to the centaur in an overly friendly voice. "We'll be on our way now."

Bram leaned into his uncle. "Just do what I do," he suggested quietly. "It worked the last time."

He quickly led them several steps down the fork to their left, paused, turned around, and walked back to the intersection. Straight ahead was the path they had already traveled. To their left lay the path to King Weador's court. Rand was clearly puzzled by such machinations, but Bram physically pulled his uncle around the cantankerous centaur and down the road that led to King Weador's court.

"Hold, foolish humans!" Both men froze. The call was followed by the familiar clatter of hooves on the path behind them.

"Thistledown gave no warning about using magic here, did he?" Guerrand whispered, instinctively preparing a spell to hold the centaur back.

"No," Bram said, "but wait a moment."

The young lord turned and gave a wide-eyed smile to the approaching centaur. "Yes? Did we forget something?"

"Yes," snapped the centaur. "Me. You'll get lost without me, so I've decided to lead you to the court."

"That's really not necessary," protested Guerrand.

"No need to thank me." The centaur scowled. "You may still get eaten before we get there."

"Shouldn't you be guarding the fork?" suggested Bram.

"I am," said the centaur simply. He trotted around Guerrand to lead them forward.

Behind the centaur's back, Guerrand raised his brows in question. Bram considered whether they should risk a spell on the creature. Deciding it was unwise, he shook his head and followed the cantankerous centaur.

The landscape changed dramatically not far from the

fork. The flat, meandering trail that had been surrounded closely by trees began to wind through the
most beautiful and diverse scenery either man could
imagine. To either side rose twin, towering waterfalls.
Just past the falls, the path was suspended on a great
cliff above a vast blue sea. The road hooked away from
the cliff and cleaved a path through more woodland,
which in turn gave way to great dunes of sand, then a
steep river banked by towering, pungent pines.

"Is the road to the court always the same?" Bram
asked the centaur.

"It always leads you to the same place—how much
more the same could it be?"

With a flourish, the centaur stepped aside and swept
his arms forward. Only then did Bram notice that they
stood before a leafy arch formed by two tremendous
oak trees. Between the oaks, the graceful leaves of a
willow closed off the arch like a curtain.

Bram and his uncle parted the willow leaves and
stepped through. Bram's breath caught in his throat at
the sight beyond the arch. At least several hundred
tuatha of all ages stood in the area, wearing a colorful
assortment of jaunty wool caps and matching tunics.
The nearest tuatha regarded the two humans curiously
through brilliant blue eyes. But the faerie folk weren't
alarmed, as if human visitors were nothing unusual.

Even though the tuatha lived outside, Bram found
himself thinking of his surroundings as a chamber, so
perfect was the natural architecture. Beneath his feet
the stony road had turned to a lush carpet of moss and
soft grasses. Overhead, the canopy of leaves formed a
vibrant, glowing vault that reminded Bram of a green
and living stained glass window. Its aspect changed
constantly like a kaleidoscope when a gentle breeze
stirred the leaves. Rich sunlight filtered down through
the leaves in thousands of tiny shafts. The bower was
bright with multicolored flowers and full of life.

The faeries weren't the only creatures living in the

chamber. Myriad forest animals mingled with the tuatha like pets: squirrels, chipmunks, rabbits, and hedgehogs hopped and ambled and climbed on or among them. Birds of every variety flapped through the air or alighted on the faeries' caps and shoulders. Bram marveled at a group of tuatha children playing tag on a reclining bear. Occasionally the animal would swat playfully at them or roll over and tumble them all to the ground in a laughing sprawl.

Bram's ear was drawn to the sound of piping. Turning his head to follow the music, he spotted a swarthy, dark-haired man leaning against a tree and playing a set of flutelike pipes. The melody was quick, yet somehow sad and beguiling. The musician was not a man at all, but another faerie creature. Tiny horns poked through his black hair. From the waist down, he had the hindquarters of a goat.

Bram suddenly noticed a young woman standing near the piper. He was surprised, in fact, that he hadn't noticed her before. She was without a doubt the most beautiful woman he had ever seen. Her features were so perfect as to be indescribable. She was neither human nor tuatha, nor did she look entirely elvish.

Bram stood entranced, staring at her flowing blond hair and her flawless figure, hardly concealed beneath the thinnest of gossamer veils. When she glanced up at the young lord, he thought his heart would burst.

Guerrand's hand squeezed his shoulder in a warning. Suddenly Bram felt acutely embarrassed to be caught gaping at this nearly naked woman. He had to struggle to pull his eyes away from her smile. When he did, he felt as if an enormous weight had been removed from his chest. Bram inhaled deeply several times, just to clear his head.

"It's best not to get drawn in by things you don't understand," Guerrand admonished. "You are a stranger here. Be cautious."

Three tuatha pressed through the throng and

approached the humans. One of them, a male with an
unruly shock of brown hair, carried an intricately
carved staff twice as tall as himself. "Bram DiThon and
Guerrand DiThon," he intoned as he stepped forward,
"your arrival is noted and your presence is requested
by King Weador of the tuatha dundarael. If you would,
follow me, please."

He turned on his heel and strode purposefully away,
followed by his two companions. Bram and his uncle
were led across the glade to a second screen of greenery.
The two faeries who had not spoken stepped to the side,
while the third parted the leaves with his staff. Bram
and Guerrand stepped through. The tuatha followed.

This second area was much like the first, only slightly
smaller. But it more than made up for that deficiency in
grandeur. Their escort marched halfway down the center of the court, then stopped and planted his staff
firmly on the green carpet.

"King Weador, Queen Listra, Grand Councilor
Allern, lords and ladies, attendants of the court, I present Bram and Guerrand DiThon, lord and regent of
Thonvil. They do humbly beg the favor of an audience
with you, Sire."

The tuatha king nodded his head slightly, and the
herald—that is what Bram took him to be—motioned
the humans forward. Weador's hair was white as new
snow and hung down his back until it brushed the
ground. Like a kender, his face didn't look particularly
old, just character-etched with straight, deep brown
creases. The effect always reminded Guerrand of a
lady's perfectly folded, oiled parchment fan.

The royal mantle that draped past Weador's thighs
was made of gopher skins, intricately stitched so that
the dash-and-stripe from the back of four pelts formed
a continuous diamond pattern that reminded Guerrand
of the view through a kaleidoscope. The mage recognized the elaborate, polished gold brooch that held it
closed. Weador obviously still favored the fine-spun

spider silk tunic and trousers dyed in muted tones of the earth. Soft, mouse-fur boots adorned his small feet.

Guerrand found his eyes wandering to Weador's fingers; each of the ten short, thick digits sported a ring. He recognized a few of the scrimshaw rings, but there were new ones of stone and wood, too.

Weador's scepter was the same intriguing one Guerrand remembered from the garden back in Thonvil. Its tip was a bleached-white turtle skull, eye sockets filled with shining gold.

At a wave of the king's hand, two servants stepped forward and placed a pair of stools behind Bram and Guerrand. Weador motioned for them to be seated.

The king held both of their gazes with his frost-blue eyes. "Welcome to my court," he said in smooth, tenor tones. "You are both looking well—prosperous, in fact."

"We have you to thank for that, King Weador," said Bram humbly.

"That's only partially true," Weador said. "I've had reports of your hard work. Remember, we tuatha can only embellish what exists."

Bram bowed his head in acknowledgment of the compliment.

"I was surprised to receive your missive," said Weador. "I believe this is your first request to come to the court. Is there something amiss in Thonvil?" he asked. "Are my tuatha causing difficulties?"

"No, King Weador, nothing like that," Bram assured him hastily. "I requested the audience because I, ah, have an important question to ask—a question to which only you can provide an answer."

Weador settled himself back in his throne. "Ask."

Bram had rehearsed a dignified speech that sounded more curious than distressed. Now that the moment of discovery had arrived, what came out of his mouth was: "My uncle was told that I am a changeling of the tuatha dundarael. Is it true?"

Weador's blue eyes didn't blink. "Yes. And no."

Bram exhaled. "With all due respect, that's no answer."

"I'll hide nothing from you," said the king, "but you must let me tell you in my own time. It is a complicated story." Weador gestured to a servant for drink.

"How many human years have you now, Bram?" the king asked when carved wooden mugs of fruit cider had been passed to all.

"The twenty-fourth anniversary of my birth has just passed."

The king nodded appreciatively. "Has it been that long? Then twenty-five years ago, in the early days of your father's stewardship, I predicted a serious decline in the well-being of Thonvil and the surrounding regions."

"You predicted my father would fail as lord?" asked Bram.

"You forget the tuatha proclivity to recognize strength of character." Weador's tone was more matter-of-fact than cruel. "However, the specifics of your father's strengths and weaknesses matter less than their long-range effects. I believed Thonvil would survive Cormac's reign, despite the decline it would cause. With that in mind, I took unprecedented steps to reverse the trend in the next generation. You were the result of those steps, Bram. And you have exceeded my hopes."

"I was an . . . experiment?"

The king shifted. "I wouldn't call it that, especially if it disturbs you."

"How can I not be disturbed by the realization that I am not human?" Bram demanded.

"But you are," said Weador.

Bram looked totally confused. "But you said I was a changeling. Are changelings not faerie babies exchanged for human babies?"

"They can be, though unlike other faerie folk, the

tuatha have never engaged in that particular random capriciousness."

Bram sank back upon the stool and crossed his arms expectantly, willing patience.

Weador recognized Bram's frustration. "I considered both Cormac's flaws and Rietta's frailties," he continued quickly. "Acknowledging the significance humans place upon primogeniture through the male line, it was magically arranged for a tuatha woman to carry Cormac's child, giving it both greater strength of character and magical abilities. Rietta was already with child at the time, and our intention was to exchange the babies. However, Rietta's and Cormac's child was stillborn just days after the chosen tuatha woman's child—you, Bram—was born healthy and entirely human in appearance. The exchange was simple to arrange in the confusion and fog of their grief."

"So you fooled them into thinking their son had come back to life!"

Weador's eyebrows raised. "He did, for one of them anyway. You were Cormac DiThon's true son."

No amount of preparation had steeled Bram for the truth he'd sought. Left to his thoughts in the darkness of his chambers, he had wondered if he might be only half-tuatha, considering his human appearance. He had even discussed it with Guerrand. But based on Cormac's lifetime of little interaction with his son, he had decided that Rietta must have been his human parent.

Bram thought of his father, who had obviously believed the same. Cormac had tainted his relationship with his true son and his wife out of ignorance, likely concluding that Rietta had betrayed him. If he'd only possessed the courage to voice those false accusations. But then, who would Cormac have asked, hating magic as he did?

Bram's eyes widened abruptly. "Does my . . . mother still live?" he whispered hoarsely.

Weador's veneer cracked for the first time, and an

unexpected look of pain flashed across his creased face. "Yes, I believe so. That is my hope, anyway."

Bram heard only "yes." He scanned the faces of the tuatha nearby. "Is she here? Can I meet her?"

Guerrand touched his nephew's shoulder again. "You already have a lot to consider, Bram. Are you sure you wouldn't rather rest before you take on more?"

"No, I couldn't rest knowing she's nearby."

"I'm afraid you must wait," said Weador. "Primula no longer lives in our community."

"Primula," Bram repeated dully. His true mother's name. "Where is she, if not here?"

"Just as with humans, there are pockets of tuatha all over Krynn. Primula left our settlement to establish her own community shortly after your birth."

"Tell me about her," Bram prompted. "Why was she chosen to—" His voice trailed off.

"Produce you?" supplied Weador. The king's frost-blue eyes took on a faraway gleam. "I confess I chose her because I favored her. Primula was a very special tuatha. Her leadership potential was recognized early on. She had begun training as a matriarch, one of the spiritual leaders of the tuatha dundarael. I believe humans would call one such as her a priestess."

Weador bent forward, leaning on the turtle shell staff. "Primula had a quick and curious mind. She was always questioning things, from the purpose of our existence to the appropriateness of our traditional dress. I suspect she agreed to carry you because I asked her to. In those days she would have done anything to please me, for I was something of a father figure to her—well, as close to one as we tuatha get."

Weador snapped back from his musings. "To recognize the significance of that, you must first understand that our sense of family differs from yours. The tuatha community as a whole shares responsibility for raising children."

"No one knows who his parents are?" asked Bram.

Weador shrugged. "We all know, but it simply isn't very important."

"If my mother was such a devoted follower of yours, why did she leave you?"

The look of pain crossed Weador's face again. "You would need to ask her that." The king leaned back in his throne. "An idea comes to me that may help both of us achieve what we seek."

Bram held his palms up. "Forgive me if I'm suspicious of agreeing to another deal, Weador."

"After seeing the success of our joint venture in your village, would you say I have failed to uphold my end of the bargain?"

Bram saw the faces of the happy and prosperous villagers of Thonvil in his mind. "No, it has been good for both our people," he conceded. "But you should have told me the truth about my heritage."

"Do we mortals ever know the whole truth of our lives?" Weador asked, more to himself than to Bram. "Anyway," he continued, "the truth would have distracted you, as you are distracted by it now. Neither Thonvil, nor we tuatha, could have waited for you to come to terms with your heritage. But you have time for it now."

"What are you proposing?" asked Bram.

"Find Primula," Weador said. "All tuatha embark on a journey of self-discovery to mark a spiritual coming-of-age. Most use the experience to determine the direction of their life's work. Though it is typically a journey of the mind only, there is no reason the body cannot search for the spirit's answers. I believe that when you meet your mother, you will also find the answers you seek."

"You said this benefits both of us. What's in it for you?" Bram asked bluntly.

"Primula's departure created a schism among the tuatha. I would see that rift mended. If that's not possible, I would like at least to know that Primula is well."

Bram looked at him in surprise. "You once told me

that there was little in the magical world to which you were not privy."

"I am not omnipotent," said Weador. "Though I haven't spoken with Primula since she left, I knew where she took her followers. In my recent efforts to ascertain her well-being, I discovered that she relocated her sect; I no longer detect her presence. I can only presume she has intentionally severed any link between us." Weador's shoulders sagged visibly beneath the fur mantle. "The alternative is too disturbing for me to consider."

And for Bram, too. He could not bear the thought that he had got this close to discovering his heritage, only to find out his true mother was dead.

"All right," the lord of Thonvil said at last. "I'll find Primula—for both our sakes."

Chapter Four

The palanquin swayed gently, pleasantly upon the shoulders of the potentate's slaves. The part of Lyim that would always enjoy the finer things in life was glad Potentate Aniirin had insisted upon sending the conveyance to carry him to tonight's gala. Lyim had initially protested the gesture on the grounds that he did not deserve such an honor. But the potentate recognized that as false modesty and pressed the point. Lyim had no choice but to agree, with the concession that the carriage be the simplest the palace possessed and not bear Aniirin's insignia.

As if anyone else in all the Plains of Dust could afford such an opulent, velvet-trimmed conveyance, thought Lyim. He leaned back among the fringed pillows and settled the warm furs higher before sipping his springwater from a pewter-edged goblet. He felt safe enough from assassins. Even so, Salimshad had arranged for Lyim's usual retinue of bodyguards to surround the conveyance on the trip to the palace.

Lyim pushed back a small, gold-embroidered patch to peer out the palanquin's peephole. The avenue to the palace was lined with waving, rag-wrapped citizens, watching the city's elite arrive for the rare gala amid swirling dust and snowflakes. Lamps had already been lit. Their bluish light mingled with the orange glow of an enormous sun setting behind the glittering palace at the end of the avenue.

The palace was such a contrast to the squalor that surrounded it. Tumbledown stone buildings and large wooden crates that served as homes abutted the beautifully maintained, sixty-foot-high granite wall encircling the palace. The streets belonged to a world far different than that of the palace.

Lyim's own district had recently looked equally rundown. He had raised the standard of living, but only Salimshad knew his true reason for doing so: There was no greater enslaver than gratitude. Raise them up from poverty higher than they could ever hope to rise on their own, let them know the price for betrayal, and they will stay with you forever. The slaves who carried Lyim now would leave their master, the potentate, in a heartbeat if they could break their chains. But Lyim's unchained followers were loyal for life.

The palanquin bearers left the last wretched citizen behind as they marched in rhythm through the filigreed gates and onto the palace grounds. The road split into a circle that surrounded a statue of Aniirin I. The palanquin stopped swaying abruptly, followed by the sounds of booted feet marching in place. The stomping ceased, the emerald-green curtains parted, and Salimshad's familiar veiled face poked inside.

"All secure," said the elf in a dark, cryptic cant he and Lyim used only with each other.

Lyim swung his legs through the opening and dropped his feet to the marble steps. Without the warmth of the palanquin's furs he shivered in the chill air. Salimshad gazed meaningfully at the fashionably flashy attire of the nobles stepping from the other conveyances, then looked at Lyim's dress with a disapproving frown.

Salimshad had tried to talk his master into wearing something befitting the occasion. "This night is in your honor," he'd reminded him.

But Lyim had insisted on his usual brown vest over a long dun tunic and flowing trousers. "Let them see I have the confidence to flout convention. It makes me mysterious." As a small concession to the occasion, Lyim had covered his stubble of hair with the elaborate and colorfully embroidered turban favored by the other amirs.

Lyim accepted but did not return the polite nods of those same men upon the steps. They were as nothing compared to the magnificent structure behind them. Strangely, it was not the exterior of the palace that impressed the viewer. There was little besides stained glass and sheer size—and five hundred thirty-two greening copper minarets—to catch the eye here. A dome had been added each year since the laying of the cornerstone, varying in size from a large observation deck to ones too small to support even a kender. The current year's minaret was always a work in progress, its size determined by the city's coffers. During the current potentate's indifferent reign, the minarets had been on the small side.

Surrounded by his bodyguards, Lyim felt the press of curious eyes as he mounted the marble steps to the towering entrance. The arched, double door was of plain, polished copper. Unlike the minarets, the door appeared to have maintained its rich color because of the protection of an overhang.

Lyim could never quite subdue the awe he felt upon entering the palace. The entryway itself would have shamed almost any house in the upscale section of Palanthas that housed the nobility. Every inch of the floors, arched walls, and vaulted ceilings were inlaid with copper and gold in intricate repeating patterns. Encircling the base of the entryway's dome was writing Lyim recognized all too well—words of magic.

Thirty columns ringed the circular entry, each topped by a capital fashioned of rolled copper, then connected by arches carved from alternating wedges of black and white marble. Though it was now dark outside, light flooded through stained glass windows set at regular intervals high above in the dome.

"Mavrus approaches," whispered Salimshad.

Aniirin called Mavrus his "manservant" because the man's male ancestors had served that function for previous potentates. But anyone who met Mavrus even briefly knew the title was inadequate. In reality, Mavrus functioned as chief vizier, counselor, and manservant rolled into one. While the potentate sought advice from no one, he spoke freely to Mavrus. He was to Anirrin what Salimshad was to Lyim, which was why both men respected Mavrus's position, if not the man himself.

Mavrus was a short, thick man in the autumn of his life. Sparse, graying hair fanned artfully across a broad forehead whose bones were all too visible through transparent skin. Tonight, as always, he was dressed in the long, formal cloak, slippers, and turban Aniirin required of his household staff. He looked soft, but he moved with the quiet fluidity of a practiced fighter.

"Welcome, Amir Rhistadt," pronounced Mavrus in the slick, modulated accent of Old Kharolian. He held up a tray that supported a single, slender goblet containing Lyim's preferred springwater.

Lyim took the glass by the whisper-thin stem and sipped indifferently.

"Potentate Aniirin has been anxiously anticipating your arrival. He awaits you in the hanging gardens. Please, follow me."

Mavrus seemed only then to notice Salimshad's presence. He regarded the black-swathed elf over his shoulder. "Your manservant may wish to join the other staff in the kitchen."

"Salimshad will remain with me," Lyim said. The elf slipped around Lyim like a shadow at such events and usually went unnoticed.

Mavrus bowed his head. "As you wish."

Lyim followed the silent-footed manservant through the largest of the black-and-white arches, into the hanging gardens. The room itself was larger than the village in which Lyim had grown up. Like the entry-way, the walls here were wrought of rare woods and veined marble inlaid with burnished copper.

Despite the cold climate of the Plains of Dust, the hanging gardens had no ceiling. Above was only the blue-black sky and first twinkling stars of early evening. There were no fireplaces, and yet the room was always warm. Tropical ferns and fig trees fes-tooned with thousands of lit candles flourished here.

The potentate used the palace's magic to keep it as warm and tropical as it had been over three hundred years before, as if no earthshaking Cataclysm had ever occurred to change the climate. Before Lyim was done with his crusade against magic, it would be as cold as a tomb in here.

The crowd of party-goers parted like a wave as the guest of honor approached. A colorful lot, each sequined velvet trouser seemed more pretentious than the last, as if to cry, "Look at me! My owner is important!" Lyim recognized most of the nobility and, of course, the other amirs and their overdressed wives. The nobles' faces were each painted into the perpetually wide-eyed smile that was fashionable these days in Qindaras.

But even face paint could not hide their expressions of suspicion and fear as they watched Lyim approach the potentate. The fear was new, and it pleased him. So much so, in fact, that Lyim tipped his glass of spring-water and smiled at the amirs and their wives for the first time, a slight, wry raising of a corner of his mouth.

The unexpectedly civil expression made them withdraw even farther.

Lyim knew they suspected him of setting up Amir Rusinias. He wanted his peers to believe he had done it, to think he could do it to them, as well. Salimshad had fanned the rumor among citizen and nobleman alike that Lyim was a man who smoldered under the surface, just waiting to erupt. That description had special significance, since the elf had also let it be known that Lyim was a powerful mage who refused to practice his Art.

The other amirs stood in a fashionably dressed cluster, like cows in a patch of shade on a hot day. They liked each other no more than they did Lyim, but now they huddled together, united against him. That suited Lyim just fine, too. They would be so occupied protecting their small holdings that they would spend no time advancing them.

Lyim could see Aniirin ahead, sitting alone among the candlelit ficus trees. In honor of the festivities, the potentate wore the same well-tailored robe Lyim had last seen him in; it still hung too high on one shoulder and so drooped over the hand of his other arm. Aniirin fidgeted upon his carved and inlaid ebony throne, centuries-old and of dwarven design.

Mavrus's mouth was open to officially announce Lyim when Aniirin leaped to his feet and rushed to pump Lyim's hand.

"Amir Rhistadt," Mavrus said belatedly. Then the manservant discreetly disappearing into the shrubbery.

"Thank the gods you're finally here!" said Aniirin. "Couldn't speak to anyone else until you'd been announced, you know. Rules of etiquette established by my beloved ancestor, Aniirin I. But let us retire from this mob," the potentate whispered eagerly. "I've something more interesting to do than stand about."

"Sire, you wished to make an announcement to all the attendees," Mavrus murmured from the trees.

"Yes, yes, of course," said the potentate distractedly.

"Tell all those other people to stop drinking my wine and come in here where they can hear me!" He gave Mavrus mere heartbeats to draw the others over, forcing them to run like street urchins after a handout.

"Tonight we toast Amir Rhistadt in honor of outstanding service rendered. To show our gratitude, we hereby announce his promotion to basha and grant him all such privileges as the title bestows."

The potentate's expression darkened instantly, as if a cloud had passed overhead. "A vicious and craven coup was attempted upon my person, but prevented by the bravery and foresight of Lyim Rhistadt. The culprit has been duly punished and his family banished. Let it be known that the name of the traitor, Amir Malwab Rusinias, shall never be spoken in Qindaras again. Henceforth, anyone caught similarly plotting, or even uttering the cursed name, will suffer the same fate."

Aniirin snapped his fingers to Mavrus, who in turn signaled to another servant beyond the trees and out of Lyim's sight. Two liveried soldiers shouldered an unadorned wooden box, too small to be a coffin, too plain to be a treasure chest, and dumped it unceremoniously on the floor before the potentate.

"Behold a traitor's fate." With a shiny booted toe, Aniirin flipped open the latch on the box. Unsuspecting men and women alike pressed in curiously. Lyim hung back and watched them, arms crossed.

All the women shrieked; two fell into faints, and one soiled her cerulean brocade gown with a mouthful of spewed spirits. The other amirs withdrew with their womenfolk, scowling at, of all people, Lyim.

The newly proclaimed basha barely leaned forward to peer down his nose at the contents of the box, though he would have bet considerable coin as to what was inside it.

Atop a bloody, twisted pile of barely recognizable body parts was the head of Amir Rusinias. His face had been painted with the pale skin and wide-eyed smile of many of the party-goers. The stench was instantly overwhelming.

Secretly, Lyim applauded the stunt. For all his childish petulance and distractibility, the potentate could show brilliant flashes of insight. The contrast between the sumptuous festivities and the pile of gore in the box was a stark reminder of the potentate's true power over his citizens. What delicious irony that the only one who recognized this was the one not loyal to Aniirin, thought Lyim. Still, he kept his face a mask of studied indifference.

"Impressive deterrent, Sire." Lyim sipped the last of his mineral water, then held his glass high, signaling over Aniirin's shoulder for Mavrus to bring him another. "The . . ." Lyim hesitated, recalling the curse upon the dead man's name, "*amir* deserved such a fate, not only for disloyalty, but for unparalleled stupidity." He accepted the glass that Mavrus held at his elbow.

Aniirin gave a distracted wave, dismissing the box containing the dead amir from his presence, as well as his thoughts. The silent soldiers hefted the remains and slipped into the dark beyond the candlelit trees.

"I asked Mavrus to schedule the jugglers and acrobats right after viewing the corpse. It will lighten the festivities again, don't you think? They're quite good. I've seen them myself. Mavrus said they've teamed up with a most impressive wizard from our very own plains. I do so love magic, you know. The whole palace is run by magic, as you must have guessed. Yet I can't cast a spell to save my life. I studied under a series of masters as a boy, but it never came to me."

The potentate took Lyim by the arm and steered him toward the front row of chairs before a small stage assembled for the occasion.

"I hear rumors that you are a powerful mage. Why is it that you no longer use magic?"

Lyim's lips pursed. "I used to have a middling skill, yes. I gave up the Art for personal reasons."

"Stuff and nonsense," puffed Aniirin, settling himself with an undignified plop into a seat. "I would find an amir with such skill very useful. Very useful, indeed. For instance, I'd be interested in a critique of the wizard we're about to see. Perhaps later you'll even show me how to perform a spell or two."

Lyim was saved from answering by the arrival of the colorfully dressed acrobats. They tumbled in, one after the other, twisting and leaping in concentric circles. Suddenly they formed a human pyramid before the potentate. The pyramid dissolved into myriad other shapes: geometric patterns, birds, even a likeness of what Lyim assumed was a mythical dragon.

Lyim watched them through bored, slitted eyes. He had seen their likes, and better, every night in his youth, upriver in Rowley-on-Torath. Such traveling entertainers had been as numerous as drunkards in the dusty tavern in which he'd been left to grow up, while his mother entertained travelers in the chambers above. That is, until she'd lost her life to one of the countless diseases that usually killed her kind at a young age.

Lyim was ten when he heard of his mother's death. He hadn't seen her since he was six. His parents had never married, in fact had done no more than pass each other in the dark one night, with Lyim as the result. Ardem Rhistadt had agreed to allow the child to take his name, for all the good it did. The man soon moved on to another town, without his child.

Though his mother's death technically made Lyim an orphan, it changed nothing. He was earning a few coins and some scraps of food as a general errand runner and clean-up boy at another of Rowley's run-down inns. It was there, one night in Lyim's twelfth year, that he saw something that would forever change the direction of his life.

A traveling sleight-of-hand artist was passing through Rowley during the short summer months.

Lyim could no longer recall his name, but he would forever remember the tall, lanky man with a dirty yellow cape and equally grimy hair who made coins appear in patrons' ears or under their tankards. When Lyim saw the magician count his evening's take—more money than the youth expected to earn in a lifetime— he knew he, too, would become a wizard.

Such memories were no longer comforting to Lyim. He dashed them away when the leader of the jugglers announced the next act.

"Ladies and gentlemen, I would introduce for your entertainment, Fabulous Fendock!"

Usually the master of composure, Lyim nearly tumbled from his chair when the sleight of hand artist entered the room. He blinked up at the stage and focused on the figure there. The man was just beginning to stoop from age, but was still quite tall. A slight paunch was pushing out the midsection of his robe; his arms and legs were thin as sticks. But the eyes were unmistakable. They still radiated the same promise of great knowledge and mystery that was so completely false.

It should not be surprising that you would meet Fendock again, Lyim chided himself, the Plains of Dust are his territory. The trickster had seemed ancient to a twelve-year-old boy; Lyim had assumed the man long dead from old age or a stab wound delivered by a jealous husband or a clever patron who'd seen through Fendock's tricks.

Fendock had the look of a man who'd been on the road too long, drank too much, and slept too little. His nose and eyes were red. His hands trembled while he performed the same tired tricks he'd reluctantly taught the small boy from Rowley. Lyim could easily recall cutting open a lime to find the copper ring inside, pouring dry sand from a bowl of water, even making a glass globe float in the air.

Actually, they weren't all trickery. Fendock used some genuine magic in his act, but it was entirely the sort that apprentices learn and perform as exercises: simple manipulations of light, sound, and weight.

When Fendock discovered that Lyim possessed far greater natural ability for such exploits than he, the magician had angrily cut off what little training he'd provided. Lyim had slipped away in the middle of the night with Fendock's prized spellbooks. Lyim had felt no guilt. In fact, he considered the books only a partial payment for the services he'd rendered the bogus mage.

Still, Lyim averted his face a little, fearful that Fendock would recognize and acknowledge him publicly. The story of his street-rat upbringing and apprenticeship to one such as Fendock would be deadly for the mysterious image Lyim had cultivated in Qindaras. Fortunately, Fendock saw nothing beyond the ends of his arms, where his shaking hands manipulated props out of habit. Besides, Lyim bore no resemblance to the wide-eyed lad of twelve who'd begged Fendock to teach him the secrets of magic.

Lyim began to feel distinctly edgy. He had the undeniable urge to slip upstairs to escape Fendock's voice. Surprised by the intensity of his own reaction, Lyim stood clumsily and muttered an apology to Aniirin. Entranced by Fendock, the potentate took no notice as the basha slipped away from the show. Once free of the humid gardens and the crowd, he sat in the relative darkness of the grand staircase, closed his eyes, and pressed his fists to his throbbing temples. What's the matter with you? he asked himself.

But he already knew the answer. Magic was calling to him—and his blood was answering. Like ale to a drunkard who'd sworn off the stuff, the pull of magic was always strong to Lyim. What he didn't understand was why it was so overwhelming tonight. Had he underestimated what proximity to a vast amount of magic—like the enchantments that coursed throughout the palace—would do to him? He'd been to the palace before, but never had he felt this. The magic beckoned him here, now. Its call was stronger than any place he'd ever been—even the Tower of High Sorcery.

"Is something wrong, Basha?"

Lyim was so distracted he hadn't heard Salimshad's approach. His head shot up. "I have a pounding headache," was all he said. There were things about himself he would not share even with Salimshad. Information was a weapon, and Salimshad already had more weapons against Lyim than made the basha comfortable.

"I'm going to find a dark room upstairs in which to meditate briefly," Lyim ground out. "Go back to the festivities. If pressed, make whatever excuse you must about my absence to Aniirin or Mavrus." Lyim frowned; he found speaking over the tumult in his head irritating.

"Another thing," he said, in the private language they had developed for their own use. "Have the magician killed when he steps foot outside the palace."

"Yes, Basha." The elf slipped away into shadow.

Lyim stood too quickly and felt dizzy. He closed his eyes briefly to collect his equilibrium, then stumbled up the stairs. Distantly, he could feel the copper pattern cut into the cool marble through the thin soles of his slippers. He held to that, focused his thoughts on that texture, anything to shut out the pain in his head.

He stepped onto the second floor landing and leaned against an intricately carved pillar. Sweat poured down his face; his breath came in ragged gasps. He forced his eyes to focus on a portion of the pattern in the mosaic floor, while his mind looked inward for calming meditation. The mosaic tiles were sharp and bright in his vision, and their crisp edges created a feeling of cool freshness behind his sweating brow. He pictured the tense muscles of his forehead relaxing and pushing the compulsive thoughts away. It slowed the pounding, but the pull was as strong as ever.

From nowhere, a slip of mist slithered across the tile at which Lyim was staring. He blinked, and his dry eyes pooled with soothing tears. The white vapor must have entered the palace through the open ceiling in the hanging garden, he told himself. The mist wavered in his watery vision until he rubbed the tears away. What he saw at that moment made him blink yet again.

It was not mist swaying before him, but a woman, lithe and fair. She wore little more than a mauvy bolt of gauze twisted around her slight frame, leaving alabaster-white limbs exposed. Her hair was as ghost-pale and luminous as mother-of-pearl. She looked like a living statue, so perfect was her beauty. Lyim felt his throat catch and the pounding in his ears dim.

The woman smiled when she saw she had Lyim's rapt attention.

"Who are you?" he called, taking a step toward her. "One of Aniirin's concubines?"

The woman pirouetted on one toe, shot him a look over her graceful shoulder, then bounded out of sight around the pillar.

"Wait!" Lyim charged after her, but when he rounded the column she was nowhere to be seen. The hallway was long, open on the right side for half its length to overlook the hanging gardens. Festive flute music swelled from among the trees below, signaling the beginning of the dance.

He could see no doors to his left, just a long stretch of wall covered with elaborate tapestries. Lyim was pondering whether the mystery woman was simply fleet-of-foot or magically conjured when he caught a distant glimpse of her at the far end of the corridor. Squinting, he waited and watched for her next move. To his surprise she didn't leave; she stood still, as if she were waiting for him.

Lyim would have called to her again, but he feared attracting the notice of the party-goers in the gardens below. Too curious to ignore the woman, he moved closer to the left wall, out of sight of any celebrants, and began following her at his own carefully controlled pace. He would not be seen chasing after any woman. Just the same, he hastened his steps to catch up with her.

As he neared the end of the open railing, she disappeared into an archway to the left. Lyim broke into a run. His head was clear of the pounding now, but he felt compelled to chase her, driven. He realized vaguely that she had bewitched him, yet he was powerless to ignore her. Sweat formed between his shoulder blades as he ran through a handful of ornate, formal rooms joined by corridors, teased by fleeting glimpses of her diaphanous gown ahead.

Lyim rounded a corner at a dead run. He skidded to a stop and nearly cried aloud in surprise. The woman was within arms' reach, standing under a mosaic archway. Smiling enticingly, she floated through the arch. She paused briefly when she noticed Lyim had not followed. Peering over her shoulder, she waved him in.

Lyim followed her into a small, windowless room. His eyes adjusted slowly. All around, the shadowy walls and ceiling were painted in a three-dimensional fresco of the palace complex, colorful and minutely detailed. The woman was seductively draped over a glass box, which was perched on a smooth, rosewood pedestal. Her paleness had a golden glow now, lit from beneath by the object in the case—a heavily ornamented gauntlet.

"Who are you? One of the potentate's concubines?" Lyim asked again. His words boomed in the small room, no larger than a dressing chamber.

The woman appeared to ponder his question. When she replied at last her words were softly musical, like wind through the trees, her answer as mysterious. *I suppose you could say I have been a mistress of sorts to all Qindaras's potentates. You may call me Ventyr.*

Lyim squinted suspiciously at the woman. "All the potentates? You're centuries old—and a sorceress, no doubt. I suspected as much."

72

A sorceress? No—at least not in the way you think.

"Why did you beckon me to follow you?"

In answer, she stretched over the glass case and extended a sensuously pale arm. *Touch me*, she invited.

Understanding came to Lyim, and he half laughed, half scowled. "I'd have to be insane to dally with one of the potentate's mistresses."

Ventyr ignored his rejection and slid her fingers into his hand. Lyim tried to pull away, but he felt . . . nothing. Nothing but air touched the flesh of his hand, yet it seemed as if his whole body was being enveloped by her soft fingertips. If this was her usual method of seduction, Lyim began to understand why three potentates had kept her around for five hundred years. The basha himself had charmed and discarded many women in his time; he knew he was under a spell. Yet he didn't care. Lyim knew he would die rather than never feel such . . . vibrancy again.

The woman withdrew her hand, and Lyim nearly collapsed.

Have you never wondered how such an unmagical potentate as Aniirin III maintains this magical palace?

Lyim gathered his composure. "I had been told he supported wizards, as well as concubines. I never imagined they were one and the same."

Ventyr sighed, the sound like a cold wind over a frozen field. *You have taken me too literally, mage.*

"I am not a mage," Lyim hastily corrected.

And I am not a woman, in the mortal sense.

She stepped away from the pedestal and directed his eyes to the glove inside the glass box. It appeared to be made of intricately carved, interlinked plates of ivory, jade, and silver. The carvings on the plates were clearly magical pictograms, but the forms were unfamiliar to Lyim. Some of the individual plates were so small they were barely discernible. They must have given the glove incredible articulation, since it appeared to contain no other linking material.

The Gauntlet of Ventyr is my true physical form, she explained. *However, I choose to appear as a woman to men.*

Lyim prided himself on being worldly wise about magic and all its forms. Still, he could not deny his surprise.

I was created by the dwarves of Thorbardin in their desperation to disarm the wizards of Ergoth during the War of the Mountain, she continued. *But before I could be used, the elflord Kith-Kanan engineered the signing of the Swordsheath Scroll, which settled the long-standing dispute between the barbaric Ergothians, the elves, and the dwarves.*

The woman stepped behind the glass case and wrapped her arms around it. *I lay unused and forgotten in the bowels of Thorbardin, passed from thane to thane, for more than two thousand years. But in the years preceding the Cataclysm, that event which Qindaras will not acknowledge, Thorbardin became heavily dependent upon the world outside the mountain for food. With available sources drying up, the thane, Beldris, searched farther east. The fertile fields of Northern Kharolis were the breadbasket of the region. What was more, Aniirin I had taken control of trade on the River Torath. A powerful wizard in his own right, the first potentate of Qindaras was less interested in adding coin to his coffers than magical items.*

Being a dwarf, Beldris was happy enough to exchange a magical item for much-needed food. You see, most dwarven clans distrust magic, though historically they have created the greatest magical items, since they are superb metalsmiths. She smiled coyly. *Being a wizard, Aniirin knew he had acquired his greatest magical treasure for two boatloads of grain.*

"What makes you so great?" Lyim blurted. "Your power to bewitch?"

Your ignorance surprises me, mage. But perhaps you are merely out of practice. Ventyr straightened and rounded the case slowly. *The dwarves created me to absorb magical energy, both virtual and realized. I can syphon power from the vast field of magical energy that suffuses the world. I am*

74

tapped directly into the magical weave that mages like your-self must work so diligently to release.

You can imagine the practical application of such a skill. The first Aniirin realized that the energy I absorb could be harnessed and redirected to power and maintain his beautiful city. Ventyr waved her arm, and Lyim saw before his feet an image of Qindaras as he had never seen it. It was a bird's-eye view, perfect in every detail, shimmering and clean.

This was particularly significant to Aniirin in the years preceding the Cataclysm, when jealousy and hatred of magic was being stirred up by the Kingpriest.

"Wasn't it unwise to increase his visibility as a mage at such a time?" Lyim inquired.

Aniirin neither advertised my presence nor his own use of magic. The Kingpriest's energies were focused on destroying the towers of magic, not some minor potentate who was rumored to practice the Art.

Lyim shook his head. "I can't believe the Council of Three were not concerned about a wizard who had the ability to absorb and redirect their own magic against them." Lyim blinked as a realization struck him. "Why, it made this palace almost as powerful as a Tower of High Sorcery!"

They were aware of that, conceded Ventyr. *Yet they, too, were consumed with defending their own towers against the Kingpriest. They didn't ignore the problem, however, but struck a noninterference treaty with Aniirin. They wouldn't insist he surrender me, as long as he didn't use my power beyond the already-established bounds of Qindaras.* Ventyr drew her legs up into a crossed position and hovered, in a sitting posture, next to the glass case. *I suspect the Orders allowed the unusual treaty because they hoped a frag-ment of magic would survive beyond the clutching fingers of the Kingpriest.*

And it did just that. It also explains the origin of Qin-daras's refusal to acknowledge the Cataclysm.

Lyim shrugged. "I assumed it was just another facet of

Aniirin's obsession with the policies of his grandfather."

The woman nodded. *That has become the truth. But it began because I was already in place, magically powering and protecting the city when the Cataclysm struck. The quakes had little effect here because of those protections. Under Aniirin's rule, the city had already been pursuing an isolationist policy, largely because of the treaty with the Orders of Magic. There were few enough people to maintain even a minimal trade of goods and ideas in the years of isolation that resulted from the catastrophe.*

Practically speaking, daily life changed very little within the city walls. A new copper dome was added to the palace each year, marking the passage of time in the same old way. There was no need to recognize an event that affected the people so little.

Lyim's mind was racing with the possibilities. "How is the gauntlet—I mean how are you activated?" he asked awkwardly, no longer sure how to refer to the woman who was not a woman.

Aniirin instructed me to absorb spent energy and redirect it to maintain Qindaras's magical effects.

"With no guards on the door to this room," mused Lyim, "it's amazing no one has ever stolen you."

Aniirin recognized that danger, explained Ventyr. *He used powerful magic so no one but the crowned potentate of Qindaras can wear or use me. Such safeguards are vital: if I'm somehow removed from the grounds without being worn by the potentate, the loss of my magic would cause the destruction of the palace.*

"So you're saying Aniirin III dons you to draw magic?"

As potentate he could, responded the woman. *However, he does not practice the Art, so he has chosen to not use me for over a century. As a result, I have expended most of the energy stored by the first two potentates. As you must have noticed, the city has suffered for my lack of power. Soon I will not have enough energy to maintain even the palace, as Aniirin I magically bade me to do.*

"Why tell me this?" asked Lyim. "The potentate is the only one with the ability to help you. Appeal to him."

I have. Unfortunately, though Aniirin is enamored of magic, he does not understand it. He has neither the abilities nor the foresight of his grandfather. He even pales beside his father, whose meager intellect was no gift from the gods.

She drifted close and settled directly before Lyim. *You, however, are smarter and stronger than Aniirin. I sensed this when you entered the palace tonight. That is why I summoned you to help me.*

"I no longer use magic, for myself or others," Lyim said in a taut voice.

Without a skilled wizard as potentate, my magical stores will be drained. The city and all who reside within will wither and die. She paused for effect. *Consider what I have said, mage.*

"I told you, I am not a—"

But the mist woman had already slipped into the glass case and was gone from his sight.

With Ventyr's passing, Lyim felt the magical compulsion lessen and vanish. It left him angry, angry at having been used by the thing he had vowed to destroy. But it also left him confused. An item that absorbed magic . . . Was that so different from his own goal?

Lyim felt too drained by the events of the evening to think beyond his anger. As he left the chamber, he thought of Fendock. The old sharp was dying on Salimshad's knife somewhere below in the city. That thought made the basha feel better, even though some would call him a monster for ordering the death of a harmless old huckster.

Lyim had a motto, a gift from Fendock himself, that he would have used to reply to any outraged accusations of cruelty. The words had held the ex-mage in good stead through the lean years: "Never explain, never defend."

77

Chapter Five

It was cold, and it was wet, and he was hungry. Bram slogged uphill over slippery, rain-soaked leaves behind the centaur, Aurestes. No matter which way he turned, the filthy weather hit him in the face. What had ever made him think their realm was always warm and green? *Their* realm . . . He would have to stop thinking of the tuatha dundarael as "they."

Bram slipped on a patch of slick, frozen leaves and went down hard on one knee. He stayed there, eyes closed, trying to gather himself and remember why he was going through this ordeal.

You're going to meet your true mother, he thought to steel himself. A damp chill is little enough to bear in order to learn the truth. You've suffered worse plowing Thonvil's fields by yourself.

At least he didn't have to be hungry, too. Reaching into the leather pack provided by the tuatha, he withdrew the first thing his fingers met with, a dried fig. Bram swallowed it in one bite, hoping it would restore his determination.

"Don't tell me you're tired already," scoffed Aurestes.

Bram looked above him to the centaur. Aurestes had picked his way up the steep hill as surefootedly as a mountain goat. Slung over one broad shoulder was a quiver filled with arrows. Across the other was a hand-carved bow. Saddlebags bulged with wooden clubs and provisions sent by the tuatha who served Weador. Aurestes's expression was bemused.

"I offered to let you ride on my back."

Bram gritted his teeth. "I told you, I don't think that would be a good idea. Frankly, I find it only barely tolerable that you're my guide."

The centaur gave an equine snort. "As long as we're being frank, one of the two reasons I agreed to lead you was because I found out you were half tuatha. That makes you only *half* tolerable."

Bram stood and, with chilled fingers, brushed off his knee. "I still don't understand why Weador insisted that you accompany me."

"I believe he explained that. Apparently your human half is too dim-witted to understand, so I'll try to say it simply: we must cross a region of utter desolation to reach the area where Weador believes Primula has settled. The region would rapidly drain a tuatha's energy, dependent as they are on the health of their environment. I am not a tuatha, so I will be safe from the effects of the area. You, on the other hand, may be affected, since you are part tuatha."

Bram nodded reluctantly. "I still don't think of myself as anything but human yet." He ran a hand through his hair. "I'm not sure I ever will."

"I don't know why you'd fight it," remarked the centaur. "Tuatha are a far more civilized and intelligent race than humans."

"That's just your centaur bias," Bram said coolly, "which is interesting, considering that your front half looks human. Tell me, how would *you* react if someone

told you that you weren't really a centaur, you were a
. . . a bugbear?"

"That would be ridiculous," said Aurestes. "Look at
me." He peered around at his flanks. "Do I look like a
bugbear?"

"Do I look tuatha?" returned Bram. "No, I look, I
feel, I think like a human. It's all I know."

For once, Aurestes refrained from a nasty reply.
Instead, he nibbled on his own stores.

"You said something about there being two reasons
you agreed to guide me," Bram recalled, breaking the
silence. "What's the second?"

"Not that it's any of your business," the centaur pronounced haughtily, "but I am in temporary service to
the tuatha as a priest of the true god, Habakkuk."

"You don't seem like the spiritual type," Bram
remarked unkindly.

Aurestes gave him an arch look. "Habakkuk says
nothing about having to be nice to stupid humans. He
does, however, expect that once during a priest's lifetime he leave friends and community to wander the
land. This time purifies the priest and teaches him the
true ways of nature. The time ends when the priest
receives a sign from Habakkuk that he has done a great
service. Toward that end, I have served my time helping Weador to restore the lands within his domain. Just
before Weador asked me to accompany you, I received
a vision from Habakkuk. He told me that leading you
to Primula would complete my missionary work."

"But Weador told me the tuatha worship Chislev.
Why would a priest of Habakkuk serve the followers
of another god?"

"Habakkuk and Chislev work in concert to restore
and maintain the natural world. Both tuatha and centaurs fiercely protect nature from those who would
destroy or squander it."

"Wait," protested Bram. "Habakkuk is also wor-
shiped by the cavaliers in Ergoth—"

"So?" barked the centaur rudely. "Knights and centaurs have much in common—bravery, valor, a fierce love of nature. Habakkuk, in fact, created the Order of the Crown of the Knights of Solamnia."

The centaur looked back over his shoulder, then began picking his way up the slope again. "If you're done resting, let's continue. We haven't even reached the devastated area yet."

Bram looked around at the gray, wet landscape in disbelief. "This isn't it?"

"Not hardly," Aurestes snorted. "But we'll be there all too soon."

Beyond the ridge the land dropped away sharply. As the pair pressed on, moving down to lower elevations, they reentered a wood. But this one was nothing like the forest they had left behind. These plants had none of the sense of harmony or perfection that had been so strong back at Weador's court. More and more, they took on a threatening appearance: twisted, gray, thorny. Hideous faces leered out from between shadowed tree trunks or down from the gnarled branches, only to disappear when Bram looked at them squarely. He found himself shuddering involuntarily and jumping every time a twig snapped beneath Aurestes's hooves.

When the forest ended a short time later, Bram wished for the frightening shadows again, so bleak was the landscape here. The sky, or what functioned as sky, was gray-black. The air smelled of wood smoke mingled with the scent of burning flesh. There were no trees or grass to speak of, only bare branches protruding from barren, black dirt. And rocks: big, jagged boulders.

"What happened here?" Bram asked breathlessly. "It looks as if the hottest fire swept over this landscape."

Aurestes took a careful step forward. He looked more watchful than usual. "Just as Weador's court reflects the organic and spiritual health of the physical world it parallels, this part of the tuatha realm mirrors the desolation of the Plains of Dust. Weador believes this area is particularly devastated because of a magic-absorbing artifact that's being used there."

Bram considered the bow in the centaur's hands. His guide had nocked an arrow for the first time since they'd left the court. "Are you expecting some trouble?"

"I always expect trouble when I travel with a human." Aurestes smirked, but his eyes never stopped scanning the bleak scene.

"I thought you'd been here before," accused Bram. Following Aurestes's lead, he withdrew a cudgel from his own pack and proceeded cautiously behind the centaur. The area prompted in Bram a feeling of silent desperation. They moved quickly, at a run, to get the desolate landscape behind them. When at last they passed back into gray, rainy slopes, Bram could have kissed the wretched, cold dirt.

Some distance into the leafless forest, Aurestes finally stopped to let them rest. The centaur's flanks were running with sweat, his lungs heaving. He dropped to his front knees and struggled to catch his breath.

Bram took the wineskin from his pack and pressed the opening to Aurestes's mouth. The centaur gulped the drink gratefully, splashing the runoff onto his hot, red cheeks. Despite the guide's protestations, Bram began to realize the creature wasn't as cantankerous as he pretended. "Why did you seem bent on keeping me from traveling first to Wayreth, then Weador's court?"

Aurestes wiped his mouth on his forearm. "My assignment was to test your mettle and determination."

"I had you pegged for a bit of a fool," Bram confessed ruefully.

Aurestes actually smiled. "You, of all people, should know not to judge on appearances."

"I owe you an apology," Bram said. "I was wrong about not needing you as a guide."

Instead of looking touched, Aurestes scowled. "I told you, I came along because I was charged by Habakkuk to do so. Somehow—and I can't imagine why—it furthers his goal of defending nature. It was *not* out of any sense of friendly concern or affection. Just get that notion right out of your foolish human head."

"Fine," Bram said, trying to hide a grin that he knew would only annoy the centaur. He retrieved his wineskin and tilted it. One last drop fell to the earth. "Next time, guzzle your own rations."

"It looks as if I'll have to, since you're out of Weador's restorative drink."

The centaur led them to the riverbank. There they turned left and followed the river downstream for what seemed like several leagues. Eventually the river plunged through a rocky gorge. At first, Bram was doubtful he could scramble down the rugged slopes, but the centaur found a route that they both could follow. After much hard climbing, they reached the bottom.

There the riverbed flattened, banked by great slabs of smooth stone. Just across the river rose a rocky cliff face streaked in shades of water-weathered gray. Propped against the stone wall was the tallest ladder Bram had ever seen, and the most primitive. The unhewn trunks of hundreds of saplings were lashed horizontally to three vertical support beams. It reminded Bram of the sun-bleached spine and ribs of a cow.

His gaze followed the ladder up to an opening in the cliff face. "Opening" wasn't the right word, he corrected himself. It looked as if the elaborate, columned entrance to a temple had been ripped away and grafted into the face of the stone wall.

"Are you just going to stand there, gaping, or are you going up to meet your mother?" the centaur demanded.

Bram jumped, startled. "I'm going." He regarded the centaur's horse quarters with a frown. "How are you going to climb that ladder?"

83

"I'm not. Your arrival here completes my service to the tuatha. Now I can return to my people after a very long year." Aurestes turned to leave.

"That's it?" said Bram. "You're going just like that?"

"Did you think we'd engage in that particularly annoying human custom of hugging good-bye?"

"No! Of course not, I—" Bram paused, flustered. He straightened and composed himself. "Fare-thee-well and thank you again, Aurestes. I hope your homecoming is all you expect and more."

Aurestes's gaze traveled up the enormous ladder, then back to the human's anxious eyes. "The same to you, Bram."

Bram watched the centaur canter away and disappear in the maze of gullies that filled the land this side of the river. He continued staring until long after the sound of hooves ringing against stone had faded to nothing.

He took his first, tentative steps up the ladder, thinking as he did that the area looked deserted. That was just what he'd expect from the tuatha, who were never seen unless they wanted to be. Weador's subjects had been helping Bram in Thonvil for years before he became aware of their existence.

With measured care, he proceeded up the ladder. At the top, he stepped through the carved archway onto a long, broad underground road.

"Hello!" he called, his voice echoing down the rocky shaft. "I have come from King Weador's court to speak with the tuatha named Primula." When there was no answer, he began walking. After a short way, Bram realized that he was not in a cave, as he originally thought, but a tunnel dug into the hillside. He quickened his pace until the spot of light at the far end grew into a distinct opening. Beyond it the world was once again green and inviting.

Stepping through the opening, Bram called out again. He felt foolish shouting to the trees, but he also thought it would be rude to barge into Primula's realm uninvited and unannounced. He trusted that the tuatha were there. Over the three years that he'd knowingly worked side-by-side with the tuatha in Thonvil, he had developed a sense of their presence. The air seemed more vibrant, electric even, when they were near. He would have said he'd learned how to detect them, but now he wondered if he hadn't inherited the latent sense.

When still no tuatha appeared, he repeated his message a third time, adding, "I mean no harm. My business with Primula is urgent."

Slowly, very slowly, Bram detected a change in the air. One leaf, then two, then five dropped from the surrounding trees and spiraled through the crisp air, as if propelled by an unseen whirlwind. As each leaf touched the ground, a faerie appeared. These tuatha were as short as, though much thinner than, Weador's subjects. They were pale and slight, even sickly. The men wore simple tunics and trousers, the women plain shifts in subdued shades of the forest. None wore the bright and whimsical colors favored by the tuatha Bram knew.

More leaves tumbled, more somber-faced faeries appeared, until at least thirty were present. A woman stepped forward to face Bram. He knew before she spoke that he looked into the face of his true mother. She had his same oddly flat nose, the feature that had always baffled him. Even Guerrand had long ago remarked that Bram's nose was the one thing that kept them from looking like brothers. No ancestor's portrait had revealed the origin of that feature. Now he knew why.

"I am Primula," she said, stumbling slightly over the pronunciations. Her voice was of medium pitch, strong yet serene. "Please forgive my slow speech. It has been many years since I have spoken the common tongue of men."

Bram simply stared. His mother had the same crystal-blue eyes of so many of the tuatha. Her chestnut-brown hair was drawn back tightly and gathered into a braid that was woven through with bright green ivy. Another length of ivy draped the pale collarbone above her brown shift.

"You bear a message from Weador?" she prompted.

Bram swallowed hard. "He told me I am your son."

"Yes."

"Does that mean nothing to you?"

"I'm sure Weador explained how we view such relationships, if he found reason to tell you of your true heritage."

"He didn't offer me the information; I confronted him about it." Bram felt the press of a hundred eyes. "Is there somewhere more private we can talk?" He scanned the surroundings for signs of shelters.

"The others will hear us wherever we are."

"Then please tell them not to listen."

Primula summoned another of the tuatha and spoke quickly in a language Bram could not understand. This one waved his arms to the others, and they all spun about and disappeared, literally, into the tree line.

"We are alone."

Bram looked around self-consciously for something to sit on. "Do you just live out here in the forest, with no shelter or other comforts?"

"We find the forest filled with comforts," she said softly. "What would you have us seek shelter from? Chislev's renewing rain? The sun that makes all things of nature grow?" She eyed his wet clothing. "For your comfort I will provide a fire and a dry seat." Without so much as a wave of her hand, a small but warming fire and tree stump appeared to Bram's left. Awkwardly, Bram settled himself, while Primula continued standing.

"I won't ask you just yet why you agreed to give me birth," he began. "I'm not sure I'm ready for that answer. Instead, I would ask why you left Weador's realm."

"You would find that the answers to both questions are the same. I did these things because I believed I was serving Chislev. However, I came to realize I was serving only Weador."

Bram bristled slightly. "For more than three years King Weador and his subjects have worked tirelessly to bring back life to my village and its people. In turn, the quality of life for his own people is good."

"You are judging accomplishments by human standards," Primula said with great tolerance. "Our community has spiritual wealth brought about by disciplined worship to Chislev. Weador's wealth is of a material nature."

"He could have left Thonvil to die, but he didn't."

"Perhaps that was Chislev's plan for you and your village." Primula placed several small sticks on the fire. "There is much you do not understand about a tuatha's service to Chislev, Bram."

"I know nothing about it," agreed Bram. "And I'm not sure I want to, if he asks his followers to value laziness and death over hard work and life."

"All things of nature must die."

"We don't need to hasten them along toward that goal," he returned evenly.

"The timing of such things is not for us to decide," Primula said. "By meddling, we are imposing our will over Chislev's. We seek to have a god's powers."

"So you would have had Weador just let us—let me—die."

"Perhaps you would have accomplished the same renewal on your own."

"What would have happened to Weador and his subjects?" Bram demanded. "It was explained to me that a tuatha's survival is dependent upon the well-being of the human community to which it is attached."

"Tuatha dundarael are nomadic by nature," Primula began. "Weador should have moved his people when things began to decline in your village. Instead, he grew too comfortable in the setting and chose not to leave it."

Primula's gaze never left Bram's eyes. "That is why I left Weador's domain. Your presence here tells me that his thinking has not changed.

"I left Weador's community," she continued, "and many chose to join me. I recognized that he had grown too dependent upon contact with humans. I fear that when kings like Weador blur the distinction between tuatha and humans, our culture will eventually be assimilated into theirs. Or worse, that we will cease to exist. Weador's decision to arrange a human-tuatha offspring to strengthen the DiThon family line eventually convinced me his was a dangerous folly."

"And yet you agreed to carry me."

"Weador was my king," she said simply. "I wanted to believe he represented Chislev's will. I came to realize the truth when I carried you in my womb. I left as soon afterward as was physically possible and have never regretted it."

The silence that followed felt terribly awkward to Bram, but had no visible effect on Primula. "How is your service to Chislev here any different from Weador's?" he asked at length.

"Our goal is to return to the traditions of our ancestors. Tuatha should never be seen by humans, but only do them small favors in return for gratuities. Our numbers here are much smaller than Weador's, and our needs are simpler. We have never allowed ourselves to be seen by the human community we serve—a small, humble village."

"I suppose, then, it's pointless to tell you that Weador is concerned for your welfare," Bram informed her. "He asked me to invite you to return to the safety and comfort of his realm."

"There is that word again—'comfort'." Primula nearly gave an ironic smile, but shook her dark head instead. "No, there is no point in your asking me to return. This is how Chislev means tuatha to live."

"Then how am I meant to live?" Bram asked.

Primula's eyes flashed pity for a split second. "I cannot answer that. You are free to choose which philosophy you will follow."

"I *am* of two cultures." Bram said it for the first time without fear or loathing. "But I know so little of tuatha ways. . . . Teach me your ways," he prompted with great feeling. "Give me the knowledge to choose wisely between the tuatha ways and the human ideals I have followed all my life. Perhaps I will even find a way to prevent your prophecy about the melding of the societies from coming true."

"I fear what you represent for the future of the tuatha dundarael," admitted Primula. "But it would be the ultimate hypocrisy to hold you responsible for your heritage. Besides, I can turn away no one who would follow the teachings of Chislev. But I must warn you: You are the only one of your kind. What you seek—to learn to become tuatha—has never been done by any human. The path will be long and difficult, and quite possibly deadly."

Bram straightened with determination. "I don't take on this quest lightly, Primula. I'll do whatever it takes," he vowed solemnly, "for however long it takes, to learn Chislev's ways."

Lyim sat at the blond-wood table in the Hall of the Councilors, absently tracing a tapered fingernail in the thick dust overlooked behind a vase. The contingent of servants sent by Mavrus had been given only heartbeats to set right a council chamber that hadn't been used in years. Vases of fragrant flowers helped to dispel the mustiness of sealed disuse.

"Basha," Aniirin began, peevishly slumped at the head of the conference table. "Tell me again: why did I decide it was necessary to meet with these dwarves? I would rather be feeding my fish in the reflecting pool."

Mavrus had managed to get the potentate into a very snug cobalt-blue ceremonial cassock. Buttons strained across his lumpy chest so that his white cotton underclothes peeked between them. Aniirin squirmed and scratched like a child in temple-day clothing.

"These sorts of trade conferences are tiresome, no doubt," agreed Lyim. "Particularly with a race as self-important and greedy as the dwarves. Nevertheless, you felt that since they were so persistent we should listen to their grievances. If we don't, we risk jeopardizing the trade agreement struck with them during the reign of your venerable grandfather. This would seriously affect the shipping revenues we receive for the dwarven trade barges navigating our River Torath."

"Yes, that was it," said Aniirin absently. His oddly shaped head snapped up. One blue eye and one green eye squinted at the doorway. "Why aren't they here yet? Don't they realize I'm a busy man? I have better things to do than wait for a passel of whining dwarves."

"Of course you do, Sire," said Lyim. "Unfortunately, the other amirs must arrive before Mavrus can show the dwarves in." He gave the door a worried glance. "I can't imagine what has kept them."

Lyim knew full well what was delaying the aldermen. Salimshad had arranged to waylay the messengers sent to the amirs and made some alterations to the appointed time on their missives.

"I'm sure they will arrive shortly," Lyim said. "They are responsible men, all. The streets were crowded, what with the festival to Sirrion being observed by the masses."

"And yet you made it on time," observed Aniirin.

"I am flawed with an intolerance for lateness," confessed Lyim. "Salimshad maintains I'm obsessed with leaving ridiculously early for appointments."

"This does not sound like a flaw to me." Aniirin plucked a handful of green grapes from the bowl before him and popped them in his mouth all at once.

Lyim coughed uncomfortably at the praise. "I assure you, Sire, it is a policy that maddens Salimshad." He looked toward the door again and frowned. "Perhaps I can determine what keeps the other amirs." Lyim stood and bowed his head briefly. "If you will excuse me, Sire, I will be only a moment."

"Instruct Mavrus to help you." Aniirin waved a

distracted hand, his attention already focused on the ticklish task of peeling a pomegranate's leathery red skin without piercing the juicy seeds inside.

Lyim stepped quickly from the room and closed the heavy gilt door behind him. Everything was going as planned. He gave a shrill whistle, the signal to Salimshad. The elf was in the small adjoining Courtyard of the Councilors, explaining to the waiting aldermen that Basha Rhistadt was still working to persuade Aniirin of the need to meet with the dwarves from Thorbardin. The amirs would have no choice but to believe it, then would be forced to acknowledge the progress Lyim had made with the potentate. Though it would be beneficial for the city and all its aldermen, Aniirin had resisted such a trade meeting, citing tedium, before Lyim's rise. But now the potentate trusted Lyim implicitly.

Timing was crucial. Lyim had to get the dwarves into the council chambers just seconds after the amirs arrived, so that Aniirin would have no time to ask the nobles about their lateness. He hastened to the audience antechamber, where Mavrus was entertaining the contingent of three dwarves.

"We are ready," Lyim announced.

A little frayed around the edges, Mavrus looked relieved to see Lyim. The crisply starched collar of the man's jacket was stretched and slightly sweat stained. Three large, empty bottles of Aniirin's best Kharolian ale stood empty on a table. Mavrus's hand was poised to pour the dregs of another bottle into a mug intended for a dwarf whose eyes were already red-rimmed with drink. That the dwarves were on their way to being inebriated only furthered Lyim's plans.

The dwarves regarded the basha with irritation at having been kept waiting. One stomped up to him, about to speak, when Lyim cut him off.

"We had best save introductions until we reach the council chamber, sir. Aniirin is a busy potentate, and I am loathe to keep him waiting."

Lyim knew this approach was risky. He gauged the dwarves' reactions to his words. As he'd intended, the suggestion that Aniirin's time was more valuable than theirs fanned their anger.

Aniirin's new heir apparent glanced at Mavrus and was further relieved. The manservant gave a slight smile of approval, having detected only concern for Aniirin's schedule in Lyim's words. So far, so good, thought the basha.

Walking before the contingent, Lyim could see the door to the Hall of Councilors close behind the last alderman. He hastened his steps and swung the heavy door open again before the amirs could do more than find seats.

"Potentate Aniirin, venerable amirs of Qindaras, I would introduce the representatives from Thorbardin."

Aniirin's mouth was ringed in red pomegranate juice. The potentate spit a seed to the table just as Mavrus hastened through the assembled group to hand him a handkerchief.

Though not known for their subtlety, the dwarves seemed able to conceal their surprise at the potentate's appearance. Lyim could scarcely suppress a snort at the sight of his pushed-in head and childishly stained face. Lyim only hoped that the dwarves would not openly insult anyone before he had the chance to plant more poisonous seeds of discontent on both sides.

One of the dwarves stepped forward. "Therin Glous, of Clan Daewar," he said in the heavily accented, rumbling baritone of most of the dwarves of Lyim's acquaintance. He wore a heavy leather doublet, striped pants, and rolled boots. "Behind me is Noshor, our minister of trade, and von Eaugur, our minister of public safety."

The potentate merely sat, blinking one green and one blue eye expectantly, so Lyim hastily introduced his fellow amirs—Vaspiros, Garaf, Calesta, Dafisbier, and Hasera, Rusinias's replacement.

"Let me also introduce myself," he said in his most suave tones. "I am Basha Lyim Rhistadt, Potentate Aniirin's legatee." He waved the dwarves toward three empty chairs at the conference table. "Please, make yourselves comfortable while you repeat to all of us the nature of your grievances."

Amidst loud grumbling, the short-legged folk struggled into the tall chairs.

Mavrus exchanged a worried glance with Lyim. The manservant had thoughtfully suggested replacing three of the human chairs with shorter, dwarf-sized ones. Lyim had quickly rejected the idea, informing the manservant that, in his experience, dwarves interpreted that sort of gesture as patronizing. Lyim merely wrinkled his lips now, as if to say, "Who could have known?"

"As we told your man Mavrus here," said Glous, "we have come to lodge a formal complaint concerning the looting of our trade barges and the murder of our sailors and merchants. Ships that have passed through Qindaras on the Torath in recent months have reached their final destinations with only half their loads and often minus a number of deckhands. We demand a formal investigation into this matter," concluded the dwarf.

"Perhaps your sailors are not as trustworthy as you think," suggested Vaspiros in his twitchy way. Like Lyim's, Vaspiros's district was on the waterfront. "Perhaps they were tired of life aboard ship and deserted after selling your stolen cargo to insure they could retire in style."

The dwarven minister of trade leaned forward to speak, his fleshy cheeks burning red with anger beneath his beard. "Sailors returning to Thorbardin reported that the missing deckhands went ashore while here in Qindaras. When they did not return, search parties were dispatched. In all cases they discovered the missing sailors slain in the streets of your riverfront districts. We reported the murders, but nothing has been done."

Calesta and Garaf, aldermen of inland districts, both visibly sighed in relief.

"Qindaras is a city of considerable size," said Alderman Hasera, who had taken over Rusinias's warehouse district on the riverfront. "This type of sordid thing happens all the time in cities."

"Perhaps in human cities," said Noshor with thinly veiled disdain, "but not in civilized cities like Thorbardin."

"Civilized!" barked Aniirin, seeming to pay attention to the discussion for the first time. "You have a great deal of nerve coming in here, demanding anything. You're lucky we let you sail your boats past Qindaras at all!"

"I'm certain His Lordship doesn't mean that—" began Garaf, struggling to calm the storm that was beginning to brew. He looked helplessly to the other amirs.

Lyim's attention turned, however, to the door. On cue, Salimshad slipped in from the courtyard and moved, with the unobtrusive grace of a surefooted elf, to Lyim's side. He looked like a shadow in his black jelaba and hood. Lyim leaned back in his chair to give an ear to Salimshad. The elf whispered to him briefly, and Lyim's face abruptly lit up. He nodded in satisfaction before waving Salimshad back through the doorway.

"If you do not give us satisfaction regarding these robberies and murders," von Eaugur was shouting, "we will be forced to consider null and void the three-hundred-year trade agreement struck with Aniirin I."

Hasera picked up the lame defense. "I'm certain the potentate shares our concern with continuing this mutually profitable trade agreement. Perhaps he has an idea that may satisfy all parties."

"Aniirin," stormed the potentate, "can speak for himself! Mavrus! Give Garaf and Hasera half-punishment for impersonating the potentate."

Mavrus was surprised at the turn of events. But ever

the trained manservant, he waved an arm through the doorway. Four armed sentries appeared within heart-beats. Mavrus pointed to the stymied and frightened amirs, who obviously remembered the sight of Amir Rusinias's remains in a blood-soaked box. Without delay, the sentries marched the anxious amirs out of the Hall of Councilors. Vaspiros and Calesta gaped like landed fish, but swallowed any words they had intended to speak.

Lyim cleared his throat, then addressed the dwarves. "I take exception to your demanding tone," he began. "The potentate moved to correct the problem of which you speak upon hearing of it from Mavrus this morning. I regret to admit that the majority of these crimes appear to have happened in my own district. Because of that, I offered my own man, Salimshad, to infiltrate the seedier sections of the district to find those responsible. He has just informed me that the culprits have in fact been apprehended and await punishment."

Lyim snapped his fingers. Four scruffy, gagged vagrants tripped through the doorway, prodded from behind by Salimshad.

Aniirin's mouth hung open, and his eyes bulged. The dwarves were astonished at the speed with which their demands had been met, particularly in light of the conversation.

"There can be no mistake?" asked Glous.

"None," Lyim said, his expression as firm as cooled metal. "Salimshad is expert at forcing the truth from even the most reluctant prisoners. The men have all confessed. Your barges will have no more trouble in Qindaras."

Lyim turned to address the potentate. "What is your will for their punishment, Sire?" Aniirin still looked stunned, obviously searching his misshapen head to remember when he had issued orders for such a search.

"Perhaps," Lyim suggested, "you would allow the dwarves to decide their punishment, in the spirit of continued good faith."

Pleased at his own clever forethought, Aniirin slammed a fist to the table. "Excellent idea!"

"I only remind you of what you yourself thought of first," Lyim insisted with carefully measured humility.

"Kill them in our presence," von Eaugur demanded. Glous and the minister of trade both nodded their bushy heads. "It is the punishment for similar, if infrequent, crimes in Thorbardin."

Immediately, the guards tossed a loop of fine cord affixed to a wooden handle around the throat of each prisoner. The handles were twisted, and the cords tightened like tourniquets. The prisoners were unable to scream, or even whisper. One by one they dropped to their knees, their faces turning bright red, then purple. Their cheeks swelled and their eyes, filled with terror, bulged from the sockets. They convulsed in their bonds for what seemed to Lyim quite a long time. He was not sure when the precise moment of death came because their eyes never closed, though they glazed over noticeably somewhat before the limbs stopped twitching.

Satisfied at last that all four were dead, the soldiers relaxed their grips and let the bodies collapse to the floor.

Lyim leaned in and dropped his voice, ostensibly so that only Aniirin could hear. "Sire, when you decide upon a punishment for my part in these shameful incidents, I would ask that you consider my loyal service. It is unforgivable that citizens of my district could think they would get away with such acts. Garaf was right: we lose sight of how dangerous the streets are, those of us who do not live in the worst of them." Lyim stood up straight. "Still, I take full responsibility."

Vaspiros and Calesta exchanged looks. They had seldom heard such a long speech from the basha, whose frequent silences they had attributed to shiftiness. Neither had they expected self-reproachment from him.

"Await me in my chambers," Aniirin pronounced with unfamiliar seriousness. For once, the look Aniirin gave Lyim was unreadable.

With bowed head, Lyim stepped over the crumpled bodies of the four innocents Salimshad had procured from the streets outside the palace. When he reached the door and slipped through it, a secret smile pulled at his lips.

* * * * *

"I do not recall giving an order to find the culprits," admitted Aniirin. His puffy body disappeared into a soft, deep chair by the hearth. The palace was warmed by magic, as always, and needed no fire, but the potentate's servants knew he liked to stare vacantly into flames. He claimed it soothed him.

Lyim squirmed slightly and adjusted his collar. Aniirin's quarters were unbearably hot. "You did so this morning, Sire. We were discussing renovating the stables when Mavrus informed us of the dwarves' arrival and complaints."

Aniirin nodded his head. "I remember that."

"We discussed sending agents into the waterfront districts," Lyim continued, "and then Mavrus claimed your attention for some other pressing court issue. I merely executed what I believed was your order and sent my men into the streets." Lyim paused and looked contrite. "I hope I did not overstep my bounds."

"No." Aniirin stood and began to pace. He tried to lock his hands behind his back, but his arms were not long enough to surround his girth.

"Since the meeting," Aniirin said, "I have been thinking of my grandfather. He would not consider me to be a good potentate." He put a hand up at Lyim's sputtered protest. "No, no, do not interrupt me in this, my good Basha."

The potentate appeared more serious and lucid than Lyim could ever remember him, as if the day's events had sobered him.

"I do not recall the last time I had real news of Qindaras, or cared to. You may not have noticed this, for perhaps I've hidden it well, but I have concerned myself only with the tax collected by my amirs, not what it represents. Are the citizens doing well? Are such murders as the dwarves described common in all riverfront districts? I know my grandfather, and my father, too, would have had the answers to these questions. A potentate should know these things."

"It is not uncommon for leaders to lose touch with their people," said Lyim, "particularly if they are unable to leave their palaces for security reasons."

Nodding, Aniirin slumped back into the stuffed chair to stare into the flames in the hearth. "I do not recall the last time I saw a citizen close up, let alone spoke to one."

Lyim pretended to be struck with a thought. "You are potentate. Who is to stop you from walking freely among your people? But, no," Lyim said with a shake of his head. "It would be too unsafe for you."

Aniirin sat forward. "Why is that?"

"What leader is free of citizens who would wrongly blame him for their own shortcomings? I am merely a humble basha, and yet I am still unable to travel even the shortest distances without bodyguards. As potentate, you would certainly be subjecting yourself to verbal abuse, possibly even bodily harm."

"Who would dare to harm the potentate?" stormed Aniirin. "There would be retribution both here and in the afterlife!"

Lyim paused meaningfully. "It may seem inconceivable, Sire, but some people are willing to chance their placement in the hereafter to get the revenge they seek in the here-and-now."

Aniirin considered that. "Few people have ever seen me. How would they know I was not some visiting nobleman?"

Lyim took in the potentate's finely made clothing. "You don't look like just any nobleman, Sire. Of course,

I mean that only as a compliment."

Aniirin's brief frown of annoyance changed to resolve. "I am potentate, and I say I will travel in a disguise. Arrange it with Mavrus." He saw Lyim's look of protest and smiled slyly. "Consider the order your punishment for allowing those culprits to operate in your district."

Lyim bowed his head. "Then I cannot refuse you, Sire. But I must insist you consider letting my contingent of bodyguards accompany you. I can personally vouch for their effectiveness."

"Would I not seem more suspicious, surrounded by guards?"

"They are trained to be discreet."

Aniirin slammed his fist upon the arm of the chair in triumph. "Then it is settled. You will see to my disguise and protection."

"Mavrus will be the harder to convince, Sire."

Aniirin waved a hand to dismiss the notion. "Mavrus will do whatever I say. Besides, he has witnessed your loyalty. He trusts you now."

Lyim bowed his head once more in obeyance. "Then consider it done, Sire."

Inwardly Lyim's smile became a sneer as he reflected that soon, Mavrus would learn the depth of his mistake.

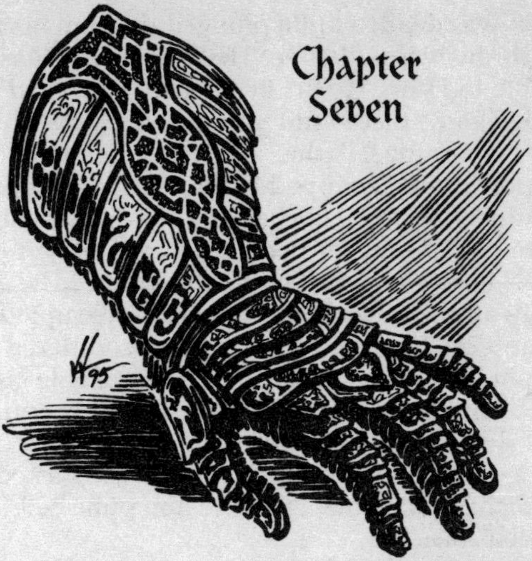

Chapter Seven

Mavrus's pale, wrinkled fingers drummed the parqueted gaming table in Aniirin's sumptuous quarters. The rhythmic noise began to fray at the already-ragged edges of Lyim's nerves. He was supposed to make a move in their game of tenstones, but he could scarcely recall what color pieces were his, much less care. He was only playing the pointless parlor game with Aniirin's manservant to occupy himself until the time the potentate was scheduled to return from his foray into the city.

Lyim knew Aniirin would never return.

At least that was what he hoped, what he had arranged. But the sun had slipped behind the last buildings visible through the arches of the west-facing windows. Salimshad was past due. The news of Aniirin's murder by thugs was to have arrived just before nightfall. Salimshad made no mistakes and was never late without good reason.

What *good* reason could there be tonight? Either

Aniirin was dead, a knife plunged through his inbred heart, or he was still alive. That possibility was unacceptable to Lyim. He unconsciously squeezed a tiny, rounded game piece until his knuckles were white.

"It is your move, Basha," Mavrus prompted.

"I know that!" snapped Lyim. His lips compressed into a tight line at the uncharacteristic crack in his composure. "I have never been much of a player of ten-stones," he explained. "I forget the rules and—"

"I am afraid for him, too," Mavrus interrupted.

"Don't mistake concern for fear," countered Lyim. "The potentate is under the protection of able guards." Lyim pushed himself away from the table and stood up. "I don't well tolerate changes in plan. There is never a good reason for them. Salimshad is responsible for tonight's timetable. I will see him punished for this inconvenience."

Mavrus toyed with the game pieces. "You forget Potentate Aniirin's capricious nature. Your man would have no choice but to obey a whim of the potentate."

Lyim frowned. Aniirin had agreed, for his own safety, to follow a prearranged sequence of events. Lyim remembered the potentate's acquiescence had come quickly—maybe a little too quickly.

The basha was anxious to know what was keeping Salimshad from arriving with the "tragic" news.

"Perhaps I should have followed at a distance in disguise," said Lyim. "Only then could we have been assured Aniirin would not veer from the planned route."

There also would have been no alibi for Lyim's whereabouts when it came time to investigate the assassination. The need for a credible witness was the only reason Lyim had agreed to sit in the potentate's stifling chambers with Mavrus, playing a mindless children's game.

An attractive young wench wearing the tight shift Aniirin preferred on his female servants glided into the room just then. She kept her face averted as she added logs to the fire already blazing in the hearth. Then the woman slipped soundlessly from the room.

Lyim frowned as the logs sizzled, then burst into flame. "Why must Aniirin keep it so warm in here?" He tugged open the strings at the neck of his tunic.

"Aniirin likes to—"

"Watch the flames, I know," Lyim finished. The sweet scent of roses became almost overpowering in the heat, thanks to the potentate's annoying penchant for surrounding himself with enormous vases of fresh flowers. "It smells like a death room in here."

The pale, transparent skin on Mavrus's face pulled up into a wry smile. "You get used to it."

The manservant stood and poured some water from a crystal pitcher atop the settee. He took a long drink, then cleared his throat as if preparing to speak. But ever the manservant, he hastily remembered the heir apparent. "Would you care for some?"

Nodding absently, Lyim accepted the glass Mavrus held toward him.

Mavrus cleared his throat again with obvious awkwardness. "I would like to explain something that has troubled me," he began. "When you first became amir of the merchant district, there was much talk of a negative sort regarding your character, particularly after the death of the amir who remains nameless. I confess I listened a little too closely to the wagging tongues and concluded that your motives were not the purest. I believed the potentate was enamored of your reputed magical abilities, and it was blinding him to your true nature."

Lyim was amused by Mavrus's discomfort. "Is that so?"

The balding man nodded ruefully. "You must understand, for so long I have been the only person the potentate would trust—could trust. There are few men who would not take advantage of proximity to the potentate's ear."

103

"Am I to presume from this confession that you've had a change of heart?"

Mavrus set down the water goblet. "I have watched you accept blame for things for which you could have seized credit. I have witnessed the loyalty you inspire. I have seen you foster in Aniirin an interest in the city's welfare that he has never before possessed."

Mavrus paused, then said in a rush, "It is a relief to admit I have been most concerned. I can see that the magic instilled by both Aniirin I and II to maintain the palace is waning. But other than gently reminding my lord, I have been helpless to do anything about it." Mavrus clamped a hand over his mouth and sank weakly into a chair, surprised at his own confession.

Lyim stared at Mavrus's fretful profile for a long moment. What a pity, he thought, that you should choose me as your confessor. I would slay any servant so free with his words about me, however well intended.

"Please forgive my loose tongue, Basha. It's just that I am so happy to see new life breathed into my lord." It was Mavrus's turn to frown at the closed door. "And I am so worried that he has not yet returned."

Lyim had similar concerns. Perhaps there was some way he could leave to locate either the potentate of Salimshad. If Mavrus saw him, Lyim would forfeit his alibi. As much as he'd like to, he couldn't very well knock the man unconscious. The room was hot enough to inspire sleepiness, but Mavrus was too concerned about Aniirin to drop off on his own. Searching his mind for alternative means to slip away, Lyim absently fingered the velvety, wilted petals of a rose in a nearby vase. An old memory sprang to mind. He had once used a handful of rose petals to cast a sleep spell.

Did he dare use magic to put Mavrus to sleep? He reminded himself to keep his goal to destroy magic foremost in his mind. His conversation with the Gauntlet of Ventyr had prompted his decision to kill Aniirin.

He wanted that gauntlet now, so that he could use it to systematically draw away all the magic from the world. There would be no second chances of this sort to kill Aniirin.

The desire to heed magic's pull was strong in the basha every second of every day. He had been vigilant against its enticements. It would have been a simple thing to give in when a fire needed stoking and there was no servant to tend it, or when his tasks took him by foot to the other side of Qindaras on a frigid winter day. Yet he knew that casting even one simple cantrip might prod him into greater enchantments. Then, before he knew it, he would be back under magic's spell. But he knew the danger now, knew what to watch for. He could control further urges, if using magic now brought him closer to destroying magic. Lyim was nothing if not in control.

Is it in conflict—or poetic justice—to use magic to destroy magic? the basha pondered. Only a diamond can cut a diamond. Besides, the goal is all that matters. As for the means to reaching it—never explain, never defend.

Mavrus was stirring the fire, his back turned. Lyim's slender fingers curled around the deep red rose blossom. He gave a sharp tug, and the fragrant petals fell into his palm like feathers. The manservant didn't notice Lyim pluck the rose. He couldn't hear over the crackling of the flames as Lyim muttered the easily recalled incantation to induce sleep, hardly more than a cantrip.

"*Vexe dorema*," Lyim breathed. The words flowed like water over his tongue. The old, familiar tingling began at his scalp, made his stubble of hair stand up. The delicious sensation spread down his body in raw waves. It had been so long. . . . He felt woozy, drunk on the effect of one simple spell.

Do not let it control you, he warned himself.

Lyim came back to himself with a jerk. Mavrus sat in

his chair as before, but his eyes were closed peacefully. The basha held a hand under the manservant's nose, detected slow, even breaths.

"Mavrus?" he whispered. The man didn't twitch.

Lyim ran to the door and slid the bolt in place to ensure that no conscientious servant would enter and try to awaken the sleeping manservant while he was gone.

The basha couldn't recall how long the spell would last, but he knew he hadn't hours before Mavrus would wake up. That eliminated traveling on foot to find the potentate. He would have to think of another spell to transport him to the appointed site. Teleportation was the only method he knew that could accomplish that. It was a difficult spell. There were rules regarding recent memorization, particularly for complex spells. Gods, how he hated rules that were not of his own devising!

Lyim looked at Mavrus and grew conscious of the passage of precious time. He banished the irritation that occupied his mind and let his thoughts roam free. He had invoked the spell to teleport often enough. It shouldn't be impossible, if he concentrated.

A spellbook's worth of arcane words came to him all in a jumble. Lyim calmly sorted through them, arranged them, then rearranged them until he had a combination that felt just right. He created and held in his mind a picture of the back alley in Amir Garaf's district, where the slaying was arranged to take place.

"*Lethodor, ithikitalkus maldifidii locitium.*" The air around him shimmered. But instead of feeling the coolness of a late autumn night in the Plains of Dust, Lyim remained in the potentate's stiflingly hot quarters. His eyes drew to slits as he contemplated the words he had uttered.

"*There's* the catch," he muttered when he realized what he had done wrong. He repeated the incantation, slightly altering the final word's pronunciation.

The air shimmered again. In the blink of an eye Lyim

stood in the coldness of a dark alley overflowing with garbage. Cheap wooden crates lined the walls, spilling rotten produce. The air stank of human and animal wastes. Dogs picked through the trash, sniffing at piles Lyim came to realize were unconscious—or dead—vagrants. The alley was otherwise empty.

Lyim's skin was shocked by the cold, as if he had jumped from a fire into an icy pond. He had foolishly left without a cloak.

"Get!" Lyim's shout scattered the dogs. Looking over their shoulders, they skulked toward the smoky lights that marked the ends of the alley.

He rushed over to the first vagrant and rolled him, half expecting to find Aniirin's corpse. Lyim snorted in disgust. He was a she, and still alive, though she stank of the decay that preceded death. Her fingers were closed about a large, crimson-stained rock. Lyim considered her filthy cloak, but rejected it. He would not walk about in too-small woman's attire.

On the next body, the basha found a suitable dark cloak with a concealing hood. This man *was* dead, his head bashed in and oozing blood—which explained the rock in the woman's hand. Lyim wrenched the man's arms from his sleeves, relieved that the poor sot had at least had the courtesy to not bleed all over the cloak. He slipped the threadbare woolen thing on.

Lyim headed for the alley door to the inn where Salimshad had intended to lead the potentate. The noise hit him in the face, along with a wave of eye-watering smoke caused by a chimney with a bad damper. Lyim remembered at the last instant to cinch up the hood of the cloak, exposing little more than his eyes, nose, and mouth. He kept his head low as he pressed through the bodies who, for lack of empty chairs in the packed inn, stood. A tipsy dwarf staggered back from his group and into Lyim's path, splashing the basha with ale. In days past, Lyim would never have suffered such an affront, but tonight he let the incident pass without a word.

Lyim spied an empty corner where he could scan the crowd unobserved. It took but a moment to realize Salimshad was not at the inn; Lyim knew the elf's stance, even in disguise. There was no sign of Aniirin, either, though Lyim spied Amir Garaf laughing and drinking with a crowd. The man caught Lyim's glance, but the basha looked away too quickly to be identified.

Annoyed, Lyim pushed his way out the front of the inn. Outside, the curving street was bathed in the odd blue light of a cold harvest moon. A stout woman in a black wool cape scurried past, head bent against the bitter wind. Oblivious to the cold, two teenage boys rushed past Lyim in short-sleeved tunics, laughing, taunting each other to enter the inn in search of women. Lyim wasn't surprised to find no one else nearby on the market district street after dark.

Now what? The plan did not call for stops at any other establishments. Lyim's mind flashed on a memory of Mavrus asleep back at the palace. How long would Lyim have before the man awakened on his own?

Abruptly, a door slammed open, followed by the distant sound of loud, drunken voices. Lyim hurried up the street, following the sharp curve. Around the bend, a large sign hung above a wooden door, bearing a carving of a storm-tossed cargo ship—the Pitching Cog Inn.

The potentate has a capricious nature.

Lyim flung back the door on a hunch and stepped inside. He knew instantly what had kept Salimshad.

Aniirin was dressed as a common citizen, his head wrapped in layers of cloth to hide its odd shape. The disguised potentate was holding court of a kind to a circle of men near the blazing hearth. Lyim could see from their scruffy faces that the men were entranced. The basha's heart skipped a beat. He pressed in, head averted, to hear if the potentate had given himself away.

"Believe this if you can, my good friends, the guards bring in a wooden chest, simple of design but strong, and quite large. The sort of chest one might expect a potentate to have in his palace, I suppose.

"And then the lid of the chest is flipped open as casually as you please. The amirs and their wives and all the other painted peacocks in the city are leaning in as close as can be, to see what fabulous treasure lies inside such a box." The crowd, of course, was now leaning in to hear what Aniirin would say. "What do they see? The amir, torn to pieces and then gnawed to shreds by wild dogs! And his face, artfully arranged atop the grisly heap, is painted in the loveliest cosmetics, as if he had come to the party as an honored guest. Which, I suppose, he had. And that, my friends, is how my master survived a treacherous plot."

The crowd roared at the story, obviously entertained at the thought of an amir begin treated so. Lyim was reassured. Even if Aniirin had openly claimed to be himself or let a hint slip, no one would have believed the man with the oddly-colored eyes and oversized head was Qindaras's potentate.

"Aniirin is still a slow boat, if you ask me," Lyim heard a younger man bray. "He's got no wind in his sails, and never has! His hands are always warm, his belly always full! He ain't got no idea how we suffer."

The basha caught his breath, certain Aniirin would not tolerate the insult, however ignorantly delivered.

Aniirin did, in fact, rise to his own defense. Still, he surprised Lyim. "Perhaps Aniirin III has not been the best of potentates, but—"

A loud round of derisive snorts swept the assembled crowd, cutting Aniirin's excuse short. The potentate paused, clearly puzzled, while the men leaned back and drained their mugs of ale.

Lyim scanned the dark corners of the inn and recognized Salimshad, though disguised, by the elf's stiff, slender pose. Near him, but not too close, were Rofer and Lorenz, two of Lyim's most trusted men. All three were dressed as peddlers.

The elf's eyes, locked on the potentate, looked a little desperate; Lyim could not hope to draw them to him. Neither could he stroll over and converse openly, for fear of drawing all eyes.

With a simple, inaudible utterance, Lyim broadcast a silent message directly to the elf's mind. Salim's head snapped up as he recognized his boss's voice. Locating Lyim in the inn, both relief and fear crossed Salim's fine, elven features at his unexpected presence.

Salimshad had joined Lyim long after the mage had sworn off using magic. Lyim refused to pacify the elf's anxiety by revealing either his methods or his mood. He merely jerked his cloaked head, an almost undiscernible motion, toward the back of the inn. *Have one of the guards warn Aniirin he has many enemies here. Tell him he must leave immediately by way of the alley. Instruct the guards to stay inside. You wait for Aniirin in the alley, but do nothing until I get there.*

Salimshad bowed his head to the order and did as instructed without delay. Lyim watched as Salim stepped up to the bar to order ale, the prearranged sign for one of Lyim's hand-picked men to do likewise; the elf did not drink spirits. Recognizing the sign, Rofer, a burly blond fellow with the thick neck of a warrior, approached the bar. Empty mug in hand, he pushed it across the polished wooden surface to the elf's right. Only a knowing eye could have recognized that a message passed between the two strangers. The innkeeper returned the filled mug. The warrior dashed it back with one long pull, wiped his mouth on his sleeve, then returned to Aniirin among the circle of listeners.

The crowd had thinned already, many having tired of the potentate's outrageous stories and moved on to other conversations. When Aniirin leaned back to catch his breath between tales, the warrior dropped something to the rush-covered floor. Bending to retrieve it, he whispered briefly to the potentate.

The color flew from Aniirin's pudgy face, and his

shoulders tensed. He vaulted to his feet, knocking over his stool in his haste. Lyim could see Aniirin's off-colored eyes darting everywhere at once, searching for telltale, hateful glances. He excused himself clumsily from the circle and began to press his way toward the back door.

Lyim knew he must not be seen following Aniirin to the alley. He waited for the potentate's slouched form to slip through the back door before slithering like a shadow through the front. Time oppressed him—Mavrus could already be awake.

Lyim sprinted up the street, turned right, then right again at the alley. Two forms were bathed in the moonlight. Aniirin's back was turned to Lyim; he was stooped, examining the bodies Lyim had found earlier. Salimshad kept quiet, listening to the potentate's tirade even as he watched for Lyim's arrival in the alley.

"These people are dead!" Aniirin cried, pulling back from them in distaste. "Is this common, people just dying in the streets?"

"It has been known to happen," Salimshad said.

Aniirin straightened abruptly, his mind already past their plight. "I'm chilled to the bone. What are we waiting for?"

"Aren't we all just waiting for death?" Lyim posed.

Aniirin spun around, his face full of surprise. "That's an odd thing to say to a stranger."

Lyim walked slowly toward the potentate. "Some of us have less time to wait than others."

Aniirin showed a mounting horror. "Who are you?" he demanded, taking a tentative step backward.

Lyim's face was concealed by his hood. His steps were slow, silent, in tempo with his carefully measured words. "None of us really chooses the time or place of our deaths. Is it the gods, or just plain bad luck that decides for us? Perhaps it's simply another man with more power at the moment." Lyim chuckled. "That would be the ultimate in bad luck, wouldn't it, Aniirin?"

"Why do you call me that? I am nothing but an old merchant," whimpered Aniirin. "Why do you try to frighten me this way?"

Lyim kept walking until he was within arms' length of the terrified man. "We both know the truth of your identity, Aniirin. We also both know that I would not have gone to such lengths to frighten just anyone."

"I tell you, I don't know what you're talking about! I don't even know who you are!" Aniirin took another slow step back and darted a desperate glance around the alley, relieved to find Salimshad nearby, until the elf slipped behind the potentate to block his escape.

Aniirin spun around to stare pointedly at the shrouded figure before him. Lyim uncinched his hood and let it drop to his shoulders. His face was bathed in blue light.

"Basha!" cried Aniirin. Paling further, he drew back again, only to bump against Salimshad's muscular form. "But I trusted you above all others!"

Lyim's broad shoulders lifted in a shrug. "Another bit of irony for this night."

"The rumors . . . Amir Rusinias . . ."

Lyim gave a wry smile. "A funny thing about rumors; there is often a grain of truth in them."

Aniirin shook his head over and over in silent denial. "But I don't understand! The position would come to you soon enough. I made you my legatee, my heir!"

"I don't recognize your right to grant me anything," snapped Lyim. "I have never met the nobleman who deserved the power and privileges to which he was born." The basha's mind flashed to another man of higher birth who had stood between Lyim and his goals. At least Guerrand had been a worthy adversary. "You are the greatest example to prove that rule yet." He laughed at Aniirin's misshapen head, his odd-colored eyes. "You *are* an accident of birth, a joke played on Qindaras by the gods. But tonight I will set things right."

Aniirin was terrified. "Hel—!"

Salimshad's gloved hand clamped firmly over the potentate's mouth, cutting off any further sound.

Lyim's hand slipped down his thigh. His fingers met with the hilt of his dagger. He had sharpened it out of habit to a razor's edge this morning, never guessing the use to which it would be put.

"Make haste, master!" hissed Salimshad, glancing around fearfully at the distant sounds of drunkards in the street.

Lyim's hand came up. The silver blade caught the blue light, then plunged into the potentate's thick chest three times.

The elf dropped the potentate's dead body next to the stiffened forms of the vagrants Aniirin had found so distasteful.

Lyim wiped the potentate's warm blood from his hands onto his coarse, borrowed robe. His hands shook, but with excitement, not fear.

It was done. He was potentate. Now Lyim could don the Gauntlet of Ventyr and direct it to absorb more magic than its makers had ever dreamed. The Council of Three couldn't touch him without breaking the treaty. They were too sanctimonious for that. Perhaps, the new potentate of Qindaras mused, there are gods of justice after all.

Chapter Eight

Beakers of mysterious, colorful liquids bubbled on burners in the narrow room, part of numerous ongoing magical experiments. Guerrand sat among the vapors and the variously sized skulls and dusty spell tomes in his laboratory. The mage's right index finger traced the arcane words of a spell entry, while the left hand adjusted the too-high flame beneath a beaker that was beginning to boil over.

Control weather enables a wizard to change the weather in the local area.

"That's just what I'm looking for," Guerrand mumbled aloud.

Components are burning incense and bits of earth and wood mixed in water.

Those items were easy enough to come by. The wizard whirled about in his chair to check the floor-to-ceiling shelves behind him in the room. He quickly spotted the amber apothecary jar marked "incense," next to "incendiary oil," right where it should be.

Unlike the wizard laboratories of stories—dark, spider infested, dusty places smelling of damp stone—Guerrand's lab was meticulously organized and usually brightly lit by direct sunlight. Years in the sunless, windowless space of Bastion had caused him to claim as his own the glass-lined gallery facing the sea on the third floor of Castle DiThon.

The view of the sea to the south was less distracting, more conducive to the concentration needed in spell-casting and study. Guerrand still found the landward rush of dark waves soothing, as he had in his youth when he had contemplated the nearby shores of Southern Ergoth from a small cove on the heath. Winter or summer, spring or autumn, only the weather altered the sea—angry black during storms, whorls of soft blue and green in pleasant weather.

Today, the sea was anything but pleasant. Huge, gray waves crashed upon the sands far below Guerrand's bank of windows. The gallery was uncharacteristically dark because of the storm, forcing Guerrand to light lamps even at noon.

The mage would have enjoyed watching the change of seasons in the fields north of the castle while he worked. Considering the spell he was trying to cast now, a direct view of the fields would have been a far sight handier. Still, he had an adequate, if uninspiring view of the colorful autumn landscape on the other side of the castle through the magical mirror he had been given years ago by the wizard Belize.

His gaze roamed from the shelves of spell components to the palm-sized shard of mirror on his desk. Through it, he could see that rain and fog hung like dirty gray cotton over the rolling fields of spelt, maize, and rye between the castle and the village of Thonvil. The foul weather had arrived just before harvest some six days ago and remained tenaciously. It now threatened to rot a summer's worth of work in the fields.

Guerrand saw signs that the tuatha dundarael had

tried to harvest the crops, but the mood of small faerie folk seemed tied to weather conditions. In gloomy weather, they, too, were gloomy and unproductive. And so the crops were still in the fields. All things considered, it was the first truly bad stretch of luck Thonvil had endured since Guerrand had returned with Bram to restore the village and castle some five years before.

Unfortunately, that very record was what was making Guerrand nervous. He had seen things begin to slip in the last two years. Things easily overlooked, like stones tumbled from walls and left where they fell, or haystacks with rot at their centers. Kirah and Maladorigar were doing their best, and a very commendable job at that. The gnome worked day and night to invent a contraption that would both husk and dry corn five times more quickly than by hand, but Guerrand wasn't holding out much hope for it.

The fact remained that neither of them had Bram's skill when it came to inspiring villagers, or the tuatha, for that matter. It had not been all that long since Kirah had been known as the beggarly DiThon who pined for the lover who never appeared. And Maladorigar was a gnome, which said it all concerning his ability to motivate humans.

Two years was a long time for the lord to be gone, particularly in Thonvil. The villagers had just got used to having an active lord after two decades of neglect. Bram was still on his crusade of sorts, searching for the tuatha mother he'd never known he had. Though very accepting of magic, the villagers had not been told the actual nature of Bram's crusade, nor had his human mother Rietta. Instead they'd been told that Bram had been called away north, to Gwynned, by the emperor. But some people were beginning to speak aloud that an emperor who is concerned about his subjects should allow their lord to return and oversee his land.

Not everyone had embraced Bram or his new policies. There were few malcontents in Thonvil, but every village suffered those who lived to find fault with the local lord. The mage knew it was only a matter of time before more people noticed the slight decline in conditions and blamed them on Bram's absence. Mercadior himself would soon begin to inquire too closely into the nature of Bram's absence.

No one knew that dilemma better than the mage. Guerrand himself had been blamed for Thonvil's decline not once, but twice. The first time was when he'd left to become a mage. Guerrand's own brother had blamed him when a neighboring lord led an attack on Castle DiThon.

The second time had been during the plague of snakes—the medusa plague, as it had come to be called. This horrid affliction first turned a victim's arms and legs to snakes before turning the entire body to stone. Lyim Rhistadt, the mage responsible for spreading this curse, had also planted the idea that Guerrand had brought the medusa plague down upon the heads of the villagers.

Guerrand had spent years earning back the trust lost through lies and superstitions. He couldn't let distrust for Bram set in while his nephew was away.

Two long years. Guerrand wondered sometimes, in the stillness of his firelit chamber, if his nephew was well, or if he intended to ever return. He had tried to contact Bram magically once, but the spell hadn't succeeded. The mage had assumed it had failed because he hadn't enough information about Bram's location to direct the magical energy properly. And so Guerrand still waited for word.

His glance snapped back to the spellbook. "None of that will matter if we starve to death this winter—which is precisely what will happen if I don't stop this bloody rain."

The mage unfolded himself from the chair and stood on tiptoe to retrieve the jar of incense, adding another container of fuller's earth, and one more with some interestingly twisted twigs Guerrand had gathered on walks. He set them on his desk, then ladled water from the washstand into a small glass dish.

The mage peered briefly into the mirror to reaffirm that farmers waited under Kirah's direction for a break in the drenching weather. He saw his sister at the fore of a three-sided shed, dirty blond hair pulled back into a tail, arm propped up on a sickle as she peered at the sky. Bless her, Guerrand thought, for trying to lead the people as Bram had. The lord would have been out with them in the mud, too, ready to chop maize with the villagers.

Just then Kirah appeared to wave toward Guerrand, as if she could read his thoughts or feel his gaze through the mirror. If anyone could, it would be his sister. They had grown closer than ever since his return to Thonvil, particularly in Bram's absence. Any resentment she had once harbored against Guerrand for leaving to study magic seemed to have disappeared.

Only Kirah knew what her brother was attempting in his laboratory. They had agreed she should round up the village men, telling them only that travelers had reported the weather breaking to the west and they should be at the ready. Though there was no longer a stigma regarding magic in Thonvil, Guerrand saw no point in advertising its use, particularly if the spell should fail.

Guerrand sprinkled a handful of incense into another small dish. Using a length of wick, he set the incense to flame from the burner on his desk. The air filled with the thick, pungent scent of myrrh and pine, so strong it made the mage cough. Holding a cloth to his nose, he poured a small scoop of fuller's earth into the water, stirring it with a stick from the jar. He drew a deep breath through his mouth, then dropped the cloth from his nose.

Guerrand uttered the incantation and stepped back in case the fuller's earth bubbled out of the bowl.

Instead, the mud plopped twice, a dull, brief boil at best. The thick finger of smoke trailing from the incense bowl lurched suddenly, as if a strong wind had burst through the gallery.

Guerrand looked expectantly out the bank of windows to the sky above the sea. He had specified clear weather with a moderate, southerly wind for drying out the soggy landscape. Though uncommon at this time of year, such a day was not impossible; Northern Ergoth often enjoyed one glorious week of unseasonably warm weather each autumn, known as barbarian summer.

Lightning ripped a seam through the thick black and silver clouds. Contrary to nature, the wind blew both east and west from that jagged white line, chasing the clouds away. Behind was revealed a small, hopeful band of blue sky.

Guerrand felt an adrenalin rush at seeing that the magical energy had been successfully directed and released. He could equate the feeling only to physical love. Guerrand had known mages in Palanthas who practiced the Art simply to feel that wave of hypnotic power over and over again. They cared less for the outward effect of their magic than its inward, physiological manisfestation.

Today as always, however, Guerrand was more interested in the effect, so he turned his mind from the wave rising inside him. His intense gaze turned down into a frown as he realized the transformation in the sky was stopping as quickly as it had begun. The contrary wind ceased, the blue seam filled again with rain-soaked clouds. The sea returned to a dark reflection of the angry black sky.

Guerrand sank into his chair, stunned. He was at a loss to explain what had gone wrong. The spell clearly had worked at first. But then it stopped, as if someone had blown out the magical fire that charged it. He had never encountered quite such an effect before. There was always a chance that a spell wouldn't work, but this one had started out so well. What, or who, had stopped it?

The mage's eyes traveled reluctantly to the hated black thumbprint that had marred the left hem of whatever he wore since he'd made a deal with Nuitari. The god of evil magic had so marked Guerrand to remind him of the debt he owed for turning the black moon on its side, thus stopping the medusa plague. Was Nuitari calling in the debt? Guerrand immediately discounted that possibility. He knew the day to pay would come, but a god of Nuitari's magnitude would surely charge him more than a little weather spell.

Snatching up the spellbook again, he reread the entry for controlling the weather. After a few moments, he leaned back and set the book down, still puzzled. He believed he had followed the directions to the letter. The incantation was straightforward, despite its length. He had cast many shorter spells that were much more demanding. Still, there were many places where a mistake could have occurred.

But Guerrand did not consider himself just any mage. There were, in fact, few spells he thought beyond his ability. Perhaps that was the problem. Had he been fooled by appearances? Had pride caused him to take the spell too lightly?

The mage gathered another round of the ingredients, then attempted the spell again with great concentration and attention to detail. He closed his eyes as he repeated the arcane words that would release the spell.

Superstition kept Guerrand's eyes tightly closed. He didn't want to see the previous results repeated, feel the surge of power from anticipated success, only to have his hopes dashed. He heard lightning snap outside, and still he didn't open his eyes. When he could stand it no longer, he cracked one eye and gazed into the magical mirror. The sky was bright blue, the dark clouds a thin line on the horizon. The fields were already alive with men and women with sickles, slashing at corn stalks and sheaves of spelt.

Guerrand spotted his wiry little sister and smiled broadly. The spell had worked. He was at a loss to explain it, but the spell had chased the clouds away.

He leaned back in exhaustion and relief. Under Kirah's watchful eye, the farmers would not waste a minute of the cleared skies.

Though relieved, Guerrand felt something nagging at the back of his mind. He might have been more deliberate in his spellcasting, but he was certain he had performed the spell the same way twice. Still, magic was a precise and demanding art. . . .

Had he become so complacent in Thonvil's restored-to-prosperity atmosphere that his skills were slipping? It had happened to him once, back before his service at Bastion, when he and Maladorigar had lived in the village of Harrowdown-on-the-Schallsea. How long had it been since he'd felt his skills taxed? When was the last time he'd had his confidence in his magical abilities shaken? Guerrand realized in a flash that it was the last time he'd had the Dream, before he'd returned to Thonvil. He'd been free of the Dream for more than two years. . . . Did this glitch in his spellcasting signal the Dream's return? He hoped with all his heart it did not.

Guerrand didn't place tremendous store in dreams, but this one had haunted and hounded him for years, ever since his Test in the Tower of High Sorcery at Wayreth. In the Dream, as in his Test, he was thrust into the role of Rannoch, legendary wizard of the Black Robes. Centuries ago, the Kingpriest had tried to break the power of the Orders of Magic by closing down their towers. But Rannoch had refused to surrender the great symbols of magic to the charlatan Kingpriest. Instead, as his brother wizards withdrew from the tower at Palanthas, Rannoch cursed the tower as he leaped to his death from the parapet.

More times than he could remember, Guerrand had

woken in a sweat, sure that he was dead from the fall that seemed so vivid in his sleep. But when Guerrand returned from Bastion to Thonvil, the dreams stopped. And Guerrand, frightened lest they begin again, tried for years simply not to think about it.

Esme, Guerrand's former lover, had said the Dream symbolized Guerrand's insecurity about his magical skills. But Guerrand always believed there was a deeper meaning to the recurring memory, one he had yet to learn. Frankly, in the absence of the Dream, Guerrand had stopped looking for it.

What was the point? Not only was he the most powerful mage in Thonvil, he was the only one. Now that it was out, he could not silence the concern that he had let his skills grow soft. Yet he couldn't see anything on the horizon to change his circumstances. At least until Bram came home and resumed his duties as lord.

* * * * *

Guerrand's fears were only heightened when, over the course of the following days, similar magical misfires happened more and more. The simplest incantations, spells that he had used since his earliest magic-wielding days, were failing. When it was something simple, like a magical light going out after only a few moments, it was troubling. But it was cause for alarm when Guerrand cast a spell of flight on himself to get a bird's-eye view of the surrounding territory and the spell failed in midflight. Fortunately, he had cast another spell that broke his fall, and that spell had worked, or he would now be dead or seriously injured. He spoke with Kirah about it one crisp afternoon in the topiary garden.

Guerrand had been settling himself for a rest in his chamber when he happened to glance out the second-floor window and spot her below on a bench. The sparse groves of trees that dotted the landscape about

Thonvil were ablaze with the colors of autumn. Bright yellow crab apple leaves drifted, with the rhythm of the wind, down around her.

Taking up his mug of spiced cider, the mage decided to join his sister. They'd had little time to talk of late, what with the harvest. She seldom stayed in one place long, so consuming were her duties in Bram's absence. Guerrand hurried down the curving staircase and through the foretower before Kirah could slip away.

Despite Guerrand's magical troubles, his weather spell had held out long enough for the villagers to harvest the bulk of the crops. Maize was drying in sheds and barns; spelt and other grains were waiting at the mill for grinding. The village was quieter than usual, the people recovering from the frenzy and beginning preparations for the annual festival of the harvest.

Guerrand stepped into the serenity of Bram's topiary garden of herbs and evergreens and sighed with pleasure. The heady aroma of rosemary alone was almost therapeutic. By unspoken agreement, the garden was being cared for by the tuatha. They faithfully maintained the shrubs originally shaped by Bram into birds, animals, castles, and mythical beasts.

Kirah sat with her feet up on a stone bench, back-to-back with a squirrel shaped of rosemary. It looked beastly uncomfortable to Guerrand, but Kirah seemed not to notice the branches in her back. Every time she shifted, waves of dark, fragrant scent filled the air.

She looked up when Guerrand sat on the stone bench opposite her. "I was just thinking about you."

"Good thoughts, I hope." He could feel the coolness of the stone through the folds of his red robe. Guerrand shifted until he found a comfortable position.

Even though the heavy work was over, Kirah still wore simple farming clothes. Her pale blue eyes were rimmed with dark circles, yet they sparkled as if lit from within. "You look tired," he observed.

"I am," she confessed, crossing her arms with a

satisfied sigh. "But it's a good feeling. The crops are in, and we can relax a little now." She chuckled and shook her head. "All except Maladorigar, that is."

"His drying contraption?"

"It blew up again," she supplied. "By the time he gets it running, the corn will have dried on its own. That's what I'm hoping anyway."

Guerrand squinted at his sister. "You weren't thinking of the gnome and his machine moments ago," he accused gently. "I saw your face from my window above. Your mind was miles from here."

"It was—in time, if not space," she admitted. "I was just realizing how much things have changed for us in the last decade. Ten years ago we were both desperate to get out of Thonvil." She gave a bittersweet smile. "Even five years ago I saw nothing but hopelessness here."

"And now we happily work to maintain the place we thought we hated."

Kirah's blond head shook in mild disbelief. "It just goes to prove we can't predict what's around the next corner. I like not knowing," she confessed. "The uncertainty makes waking up worthwhile. I tell myself, 'maybe something unexpected will happen today'."

"No regrets?"

Her shoulders, now wiry with muscles from work in the fields, lifted into her trademark shrug. "Little things perhaps, like why didn't I go to Gwynned to study or attend court, or failing that, why didn't I run away as a merchant seaman on one of Berwick's ships. Nothing big. At least nothing that I'd take the opportunity to go back and change."

Guerrand watched her closely over the rim of his steaming mug. "Not even marriage?"

His sister's work-tanned face lost its brightness for an instant so brief, only Guerrand would have noticed. "No one that I cared to marry ever asked me," she said in a clipped voice. "How can I regret a choice I was never given?"

She saw his skeptical expression and scoffed. "You can't be thinking of that old dolt Rietta arranged for me to marry while you were away in Palanthas."

"I wasn't."

She examined his face. It was inscrutable as always, a trait that seemed to increase with his immersion in magic. "Look, I know you think I had some schoolgirl crush on Lyim Rhistadt, but the fact of the matter is, I didn't. I confess to being lonely and gullible both times he came to Thonvil to see me, but that's all!"

Annoyed, Kirah jumped up from the bench and began to pluck dead purple flowers from the last of the fall basil. "You never did tell me what became of Lyim after he poisoned Thonvil with the medusa plague."

"I don't know for certain," confessed Guerrand. "The last time I saw Lyim, he was in Bastion and the walls were crashing around our heads. The conclave of twenty-one wizards all suspected he escaped back to the Prime Material Plane with his hand restored."

Guerrand's face reddened with the half-truth. Secretly, he believed the Council of Three had sent assassins after the renegade mage and that Lyim had been slain years ago. He more than suspected it, because Par-Salian had said, "Lyim Rhistadt will be dealt with in the manner of all renegades." According to the laws of the Orders, that usually meant death; the only exception was that the Black Robes were known to try converting renegades of other robes to their order, killing them if the offer was rejected.

"What about you?" Kirah asked abruptly. "Any regrets about marriage?"

He repeated the question dully. "Some. I've told you it wasn't my choice that Esme and I parted ways."

"There's been plenty of time since for other women," Kirah pointed out.

"Time, perhaps," nodded Guerrand, "but neither opportunity nor desire." The mage leaned back and folded his arms. "If it had been important just to marry, I might have wed the 'Bucker princess,' " he said, chuckling at Kirah's long-forgotten nickname for the Berwick woman Cormac had plotted for Guerrand to marry.

Kirah dropped a handful of plucked petals to the ground and brushed her hand. "It's up to Bram, then, to provide the DiThon heir, since he'll get no help from us. That is, if he ever comes back from wherever he's gone."

"You've had that thought too, eh?"

"Who hasn't?" she said. "Even the villagers are beginning to wonder. I heard them talking during the harvest."

"I was afraid of that. I've tried to contact Bram myself, but the spell failed." Guerrand sighed. "Actually, I'm not sure if the spell failed, or if I did. My skills seem to be slipping," he confessed, thinking he might feel better if he spoke his fear aloud. In fact, he felt worse.

Kirah shook her head. "I don't understand. You changed the weather. That can't have been easy."

"It wasn't, and that's just the point. I had to cast the spell twice."

"You've never had a spell fail the first time?"

Guerrand's expression was grim. "Not the way this one did."

"So it was one spell. You were under extreme duress to get it right, and fast."

"It wasn't just one spell, Kirah." Guerrand told her of the other problems he'd encountered with far simpler incantations.

"So what's the solution?" she asked.

Guerrand stood to pace. "I don't know. I've tried to determine if it was lack of concentration, or bad components, or just plain rusty spellcasting skills."

"The problem isn't you, Uncle Rand."

Both Guerrand and Kirah snapped around at the unexpected voice. A man who was familiar and yet a stranger slipped, as quiet as a child's breath, into the garden. He wore a robe of blended brown hues that seemed to spring from the earth, resembling a sturdy oak; thick at the hem, tapering upward to arms that brought to mind branches. In one hand was an elaborately carved staff. Guerrand's eyes followed the folds of the robe upward to the man's face.

"Bram," he breathed. The change in Guerrand's nephew was astonishing. His hair was much longer than Guerrand remembered, a charcoal color draping Bram's broadened shoulders in a manner that reminded the mage strongly of the way bark hugs a tree. His face had thinned; his cheekbones and jawline looked molded from steel under his naturally swarthy skin.

"You're back." Guerrand was at a loss for words.

As usual, Kirah was not at a loss for action. She threw herself into Bram's arms. His wooden staff flew from his hands and clattered to the ground as he caught her. "Bram!" she repeated. "You look incredible, so different from what I expected!"

He smiled fondly, a slow, lazy lift of his lips. "Did you think I would return in the pointy felt hat of Weador's tuatha?"

Kirah blushed furiously, confirming the answer. "Of course not," she denied nevertheless. "Where have you been all this time?"

"On a journey to find my soul."

Her eyes twinkled. "I was actually wondering where your body went."

"That's much less important, and more difficult to explain."

Bram sounded so much more serious than usual, even Kirah paused uncomfortably. "So did you find your soul?"

"As much as I believe any man is meant to find his, yes."

Guerrand watched his nephew, and still he could not think of the words of welcome he'd rehearsed so often. Two years explained hair growth and weight loss, but those were the most superficial changes to Bram's appearance. Bram's attitude—his aura—was different than any the mage had encountered. His new confidence went beyond the experience of travel to an earthiness that seemed organic, not donned like his new cloak.

"Did you find her?" the mage asked quietly, finding his voice at last.

Bram smiled serenely at his uncle. "Yes."

"Was it—"

"Frightening? Wonderful? Unpleasant? Fascinating? Enlightening?" Bram bent down to retrieve his staff. "Yes. I can't honestly say whether, on balance, it was good or bad. It was, however, necessary that I go and stay long enough to learn from Primula."

Guerrand refrained from asking Bram what his mother was like. He felt certain his nephew would reveal these things in his own time.

"Does this mean you're back to stay?" Kirah asked Bram.

The question obviously surprised the lord of Thonvil. "I have no interest in living among the tuatha for the rest of my life, if that's what you're asking. I missed Thonvil more than I would have thought possible. There is much I can do for this region with the skills I have learned. We won't need to rely so heavily on Weador's tuatha, or they on us."

"Can you use magic now?" Guerrand asked.

Bram nodded. "I have skill wielding magic of a different sort than yours, similar to but not the same as a druid's. Tuatha magic springs from the earth and Chislev, the goddess of nature," he explained, "not the moon gods of the Orders of Magic who require practice for successful spellcasting." Bram held out his staff, an elaborately carved length of wood topped with an uncut, glittering gem. "I shaped this myself as a channel through which my magic flows; I can't cast spells without it. It also helps me focus my thoughts."

"Perhaps that's been my problem," Guerrand said.

"Lack of concentration has been hampering my spells."

"You aren't to blame for the glitches in your magic, Rand," Bram repeated firmly. "Something odd is happening in the magical cosmos, the fabric from which all magic springs."

Guerrand was flabbergasted. "Your magic is misfiring, too?"

Bram shook his head. "The faerie realm is inherently magical, so all tuatha notice a 'wrinkle' in the fabric, so to speak. I confess, it has not affected tuatha magic—yet, anyway. Because of that, I believe the problem lies with the moon gods, and not the nature of all magic. Weador believes this, too."

"Is that why you've come back now?" Guerrand recognized the offended gleam in Kirah's eyes. All her life—since she learned of her mother's death during her own birth—the young woman had been touchy about people's motivations for leaving or returning. In fairness, Guerrand had to admit she had reason. He, himself, had fueled that obsession.

"I returned to see what I could learn about this on the Prime Material, yes," Bram said. "But also because I was ready to return home. I thought of you both, often."

Kirah's shoulders visibly relaxed. Despite Bram's ominous missive, Guerrand could not help but feel cheered by his nephew's presence.

He clapped Bram on the shoulder. "Welcome home! We've all missed you greatly. It's obvious the trip served you well. You look like a new man."

"I am happy to be back, delighted to see that I was right to leave things in such capable hands." His gaze traveled from the nearby topiaries to the harvested fields, to the sprawling village beyond. "Thonvil looks just as I remember it—better, even," he added kindly.

"We would have had a celebration," Kirah said with an edge of a pout in her voice, "had we known you were returning today."

129

"I don't need a celebration," said Bram. "I'd feel more comfortable if I just slip back into my role as lord. I'm eager to see the progress you've made, Kirah. Perhaps you'd spend this evening reacquainting me with the ledgers and books."

"Of course!" she said, her eyes shining happily.

Bram turned his peaceful gaze on Guerrand. "First thing tomorrow, I'd like to speak with you at length about magic, one wielder to another."

Guerrand smiled. "I'd enjoy that, Bram."

His nephew nodded in satisfaction. Kirah looped her arm through Bram's and led him away toward a side entrance to Castle DiThon, chattering the while.

Guerrand watched them go, thrilled beyond memory to see Bram back where he belonged.

Then why could he not silence the tiny prick of foreboding the discussion of magic had set to tapping at the edge of his happiness?

* * * * *

For the first time in more than five years, Guerrand's dreams placed him upon the Death Walk that encircled the Tower of High Sorcery at Palanthas. As always in the Dream, the mob stood below, anxiously anticipating their first glimpse of the wonders inside the magical tower. Any moment now, the regent of Palanthas would turn over the key to the wizards' storehouse of knowledge. Eyes fastened on the prize, the mob did not see Guerrand atop the tower, ready to throw himself from the walk in the name of the Art all wizards loved.

As usual in the Dream, the Head of the Conclave, a wizard of the White Robes, used a silver key to close the gates of the tower for the last time. The regent reached out his hand, eager for the key.

Rannoch's voice, ringing clear and cold from atop the Death Walk, stopped the crowd short. They looked up in disbelief as his words echoed across the tower's courtyard, to the Great Library itself.

"The gates will remain closed and the halls empty until the day when the master of both the past and the present returns with power!"

Even in his dream state, Guerrand knew what to expect next. He raised his robed arms like the wings of a bird. But, unexpectedly, the Dream departed from its usual course. For a brief moment, Guerrand stood both in the body of the wizard and below among the crowd, peering skyward.

The wizard leaping from the tower wore a red robe, wore Guerrand's face.

This time he was not Rannoch as he plummeted from the walk. The spikes atop the gates spinning dizzily toward him were talons eager to tear his own chest.

This time when Guerrand awoke, he was not afraid. There was only a strange calmness borne of knowing he'd received a piece to the puzzle of the Dream.

And an unshakable premonition that Justarius would be contacting him soon.

Chapter Nine

"Damn this place," the man cursed softly to himself. Dry, powdery snow mixed with dust rose to his muscled thighs, making travel worse than difficult. He couldn't tell if it was still snowing, or if the wind was whipping up already fallen snow. The cold bit into his legs and face. Ice had formed on the upturned sheepskin collar of his cape, and he stretched his neck to avoid its needlelike scratchings. He tugged the bottom of his fur-lined cape closed, a futile gesture, for it was pushed back open by snow with his next plowing step.

Isk plunged ahead anyway. He would have preferred a job farther north at this time of year, but he had been unable to turn down the incredible coin offered for this one.

Now Isk knew why it paid so well. He'd heard the weather was bad in the Plains of Dust, but he hadn't expected near white-out conditions. The assassin feared he might miss the city, even though he was following the western bank of the river on which Qindaras was situated. Poor visibility forced him to follow the frigid, rushing waters of the Torath more by sound than sight. How big could Qindaras be, anyway, out here in the middle of nowhere?

It was strange, Isk reflected, that no matter how civilized an area considered itself, a man in his line of work could always find employment. Death was the final argument, and Isk had been the agent of death for more people than he could remember. Uncivilized folk do their own killing; the civilized ones pay me, he mused.

The mages who hired him for this mission certainly thought themselves civilized. Still, in this kind of weather, they could have used their magic to deposit him a little closer to the mysterious city. He'd be lucky if he wasn't frozen by the time he got there. The old wizard with the white hair had said they dared not use their magic any closer to Qindaras, for fear it would be detected, or even absorbed. They believed the ruler of the city had a device that consumed magical energy, though he professed to no longer use magic himself.

Of magic, Isk knew only that it had never before prevented him from doing his job. Like most decent folk, he distrusted it. Isk had tracked men across whole continents with only his own sense and cunning. Three leagues hadn't sounded far to walk when he was back in a warm villa in Palanthas.

The wizards had obviously left out a few details.

He couldn't say they had lied. In fact, they'd been brutally honest about the two assassins sent to kill the man who was now potentate of Qindaras. Mages both, they'd reputedly died hideous deaths. That fact bothered him less than did the depth and fury of the snow.

Damn it, he wasn't dressed for a storm so severe! Isk didn't like being unprepared. It could prove deadly in his business. What else about this job was he unprepared for?

Through the impenetrable whiteness Isk sensed that the river was slowly bending east, the beginning of the forks between which Qindaras was situated. The mages had told him to look for a bridge that arched over the eastern fork. Isk thought that a foolish bit of advice now, since he could barely see one step ahead.

A dark shape appeared in the unbroken expanse of white. As Isk advanced toward the shape, it slowly grew into the curving form of a wide bridge, arched high to accommodate ships. Though surprised, Isk was a superstitious man who saw the miraculous appearance of the bridge as a sign that his luck was about to change.

The belief was furthered when a man in a furry hat poked his head out from a small guardpost. Obviously reluctant to brave the storm, the man just waved Isk across.

Further heartened, the assassin proceeded across the bridge. Snow on the decking had been recently flattened by wagon wheels. The waters of the Torath roared below.

Once across the midpoint, the bridge sloped downward, and Isk could almost make out the closed gates of the city ahead. He could also see another guardpost, built into a towering wall that stretched off into snowy obscurity to Isk's right. The mages had said that Qindaras was surrounded by an impressively thick city wall. The storm seemed less severe here. Though the wind still howled, the snowfall grew noticeably lighter as he approached the second guardpost.

This time, however, the assassin was not waved through. A stout soldier with snow-covered mustache and eyebrows stepped from the guardpost and placed himself between Isk and the closed gates. The soldier pushed back the brim of his furry hat to scrutinize the ill-dressed stranger.

"Welcome to Qindaras," said the man, looking down his thick, red nose. "Where do you come from on foot, so poorly dressed for a blizzard?"

The mages had prepared him for at least part of the question. "I was following the Torath from Shrentak, on my way to Tarsis to purchase some of the city's prized warhorses for my lord," Isk said. "My own sorry mount died beneath me some ways back. I'd heard the weather here was unpredictable, but I confess I hadn't considered the possibility of a blizzard when I left home some days ago." Isk stamped his cold feet. "Thankfully I stumbled upon the bridge, or I might have suffered my horse's fate. What city did you say this is?"

"You have come to Qindaras," the guard informed him. "How long do you plan to stay here?"

Isk started. "I hadn't planned to be here at all, so I can't say. Long enough to purchase a new mount and restore my health and supplies." Isk's eyebrows knit into a line. "I have traveled far and wide for my lord, but never have I been asked that question by a city guard."

The guard shrugged. "We are required to ask for the census." He ducked his head into the protection of the guardpost to scribble something on a clay tablet.

The guard turned back to Isk. "Are you bringing any weapons into Qindaras?"

The guard could clearly see the scimitar strapped across Isk's back, and so the assassin had no choice but to nod and point.

Frowning, the guard made another note on the tablet. "Visitors are required to check their weapons at the gate. They'll be returned when you leave Qindaras."

"I've never heard of such a thing!" exclaimed the assassin. "Do many people comply with this rule?"

The guard shrugged again. "Either they hand over their weapons, or they are not allowed to enter the city. Three short years ago Qindaras was the most dangerous city in the Plains of Dust," he explained. "Why, even our own ruler, Potentate Aniirin III, was slain in the street! Because of that, Aniirin IV's first official action was to pass a law requiring all citizens to surrender their weapons. Further, no visitors would be allowed to bring them into Qindaras. Some citizens were opposed at first, but crime is almost nonexistent now. We have no need for constables anymore."

"What happens if a citizen is caught with a weapon?"

"The penalty is death."

Isk whistled appreciatively. "Severe, indeed!"

The guard brushed the accumulating snow off his arms. "It works."

Isk briefly considered killing the guard, his usual method for dealing with overly conscientious lackeys. But a scimitar was a difficult weapon to hide; he would only be stopped later and punished for the offense. Resigned to the loss, he slipped the scimitar from his back. His fingers lingered on the beloved weapon. It had served him well since he had acquired it, during his first mission as a professional. Isk knew he would never see it again, since his task here would require a hasty departure. Still, he had no choice but to hand it over, particularly if he wanted to prevent a search that would reveal the dozen or so other weapons he wore concealed between his layers of clothing.

"Take good care of her until I return," Isk said with forced cheerfulness as he handed the scimitar to the guard.

Nodding absently, the man took the weapon, set it on the floor of the guardpost, then made a mark on his ledger. "Is that it?" he asked without looking up.

"A man traveling to trade for horses doesn't expect much trouble."

"I'll just need a name so that you can retrieve your goods when you leave," mumbled the guard.

"Tels Maviston of Shrentak," Isk said, supplying him with his favorite alias.

The guard pushed up the block of wood and began to shoulder back the gate. "Enjoy your stay in our fair city, Tels Maviston."

Snorting to himself about the man's description of Qindaras as "fair," Isk strode through the gate.

He couldn't have been more dumbfounded.

In the span of a heartbeat the tempest stopped. Inside the gate it felt as if a dome had been slammed over Qindaras, sealing it off from the rest of the Plains of Dust. There was no snow here, nor wind, nor frigid air. In fact, the temperature inside the gate was nearly balmy. Isk was at a loss to explain it, but he couldn't deny the truth of it when the ice on his sheepskin collar began dripping down the inside of his tunic.

The assassin bent over and brushed the remaining ice to the ground before it could soak into his clothing. His eyes traveled with wonder over his new surroundings. Clean streets, completely clear of snow, radiated away from the gate in four directions. People and animals moved about in normal, everyday bustle, oblivious to the howling storm just paces away. Isk looked up and over the gate: snow swirled and raged, but stopped at the wall as if an impenetrable barrier encased the city. This was magic of a very useful sort, Isk told himself. But there were other things even more remarkable than the lack of snow. Isk saw people moving about in light spring clothing, so he pulled off his snow-caked cloak and shook it vigorously, showering several nearby women with bits of snow and ice. And in the merchants' stalls Isk saw fresh fruit, fish, and vegetables. Clearly, there was much more to Qindaras than he had been told.

Isk moved down the tree-lined avenue in a bit of a daze, taking in the sights and sounds of the bustling but pristine city. It seemed a miracle to find himself in such a beautiful oasis after crossing the leagues of wasteland that made up the Plains of Dust.

The people Isk passed looked no different from people anywhere, aside from the distinctive flowing robes that were the local dress. They smiled and chatted freely among themselves, but he noticed a watchfulness that seemed out of place in these surroundings. After walking quite a few blocks, Isk decided that what he first took for urban cleanliness might almost be considered sterility.

Still, there was an undeniable appeal to the place. The warmth, the light, the very freshness of it made the city seem like a garden.

Which was why Isk was shocked when he turned a corner onto a side street and found himself strolling along a wall adorned with human heads. He had seen plenty of corpses, and these were no worse than any others; they just seemed surreal in this place. Wooden stakes the height of a person lined the right side of the street. Atop most of the stakes were severed heads in varying stages of decay. Some were obviously fresh, while others were little more than skulls with wisps of hair. Maggots and other insects crawled and buzzed on the grisly trophies. From what he could still make out of the hairstyles and apparent ages of the victims, combined with what he had been told about the potentate, Isk judged that these were mages who had been foolish enough to get caught in the city.

The second incongruity Isk noticed was the guards. He knew that an assassin's most crucial skill was the ability to detect people who were looking for assassins. There was no mistaking that the men who appeared to be idlers at the intersections were, in fact, soldiers. They didn't dress or act like guards, but that's what they were. He circled the same block several times and saw the same four men, looking for all the world as if they were just passing the time, who were clearly patrolling the area and keeping an eye on things. Their hands were too little callused to be the laborers they were posing as, their clothes a bit too clean. But even more than that, they had a military bearing and watchful eyes that Isk found unmistakable. So Qindaras does have constables, he thought, they just don't advertise their status.

A woman carrying a basket of apples shouldered her way past Isk. Her raven hair and dark dress reminded him strongly of the black-robed wizardess in Palanthas.

"The potentate is said to never leave the palace. What's more, heavy magical protections will prevent you from stealing into there," LaDonna had told him. "Don't waste your time in either pursuit. Instead, cross the bridge and make your way to the riverfront. The man you're after was once an amir from the merchant district. Some of his old constituents may have useful information regarding his likes and dislikes, or may even have access to him still. Make contacts there."

Isk would have liked to waste some of his time with the seductive wizardess. He remembered thinking it because she had frowned at the exact moment the idea crossed his mind.

"Don't be so transparent with your thoughts when you meet the potentate," she had warned him icily. "He was a mage of considerable power and could read your feeble mind as easily as I."

Isk had been a whole lot less attracted to LaDonna after that.

The assassin asked a boy for directions to the riverfront and was nearly there when bells started ringing all over the city. Instantly, people closed up their stalls and shops, bundled their wares, hustled back home with their pushcarts, and generally scurried about on the errands that eventually close down a city. In a very short time, the streets looked as if today were a holiday. Every business was closed; there was not a vendor to be seen. Yet the streets were clogged with people, all moving briskly in the same direction, apparently with the same goal in mind. In droves they streamed toward a gate in an ivy-covered wall.

Isk followed the crowd. Beyond the gate was a complex of buildings with high arches and open doorways. On the frame above the gate were the words "Misal-Lasim," etched in stone. The complex looked similar in design to temples Isk had seen in other big cities, but the unfamiliar words gave him no clue to its real function. He was not a religious man—so few people were anymore—but the citizens of Qindaras seemed to be. Isk had never heard of a god called Misal-Lasim, either of the old pantheon or among the new Seeker gods to the northwest in Abanasinia.

The assassin stood pondering for a few moments as citizens shouldered their way past him. He considered stopping someone to ask what the bells signified, then remembered the plain-dressed soldiers who remained in place while the streets emptied. The assassin joined the tail-end of eager citizens moving into the structure, squeezing through the doors just before they swung shut.

Once inside the building, Isk moved with the crowd and entered the building at the center of the complex. To contrast—or to spite the ornate beauty of the building's exterior, the interior was simplicity itself. Stone walls enclosed a large, square room, empty of any furniture. The chamber was overfilled with men, women, and children who were kneeling on the floor in supplication. All heads were bowed toward a simple stone dais, really just two steps leading up to a square platform. Murky, gray light seeped in through arched windows and cut at regular intervals the length of the room. Behind the dais, hundreds of squat candles cast a golden glow.

Isk grew suddenly conscious of being the only one standing among the group of worshipers. He toed his way through the bowed bodies to within three rows of the dais, dropping to his knees between a large, sweating man and a willowy young girl. Lowering his head, Isk kept one eye on the platform, half expecting to witness some extraordinary event.

Isk's knees, pressed to the cool stone floor, had begun to hurt, when the assassin noticed a change in the room's mood. Stealing a glance toward the platform, Isk saw a slender man step through a doorway and climb the dais. He looked like a priest of sorts, wearing a red robe beneath a human-sized feather mask of a red condor. The man's hands were tucked into the opposing cuffs of his robes.

The priest stopped before the altar and raised his arms toward the ceiling. In a powerful voice he intoned, "Great Misàl-Lasim, overseer of lands that test men's will, you who have tested the will of Aniirin IV and found him to be the greatest of men, hear our humble supplications and protect us against the pernicious influence of magic."

Isk listened carefully to the service that followed, all the while paying close attention to the worshipers around him and copying their motions and responses. Gradually he pieced together the idea that Misal-Lasim was the same deity that in northern regions was called Sargonnas or Argon. He was a nasty god of vengeance, usually revered in places that had some link with fire and heat: deserts or areas near volcanoes. Hearing his name chanted in such a frigid region came as a surprise.

But what really startled Isk was the association of Misal-Lasim with the magic-hating theme of the sermon. The focus of the priest's message was that Qindaras's newfound prosperity, even the change in climate, was the result of Misal-Lasim's pleasure at the rejection of magic. Isk's business took him to the far corners of Ansalon. As far as he had seen or heard, none of the old gods of Krynn—and some of them were pretty hostile—was particularly opposed to magic. This was a new twist, and it shed some light on his employers' desire to have this Lyim, known here as Potentate Aniirin IV, assassinated.

As the service progressed, Isk felt a powerful wave of emotion sweeping through the crowd. It was difficult to resist the urge to join them, whatever their cause. This temple meeting seemed the key to the potentate's hold over the citizens. That realization gave the assassin an idea.

Isk waited unobtrusively against a wall while the other worshipers filed out of the back of the temple.

The man in the condor mask remained at the dais, patiently watching the followers of Misal-Lasim depart, faces lowered. Behind the priest, two young men in red-and-black robes wordlessly snuffed out the scores of candles.

Isk quietly slipped up to the priest. "I was very moved by your sermon about our beloved potentate," he began.

The priest, his gaze fixed across the temple, did not appear to hear him.

"Aniirin IV must have the strength of a god, to never use the incredible magical skill he is said to have once possessed. I can only imagine the inner struggle he suffers daily to reject magic's seductive promises."

The priest still said nothing.

"How can I better serve both Misal-Lasim and Potentate Aniirin IV in his quest to eradicate magic?"

"Continue to attend worship daily when the bells ring," the priest said coldly through the mask, still without looking at Isk.

"I will do so happily," said Isk, "but I would like to serve in a more meaningful way. Perhaps you can tell me how I might study as an initiate, so that I may one day realize my dream to become a priest like yourself."

The priest looked over at last, evaluating Isk through the small eye holes in the condor mask. "Potentate Aniirin prefers to choose novitiates himself. He selects his priests from the ranks of novitiates as openings become available."

"So you have met our great potentate." Isk attempted to look both excited and unworthy at the same time. "Tell me, how can I make myself worthy of Aniirin's notice?" He wished the man would take off the disconcerting bird mask so he could read his expression.

"Neophytes perform the lowest of tasks: sweeping floors, lighting and extinguishing the candles for services, and tending to the material needs of the ordained priests." As the priest spoke, the novitiates behind him finished their task and retreated through the doorway.

Isk bowed his head. "I am at your immediate service."

"As you will." The priest led the assassin through the doorway behind the dais and into a small room, where he handed Isk a broom and a wooden bucket with a brush inside it. "After you have swept and scrubbed the entire temple floor, you may do the same to the doors, shutters, benches, and walls. Do not touch the altar or the icons behind it. The novitiates' sleeping chamber is through this door," he said, pointing to another opening behind him. "Address any questions to one of the other novitiates. If, after a few days, you find that this life suits you, you will be outfitted with the red-and-black robe that the other novitiates wear."

Isk took the bucket and broom happily. Things were moving along more quickly than he'd expected. "When will I meet the potentate so that he may approve my appointment as novitiate?"

The priest paused with his hand on the knob of the door that led to the sleeping chamber. At long last he tugged at the neck of his feathered mask and lifted it off, settling it under one arm before speaking. "Soon. Very soon."

Isk was startled, and not by the answer. The priest he'd assumed was human was a dark-skinned elf, Kagonesti unless Isk missed his guess.

* * * * *

Isk was awakened by a hard kick in the ribs. He had not slept very soundly on the cold stone floor of the novitiate's chamber. Still, he managed to come awake with an understanding of where he was and who he was supposed to be. Too many surprises in this city, he thought painfully.

Isk curled into a ball away from the offending foot and squinted up into a flickering bright light. "Is it time to sweep the floors already?" he moaned. "It still feels like the middle of the night."

"It *is* the middle of the night. Get up, Tels Maviston." The unfriendly voice accented Isk's alias with obvious suspicion.

The assassin sucked in a breath, both from the pain in his side and the surety that he had given his name to no one but the guard at the city gate. A skilled pick-pocket could have searched him while he slept, he supposed, but Isk was careful to carry no identification that would tie him to one alias. It meant only one thing: the priest had found him suspicious enough to go to the trouble to learn he was not a citizen of Qindaras. The speed at which the priest had discovered that fact in a city this size, and presumably without the aid of magic, was impressive.

Two guards yanked him to his feet.

"Is it time for me to meet Potentate Aniirin IV?" he asked in his most innocent voice. "The priest had said it would be soon, but I had not expected it *this* soon."

"You are going to the palace, yes."

Isk fought down a cold chill of premonition. He reminded himself that a trip to the palace was what he sought. He'd just hoped for better circumstances.

The trained assassin went easily with the guards, if only to prevent a thrashing that would reveal his hidden weapons.

The sun was barely up as Isk was led through the streets. Along the way he had the chance to see much more of the city than he had the day before. He was impressed with its extreme cleanliness and excellent repair, two features that were frequently lacking in most large cities he had visited.

The palace rose up, dominating the landscape. Isk had traveled far and wide, yet even he had never seen a palace of such grandeur. Hundreds of brilliant gold onion domes glowed with pristine perfection, as if newly gilded, in the clear blue dawn light. Trained to assess structures for their potential for entry, Isk noted that the palace appeared impenetrable. There were no windows on exterior walls on the first floor. Only the upper floors were marked by balustrades and smaller parapets. The assassin was not magically inclined, but he had good intuition. His instincts told him the palace was the heart of Qindaras in every respect, including its magically moderated weather.

It briefly crossed Isk's mind that the Council of Three must have reason to fear Aniirin IV. A man with the skill to singlehandedly revive Qindaras, as Lyim reputedly had, might also have the power to realize his goal to destroy magic.

To his surprise, the trip through the city to the palace gates brought him only halfway to his destination. The palace was far more immense than it appeared, and it had looked big enough. Isk walked at least as far through its winding corridors and open-air gardens as he had through the broad city streets.

Finally, he was stiffly told to sit near the reflecting pool, among the colorful, strutting peacocks and lush, green plants. He had been in tough spots before, thrown in rat-infested dungeons, tortured on a rack. But never had he been offered bountiful repast in a magnificent setting as a prelude to interrogation. It made him even more nervous. He resisted the food and his growling stomach out of an assassin's fear of being poisoned.

Though he'd heard no sound, Isk sensed a presence and looked up suddenly. A man stood so close Isk could have reached out and touched him.

"Hello?" Isk asked the question because the man looked neither like a ruler nor a servant. His head was shaved to a short stubble, conspicuously devoid of the turban the locals favored. He was dressed simply, if tastefully, in a plain dun tunic, brown vest, trousers, and slippers. The only unusual or outstanding thing about him was the glove on his right hand, made of interlocking plates of jade, silver, and ivory. Isk noticed the glove, but consciously strived not to stare at it.

"So, Tels Maviston of Shrentak, you are interested in joining the priesthood," the man said, his tone conversational.

Isk recognized the potentate's subtle method of interrogation, the deliberate lack of introduction. He had played this game of intimidation with captives himself. The seasoned assassin did not react. Still, since they had already connected him with the alias he had used at Qindaras's gate, he measured his answer carefully. "I was moved as never before by yesterday's sermon in the merchant district temple."

"Moved enough to forsake your mission to purchase prized warhorses for your master?" The potentate clucked his tongue reproachfully. "You appear to switch allegiances easily."

Isk stiffened, but kept his tone humble. "The priest was most compelling."

"I will have to commend Salimshad for his persuasive abilities," remarked the potentate. He picked up one of a number of miniature sailboats on the bank of the reflecting pool. The hand in the ornate gauntlet stroked the smoothly polished wood of the boat. "I have a servant whose sole job is to carve these for me. He lives in his own apartments here at the palace."

Aniirin IV knelt down and set the boat on the crystal-clear water of the reflecting pool. "What skills do you propose to bring to the priesthood—besides slaying people in their sleep or in dark alleys?"

The potentate's tone was so incongruous to the question, Isk was momentarily unnerved. "I don't know what you mean."

"Your skill as an assassin," the potentate supplied, his back to Isk as he calmly gave the boat a push. It lurched away, rippling the water, then slowly floated to a stop in the absence of a breeze. "I was just wondering which of your mercenary talents you might find particularly useful as a priest."

Isk's heart jumped in his chest. His hand traveled to the knife he kept strapped to his thigh.

"You'd be dead before you even pulled it clear of its sheath."

Isk froze, his eyes scanning the garden for an escape route. He spied at least two dozen guards inconspicuously placed among the potted palms.

"I'm sure you realize there's only one way you'll leave the palace now." Aniirin glanced at the food trays with a disappointed frown. "You haven't eaten anything."

Shrugging, the potentate picked up a slice of melon and took a bite. "It's not your fault you were found out, you know. The Council isn't playing by your usual rules. I suspect—and you should remember that I've had dealings with the Council of Three in the past—that someone on the Council cast a spell on you. Enchanting unsuspecting people is their preferred method of doing business. I can't imagine how else they got a smart assassin like you to undertake such a suicide mission."

Aniirin paused to finish the slice of melon. When the last bite was gone, the potentate spoke. "I must credit them for not sending another mage after what happened to the previous two, before I became potentate. In your profession, some unpleasantness is to be expected. Still, their actions so far tell me that Par-Salian and his compatriots are willing to throw away good men on rash gambles like this. In some regards it's useful, because it tells me the measure of their desperation. I'm almost flattered." He passed his hand tentatively over the fruit plate, but then paused. "Actually, I should be flattered, having seen the caliber of man they are sending now."

Isk calculated the time it would take to sprint across the courtyard; the guards would be on him before he even made it to the first ring of potted plants. There was a chance, though extremely remote, that he could draw one of his hidden knives and stab the potentate before a guard could reach him. Still, they would kill him instantly afterward. Isk was not ready to die just yet.

Aniirin continued. "Your presence here is something of a watershed, actually. You're the first assassin the Council has sent since I became potentate, significant because it means they are no longer honoring the treaty. They were within their rights to try to kill me when I was but an amir, but attacking the potentate is a flagrant violation of the terms signed by the Council and the first potentate of Qindaras. Either that, or they think I've broken it, and so don't have to honor it anymore." Aniirin's gaze played across Isk as he mentioned the treaty, but Isk displayed no reaction.

Aniirin stood and wiped his hands dry on a towel laid next to a tray. Then he leaned close and locked his eyes with Isk's. "Par-Salian can't stop me. None of them can. They can't know what I've accomplished here, or even how I'm drawing away their magic. They've been unable to scry into Qindaras since I became potentate. That's why they couldn't tell you anything useful about what you would find here. How I'd love to witness their impotence firsthand.

"Melon?" The potentate held out a pale wedge of casaba. He didn't wait for an answer, but nibbled the fruit himself.

"Are you hoping I'll reveal something useful about them before you slit my throat?" Isk saw the first flicker of emotion in the potentate's eyes.

"I don't need you to tell me anything about the Council of Three. I lived with them, studied under them, suffered from their lies just like you."

"Is that why you hate magic enough to decry it in the temples? Why you profess never to use it, yet the city seems to thrive because of it?"

Aniirin's eyes narrowed. "You weren't listening to the priest yesterday: I no longer cast magic. The city thrives because Misal-Lasim has smiled upon it. What's more, my methods and motives are far beyond any simple, emotional desire for vengeance. I don't believe they can really be understood by someone who hasn't studied and mastered the Art."

Aniirin sat down on the ledge surrounding the pool, within reach of Isk. "You have good reason to despise the Council, too. They twisted your will with their spells, then sent you here knowing it would very likely mean your death. In their arrogance they judged that their magic was more important than your life."

The assassin had never considered that the mages had used magic to make him take the job. "If what you say is true, then why am I still alive?"

Aniirin's voice swelled. "In part because it amuses me to thwart the three most skilled mages alive. However, that is never reason enough to do anything for long," he said, dipping a finger into the pool and watching the ripples. "You are alive because you're a skilled and valuable man. I have respect for your special talent."

For the first time since awaking, Isk felt a little less ill, a twinkle of hope.

"I have been considering ways to pursue my goals beyond Qindaras without leaving the palace. I have already freed this city of all who practice magic. You may have seen their heads on gates all over the city." The potentate tapped his chin thoughtfully. "I would have you pursue the same goal in other areas of Ansalon."

"You want me to kill wizards."

"Why so surprised?" chuckled the potentate. "Isn't that what assassins do, hire themselves out to kill people?"

"If I agree," Isk asked haltingly, "who will save me from the wrath of the Council of Three?"

"I think you would be wiser to consider what will happen to you immediately if you *don't* agree."

Isk was forced to nod at that.

"Any of my followers could tell you that I reward loyalty lavishly," the potentate said. "You would live better than you could hope for if you worked without rest as a freelance assassin. You will want for nothing, just like the man who carves my ships." The potentate returned to the reflecting pool. He flexed the fingers of his right hand inside the gauntlet. A breeze rose as if from nowhere, sending the small boat sailing swiftly to the other end of the pool.

"However, you should know I have only one response to betrayal on any scale: swift and painful death. Your predecessors here would corroborate that were you to meet them in the afterlife. Keep that in mind after you leave Qindaras. You have seen the length of my reach."

Aniirin pursed his lips in thought. "You wonder why I detest the Council," he murmured. "I detest them because they symbolize the unthinking subservience to magic that has blinded so many men to its corrupting effect. They are beyond symbolizing it—they are its highest expression. The council members are living testaments to the ways that magic warps a person's notion of reality."

Aniirin stepped up directly in front of Isk and looked squarely into his eyes. "The discipline of magic twists your perception until you believe that because you are gaining knowledge and power, you are becoming wise. But true power grows out of wisdom borne of adversity and struggle."

The ruler stepped back. "In spite of what the Council undoubtedly told you, I am not a maniac obsessed with revenge. I am going to change the world."

It was a choice between life or death. Only a fool would choose the latter. Isk was many things, but he was no fool.

"Tell me where to begin," he said.

Smiling, Aniirin reached out with his gloved hand and picked up the tray of fruit. "With breakfast."

Chapter Ten

"Quite a view, isn't it?" Bram commented to his uncle.

"Breathtaking," Guerrand agreed distantly. The mountain air was chilly, so the mage cinched his red robe tighter, then leaned back against the support rail to soak in the panorama.

Guerrand was impressed by the beauty of their surroundings. He would have enjoyed it more, he thought, if only the air were dense enough to breathe. Palanthas, where he served his apprenticeship, was ringed by mountains, yet those heights were mere foothills compared to these magnificent snow-capped peaks. Nestled between and hidden by the massive ranges were lush green valleys, and streams as clear and cold and blue as polished turquoise. As much as Guerrand loved his native Ergoth, he could also see why highland people were so attached to their land.

Amid this tremendous natural beauty was a singular artificial structure. Built into the mountain behind Guerrand and Bram was the largest bank of solid glass mirrors Guerrand had ever seen. The beauty of the mountainscape was reflected in that rectangular block, but the glass gave no clue as to what lay behind it.

Guerrand's mind was not entirely on the view, or even this mysterious location to which Justarius had summoned them.

"I understand why Justarius sent for me," Guerrand said. "In fact, I expected word from him, though I'm anxious to learn the exact reason for it." He shivered involuntarily, recalling the return of the Dream that had given him a premonition of the summons. "But what could the Orders of Magic possibly expect of you?"

Bram smiled softly. "I won't take offense, since I know you didn't mean that the way it sounded."

"Of course not," Guerrand said, frowning. "I'm just a little anxious to find out what the Council wants."

"Where did Justarius teleport us to, anyway?" Bram asked. "This isn't Wayreth," he said, comparing those flat woodlands to this mountainscape. "Another Tower of High Sorcery, perhaps?"

Guerrand shook his head. "As far as I know, there are only two of those still standing: Wayreth, as you mentioned, and the tower in Palanthas." The mage closed his eyes at the memory of that black, accursed place, which he had visited so often in his nightmares.

Feeling jittery, Guerrand opened his eyes and saw his nephew's peaceful pose. Lord DiThon stood impassive, oblivious to the cold air in his heavy brown wool cape. Bram had changed a great deal in the two years he'd spent with his mother and the tuatha dundarael. Guerrand noticed the difference daily, in little gestures, Bram's more somber but less seen smile. Guerrand knew some of Castle DiThon's servants didn't entirely appreciate the changes in their lord. They interpreted his new sense of composure as distance or even disdain.

It was true Lord DiThon moved more quietly and spoke less often to his people. He kept to himself more, tending his gardens, sitting by the sea in contemplation. Guerrand's nephew said he was meditating to the goddess Chislev, nature incarnate. Bram had an inner peace that his uncle envied, especially now.

Guerrand frowned at the glass again. "Where are those people?" he muttered. "I'm freezing out here."

Just then, the head of the Conclave of Wizards himself stepped through an unseen doorway in the bank of mirrors and joined Bram and Guerrand on the polished flagstones of the observation deck. He shook hands with Guerrand first, welcoming him heartily.

Guerrand held a hand toward Bram. "You remember my nephew, Bram DiThon?"

"Of course," Par-Salian said quickly. "Our first meeting may have been brief in time, but weighty in its significance. Thank you both for responding so promptly to Justarius's missive."

"I had a feeling I was to hear from him," confessed Guerrand.

Par-Salian cocked his head in surprise. "Do you know why you were summoned here?"

"Not specifically," said Guerrand, "but Bram and I both suspect it has something to do with the magical disruption we've been experiencing."

Par-Salian's lips pursed as he nodded. "All will be revealed to you shortly," he said in his distinctively clear but quiet voice. "I apologize for the delay. Several issues surfaced at the last minute that will impact our discussion. However, we are ready for you now."

Guerrand took one last look at the view. "I'm guessing we're still on the Prime Material Plane. What mountain range is this, Par-Salian?"

"The Khalkists," the old mage told him. "I'm surprised you don't know that, Guerrand. Weren't you a part of the construction of the second Bastion?"

"No," said Guerrand. "I relinquished my position as sentinel to Dagamier and returned to my homeland before construction began."

The old man waved his hand distractedly. "Yes, of

course, I recall that now. Forgive me, my attention has been much diverted by the events of late, and I forget things. . . ."

Frowning, Par-Salian bustled them toward the wall of mirrors, which reflected the mountain range. "Speaking of which, I'd better get you inside or LaDonna and Justarius will have my head for delaying things further. Recalling Bram's first trip to meet us, we have prepared a repast." Seeing Bram redden, the old mage's wrinkles stretched into a mischievous smile.

Puzzled, Guerrand looked between the two men.

Blushing through a grin, Bram explained. "By the time I got to the tower at Wayreth when I was looking for you, I hadn't eaten for three days, so I filched some cookies from Par-Salian's desk."

"I was to blame for not offering him food," said Par-Salian. "Come inside, so I don't repeat the mistake."

At a wave of Par-Salian's hand, the doorway reopened in the mirrors. On stepping inside, Guerrand found himself in a huge chamber, several stories tall. The outer wall was formed by the bank of mirrors, which were transparent from this side. The whole, magnificent vista that Guerrand had enjoyed outside was visible from this chamber, only without the icy wind to probe through layered cloaks. A suspended walkway spiraled gently up to three observation platforms where, he suspected, the view was even better than it was from the floor. There was no apparent structure supporting either the walkway or the platforms; instead they seemed to float in the air.

Par-Salian escorted them across this foyer to a long hallway that appeared to bore straight back into the mountain. The corridor ran straight for many dozens of paces, sloping steadily downward, before coming to any doors. The walls were smooth and dry, yet appeared to be natural rock. "Dwarves helped us a great deal with the basic excavation," Par-Salian explained. "We could have done it faster with magic, but I doubt as well."

"So this is the new Bastion," Guerrand breathed in awe. "The view outside is quite an improvement over the blackness of the demiplane of shadows where the first Bastion was located. I'm curious to know why you placed it on the Prime Material this time, but I can't wait to see what the rest of it looks like."

"We endeavored to correct our mistakes in both intent and design from that first fateful experiment," Par-Salian explained. "But I'll let Dagamier tell you more about Bastion when she gives you the tour. She is understandably proud of the place."

"Dagamier is still here?"

Par-Salian's white head bobbed. "You were right to recommend her, Guerrand. She is an excellent high defender."

"Wasn't she that dark and dour wizardess of the Black Robes?" Bram whispered for his uncle's ears only.

Distracted, Guerrand nodded vaguely, his thoughts on the past. He had detected no indictment of himself in Par-Salian's kind words about Dagamier, yet he suffered a twinge of jealousy. He considered his own tenure as high defender something of a failure. Who wouldn't in his place? First he'd fallen for the trick that had allowed Lyim Rhistadt into the fortress. Worse still, Lyim had made it to the gate of the Lost Citadel, an occurrence Guerrand had pledged his life to prevent. Lyim's trip there had caused the gods to destroy the first Bastion. All this had happened during Guerrand's watch, which made him responsible. He considered his time as high defender an ignominious addition to his list of credentials.

"Don't let regrets about the first Bastion trouble you, Guerrand," said Par-Salian, as if reading his mind. "We all have them. You were not the first person, nor the last, to be fooled by Lyim Rhistadt." His soft voice was ripe with meaning. "Besides, those tragic events helped us see the flawed logic behind the construction of the first Bastion."

"For that, I am eternally grateful," said a woman's deep, vaguely accented voice.

Guerrand spun around. "Dagamier!" he cried, moving forward to shake her hand warmly. "The position of high defender obviously agrees with you," he said, studying her with obvious approval. Her straight black hair was still shoulder-length, and a great contrast to her pale-as-marble skin. She wore the same tight, black silk robe as always. And yet something about the young woman was different. Guerrand concentrated his gaze on her eyes and there found his answer.

Dagamier had always seemed to Guerrand to suffer from a cynical sadness, as if she had witnessed more of the world than anyone so young should. But the Dagamier who stood before him, now five years older, seemed to have grown into her eyes. She was not quite warm—that would never be in the black wizardess's nature—yet she was obviously happy to see Guerrand. And she remembered Bram.

"You've changed very little, Guerrand," she said. Her gaze turned to Bram. "But your nephew has undergone some metamorphosis. I see it's true, he does possess druidlike magical skills now. I applaud the improvement."

"News travels fast," Bram observed wryly.

"It does in the magical world," agreed Dagamier. "But then, you must have guessed that's why you were asked to accompany your uncle here."

Both DiThon men looked at each other in puzzlement. "We're still waiting for the answer to that question."

Par-Salian's face darkened. "Now, Dagamier, you've gone and confused them. Let's get to the dining hall before things get any more muddled."

"Yes, Par-Salian," the young woman sighed. "The tour will have to wait until after the conference. The other sentinels have ongoing tasks and will not be part of this discussion, but Ezius of the White Robes will be particularly glad to see you, Guerrand." Dagamier slipped a pale white hand through an arm of each visitor and gave them a warm smile as she led them toward the dining hall.

Apparently a lot of things had changed in the new Bastion.

They walked farther into the mountain, crossed through a magnificently sculpted threshold, and into a large, high-ceilinged room. Justarius and LaDonna sat waiting at a large table. Both remained seated, Justarius because of his crippled leg, LaDonna because it wasn't in her nature to stand for anyone.

"And who is there but Par-Salian that I should stand for, Guerrand DiThon?" she asked, once again reminding the mage of Thonvil that these powerful wizards read minds like other people read books.

Guerrand bowed his head in respect for her position as Mistress of the Black Robes. "Well met, LaDonna," he said calmly, taking her gentle rebuke in stride. She had changed not at all since last he had seen her; LaDonna's black hair was still woven into an intricate braid that coiled about her delicately shaped head.

Guerrand turned a fond smile on his former teacher, Justarius. The archmage's salt-and-pepper beard had grown overlong and rested on his ever-present white neck ruff, but his red linen robe was as crisp and clean as ever.

Guerrand extended his hand. "It is good to see you looking so well, Justarius."

The Master of the Red Robes pulled a disbelieving frown, yet his dark eyes sparkled with pleasure. "Not with this mop of hair graying so quickly. I suppose I could alter it magically, as some do, to conceal my years," he said with a mischievous glance at LaDonna. "Yet why should I bother, when I know the truth of my age?"

"Why bother, indeed," snapped the raven-haired wizardess, whose looks had always defied her years.

"You'd still be ugly as an owlbear."

"Denbigh, the owlbear who runs my household, would take exception to that," Justarius chuckled good-naturedly.

Guerrand had never seen the council members jibe each other so readily before. In the past, their differing philosophies had usually put them at odds. But this unexpected sense of camaraderie lifted Guerrand's mood and made him believe that perhaps the reason for their summons was not as dire as he'd expected.

Such serious reflections were interrupted by the arrival of servants carrying trays of food. Guerrand's mind turned to his surroundings while he dined on a perfectly prepared pheasant. Unlike in Castle DiThon, no smoky torches lit the dining chamber. Instead, the room was bathed in natural light from a long, solid window that gave a magnificent view of the Khalkist Mountains.

"How do you accomplish that view?" Guerrand asked. "Unless I miss my guess, you walked us into the mountain, not toward another promontory."

"Magic, of course," said Justarius. "Have you been away from my tutelage for so long that you've forgotten anything is possible with the Art?"

"Of course not," Guerrand said a trifle defensively.

"Tell me what you see when you look around this room," Justarius charged him.

Guerrand was puzzled by the question, but his apprenticeship with Justarius had taught him to answer every question the master asked, however odd. So he described the room, its tall window looking out from the mountain, and three natural rock walls.

"That's interesting," mused Justarius. "It reminds me of the open-air peristyle in my villa in Palanthas."

Guerrand remembered the serenity of that lush garden, with the goldfish pond in its center.

"To me this hall appears totally enclosed," supplied LaDonna, nibbling a chicken bone, "lit only by the soothing yellow light of torches."

Guerrand glanced at the sunlit bank of windows.

"I see the Hall of Audience in the Tower of High Sorcery at Wayreth," added Par-Salian, watching Guerrand's reaction to these revelations.

"In case you haven't guessed it," said Dagamier, "this Bastion is magically imbued to appear pleasant and comfortable to everyone who enters it."

"I understand," said Bram, nodding thoughtfully. "Someone who likes sunshine and a feeling of openness has a different vision of this room than someone who likes cozy, dark places."

"Exactly," pronounced Justarius.

"You can imagine how much easier this is on sentinels than the environment in our Bastion, Guerrand," said Dagamier. "Both Ezius and I are still here. The sixth sentinel, a Red Robe named Feldner, replaced you five years ago and has showed no signs of stress. We feel much less isolated here and can actually take short leaves, another of the many reasons the Council kept this Bastion on the Prime Material Plane."

"Actually," interrupted Justarius, "that decision had to do with the change in Bastion's purpose from its first incarnation. Then it was a physical roadblock between the Prime Material Plane and the Lost Citadel. However, we discovered the defenses were susceptible to being overwhelmed by a massive assault or bypassed completely." Justarius took a long, contemplative sip of his drink. "As Lyim Rhistadt discovered."

Guerrand noticed that Justarius was ignoring the bounty of food in favor of his usual brewed lemon water. That had always been a sure indication that the head of the red mages was distracted and concerned about something, despite his outwardly calm demeanor.

"Now Bastion functions more as an early-warning system," said Dagamier, continuing where Justarius had left off. "Defenders monitor magical activity through spells. We are no longer frontline soldiers fighting alone, but more like scouts. When we detect disruptions in the magical cosmos, anywhere on Ansalon or near the Lost Citadel, we alert the Council."

"I assume, then, that you have experienced the magical disruption Guerrand experienced at Thonvil," said Bram.

Par-Salian's expression was grim. "We have all witnessed a sporadic drain in our magical abilities."

"Even King Weador knew of it in the faerie realm," Bram said.

"We've heard from Weador," acknowledged the head of the Council. "And Lorac, the Silvanesti elflord. And the ruling thane of the Daewar dwarves in Thorbardin. Even Solostaran of the Qualinesti has expressed his fear that the magical drain will spread to his realm. It was his missive that delayed our meeting today."

Guerrand looked at Dagamier. "You've isolated the cause of the disruption?"

She nodded.

But it was Justarius who answered solemnly, "Lyim Rhistadt."

"He's alive?" Guerrand gasped.

"He's alive and apparently doing very well for himself in the Plains of Dust," said Justarius.

"That's where he grew up," Guerrand muttered. He turned on Par-Salian with an expression of disbelief. "But you said at the conclave where I relinquished my position that if Lyim were alive, he would be dealt with in the manner of all renegade mages! I assumed that he had been killed, either during the destruction of Bastion, or . . ." Guerrand's voice trailed off.

"I've lost count of the number of assassins the Council has sent after Lyim," LaDonna assured him. "Three—one from each order—left immediately after Par-Salian spoke those words."

"And none of them has been able to touch him?" Guerrand asked, incredulous.

"I know it sounds improbable that anyone could

avoid a stream of assassins for so long," said Par-Salian, "but none of this is as straightforward as killing an ordinary renegade mage. Lyim Rhistadt is no ordinary man."

Par-Salian pushed his plate away. "The first three assassins had nothing on which to base their search. They weren't even sure Lyim was still alive. One was murdered in a street fight, pursuing a false lead in Neraka. Another had the ill fortune to drown in a shipwreck in New Sea. But the third finally traced Lyim to Qindaras, the largest city in the Plains of Dust."

"That was the black-robed assassin," supplied LaDonna proudly. "He reported his findings to the Council and was about to accomplish his mission when Lyim recognized him for what he was."

"So?"

"So," she continued, "Lyim gave the Black Robe two messages for us. First, he said that he had renounced his magical abilities and no longer practiced the Art, so we should reconsider the need to slay him as a renegade. Of course, he already knew we could not reconsider. His second message was to have us check the Orders' records for a pact signed over three hundred years before between Qindaras's potentate and the wizards who then comprised the Council of Three."

"Surprised by the turn of events," Par-Salian said, taking up the story, "we nonetheless did as he suggested. We discovered that Qindaras's potentate, a powerful wizard, had come into possession of a magical gauntlet through a trade agreement with a dwarven thane in Thorbardin. The dwarves had apparently forgotten that the gauntlet made by their ancestors had the power to draw magical energy into itself."

"The Orders had to be concerned by the existence of such a powerful artifact that seemed in opposition to the Art," observed Guerrand. "But the potentate was a wizard and so subject to the rules of the Orders. Why didn't they just demand that he relinquish the article?"

"I'm sure they tried that," said Justarius, "but consider the time. This was just before the Cataclysm, when magic was feared and hated. One wizard and his gauntlet probably paled in comparison to the Council's struggle with the Kingpriest. Besides which, simple possession of such a powerful item made the potentate immune against almost anything the Orders could summon against him. Distracted by the Kingpriest and confounded by the gauntlet, the Council of Three struck an agreement with Potentate Aniirin I: the Council would not interfere in the internal affairs of Qindaras or its citizens if the potentate vowed never to use the gauntlet's powers beyond Qindaras. Since then, two more potentates have come and gone, but the agreement has never been broken."

Bram tapped his chin. "Lyim *is* no ordinary man. Somehow, he discovered the one place on Krynn where the Council could not attack him without breaking a centuries-old pact."

"So you just let him go?" Guerrand asked.

"Of course not," said Parsalian with a frown. "We instructed the assassin to watch Lyim closely and wait for him to step foot from the city. But in five years he never has. The assassin said Lyim never performed a magical spell, and had, in fact, spoken out publicly against magic. Nevertheless, though we never moved against Lyim, that assassin mysteriously disappeared, as have the countless others we've sent in an effort to maintain observation."

Bram shook his head. "I'm not sure I understand what you're leading up to here. What is Lyim doing in this city if he's not practicing magic? And how does he relate to this magical gauntlet of the potentates?"

"According to our spies, Lyim raised himself up to a position of political power," explained Par-Salian. "He caught the potentate's attention during a suspiciously convenient attack on the ruler, who then made Lyim his legatee as a reward. Not very long after, the potentate himself was slain under very suspicious circumstances, and Lyim ascended the throne."

Guerrand whistled sharply. "None of the previous potentate's retainers questioned these events?"

LaDonna shrugged. "His first order of business was to have all loyal followers of Aniirin III slain. Concubines, servants, wizards, viziers, astrologers, even bakers and artists were dispensed with in one fell swoop."

"And still he had done nothing to break the pact," said Bram, beginning to understand the dilemma.

"Nevertheless, we might have found a way to get around that agreement, but for one thing." Par-Salian wiped his lips with a white linen napkin, then pushed himself back from the table to pace. "Lyim now wears the gauntlet that draws magic. Assassins from the Orders of Magic are powerless to use their magic against him. What's worse, it appears he has somehow recruited to his cause the mundane assassin we sent, who is now going about Ansalon killing mages."

"As potentate, Lyim is the most powerful man in the Plains of Dust," said Guerrand. "What else does he want?"

"He seeks to destroy magic," pronounced Par-Salian without preamble. "And with that gauntlet, he may have the power to do it. We realized just how far Lyim's influence had reached when Dagamier contacted us."

Dagamier took a sip of frothy green wine. "Lyim's gauntlet is drawing enough energy from the magical fabric that Bastion—even the Tower of High Sorcery at Wayreth—is going to become difficult to defend," she explained. "If he breaks the pact and moves his crusade beyond Qindaras, he could attack the towers directly."

"A case could be made that Lyim has already broken the pact," suggested Guerrand. "Why hasn't the Council of Three pooled its skills to overpower Lyim and seize or destroy his gauntlet?"

"Of course we've considered that," Par-Salian said patiently.

"But wouldn't your magic only feed Lyim's gauntlet?" asked Bram.

"Exactly," exclaimed the Head of the Conclave. "But this, too, is more complicated than it initially sounds. Lyim has developed a devoted following among his citizens. His power over them can be likened only to that of the last Kingpriest of Istar. Our dilemma is not dissimilar to that of the Council that made the pact with the first potentate of Qindaras. The majority of Ansalon's citizens still distrust magic. It wouldn't help that image if magic's ruling council openly slew Qindaras's beloved savior, a man who has attracted his following based on a pledge to destroy magic.

"No," Par-Salian said, shaking his white head, "Lyim's downfall must be brought about more covertly."

"That's where you and Bram come in," Justarius said bluntly. "The Council believes that you, Guerrand, are the only person who might distract Lyim sufficiently to defeat him."

"We were friends once, long ago," agreed Guerrand, "but Lyim hates me now."

"Hatred is as much a distraction as love," observed LaDonna. "So far, our assassins have engendered only ambivalence or have been recruited to Lyim's side, which is something we know would never happen to you."

"I can't imagine a circumstance that would cause me to see things as Lyim does now," Guerrand muttered, more to himself.

"So you want my uncle to go to Qindaras and kill his old friend," said Bram.

"That's one option," explained Justarius, "and probably the best one. If Lyim can't be killed, stealing his gauntlet would prevent him from absorbing any more magical energy. We suspect that removing the gauntlet by itself from the palace could destroy either the palace, the gauntlet, or both."

"Good luck separating the two," Guerrand said wryly. "If I can't get near enough to kill him, I'm at a loss to see how I'd get the gauntlet."

Bram leaned forward. "And I'm pressed to see where *I* fit into this scheme."

"May I explain that?" Dagamier asked the Council. Par-Salian nodded.

"It's because of your new magical ability," she said quickly. "When a mage casts a spell, the words and motions and components of that casting serve to draw and focus ambient magical energy into a specific effect. Lyim's gauntlet absorbs magical energy. The spell failures that we've experienced are caused by a lack of ambient energy. It's as if we're lowering a good, waterproof bucket down the well; but if there's no water at the bottom, the bucket comes back empty.

"As I'm sure you know," Par-Salian interjected, "a tuatha's magic is not powered from the same source. In effect, tuatha have their own well, shielded from use by humans and elves and protected against the kind of poaching the gauntlet is doing. King Weador believes the gauntlet draws only magic derived from the moons."

Bram nodded his head slowly in understanding. "Tuatha magic stems from the earth and Chislev, not the moons."

"If that's so," puzzled Guerrand, "why don't you ask King Weador to lead an army of tuatha against Lyim?"

"I think I can answer that one," Bram said softly. "It isn't in the nature of tuatha to so drastically alter what is. They—*we* only embellish what exists. Remember, Rand, when Weador explained that tuatha thrive on positive energy and good deeds. Weador's subjects would quite literally die if forced to attack Lyim's city."

All three members of the Council were nodding their heads in agreement. "We suspect that Bram's half-human side would spare him that fate," said Par-Salian.

"But you don't know that," charged Guerrand. "You want Bram to risk his life casting spells where I cannot, so that he can save a type of magic he doesn't even use."

Par-Salian cleared his throat awkwardly. "The death of magic would affect everyone in the world in ways we cannot now imagine, Guerrand," he reminded the mage gently. "Magic plays an integral role in maintaining the balance between good and evil."

Bram turned to his uncle, surprised by his objections. "Why is it so different for you to risk your life in Qindaras than for me to risk mine?"

Guerrand had readied himself for this task before he'd even known what it was. He had pledged his life to the Art. Besides, he had waited since his Test at the Tower of High Sorcery to discover the meaning of the Dream. But his nephew was different.

"Your skills are new to you, Bram," Guerrand said, concern creasing his brow. "Are you sure you're ready for this?"

Bram looked unperturbed. "Were you ready when you took on the archmage Belize at Stonecliff and kept him from entering the Lost Citadel?"

"I know Lyim well, Bram," Guerrand said. "He nearly killed me more than once and has survived tribulations that would have felled a dozen lesser men."

Bram stood firm. "No one said this task would be easy. But it seems that, together, we're the last, best hope."

Guerrand saw the determination in his nephew's eyes and felt reassured. He squeezed Bram's shoulder encouragingly. "Together we *can* defeat Lyim," Guerrand vowed, "just as we beat the odds and resurrected Thonvil."

Chapter Eleven

Lyim sank back with a gratified sigh among the herbal bubbles. Despite a certain loss of freedom, being potentate had much to recommend it. In addition to ordering the torture of anyone he liked—or rather, didn't—without retribution, the palace's private bath was one of the position's greatest perks. Servants had revealed that Lyim's predecessor had seldom taken advantage of this room, more proof of Aniirin III's idiocy.

The bath chamber, totally enclosed to hold the steam, was not large. In the middle of the room was the pool, a perfect square, which stretched the length of two men. The deck was perhaps as wide, though a bit crowded with lush tropical plants in bronze urns. The first potentate had chosen a big, bold, serpentine black-and-cream tile pattern.

Sweat beaded up on Lyim's brow as he relaxed in the water, heated by the boiler stoked by servants in a room beneath the pool. Sitting in a corner of the basin, Lyim held his arms above the water by propping them on the cold mosaic deck. He dared not risk getting the gauntlet wet, and he dared not take it off. Not that he wanted to.

Opposite the potentate, an auburn-haired woman lay casually on her side on the deck, her head supported by an angled arm. Ruby gauze, the color so rich it looked as if real gems had been crushed to make the dye, draped her lithe form.

Never particularly modest, Lyim had still found it disconcerting at first to dress and undress before a woman who stared at him so blatantly. He had grown accustomed to it, though, especially in light of the fact that Ventyr was not real. At least not a real *woman*. It was a difficult thing to remember, since she appeared to every man who wore the Gauntlet of Ventyr as his ideal of the perfect female. Lyim's eye always sharpened keenly after wenches with red-gold hair. Beyond her physical attributes, Ventyr touched his mind—even his soul— with the slightest caress of her misty limbs. She satisfied his needs in a way no human woman ever had, and he had spent a great deal of his youth in that pursuit.

If you ask me, you've become too dependent on me for companionship since you had the amirs tortured to death, Ventyr remarked, her voice whispering like wind inside his head.

"I don't recall asking you," Lyim snarled good-naturedly, paddling hot water with his left hand so that it lapped over his half-submerged chest.

How are you going to produce any heirs? she pressed. *You had all of Aniirin's concubines slain, too.*

"I remember fondly." Still, Lyim made a mental note to engage some tolerable-looking female from the city at his first opportunity, if only to keep Ventyr from becoming too sure of his dependence on her.

The potentate stretched out a leg and used his big toe to turn the tap, releasing more hot water. He heard the whistle and rattle of pipes just before steaming water spurted through the copper spigot. Lyim watched it with great satisfaction, though he was careful to keep his foot from getting too close to the scalding water. But his look of satisfaction turned to one of puzzlement as the white stream turned an odd shade of pink, then brilliant red. With a shout of dismay, Lyim leaned forward and closed off the spigot, then sprang from the tub to escape the eerie water.

Ventyr sat up, her beautiful face creased with concern.

But before Lyim could ask her what was happening, Isk, on temporary leave from his travels to slay wizards throughout Ansalon, ran into the bathing chamber without preamble or excuse. The man skidded over the mosaic tile, which was moist with condensation. His wavy dark hair, bobbed at the jaw, was wet and streaming over his face, smeared with bright red blood and soot. The sleeve of his tunic was ripped, a fresh wound oozing.

"Potentate, there's a . . . disturbance in the boiler room below! One of the stokers is dead, and the other ran to alert me—" Isk's eyes fell to the bloody water in the pool. "You'd best get yourself to safety."

Lyim looked to the vision of Ventyr that only he could see. *We have visitors*, she said ominously.

"Assassins?" he asked aloud.

Worse.

"I don't think so—" Isk said, thinking Lyim had addressed him.

The potentate snatched up his robe. "Take me to the boiler room," he instructed Isk.

The man hesitated only briefly, knowing better than to contradict the potentate. Just outside the bathing chamber, the assassin led Lyim down a narrow flight of enclosed stucco stairs.

Isk kicked open a door, and they plunged down three more steps into near darkness. Lyim had never been in the boiler room, which was situated underground beneath his bath. Steam billowed and roiled. A few steps in, Lyim could see a red-hot fire of coals burning beneath an enormous copper pot contorted into the shape of a still. Stuck through the side of the pot, like a hideous cork, were the picked-clean bones of a man, presumedly the stoker. Steam hissed around the moist, red bones.

Above the hiss of the boiler could be heard heavy, hideous breathing. And unmistakable slurping. Lyim was not a man easily frightened, but the scene chilled him.

"What happened here?" he demanded of Isk.

Lyim's head of security trembled visibly. "Just before he passed out from his torn arm, the stoker who found me described a grotesque monster bursting through the wall behind the boiler. He said the thing raked out with claws and snatched up the other stoker. The creature slammed the man's head through the boiler, then proceeded to devour what remained outside it.

"Of course I didn't believe him." Isk's filthy face contorted as he viewed the chewed legs. "Until I saw this for myself. And then the thing raked out at me." He held up his wounded arm.

"What kind of creature is it?" asked Lyim.

Isk directed Lyim's gaze to the wall behind the boiler. The shimmering blue color that covered the wall was unmistakable to someone with Lyim's background. It was a gate, a magical doorway to another dimension. It shimmered and dimmed while it formed, as if the doorway were a living thing that had not yet reached maturity. Its edges pulsed with unearthly, cyan light. A dark shape twisted and churned at its center. Occasionally it slowed enough to reveal glowing eyes, glistening fangs, and long, clawed, grasping arms. Lyim and Isk scrambled farther back as one dripping talon snaked out of the wall toward them.

Nabassu, Ventyr answered Lyim at last. *Fiends from the Abyssal plane.*

He looked at the mist woman in surprise. *You know of these beasts?* he asked her mentally in Isk's presence.

I've spoken with their kind telepathically, she responded.

170

It would appear that the concentration of stored magical energy here at the palace has weakened the wall between the Prime Material Plane and their home in the Abyss. The nabassu are trying to emerge through it, but the bulge hasn't quite burst to give them total access—yet.

It's your job to power and protect the palace, accused Lyim. *Can't you stop them?* He considered the claw that raked the boiler room. *Patch the bulge at least?*

Temporarily, agreed Ventyr. *But the magical energy you've directed me to store here has to be spent, or it will overflow again. It's only a matter of time before the nabassu and others like them try to emerge in the weakening created here.*

Just do what you need to do to protect the palace and the stored energy, ordered the potentate.

With no visible effort on Ventyr's part, the blue light faded. The edges of the portal contracted until they met at the middle, and then the doorway disappeared.

Lyim ordered Isk to see to the removal of the body and the repair of the boiler. As the assassin departed down the corridor at the top of the narrow staircase to execute the potentate's orders, Lyim stepped back into the bath chamber. Tension had returned tenfold to the cords of his neck. He caught sight of the cold, red pool of water and wrenched the door back open with a scowl.

"Have the pool drained and scoured, as well!" he called after the head of security.

They'll come back, Ventyr whispered at his side.

Lyim jumped. He'd nearly forgotten about her. "Can't you just seal them out again?" he asked aloud.

I told you, not if many more come—and they will. Ventyr reappeared across the pool. *But, like any fiend, nabassu can be controlled by a powerful mage.*

"Or a powerful artifact?"

Ventyr merely smiled.

Lyim removed the robe thoughtfully and slipped his clothing back on. "There may be a day in the not-too-distant future when creatures like that could come in handy," he mused.

* * * * *

Bram sat at the desk in his study, staring vacantly at the marble mortar and pestle he used to grind herbs. He seemed unable to focus on one thing for more than a fleeting thought, before his mind leaped elsewhere.

The lord of Castle DiThon snapped back to the present. *What is the matter with me?* he asked himself. *I haven't time to be daydreaming like a schoolboy. Guerrand will be expecting me in the gallery at any moment, bags packed for Qindaras, and I'm not nearly ready. Why not? What's holding me back?*

He had started his meditations for mental strength several times, but let himself get distracted after the initial mantra. He was thinking of the confrontation that was to come instead of preparing for it.

Primula's training told him to consider the reason for his distraction, not just banish it, or it would only return. It wasn't caused by fear. There was no tightening in his throat or quickening of his pulse when he thought of what he must do.

He had never killed a man. Was that it? Killing another living thing was in opposition to tuatha philosophy. Bram had spent years trying to save all life in Thonvil. Even before his sojourn among his mother's people, he had believed that nature should determine the cycles of birth, growth, and death.

Despite all that, Bram had to admit he felt no ethical conflict at the thought of killing Lyim Rhistadt. First, the man posed an enormous threat to magic and the balance of good and evil. Second, he had caused endless suffering to Bram's family, not to mention the village of Thonvil.

Bram recognized, then, the cause of his distraction. He might never see this place again. He had learned many things from Primula, but he would never be nomadic like her. His human grandfather, Rejik, ran too deep in him. Bram's father, Cormac, had frequently told him as a child that Rejik used to brag lovingly about the extent of his holdings.

Bram had none of his grandfather's vanity for his position, but a great deal of pride in what had been accomplished. Things were very different around Thonvil than they had been in his father's time.

Even Cormac's study would have been unrecognizable to the former lord. Upon his return from the tuatha realm, Bram had tried to reclaim the sunny, multiwindowed gallery facing the sea. But Guerrand had already staked out that spot, and he'd insisted the lord of the manor must occupy the study on the second floor, as always. Bram had agreed reluctantly, but vowed to make some changes.

Those changes included removing the heavy wood desks and bookcases that had cluttered and darkened the room. He had chipped away at the narrow windows so that they afforded a full view of the fields between the castle and the village, as well as enough light to sustain the vines and various plants that now filled the study. He relied on the scent of plants to awaken his senses each morning like other people used chicory or ale. These days he trekked to the herb garden for solitude, not spell components, since he grew most everything in clay pots on his windowsills. Cormac's old study was now a cheerful place kept warm by sunlight.

Bram's longing for Thonvil had nothing to do with his power or position as lord. This was the only place he felt totally at peace with both sides of his heritage. With Primula, he had always been acutely aware of his human half. She had never criticized him for it, even during his first stumbling attempts at spellcasting. But he could never quite forget that she had left Weador's domain to distance herself from humans.

Here, in the privacy of his study, however, he was free to find his way as a human with tuatha skills. Outside this room the Orders of Magic had expectations of him. Bram was forced to admit that fear did play a part in his distraction now. He was not afraid of Lyim, or even of death, but of failing. He could not let that happen.

Bram called to mind the plan he and Guerrand had devised so that he could bring the necessary supplies. The Council of Three had informed them that they had no time to waste in Qindaras, since Lyim's defenses would almost immediately signal the presence of a mage. Spies had informed them, before mysteriously disappearing, that mages were immediately slain without benefit of a trial. That meant Guerrand had to seek a face-to-face audience with Lyim first and hope the former mage of the Red Robes would be curious enough to meet with his old friend. Neither Bram nor his uncle had any doubt Lyim would order Guerrand slain, once his curiosity was satisfied. They would have only the one chance, a heartbeat long, to slay Lyim first.

Just then, an image appeared in the window before Bram, as if it were a reflection in the glass. It was Guerrand's face, lined with worry, and it spoke to Bram with a hollow-sounding recreation of the mage's voice. "I expected you to be here by now. Is there a problem?"

"I'm sorry," Bram said hastily, filling a calfskin pack as he spoke. "I spent longer meditating than I'd intended."

"Finish whatever you need to," Guerrand said, "but do it with the least amount of delay."

"Yes, Rand." Bram tossed a long dagger onto his pile of necessary equipment. "I'll meet you in the gallery just as soon as I say good-bye to Kirah and . . . just Kirah." Bram had thought about stopping by Rietta's chamber, then changed his mind. She knew nothing about Primula, yet things had never been the same for either of them since his return from Weador's realm.

Guerrand's image faded away and Bram finished gathering up the few things he thought might be useful, then tied up the bundle and slung it over his shoulder.

Pausing, Bram touched a finger to the leaf of a rich, green herb. Tomorrow, Maladorigar the gnome would take over the care of these plants until Bram's return. They would be in good, if excitable, hands.

With that thought, Bram left in search of Kirah.

* * * * *

Bram arrived in the bright and sunny main hall a short time later with a puzzled expression on his face. He dropped his pack onto Guerrand's crowded table, where the mage sat penning a letter.

"Thank the gods. You're here at last," his uncle mumbled. He brushed the drying sand off the letter, then folded the sheet neatly into thirds. "Let's get going," he announced briskly, pushing himself up from his chair.

Bram scarcely heard his uncle. "Do you know where Kirah is?" he asked distractedly, rubbing his chin. "I've looked everywhere: her chamber, the counting house, the kitchen. No one has seen her this morning."

Guerrand shrugged as he moved to the back wall and selected a double-edged long sword from the assortment of weapons racked there. It seemed many lifetimes ago that he had trained with this blade as a prospective cavalier. But if his magic would do him no good in Qindaras, perhaps the sword could. "Kirah seldom keeps to any predictable schedule," he said, strapping on the sword. "She could be in the village, in the drying houses checking on crops, speaking with one of the tenants, sitting in the cave by the shore . . . I said my farewells to her last night, and that was difficult enough."

Bram shook his head. "I was sorry we had to tell her the reason for our absence when we asked her to assume my duties again."

"I tried to avoid the details, particularly about Lyim," Guerrand sighed. "But you know your aunt. She's never satisfied until she ferrets out the whole truth. She always knows when I'm lying."

Guerrand fidgeted with the sword belt, adjusting it meticulously as if the weight bothered him. "She was very angry about not being able to help destroy Lyim," he recalled. "I didn't realize how much she still hated him for tricking her during the medusa plague."

"Maybe she's still a little bitter that I'm going with you, but she's not." Bram said. "I'm just relieved she finally recognized the need to remain here to keep things running smoothly until we return from Qindaras."

"We're traveling the faerie road, so we'll be back in a matter of days," Guerrand assured him. "Kirah has grown up a lot since suffering the plague; she's not nearly as headstrong as she used to be. She knows what she's doing with the estate, if that's troubling you."

Bram shook his head slowly. "I'd just feel better if I could speak with her first."

Giving a resigned shrug, Bram hefted his pack full of herbs and other supplies onto his back and arched a brow at his uncle. "Ready?"

Guerrand reached for the strap of his own leather knapsack, stuffed to capacity. "I just have to pack the mirror Belize gave me, and we're all set."

"Gods, yes, don't forget that," said Bram. "We'd have little hope of defeating Lyim without it."

Guerrand gingerly slipped the shiny, palm-sized fragment of precious magical glass into a blue velvet sack for protection. "If Belize had known how useful this bit of glass would prove to me over the years . . ."

Bram shrugged. "He couldn't have predicted it, since he expected you to die shortly after he gave it to you."

Guerrand paused, his dark eyes taking on that faraway look again. "Lyim's master expected me to die many times over."

"So has Lyim," charged Bram. "But you've defied them both quite handily."

"So far," Guerrand agreed. With great determination, he slipped the mirror into his bag.

"You're not having second thoughts about our plan, are you? You do think it will work."

"Not if we don't get there." Guerrand stuffed the

cumbersome bell-shaped cuffs of his gray wool robe through the straps of his pack.

With a frown, Bram stared at his uncle. "Are you sure the mirror's magic won't be affected by Lyim's gauntlet?"

"I'm not sure of anything," Guerrand admitted. "I don't *believe* the mirror will be affected, nor does Justarius, because the mirror neither gathers nor disperses energy. It is either charged from within, or it draws energy from the strange dimension that it constantly borders and opens into. Unless the gauntlet's effect is far more pernicious at close range, I expect the mirror will function just as it always has."

Guerrand adjusted his full pack to a comfortable position between his shoulder blades. "I'm nearly ready," he announced. "Where are we joining the faerie road?"

"The herb garden," Bram replied. He turned toward the door and placed a hand on the knob.

Guerrand cleared his throat. "Wait a moment, Bram."

"Yes?"

Guerrand had a long rectangle of sealing wax in his hand. He held one end to a lit pillar candle. When it was suitably softened, he dabbed the butter-yellow wax to the flap of the letter he'd folded when Bram had first arrived. He sealed the letter by pressing the face of his ring into the melted wax, leaving the outline of a sea gull in flight.

Bram recognized the imprint of Zagarus, which Guerrand had commissioned to honor his familiar. The wily sea bird had died while trying to save Guerrand from the poisonous blows of a naga during the destruction of the first Bastion. Yet another in a mounting list of crimes caused by Lyim Rhistadt.

Guerrand turned the folded letter over and quickly scrawled Bram's name on the front.

The mage held it toward his nephew. "You are to read this in the event anything happens to me in Qindaras," he said calmly.

Bram scowled. "Then I'll never read it. Nothing is going to happen to you that won't happen to me, too."

"I hope not," Guerrand whispered, his tone hardly consoling. He slipped the letter into a narrow drawer beneath the table. "In any event, you know where it is." Guerrand blew out the candle, then watched the plume of gray smoke drift about his sunny study. His eyes settled on the view of the sea; a hand lingered on the spine of a dusty spellbook.

"Let's go," he said abruptly.

Bram opened the door, and the two men exited the gallery. They passed no one, not even a servant, as they walked through the cool, silent corridors, down the sweeping staircase. The unevenly worn stone landing led to the northeast door and the herb garden beyond.

Bram stepped between two towering rosemary bushes. He'd trimmed them years ago into the shape of enormous horses' heads and painstakingly maintained them ever since. Maladorigar had trimmed the pungent shrubs during the two years Bram had spent with Primula. Bram looked out over the vast expanse of his holdings, the late autumn fields, harvested just before his return. He was leaving it all again so soon.

"Take my hand," Bram said abruptly, holding his right one out to Guerrand. He needed no coin to travel the realm of the tuatha as he had the first time, now that he was one of them. But his uncle was different.

"Don't let go for any reason," Bram cautioned him. "You aren't protected in the faerie realm without me."

Guerrand gave an ironic chuckle. "In that regard, the faerie road is not much different than where we're going."

"Qindaras," Bram supplied, thus opening the faerie road by speaking their destination.

The assassins from Thonvil were on their way.

The crowd of citizens had been gathering in the courtyard at the edge of the palace for two days, ever since the notices that the potentate would address the people had been posted on every pillar and shop front in the city of Qindaras. Some had come out of curiosity. Most had left their homes early for a prime seat to view the potentate to whom they were totally devoted but had never seen.

"I still think this is folly, master," Isk said nervously, chewing a thumbnail. Lyim found the habit particularly irritating. "It would be too easy for a determined assassin to get to you—"

"I'm on a balcony high above them!"

"Couldn't someone fire off a spell?"

"First, we've slain all the mages in Qindaras," Lyim reminded him, speaking slowly as if to a child. "Second, if one happened to get by you, I'm wearing the gauntlet. It will protect me. Besides, I'd only look better for having survived an assassins's attack and destroyed a bit of magic before their very eyes. Now that I think of it, I should have arranged such a demonstration."

Isk raised a brow. "The Council of Three may have arranged it for you. It's only reasonable to assume that they haven't given up trying to kill you."

Lyim shrugged. "I have no reports from the gate guards of newcomers. Besides, I'm certain the risk, however small, will be worth it. After I remind them of all that I've done for them. That is," he smirked, "all that devotion to Misal-Lasim I inspired in them has brought. The citizens of Qindaras will do whatever I ask."

No one could deny that Qindaras and its citizens had undergone tremendous change during the two years of Aniirin IV's reign. The potentate's priests explained daily during mandatory afternoon prayers that the city's improvements were gifts granted by Misal-Lasim for Qindaras's rejection of magic. For one, the climate was warmer, and not just inside the palace; snow no longer penetrated the city walls. Though it was the dead of winter today, no cloaks were required, the day warm and sunny, as most were. For that reason alone, few citizens found reason to venture beyond Qindaras's walls.

And why would they want to leave? Crime was nearly nonexistent. Businesses thrived in a city spilling with lush trees and bathed in the warm yellow light cast by the palace's five hundred thirty-four onion domes whose finish had been meticulously restored.

As a result, new temples to Misal-Lasim were going up daily, providing jobs aplenty. Anyone who wanted employment could always find it with the city. Scores of able-bodied men were paid to maintain Qindaras, though it no longer seemed to need human attention. Those who remarked on the folly of paying workers to scrub sidewalks that never got dirty, or to walk behind livestock whose leavings mysteriously disappeared, were never seen again. Most considered silence a small price to pay for the new quality of life in Qindaras. They were content enough with their new wealth not to question the priests or the potentate's godlike status. That they had come out in droves today to meet their ruler proved this.

Lyim stood above them, impatiently waiting for Salimshad to whip the crowd into a frenzy sufficient for his first public address. He tugged at his collar, feeling confined in the ceremonial garb. Once Lyim had dressed flamboyantly every day. He wondered now how he'd ever tolerated it.

Lyim had devoted an inordinate amount of time considering his clothing for this appearance. He had not thought about it so much since his days as an apprentice who drew the ladies. It was important he look the part of a potentate, yet it was vital no one draw similarities between him and his predecessor.

Lyim had settled upon a costume that was simple, yet regal. He abandoned the loose tunic and trousers that had become his uniform since coming to Qindaras in favor of a long frock; the garb was loose, almost puffy around his legs, but snug like a doublet around his chest. Though uncomfortable, Lyim thought his attire flattering.

Anxious to get started, Lyim peered through a split in the blue velvet curtain that kept him screened from the crowd. He gasped, then smiled with great satisfaction. The courtyard beneath the balcony was jammed beyond capacity, a veritable swaying sea of humanity. No one but the old and infirm must have stayed home today.

Lyim needed them, each and every one, to serve in the army he hoped to mobilize. After two years of waiting in Qindaras, he had grown impatient to destroy all magic. He had been pondering moving his mission beyond Qindaras for some time. The decision was made, though, just after the incident with the nabassu erupting in the boiler room. Ventyr had informed him that she had drained away nearly all of the magical energy that she could easily access from Qindaras.

He knew a great deal more about the Gauntlet of Ventyr than he had on his first meeting with her. Ventyr told him that she functioned much like a grazing animal. Before Lyim had worn the glove, she had drawn the magic in small, unnoticeable bits from the vicinity of Qindaras itself. The drain was so minor that the mages in the city never noticed it.

That had all changed when Lyim became potentate. He had learned early on that, unlike his first impression, the gauntlet did not draw its power from spells as they were cast. When wizards cast spells, they drew energy from outside themselves and shaped it into a desired effect. The gauntlet drew the bulk of its power from the overall pool of magical power that all wizards accessed. Though quite a bit of energy was needed to run the palace, the amount was small compared to the total quantity available, and so its loss had never been noticed.

But Lyim had been deliberately using the gauntlet to increase its demand for energy. This had consumed the magical supply within the gauntlet's range. Ventyr searched farther and farther afield for new sources, concentrating her efforts on those areas rich in magical energy. But the strongest supplies—Palanthas, the Tower of High Sorcery, Bastion—pushed Ventyr's range. Lyim wanted the gauntlet to do more than disrupt their functions—he wanted to shut them down.

Lyim meant to move against these places soon, because his informant at the tower had told him that the Council of Three was aware of his plan to destroy magic. He didn't fear their reprisals, of course. He had the gauntlet, and they could not use magic to destroy him or Qindaras. But they could fortify their strongholds, making it harder for them to be breached when he marched his followers to destroy them.

Lyim's plans relied heavily on the willingness of these citizens to follow him, literally, to the ends of the world. He felt the pressure to give a speech that would bring the citizens to their knees in adulation, then send every man, woman, and child straight to the tables where the potentate's priests were waiting, quills in hand, for all to sign away their lives in Lyim's service.

Lyim smiled, supremely confident, when Salimshad called him from behind the lush curtain, saying "I give you Potentate Aniirin IV!"

He flexed his fingers inside the gauntlet and tugged at the cuff, a habitual preparatory gesture, then stepped through the luxurious blue curtain.

"People of Qindaras, faithful followers of Misal-Lasim, and loyal subjects: our blessed city stands at a crossroads. Never before, not even in the long-ago age of myth and legend, have the forces for change converged so completely in one time and place, or focused themselves so tightly onto one small group of people.

"This convergence is not the product of chance. We are not gathered here, in this most fortunate of cities, as the haphazard result of random fate. Rather, it is destiny, guided and shaped by one, single, overriding force, that has placed us here. That force is Misal-Lasim, whose favor shines on us in Qindaras like the sun.

"Destiny, wrought by the will of Misal-Lasim, has positioned us at this most crucial turning point in the annals of Ansalon. We possess the power to change the world forever. We can burn down the corrupting structure of magic as Misal-Lasim burns out the weak and unworthy with his cleansing fires of vengeance. His torch is in our hands; he waits for us to touch his flame to the dry tinder of humanity grown weak and insolent, enslaved by its own dependence on magic.

"Those who are caught in the crushing grip of magic's vise cannot break free on their own. They are wooed by its mystic promises, seduced by its silken beauty. But its beauty is all illusion, and its promises are hollow chants and lies.

"We in Qindaras have discarded all magical trappings and endeavors. We have placed our trust in the strength of Misal-Lasim, and we see how he rewards our faith. Our granaries are full, our streets are safe. We are protected day and night from the ravages of weather. Misal-Lasim has given us his sign. He has brought us to this unparalleled position. From him we have the strength, we have the means, and we have the clear indication of a goal: the destruction of all magic!"

The crowd roared its support. Lyim's lips turned up in a haughty smile. He would have no trouble recruiting followers willing to die for his cause.

* * * * *

Since protections on the palace had prevented them from entering it directly, the faerie road deposited Guerrand and Bram safe from prying eyes near a bridge outside the city. The bridge arched over a murky brown river, flowing with ice chunks. More than a foot of snow mixed with gray dust blanketed the barren landscape, though a path had been beaten from where the Ergothians stood, leading to the bridge. The air was cold, but the late-afternoon sun warmed Bram's face.

"The Torath," he said aloud, recalling the name of the river from a kender-made map Justarius had pronounced reliable at Bastion. He pointed to a small cubicle to the right of the bridge. "There's the first guardpost. You won't be stopped there, but you'll have to give a name and your purpose for visiting Qindaras at another post across the bridge."

"I remember Justarius's briefing," Guerrand said. "It's time, Bram."

The lord of Thonvil glanced sideways at his uncle and saw the small shard of mirror reflecting sunlight in his palm. He grimaced. "I know I've got to get into the mirror before I'm spotted with you by a guard. But I hate the thought of leaving you to negotiate your way to the palace by yourself."

Guerrand chuckled. "I've been in worse spots,

believe me. If Justarius's information is correct, it won't be long before I get in to see Lyim, either of my own doing, or because his guards alert him to the presence of a mage. Just remember to stand still in the mirror and listen for the signal we rehearsed. If an impossible amount of time seems to pass, assume I've failed. You know what to do then."

"Recall a mirror in Castle DiThon," Bram said, repeating the rest of Guerrand's instructions. Bram stared hard at his uncle. "You know I won't leave you there."

"I'm afraid you won't have any choice, Bram," Guerrand returned solemnly. "You haven't seen any mirrors inside Qindaras to envision and step through, and you won't be able to exit the mirror without being called by my voice. If you don't eventually return to Castle DiThon or some other looking glass of your memory, you may be trapped in the mirror world."

Bram shifted the load on his shoulders. "Have you considered that your possessions might be confiscated before you're allowed to see the potentate?"

"I won't carry the mirror in my pack," Guerrand assured him. "No one will find it." The mage squinted toward the sun dropping in the west. "Step into the mirror, Bram, before someone crosses the bridge and sees us together."

He reached toward Bram, dropped his hands, then reconsidered again and drew his nephew into a brief embrace. "Good-bye."

Puzzled, Bram grasped his uncle by the elbows and searched his face. "Good luck, certainly, Rand, but not good-bye."

"Yes, of course," Guerrand agreed quickly. "I'm just anxious to get this over with."

Bram patted his uncle's shoulder one last time. "We'll be dining on Castle DiThon's winter grouse before the week is out."

"That reminds me," Guerrand said, snapping his

fingers. "Don't forget to ration your food supplies."

"I can stretch them if I need to," Bram assured his uncle with a wink, referring to his magical skills. That said, Bram tipped his head toward the mirror in his uncle's palm, feeling odd that he believed he could fit inside the small surface. But he immediately felt the pull on his head and shoulders, felt his feet slip from the ground, though there was no sense of him falling.

Preoccupied as he was, he didn't hear his uncle call again, "Fare-thee-well, Bram."

* * * * *

I'm inside. So far, so good, Bram thought. Lyim's gauntlet hasn't seemed to affect the mirror. He staggered a bit in the disorienting fog. All around him was a world of gray. It was impossible to judge distance. There were no landmarks of any sort. The ground was flat and smooth and practically invisible, being the same color as everything else.

Bram stood just steps from where he'd entered the mirror world, arms crossed casually, shifting his weight from one leg to the other. He felt foolish when he recalled that his uncle had said it could be days before he heard Guerrand calling to him from inside the palace.

Bram sank to the ground near the big heap of sticks that had been the nest of Guerrand's sea gull familiar, Zagarus. Crossing his legs, he closed his eyes and began to meditate.

He was halfway through the mantra when a noise, intangible as the fog, pricked the edge of his senses. Bram cracked one open and looked about. He held very still.

Light, irregular footsteps.

Bram opened both eyes wide. Guerrand hadn't mentioned that anyone else could travel through the mirror world. His fingers locked around a thick branch protruding from Zagarus's nest.

A misty shape shifted in the fog.

Bram rose to a crouch.

The shape moved, grew larger.

He wrenched the branch from the pile and raised it above his head, every muscle tensed. "Is someone there?" Bram whispered. "Don't come any closer."

"Wait! Don't hurt me!" a voice squealed. Something light but solid smashed into Bram's chest before he could see it clearly. Arms scrabbled to loop around his neck. He grabbed the scrawny limbs and pushed the creature back.

"Kirah!"

She dropped away, a sheepish look on her face. She was dressed in men's clothing, but that wasn't unusual for his aunt.

Bram folded his arms in an angry stance. "Who's watching my holdings?" he demanded.

"Maladorigar, of course," she said. "Don't worry, he's capable, and the people have got used to his odd way of speaking." Kirah tried briefly to disarm him with a smile, but she gave that up with a shrug when her efforts met with a cold stare.

"We're in Qindaras, aren't we?" she asked artlessly. "That's why you're in here with me now."

Bram scowled. "No, I'm here with you only because you totally ignored Guerrand's and my wishes, not to mention those of the Council of Three."

"You didn't give me any choice," she said simply. "I overheard your plan to use the mirror last night after my argument with Guerrand. I went to the gallery this morning to try one more time to talk some sense into him, but he wasn't there. Is it my fault he left the mirror sitting on his table, where it could catch my eye?"

"Gods, Kirah," Bram breathed, running a hand through his hair, "Guerrand would strangle you with his bare hands if he knew you'd defied him."

Kirah curled into herself, as if to make herself invisible. "I admit it was rash of me to slip inside the mirror," she conceded, as near to an apology as she was capable. "But I couldn't just sit back at Castle DiThon, embroidering like good womenfolk are supposed to, while you and Guerrand risk your lives to kill Lyim!"

"That's not why you stowed away in the mirror," Bram replied evenly.

"It's at least *half* of the reason," Kirah countered churlishly. "I can't believe you, of all people, would question my motives. You were the one who took care of me when my limbs turned to snakes because of Lyim." She leaned in. "You saw what he did to your friend Nahamkin."

Bram closed his eyes against the memory of his friend's tortured death. "I don't question your reasons for hating Lyim," he said. "But this isn't some romance adventure story, Kirah. I know you think it's going to be like when you and Lyim fooled Berwick into thinking you were his daughter Ingrid—I've heard you speak of that often. But this is nothing like that. Lyim is trying—and so far, succeeding—to destroy magic. Even the Council of Three fears his power."

Kirah straightened her thin shoulders. "I'm not afraid of him," she said fiercely.

"That's what worries me," remarked Bram. "You should be. He's not the man you believe you knew. He's not even as reasonable as when he spread the plague in Thonvil."

"Nevertheless," Kirah said, her chin jutting stubbornly, "I know I can distract him so that you and Guerrand will have opportunity to kill him."

Bram's dark hair was already swinging from a prolonged shake of his head. "That's not going to happen, Kirah, so just give up the thought right this minute. Even if I were crazy enough to allow you to help, Guerrand would never agree to it."

Kirah laced her fingers together before her and looked around with wide-eyed innocence. "I don't see

Guerrand here to stop me."

Bram said nothing, not willing to admit the truth of her observation. He had to acknowledge, though, that his options here were few. He didn't dare use his magic to send her away or keep her inside, for fear of somehow alerting Lyim or his gauntlet. Kirah could return to Castle DiThon through the mirror, but there was no way to force her into mentally imagining a mirror there and stepping through it to safety. He knew better even than to raise the question. What was worse, Bram had no way to contact Guerrand and alert him of Kirah's presence.

"Guerrand may not be able to stop you, but I can," he said firmly. "I'll tie you up in here if I have to, to keep you safe."

"You wouldn't."

He gave a threatening squint. "Don't test me on this, Kirah. It's vitally important, both to your safety and to the success of what Rand and I are trying to do, that you stay here. Our plan simply doesn't allow for any modifications. I will ensorcel you, if I must."

Kirah raised her eyes to meet Bram's steely gaze in challenge and held it for many heartbeats. She wavered, then finally was the first to look away; Kirah took a breath and abandoned the fight. "All right, you win," she hissed. "I'll be a good girl."

Bram actually threw back his head and laughed out loud. "I think it's a little too late to hope you'll ever be that, Kirah DiThon."

* * * * *

The plan was simple: get to the palace as quickly and unobtrusively as possible, then request an audience with Lyim under his own name. It was possible, Guerrand supposed, that Lyim would order him killed instantly, as Justarius's sources reported was standard procedure with mages in Qindaras. But he was banking on Lyim's curiosity.

After Bram slipped into the mirror, Guerrand hastened toward the bridge, where the first guard merely waved an arm out the small guard post. The man's sleeve was quickly covered with falling snow and dust. Guerrand tipped his hat and continued over the bridge.

He was not as lucky at the second post, but he was prepared. He gave his name as Enoch, and said he was a glass blower. He reported he would stay no more than a fortnight while studying local glass-blowing techniques. There was nothing about his appearance to suggest that he was lying. He wore tunic and trousers under the drab-colored robe, and he carried no magical equipment. The portly guard in ceremonial soldier's garb made a few notes in a ledger and let Guerrand pass.

"Excuse me, sir," Guerrand said before leaving. "Can you tell me the way to the palace? I've always wanted to witness its splendor with my own eyes. It would be a shame to travel all this way and miss it."

The old guard responded without looking up. "All roads lead to the palace, but the Avenue to Enlightenment is the most direct. It's straight ahead, through the bazaar. You can't miss it."

The guard looked up. "However, this might not be a good time for a viewing, since every citizen of Qindaras—but me," he added a tad bitterly, "is gathered in the courtyard there to hear Potentate Aniirin IV's public proclamation." The guard spat. "Just my luck our great leader makes his first public appearance during my watch."

"You mean no one in Qindaras has ever seen Ly-Aniirin?" Guerrand stumbled, stunned.

The guard studied him closely. "Some have. He has retainers and such." He squinted through the doorway. "You're awfully curious for a glass blower."

Guerrand put his hands up, adopting an expression of innocence. "Idle curiosity, I assure you." He ducked his head from the man's view. "Well, I must be off.

Thanks for the advice."

Guerrand walked with great purpose through the broad gates and headed down the Avenue of Enlightenment. He noticed the improved weather first; inside the walls it was warm enough for just a tunic and trousers. Guerrand's second thought was that Qindaras seemed unnaturally clean. There was no rubbish in the streets. Many of the major thoroughfares had elevated walkways, so pedestrians could avoid any unpleasantness that might, but hadn't, collected in the roads.

The guard was right: nearly everyone else in the city had gone to the palace. Guerrand walked through empty market stalls that should have been teeming with people, but now were eerily silent. He saw less than a dozen people in as many blocks.

Guerrand rounded a shallow bend in the Avenue to Enlightenment, and the palace rose up directly ahead. The enormous edifice shimmered in a way that reminded Guerrand instantly of his brief view of the Lost Citadel—not in design, but both magnificent fortresses glittered with a visible aura of magical energy. Considering how much Lyim had robbed from the magical fabric, the Palace of Qindaras now had a lot in common with that most magical of places.

Guerrand passed through a massive gate in the palace wall. He was instantly confronted by a throng of humanity, filling an interior courtyard that was several times the size of the parade field outside Castle DiThon. The whole expanse was crammed with people of every age, sex, and race, many thousands in Guerrand's estimate, perhaps tens of thousands. He wasn't sure how large Qindaras's population was because none of the council members had bothered to say.

The mage began ruthlessly elbowing his way into the crowd. Before long he could hear that someone was speaking up ahead. Guerrand drew many angry scowls and curses as he pushed and squeezed his way forward. Eventually he could understand what was being said and could even see the somberly decorated balcony. The speaker appeared to be an elf, and a religious figure of some sort, judging by his garb. Then Guerrand heard him introduce the potentate, Aniirin IV; the mage from Thonvil strained to get the best possible view.

At first, Guerrand wasn't even sure that the man on the balcony was Lyim. His appearance had changed dramatically. The shaved head and somber clothing were unlike the flamboyant apprentice or the superbly confident mage Guerrand had known. But when he heard the voice, there could be no question that this was Guerrand's old friend-turned-enemy. At this distance he could just barely make out the magnificent glove on the speaker's right hand, occasionally reflecting the sunlight as Lyim waved his hand or raised it in a fist.

Lyim did not speak long, but his words made Guerrand shiver as if cold fingers had played across his bare neck. The crowd, too, seemed moved, but in a different way. Their applause as the potentate disappeared behind the large blue curtain continued without a break. The citizens filed like lemmings to the tables where priests waited to sign them to Lyim's army.

Guerrand gently patted the mirror against his beating breast for reassurance before pressing his way through the swaying crowd.

Chapter Thirteen

Guerrand waited for the crowd to recede before he crossed the courtyard and followed the road around to the palace's entrance. To his right, the Avenue to Enlightenment branched around a bust of Aniirin I. The cobbles rejoined at the base of a marble staircase leading to the palace's towering entrance.

The steep stairway had an aura of not having been used in a some time. Gazing up, Guerrand spied an arched, double door of lustrous orange copper at the top of the steps. There was no guard, and no other obvious means of entrance. The mage hurried up the hard steps.

Guerrand's plan with Bram was simplicity itself. Just get inside, he told himself. Request an audience with Lyim, Bram will spring from the mirror, and—Guerrand reached forward to open the door, but there was no knob. He banged boldly on the cold copper panel.

The mage had waited only a few moments when he heard a scraping sound from behind the doors. Then there was a slight clang, and one of the doors creaked open a hand's-breadth.

An aged servant stood behind it, his expression annoyed. "Yes, what is it?"

Guerrand cleared his throat. "I've come to see the poten—"

"The potentate's announcement was in the square, but it's over," snarled the man, starting to swing the door shut in Guerrand's face. "Go home."

"You don't understand," Guerrand pressed, stabbing a booted toe through the doorway. "I'm an old friend of Aniirin's."

"The potentate sees no one whose presence he hasn't requested." The man frowned at the foot in the door and pushed harder.

Guerrand leaned into the opened door. "Just tell him Guerrand DiThon says, 'Never explain, never defend'," he pressed. "If Aniirin still doesn't want to see me, you have nothing to worry about. But I wouldn't want to be you if you turn me away offhandedly and the potentate finds out," he added slyly. The mage pulled his foot from the threshold.

The man considered the request with pursed lips as the door closed. Guerrand heard fleeing footsteps, unsure if he'd just made it easier for the servant to shut him out, or if the man was passing the message. He waited with growing impatience and was nearly convinced that he'd have to try another approach when the copper door swung open again with greater intent.

Holding it was a person altogether more disconcerting than the annoyed servant. Guerrand recognized the elven priest who had introduced Lyim before his speech. The elf looked more like a shadow than substance. Dark, delicate elven features were outlined by a pitch-black version of the white headwrap Guerrand had seen in abundance in Qindaras. Black robes, belted at the waist though flowing at the feet, covered a wiry frame. He was at least a head shorter than Guerrand, but the mage could not help but feel threatened by the severe gaze of his slanted elven eyes.

"Come with me. Aniirin will see you."

Guerrand's heart hammered as he crossed into the entryway behind the mysterious elf. Despite his nerves, he noticed the stark contrast between the interior and exterior of the palace. Every inch of the floors, arched walls, and vaulted ceilings were inlaid with intricate repeating patterns. Thirty columns ringed the circular entry, each topped by a capital fashioned of rolled copper, then connected by arches carved from alternating wedges of black and white marble. Light filtered through stained-glass windows high above. Guerrand spied the magical text at the base of the dome. He recognized the protective spell and made a note of its presence in the palace.

Guerrand followed the silent elf across the entryway and under a towering arch. Just inside was an open-air hanging garden, squared in on all sides by balconies. His guide turned left up an ornately curving staircase. Guerrand peered over the railing at the gardens; ficus trees in enormous pots soared three stories toward the sky.

"How large is the potentate's palace?"

The elf didn't answer, but kept walking with the quiet purpose of the ensorcelled specter he resembled. It left out any need to correct the missed opportunity for introduction. Guerrand suspected the elf already knew who he was, anyway.

They passed through endless corridors and bedchambers, a library, a natural-spring bathing room, gymnasium, and dining room, with its impossibly long, polished table. Guerrand wondered if the palace were really a tangled maze, or if he were deliberately being led along a route that would be difficult to recall.

"My master instructed me to bring you along the most direct path," the elf explained, as if he could read Guerrand's mind. "The corridors can sometimes be the longer route."

They traveled one by one through doors, empty salons, and deserted bedchambers. Dust lay undisturbed on marble pediments. A thousand rooms never used.

At last they came to the most elaborate bedchamber of all. Blue velvet curtains edged with gold satin tassels covered arched windows nearly two stories high. An enormous canopied bed, heaped with golden down coverlets, dominated one wall. A small rosewood table, sufficient for one person to dine upon, stood in a corner, covered with the remains of a light dinner served on expensive china. A half-spent cigar lay on the plate, still trailing smoke.

Guerrand knew he was near Lyim now. He could sense the renegade's presence.

The elf led him through a small door to the left of the bed. The room beyond was long and narrow, with a vaulted, two-story ceiling with recessed coffers. Both walls were flanked by a handful of evenly spaced marble pedestals supporting half-finished busts of people and other sculptures. Lush green plants gave the room the feel of a tropical garden. Behind the statues along the right wall a bank of windows allowed light to stream in broken rays to the midpoint of the room.

Bathed in that light was a man seated on a stool, his back to the elf and mage. The man was bent slightly sideways. He held a chisel to a bust that was angled to catch the rays of the sun.

"Hello, Rand," said the man on the stool. He swung his stubbly head up and around. A familiar smile displayed still-perfect teeth. "I would ask what brings you to the Plains of Dust, but I think we both know the answer to that."

Lyim turned back to the statue, brushing from it dust and stone fragments. "Frankly, I was not surprised to get your message," he said. "I have been thinking of you a great deal lately." Realigning the chisel, Lyim drove a mallet into its end, sending chips of marble flying. Guerrand made note of the hand holding the mallet; it wore an elaborate silver, jade, and ivory glove: the gauntlet. Its workmanship was such that it would have been a treasure even if it had no magical ability.

Guerrand took a step toward the windows, so that he could address Lyim directly. The elf who had escorted him grabbed at the strap of the mage's satchel.

"Take the pack, Salimshad, if Isk insisted you must for security," Lyim said. "But Guerrand DiThon can do me no harm. His magic is useless while I wear the glove. And I have seen him fight hand-to-hand." Lyim took the chisel away from the bust while he chuckled, his shoulders shaking in his simple brown tunic. "In fact, you may leave us alone, Salim. I will be perfectly safe."

Guerrand felt the cold glass mirror he had secured to his right wrist. He dropped the pack off his shoulder and handed it to the elf. Taking it, Salimshad stared coldly at Guerrand, obviously reluctant to go. At length he slipped from the room like dark fog.

Guerrand strode casually between the pedestals. "Has sculpting filled the void of the Art you claim to no longer practice?"

Lyim looked up. After a moment he nodded, his profile to Guerrand. "I have never thought of it that way, but yes, I suppose it has. Magic made me feel powerful. That is, it did until I discovered that the magic blinds a mage into believing he controls the Art, when in fact it is the other way round.

"But the marble can't lie," he continued. "I start with a raw block, and it is altered only where I chip it away. You see?" He sliced at the slab before him to demonstrate. "I control the marble. I can shape it into my own vision."

Guerrand traced a finger down the perfectly smooth, aquiline nose of a piece two pedestals down from where Lyim worked. "I noticed that most of your busts seem to be missing features." The one the mage was touching had been shaped with only one eye. The next statue down the line had only half a face. "They aren't finished, are they?"

Lyim chuckled again, a dry sound in the back of his throat. "We are all works in progress until the moment we die, none of us complete until that precise event.

"I find my greatest inspiration from people I have known," Lyim continued conversationally. "That bust, for instance," he said with a nod toward the one Guerrand still touched. "He was a man named Mavrus, my predecessor's most-trusted servant. Though he had the use of both eyes, he was effectively blind—to his master's shortcomings, then to my motives. This myopia led first to his master's death in an alley, like a common vagrant, then to his own. Interestingly, Mavrus died from a knife thrust through his left eye."

"What a coincidence," Guerrand muttered, dropping his hand from the statue.

"This one is finished," Lyim pronounced, dropping the mallet and chisel to the floor. He slid from the stool and stood with his back to the windows as he considered his newest work. "I think you will find this one particularly interesting. Come have a look, Rand." Lyim's arms were crossed, his chin cupped in one hand thoughtfully.

The mage approached Lyim with caution, suspicious of his good mood. The front of the bust came into view. Guerrand drew in a sharp breath. The marble had been shaped into a near-perfect rendering of Guerrand's likeness as a younger man, with one exception.

No mouth had been carved.

"I remembered you best from our days in Palanthas," he explained, as if Guerrand's age were the statue's greatest distinguishing feature. He traced a gloved index finger over Guerrand's marble locks, past the temple, to the left cheek and stopped. "You may have noticed the absence of a mouth," he remarked without waiting for a reply. "That is how I see you in my mind's eye, Rand.

"Surely you can see the symbolism," Lyim continued. "You have remained silent at so many crucial junctures. Shall I list them?" Lyim extended the fingers on his gloved hand, to tick off items as they were recounted. "You agreed to remain in Palanthas while I cleared things up in Thonvil—"

"At your insistence!"

"Nevertheless, your decision," Lyim returned smoothly. "You regarded my mutated hand with silence. Then, when you could have set things right at Bastion—all you needed to do was open your mouth and say 'yes' to my request! You refused. Silence of a sort again, Rand."

"I wouldn't have remained silent if I'd realized what a snake you had become," Guerrand spat.

Lyim looked up in surprise. "You're angry with me! That's a switch for us, eh, Rand?" Lyim untied the dusty apron he wore and slipped it over his head. "Anger is an emotion I seldom feel the need to indulge these days. I suppose I have you to thank for all this," he said with a sweep of his gloved hand. "You and this gauntlet."

Guerrand was at once conscious of his goal here and the passage of time. But he couldn't suppress a shot. "You profess a hatred for magic so great you would see it destroyed, yet you owe your pampered existence here to the magic your gauntlet absorbs and redirects. Isn't that a bit hypocritical, even for you?"

"As you noted so aptly: 'never explain, never defend'. I would add that only a diamond can cut a diamond. Frankly, I view magic's destroying itself as a delicious bit of irony. Icing on an already sweet cake, if you will. I am breaking my rule to tell you this," Lyim added, his eyes glinting with malicious humor, "only because of our long-standing friendship."

"We were never friends," Guerrand responded, though he knew Lyim's comment was facetious.

"No," agreed Lyim, "I have only one friend, and I wear her on my hand." He held the gauntlet up to the light. "Have I told you about Ventyr? Only *she* speaks the truth."

"It speaks to you," Guerrand repeated, looking from Lyim's face to the gauntlet oddly. "You must know from your training the power magical artifacts can have over the mind, Lyim."

"Is that concern I hear in your voice?" Lyim sneered. "Save your compassion for someone who needs it. I control the gauntlet, because only I, as potentate, can wear it. Even the Council of Three is frightened of my power."

"If it's true you're in control," Guerrand charged, "take off the gauntlet. Prove that it isn't stealing your free will."

A spark grew in Lyim's eyes, signaling the rekindling of his old competitive spirit. Then he wagged his finger at Guerrand. "Nicely done. Almost."

Instead of removing the gauntlet, Lyim pushed it more firmly onto his hand. "How can I ever take this off, with all the assassins the Council sends after me?" He looked slyly at the mage. "You aren't an assassin, are you, Rand?"

Lyim snorted. "No, you're far too good for that. In fact, I've always found it odd you ever chose to don the red robes. You're more suited to white, though I can certainly see why you found Justarius more inspiring to follow than that old walking stick, Par-Salian." Lyim actually hunched up his shoulders and squinted, trying to imitate the master of the White Order. But when he got no reaction from Guerrand, he dropped the charade, obviously irritated. "You're no assassin, Rand."

Guerrand acknowledged that possibility as well. In moments Lyim would dispense with him first. Guerrand pretended to scratch his right forearm, releasing the catch that held the mirror in place. It slid quickly to his cuff, where he caught it in his cupped hand. He was sure his heart was beating hard enough for Lyim to see it banging against his tunic.

Guerrand slowly turned his hand over. Sunlight glinted off the mirror in his trembling palm.

Lyim squinted suspiciously. The light caught him in the eye, blinding him.

Guerrand repeated the phrase he and Bram had agreed would lead Bram to him through an opening in the foggy mirror world. "I've brought you a message from the Council."

Guerrand's heart skipped a nervous beat. He looked from the mirror to Lyim's darkening face, and back to the mirror. Finally he felt the mirror shake slightly in his hand, and he set it on the floor. Bram's head and shoulders popped from the mirror, followed immediately by the rest of him. He held aloft his carved wooden staff and spun around quickly to get his bearings.

"What are you—?" Lyim's shout was cut short when Guerrand smashed him in the mouth and nose with his fist. Lyim dropped to his knees, holding his bleeding face.

Bram cast his first spell before Lyim could recover. There were no gestures or arcane words to reveal Bram's intent as when a wizard drew from the magical fabric. But Guerrand knew, he recognized the subtle shift of Bram's staff and posture.

With a sound like rushing water, a ring of tiles along the walls of the studio burst up from the floor for a length of at least a dozen paces in both directions from Bram. Two more lines cut off the long hall from the doors at both ends. In a matter of heartbeats, the shattered floor was covered with twisting vines that were hard, woody, and bristling with thorns. They climbed the walls and intertwined themselves in needle-studded lattices across every window and formed two walls across the hallway. The barricades were so thick that the ends of the hallway could no longer be seen.

Within heartbeats, the three men were sealed off by the writhing branches, their long, curving thorns threatening to tear at any flesh that came near.

Lyim's expression revealed he had no explanation for what was happening. Guerrand could see his nephew evaluating the surroundings for potential, taking in the green plants, floor tiles, and massive marble statues.

Guerrand's eyes shifted for a flicker to glance behind Lyim, where enormous potted ivies, knocked over by the upheaval in the floor, were stretching their thick, green tendrils toward the potentate. Their leafy vines were becoming thick and ropelike, and raced toward Lyim with the speed and menace of unearthly snakes.

"Magic *can't* work here!" Lyim roared.

The potentate lunged straight toward Bram, with the gauntlet extended menacingly. Guerrand jumped to interpose himself between the two, but the move was unnecessary. The vines writhing across the floor had snagged Lyim's ankle as he leaped, toppling the suddenly unbalanced potentate to the floor. He hit the stones hard, but seemed unfazed. Lyim whipped over onto his back and stabbed his gauntleted hand toward the plants. The thick vines surged forward without pause and snaked around Lyim's shoulders, trying to pin his arms to his sides. He struggled against them ferociously, rolling from side to side, but made little progress. Each vine that he threw off was replaced by two more wrapping around his limbs.

"Ventyr!" he cried mysteriously. He cocked his head as if listening. Abruptly Lyim's eyes widened, and he looked up toward Bram in fresh understanding. "You aren't a mage!" Anger, first at the intruders and then at himself for underestimating Guerrand and overestimating his gauntlet, seemed to release in Lyim the power of many men. He tore at the entrapping vines like an animal. The gauntlet ripped away handfuls of writhing greenery, and was now shredding the attack-

ing plants more quickly than they could attach themselves. In moments, Lyim would break free.

"Guards!" Lyim screamed again. He flung a handful
of crushed greenery at the wall of thorns covering the
hallway and cursed aloud.

Guerrand glanced desperately at the doors. "Hurry
and finish what you've started!" he said hoarsely to his
nephew. It was a race against time now. Guerrand
knew they held the upper hand, but if the first spells
expired or Lyim tore free of the trapping vines before
Bram could craft another spell, the course of the fight
would change completely. Guards were already chopping at the thorns from the other side.

Then the mage spied the sculpting mallet and chisel
on the floor, near where the mirror lay. He snatched up
the mallet, intent on delivering a killing blow before
Lyim could regain his feet.

"Get back, Rand!" cried Bram, speaking for the first
time since leaving the mirror. "You'll be caught in the
spell!"

Guerrand leaped back to a safe distance. As he did
so, he caught movement out of the corner of his right
eye. Thinking someone had managed to cut through
the brambles, Guerrand, the mallet raised high above
his head, spun around to face the intruder.

And stumbled over something on the floor, something that hadn't been there before.

Wearing men's trousers and tunic, Kirah DiThon
was crouched on her knees next to Guerrand's magical
mirror. Her eyes were locked on Lyim as he continued
shredding the vines.

"What in the Abyss are you doing here?" Guerrand
demanded as he picked himself up.

Bram looked up at the sound of Guerrand's voice,
his concentration broken. He saw Kirah on the floor for
the first time. "You promised to stay in the mirror!" he
raged.

"I meant to, but the walls in there closed in on me,

and then it just sort of spit me out!" she cried.

"Stand back, Kirah!" Bram yelled, seeing that she was now standing almost directly between him and Lyim. "I can't cast the spell with you so near him."

"Too late," Lyim said through blood-flecked lips. He burst free of the last vines and sprang to his feet. Kirah screamed and punched, but she was no match for Lyim's strength and speed. His arms were wrapped around Kirah before Guerrand could reach her. Holding her slight, wriggling frame before him as a shield, Lyim skipped sideways behind a row of statues.

"Things have certainly taken an interesting turn," said the potentate a bit breathlessly.

"Let her go, and deal with us," Guerrand said softly, nodding toward his sister.

Holding Kirah tightly from behind, Lyim laughed into the hollow between her neck and shoulder. "She may look angry, but from the way she's pressing herself against me, I don't believe the lady wants to go," he said with a wicked smile.

"Take me instead," Guerrand prompted.

Lyim signaled his rejection of the idea by jerking Kirah hard. His head shook with mock sadness. "Poor Guerrand. You really don't understand, do you? Not only wouldn't you be as distracting as Kirah, I already have you. All of you." He jerked his head toward the end of the hall behind Guerrand and Bram.

Both DiThon men looked back anxiously. The guards with axes and pikes had made great progress chopping and prying apart the wall of thorns. Shreds of the unnatural plants lay over the floor. In moments the guards would be through.

Kirah yelped. Both men swung around but couldn't find her where she'd last stood with Lyim.

"There!" cried Bram, pointing to a dark shadow on the floor of the studio. Guerrand saw that a statue had been shifted aside, revealing a shaft leading down and out of the closed-off hallway.

The guards forced their way through the last of the wall of thorns. Three angry, sweating men with axes leaped through the opening, followed by the dark-robed elf, Salimshad, two more guards with spears, and the man who had originally met Guerrand at the copper door. Shouting and pounding feet could be heard beyond the thorn wall, racing down the hall.

"Into the mirror!" Guerrand ordered Bram, reminding him of the way they had planned to escape. Once inside, they could jump through another mirror in the palace, or one back in Thonvil. Bram placed a foot on the shard, expecting to slip inside. His boot landed on the hard surface of the glass and stayed there. He looked helplessly at his uncle.

The soldiers dived at Bram first, knocking him to the floor. His arms were pinned before he could fashion another spell.

Guerrand dropped to his knees and bowed his head to the floor in a gesture of abject surrender. As the guards rushed toward him, he groped for the shard of mirror, hoping to tuck it unnoticed into his sleeve. But a boot crashing into his ribs and flipped him onto his back. He raised his arm to shield his face from a second blow, but the hob-nailed boot made it through his desperate defense, knocking him into unconsciousness.

Chapter Fourteen

Safely inside his bedchamber, Lyim loosed his grip on Kirah, turning her about to face him. The young woman twisted and strained to free herself but stopped when she realized Lyim was enjoying her fruitless struggles.

Kirah scowled up into his smug face. He looked nothing like the lighthearted young man she had first met in a cove on the windy shore of the Strait of Ergoth. Strangely, he was not dressed all that differently— casual tunic and trousers, soft boots—though Guerrand had once told her Lyim liked to dress elaborately.

Once, luxuriant locks had flowed over Lyim's broad shoulders like a river of black ice. He had looked dashing, where now he merely called to mind a pirate with his shadowy stubble. Beyond anything else, Lyim looked powerful . . . and dangerous.

She stared fearlessly up into his dark, penetrating eyes. "I believe I want you dead more than Guerrand and Bram."

Lyim threw back his head and laughed at her brave

words. "Even more than the Council of Three?"

"I don't know any of them," Kirah snarled, "but I'm sure they can't hate you more than I do."

"I think 'fear' would more accurately describe their current feelings for me," Lyim said loosely.

Kirah squared her shoulders defiantly. "I don't fear you."

Lyim regarded her intently. "You never have." He let her go abruptly and walked to a small table covered with the leavings of his dinner.

Kirah watched Lyim pick up a pitcher and consider it briefly, putting it back down. He strode to the far door, opened it, spoke to someone outside. Within moments, a bottle of amber liquid passed through the door. Lyim took a swig while walking to a tall, arched window. He parted the blue curtain fringed with gold tassels and stared beyond.

Kirah stood perfectly still, but craned her neck to consider the door behind her, wondering if it was locked. The portal was not very far away, closer, in fact, to her than Lyim.

"You'll find guards beyond both doors now," he informed her, still looking out the window.

She gave him a cagey glance. "I thought you no longer used magic."

"I don't," he said. "It doesn't take a wizard to guess that escape is on your mind." Lyim took a long, slow pull on the bottle, wiping his mouth on the sleeve of his tunic. "It would be on mine."

"That's the difference between you and me," Kirah said imperiously. "I was actually thinking about how I was going to rescue Guerrand and Bram," she lied.

He shrugged. "Then you're not as intelligent as I gave you credit for being."

"Why?" she demanded. "Because I might care more about someone else's safety than my own?"

"I learned long ago that the only person you can count on is you," he said, still gazing vacantly outside. "Any evidence to the contrary is merely a temporary illusion."

Kirah couldn't suppress an unexpected shudder of pity for the man she had so admired. The horror of his mutated hand had obviously turned his zest for life into a bitter cynicism. She said nothing, knowing the thought would only anger her captor.

What she said instead was, "What are you going to do with all of us?"

Lyim looked away from the window at last. "That question requires three very different answers." He strode to the table, splashed amber liquor into two goblets. "I don't choose to consider Guerrand's and Bram's fates while in the presence of a beautiful woman." The potentate held one of the goblets toward her.

Kirah squirmed under his gaze, but forced her feet forward and took the glass, assiduously avoiding Lyim's hand. Kirah took a drink so that he would not see her embarrassment, though she suspected Lyim saw everything. The liquor was strong and burned her throat. It warmed her belly, however, and steadied her nerves.

"Don't potentates have rooms full of concubines waiting to do their bidding?" she asked artlessly.

"I did," he agreed, "but I have no interest in women who are not of my choosing. Aniirin III's wives were . . . released from their duties when I became potentate."

Lyim's eyes traveled over her thin tunic, settling at last on her face. "You've changed, Kirah. Grown up. And very nicely, too." He raised his left hand to almost tenderly brush a wisp of blond hair away from her face.

Kirah stepped back. "Having your limbs turn to snakes gives you a new perspective," she snapped bitterly. "I trusted and admired you, and you tried to kill me!"

"No one knows the pain of having that happen better than I," Lyim said soberly. "Don't forget that Belize was my master. Because of him my right arm was a snake for nearly a decade. It changed my life irrevocably.

"Believe it or not," he continued smoothly, "I am relieved to see you alive. I always regretted having to give you the plague," he confessed softly. "You were caught in the middle of a struggle between your brother and me. Isn't it an odd twist of fate that you still are?"

Without waiting for an answer, Lyim stood and began pacing. "You asked before what I intended to do with Guerrand and Bram." He stopped before her with his arms crossed, gloved right hand glittering on top. "I believe I've come up with a solution that benefits us all."

Kirah leaned forward eagerly. "Yes?"

"Stay with me."

She scoffed. "I wasn't aware I had a choice."

Lyim rounded on her. "Everything in life is a choice," he spat. "I believe I corrected your brother on that point once."

Lyim visibly struggled to lighten his tone. "Correct me if I'm wrong," he said, "but I gathered from Rand's reaction in the studio that he wasn't aware you had come along. Why did you choose to come to Qindaras, Kirah?" he asked, watching her reaction closely.

"To kill you, of course," Kirah assured him affably.

"Had you so little faith in Guerrand and Bram's ability to accomplish that?"

"No, of course not!" she sputtered. "It's just that I—"

"You wanted to see me again," he finished for her.

Her eyes blazed. "I wanted to see you dead, is all!" Despite her harsh words and her best resolve, Kirah found herself warming to their old cat-and-mouse ways. The realization angered her as much as the fact that Lyim, in his arrogance, had noticed it first.

"What is this choice I have?" she demanded skeptically.

"I can order any woman in Qindaras into my bed," Lyim began.

"Are you bragging?"

Lyim lips cracked briefly in amusement. "Just stating

a fact I've had little interest in pursuing. Right now, you are the only woman in Qindaras who would not come to me simply because of who I am. I find that very . . . intriguing."

"But I told you that I hate you, that I want you dead!"

Smiling, he shrugged away the notion. "And I told you that I don't believe you. I enjoy a challenge. Besides, I find you much more interesting as a spitfire than as the doting little sister I last knew."

She squinted at him in disbelief. "I thought you didn't trust anyone but yourself."

"Don't ever confuse desire with trust, Kirah," he advised. "It can be a fatal mistake."

It almost had been for her, she admitted, recalling that her feelings for Lyim had caused her to blithely drink the poison he had presented to her as medicine.

The memory renewed her anger. "You know I would agree to stay only to save Bram and Guerrand. That's no choice, it's extortion! Why is that any more intriguing to you than ordering a woman from Qindaras to—" her mind stumbled for the words "—to join you?"

Lyim laughed at her. "Because, my dear, unlike them, you do have a choice. Come to me of your free will, or let Br—" Lyim stopped. And smiled. And cleverly left the threat unsaid. Almost. "We have some very talented torturers here in Qindaras."

Her eyes flew wide.

Before she could move, Lyim had Kirah in an unrelenting embrace. "I'm a practical man with a lot less vanity than I used to have. However, I have enough left to be certain you aren't as unwilling as you profess."

Kirah's mind and heart raced, fought. There was no point in denying to herself that her thinking was flawed where Lyim was concerned. She had no reason to believe he spoke truthfully about letting Guerrand and Bram go free; he had lied more than not in the past. Yet, she was certain it wasn't vanity that made her believe he had a weakness for her, too. Perhaps, in time, she could persuade Lyim to let them all go.

"I'll stay," she said, her voice trembling.

Lyim's lips traced a warm path down her left temple. "I can be very generous, Kirah. And very vindictive. That's something for you to remember if you accept my offer with the idea of betraying me."

"How long must I agree to stay?"

Lyim shrugged. "As long as it amuses us both."

Lyim's arms tightened around Kirah. She could not fool herself that she tolerated Lyim's attention only to save Bram and Guerrand. This was something she had dreamed about in her days as the village crazy who stared out to sea, watching for her lover's return. Kirah didn't trust Lyim, didn't know where this folly would lead her, but in keeping with a life marked by imprudent acts, she didn't care.

She was saving Guerrand and Bram's lives. Beyond that—beyond this moment—Kirah just didn't care to think.

* * * * *

Bram was in a foul mood, too angry to meditate to calm his spirit. He had no idea how to get out of this cell, let alone resume their plan to kill Lyim. And then there was the question of Kirah's safety. . . .

One thing was clear: Bram would solve none of his problems until he conquered his anger. He forced his eyes closed and slowly repeated the words of the calming mantra. The tension in his muscles gradually eased; the pounding in his temples subsided. When he opened his eyes again, his thoughts were clearer.

The cell in which he and Guerrand had been deposited was clean, by dungeon standards, the rushes sweet smelling. There were padded stools, two small rope beds, a basin of fresh water, even bread and cheese. Bram ignored them, despite a gnawing hunger.

The guards had taken his staff, the one Bram used as a channel for his magic. Without it, he couldn't cast spells, couldn't magically awaken Guerrand, or even heal the lump on Rand's head that had rendered him unconscious. Bram's pack had been taken as well, so he was without curative herbs or smelling salts.

Bram almost envied Rand his oblivion. Reluctantly, he walked over to one of the rope beds and shook his uncle gently by the shoulder. "Rand," he said, "can you hear me? You've got to wake up."

Guerrand muttered, rolled his head from side to side, but didn't open his eyes. Bram patted his cheeks, rather vigorously. Groggy, Guerrand batted Bram's hands away, until finally his eyes popped open. He stared up at Bram in confusion.

"Where are we?" the mage asked, blinking.

"Dungeon."

Guerrand pushed himself up on his elbows, then sank back down when his head started throbbing. Wincing, he gingerly touched a finger to the lump there. "One of them clubbed me, didn't he?"

Bram nodded, didn't tell his uncle how many of Lyim's faithful guards had kicked him while he was dragged unconscious through the halls and down several flights of stairs to the dungeon. Guerrand would realize that soon enough when he tried to move.

"Please tell me I'm remembering some awful dream, that Kirah didn't really spring out of the mirror," he begged, wincing against the pain even speech brought.

"I wish I could tell you that," Bram said softly. "I found her in the mirror world shortly after I slipped inside at the gates. There was no way to warn you, but she promised to stay there. She said the walls in the mirror world closed in on her, and she was forced out."

Guerrand nodded. "I wasn't sure what effect Lyim's gauntlet would have on the mirror." His eyes popped open. "Why didn't you order her to envision a mirror in Castle DiThon and return through the mirror world straightaway?"

Bram frowned. "I tried. Have you ever successfully forced Kirah to do anything against her will?"

"No, I suppose I haven't," Rand said, sighing in resignation. "So what's our situation?"

"We're in the palace's dungeon," Bram repeated. "They've taken all our belongings, including my staff."

"The mirror? I was trying to pick it up—"

"Last time I saw it," Bram said, "it was on the floor of the studio. I assume Lyim has recovered that, too."

"Damn!" Guerrand cursed softly. "That's to be expected, I suppose. At least Lyim hasn't had us summarily slaughtered. We can be thankful for that, anyway."

Bram drew in a breath. "He's got Kirah someplace."

Guerrand sat straight up at that, ignoring the pain in his head. "You're sure?"

Bram pursed his lips. "Unless she's unconscious, too, I'm fairly certain she's not down here in another cell. I've been calling through the slot in the door. I've heard from an old prisoner named Yarlsruh, but no Kirah. I suppose she could have escaped, but—"

"I doubt it." Guerrand scowled. "Lyim's probably holding her as insurance against our giving him information about the Council of Three. She should be all right for a while."

Bram couldn't help but notice his uncle's tone wasn't as confident as his words. "What do we do now?"

"Get your staff back, of course."

"No problem," Bram said wryly. "I'll just ask that nice guard who brained you senseless to give it back."

Guerrand glowered at him. "Just give me a chance to think, will you?" he said, grabbing his head again.

"Maybe you'd feel better if you ate something," Bram suggested. "I know I'm starving." He considered the victuals on the table next to Guerrand's bed, then drew his hand back. "Do you think they're poisoned?"

Guerrand shook his head gingerly. "You read too

many of Rejik's cloak-and-dagger novels before Cormac burned them all. If Lyim wanted us dead, he wouldn't have to resort to poison, would he? He already has us locked up."

"I suppose," Bram muttered, feeling foolish. Recalling those well-loved stories, he came up with an idea. "What if you pretend to still be unconscious, and I call the guards in to check on you, and—"

"Then we knock them out," Guerrand supplied. "It's a bit hackneyed. The oldest trick in the world, in fact, but I suppose it could work." He rubbed at his aching muscles. "We'll have to be very convincing, because we won't get a second chance to fool them. You'll have to dash out their brains alone from behind, since I'll be flat on my back. Do you think you can do it?"

Bram's eyes twinkled. "I think I can recall some of my brief cavalier training from nearly twenty years ago."

"That wasn't exactly the vote of confidence I was hoping for," sighed Guerrand. "But it'll have to do. Maybe some props will help." Guerrand took a mouthful of bread and cheese, chewed it thoroughly, then spit the mess back into his hand. "This ought to make anyone believe I'm sick," he said as he smeared goo on his lips and chin, then plopped the remainder on the mattress near where his head would lie.

Bram moved to the door as Guerrand arranged himself on the bed. With one last look over his shoulder, he called, "Guard! I need help! Please, I think there's something really wrong with my uncle!"

A heavy scuffling sound in the hall was followed by footsteps and jangling metal. Then a voice replied, "Of course there's something wrong with your uncle. He's down here, isn't he? If things was all right, he wouldn't be here. Now shut up and behave yourself, or I'll give you a damned good thrashing."

Bram banged on the door. "Wait! You don't understand. He was hit in the head, and now he's throwing up. I think he's really hurt."

The guard chortled. "Well, I tell you what. Tomorrow when we strap him to a table down the hall, we'll make him forget all about his upset tummy."

Bram glanced at his uncle, who threw him a stern look and made a fist. Turning back to the door, Bram assumed his best, commanding voice, the one he used when addressing uncooperative subjects.

"Listen to me, you great oaf. There's a man in here who is very important to your so-called potentate. He may be dying because of your cruel treatment. If Ani-irin comes down here to interrogate him, as he surely will, and finds him dead or too badly hurt to answer, where do you think the potentate's wrath will fall? On another valuable prisoner like me, or on a no-account bully of a guard who is easily replaced? If my uncle is hurt as badly as I think he is, you don't have much time to ponder that."

There was an uneasy silence in the hall. Then, as Bram had hoped, he heard the bar being lifted from the front of the door. The guard's voice, a bit shaky now, warned, "We're coming in. Back away from the door, d'you hear?"

Bram quickly complied, backing up against the empty bed within easy reach of the basin and water pitcher. Guerrand tossed his nephew a wink, then closed his eyes and began moaning softly as the door creaked open. The burly guard poked his head through the doorway and checked to see that Bram was out of the way before looking at Guerrand. His gaze fell for several moments on the smear of chewed food, the bruised temple, and torn clothing.

"Mercy, what a mess we got now," he muttered, then swung the door open. "Keep an eye on that one," he admonished. Bram was momentarily surprised to see that the jailer's helper was a boy, probably in his mid-teens, who looked far more frightened than Bram felt in spite of the spear he held before him.

As the guard knelt to examine Guerrand, Bram snatched the water-filled pitcher and swung it as hard as he could, smashing it straight down atop the guard's head. The man crumpled without even a groan, amid the splashing water and clattering porcelain fragments. Guerrand lunged forward and grabbed the spear with both hands, wrenching it away. The boy retreated, wide-eyed and whimpering, to the far corner of the cell.

Bram picked up the heavy basin and eyed the frightened lad, but Guerrand told him to set it down. "We can gag him and tie him up. We don't need to bash in his head just to keep him quiet, much as I'd like to."

Immediately Bram went to work on the guard, using ropes that he stripped from the bed frame and stuffing the better part of a sheet into the man's enormous mouth.

Meanwhile, the boy submitted to having his arms, thin as straw-sticks, lashed to his sides. "There was a young woman with us," Guerrand said as he knotted the ropes to the bed frame. "Was she brought down here?"

The boy shook his head, then whispered, "No, we've got no ladies in here at all." As Guerrand prepared a gag, the boy spoke again. "Please, sirs, if it's not too much to ask, could you knock me about like you did Murtzy? The soldiers will thrash me something awful if I don't have a knot on my head."

Guerrand picked up the basin, than passed it to Bram. "Get it right the first time," he advised. After a dull *clong* sound, the boy slumped in his bonds.

Once out of the cell, they quickly located their belongings near the guards' table. Bram's fingers ran the length of his meticulously carved staff, lingered over the rough gem set in the top. He hadn't realized how mentally dependent he'd become on the staff he'd fashioned as a focus for his magic. He had felt vulnerable without it, despite the relative ease of their escape.

"Finally, the fates would seem to be on our side," Bram remarked. "That old trick worked beautifully."

"Maybe a little too beautifully," mused Guerrand.

Bram turned on him. "What do you mean?"

Guerrand looked pensive. "I've just been thinking how odd it is that Lyim would have assigned such foolish guards to our detail."

"You think he arranged it so we could get out?" Bram asked. "But why?"

"Because he enjoys playing games. Because he would find it more interesting to give us hope, then squash us like mice running through the corridors of his palace." Guerrand gave a little shrug. "Don't ask me to try to think as Lyim does."

"Maybe you're overestimating how much he regards us as a threat," Bram countered.

"I don't think so. We can't afford to take anything at face value from here on out."

Bram wrapped his fingers around his staff and headed for the stairs.

"Wait a moment," his uncle said, stopping him.

Bram turned around a bit anxiously. "What is it? We've got to move before any more guards or soldiers come down here to check the area."

Guerrand cleared his throat awkwardly. "Remember Lyim's unpredictability," he said, "and you won't be surprised by any situation that arises, or anything I do. You have to be prepared to leave me if you must."

Bram looked at his uncle strangely. "We've been over this. Let's just hope I don't need to make that choice." He headed for the torchlit staircase.

Bram didn't see his uncle's grim expression as the mage followed him up the stairs.

Chapter Fifteen

Guerrand felt as though every nerve was at the surface of his skin. He expected something to go very wrong at any moment. He was waiting for it around every corner he and Bram turned as they crept through Lyim's palace, searching for Kirah. Guerrand's sword, retrieved from the guards' station, was thrust through his belt, but Bram carried only his staff.

Guerrand could not shake the thought that their escape from the dungeon had been entirely too easy. There might as well have been no doors on their cell or guards outside, for all the good either had been. Lyim hadn't risen so far in so short a time by being so careless.

How was it, in a palace the size of Thonvil, that they had easily avoided both sentries and servants?

Guerrand could scarcely contemplate the possibilities through the pounding in his head. He had been suffering since awaking in the cell. Through the headache, he sensed a strange, undeniable pull. Some force, undoubtedly magical, was leading him through the palace. The mage hadn't mentioned this to Bram; it was a sensation too vague to describe, let alone credit.

How he wished he could cast just one spell to determine if they were being led into a trap, or if this strange pull was just his imagination. The palace was, after all, powered by an immense amount of magic. Perhaps his senses were being skewed in the presence of so much arcane energy. Above all these considerations, his head just throbbed. His thoughts were twisting into a coil he couldn't untangle.

The mage and his nephew came to a second floor landing just above the hanging gardens. Guerrand dropped onto a step briefly. Sweat ran in rivulets down his temples, matting the dark hair around his face. They hadn't traveled particularly far or fast, so the mage's condition was surprising to both men.

"Are you all right?" Bram whispered at his side.

"I've got a terrific headache," Guerrand ventured back, his voice raspy, "undoubtedly the result of the guards' delicate handling."

Bram looked concerned. "I could give you a curative herb concoction, or try a spell to ease the pain."

Guerrand winced his refusal. "Thanks, but I have the feeling neither would help." He cradled his head in his hands momentarily, but the longer he sat, the worse the pain became. He was comforted briefly at the thought of the vial Dagamier had prepared for him at Bastion, safely tucked into his tunic, but nothing could overcome the torment in his skull for more than a breath or two.

Bram shrugged. "Maybe we should find someplace out of sight for you to rest, while I continue looking for Kirah." He stood in a crouch, looking for a doorway or dark alcove.

"No!" Guerrand hissed. "You don't know where to go!"

Bram cocked his head in surprise. "And you do?"

Pressing his palms to his moist temples, Guerrand

told Bram of his sensation of being drawn through the palace. "You believe me, don't you?"

Bram frowned at his uncle's anxiety. "Of course, Rand. I've been around magic long enough to believe almost anything. But this makes me nervous. Nothing good can come of us following this . . . feeling. Why haven't we been pursued from the dungeon? Why haven't we seen even a single person in this place? Why would anyone here lead us anywhere but into a trap?"

"I've thought of all that, of course. But we were already in a trap," Guerrand reasoned. "Why would anyone make it easy for us to leave one, only to send us to another?" He shook his sore head, stopping abruptly when the throbbing increased to a roar. "No, there's something else afoot here."

"Another mage, perhaps?" Bram suggested.

"I don't see how, with Lyim wearing the gauntlet," said Guerrand. "But we won't know until we get to where I'm being led."

"Do you think that's wise? Perhaps we should find our own way."

Guerrand grimaced. "I don't have a choice," he said, standing with effort. "I tried to force myself to stay here and ignore the pull, but the pounding in my head only got worse. I'm afraid my skull will split open if I don't keep moving."

Without a thought toward caution, Guerrand stumbled down the corridor. At this point, he felt willing to do almost anything if it would make the pounding go away. Certain directions in the palace seemed, somehow, to hold out the promise of relief.

"This way," Guerrand muttered, rounding a corner. A slip of mist slithered across the floor at his feet. He stopped and blinked, but the mist remained.

He rubbed his eyes and looked again, then staggered back a step. It was not mist he saw, but a red-haired woman in a pale pink gown, very like the kind Esme had favored back in Palanthas. The woman resembled a cloud, a rosy cloud at sunset, with slender, pale arms trailing like misty tendrils.

She smiled at him. Guerrand's heart thumped in his chest, and the pounding in his ears diminished.

"What's wrong?" demanded Bram, behind him. "Why did you stop?"

"Can't you see her?" Guerrand asked.

Both men looked down the hallway, but only Guerrand gasped in dismay. "Where did she go?"

"Who? I didn't see anyone."

"But you must have! She was right in front of me!" Guerrand spun about, but saw only empty corridor in all directions. "Damn!"

"Maybe your eyes have been affected by your headache. That happens with migraines, you know. Are you sure you don't want to take some of my herbs?"

"No, I want to find that woman," Guerrand said fiercely, breaking into a run down the corridor. The hallway was long, open on the right side for half its length to overlook the hanging gardens. There were no doors to the left, just a long stretch of wall covered with elaborate tapestries.

Guerrand thought he caught a glimpse of pink tulle at the far end of the corridor. "There she is!" he cried, anxious beyond all reason to speak with the mysterious woman. He ran after the tuft of pink fabric.

"I don't see anything," Bram protested behind him. "Let's not be hasty, here, Rand."

"I have to follow her," Guerrand insisted. "Stay behind if you must." His headache was gone now, but his thoughts were jumbled and overwhelmed by the pull he felt on his heart. Teased by fleeting glimpses of her pink gown ahead, Guerrand led them through more ornate rooms joined by corridors. Somehow he felt that if he could just talk to her, all the questions he had ever had would be answered. Even the purpose of the Dream . . .

Guerrand rounded a corner and stopped. He recognized this hallway as the one the elf, Salimshad, had brought him to earlier. The woman stood before Lyim's chamber door, between two armed sentries who seemed not to see any of them. Guerrand was not surprised by their oblivion, given the magic he was certain had led him here.

Bram skidded around the corner behind him and saw the guards standing at attention, legs spread, hands behind their backs. "Great Chislev!"

Still the sentries seemed not to see or hear them.

The woman, who was within an arm's length of Guerrand, waved the mage toward her as she slowly opened the door and slipped inside. Guerrand was so desperate to follow that it carried him straight toward the room past the unseeing guards.

"Please, Rand, wait!" Bram hissed softly.

"I have waited," Guerrand responded, "ever since my Test at the Tower." He knew his answer would only confuse Bram, but there wasn't time to be more clear. Bram seemed to understand anyway, or at least recognize Guerrand's determination. He released his uncle's arm.

The mage had spent months preparing himself for the events he felt certain lay ahead, and so he was strangely calm as he took mesmerized steps and pushed through the door behind the woman. His serenity didn't last long, however. Nothing could have prepared him for what he saw behind the door.

Guerrand stepped into Lyim's chamber, looking for the mist woman. He found her standing on the far side of the enormous, canopied bed. Lyim was in the rumpled bed itself, his back to Guerrand. The potentate was obviously unaware of the mage, as he rolled himself to the side where the mist-woman stood. Barebacked, Lyim still wore the elaborate gauntlet, a fact that Guerrand might have overlooked but for one thing. While he watched, the woman coalesced into one brilliant red spiral of mist. She hung suspended above

Lyim briefly. Then the rosy whirlpool coiled like spun cotton into the magical glove on Lyim's right hand.

"So you're back, Ventyr," Guerrand heard Lyim say. "Off running the palace while I indulged in a little distraction?"

Guerrand scarcely had time to make the connection between the mist woman and Lyim's gauntlet, when something stirred beneath the sheets in the middle of the gigantic bed. He almost stepped back, oddly embarrassed at having intruded upon Lyim's philandering, when he heard a voice ask with drowsy familiarity, "Who are you talking to, Lyim?"

Kirah pushed herself up under the weight of heavy golden damask covers. Looking for Lyim, she turned her head and gasped at the sight of her brother, standing openmouthed at the door. Her usually pale face had been flushed with pleasure, but it drained entirely of color. She gathered the covers modestly, dispatching to the rug the tunic that had been discarded on the bed.

"What is it, my dear? An intrusive guard?" Lyim looked casually over his shoulder, then jumped to his feet, unconcerned by his state of undress. "Oh, I see. Only a morally outraged brother." Bram burst breathlessly into the room behind the mage. "And nephew. Ah, well."

Guerrand shook with silent rage while his face boiled red. He was incapable of speech.

"You're all suited up for righteous battle, I see," Lyim said, gesturing to the weapon in Guerrand's belt. "We have all the players for a melodrama, don't you think? The virtuous ingenue, unrepentant villain, irate family. Something you might see in Qindaras's theater district, if I allowed such disruptions anymore."

"Shut up and get dressed, you bastard!" Guerrand barked, finding a voice for his anger at last.

Lyim's eyes narrowed with that glint Guerrand recognized when Lyim was amusing himself by manipulating others. Something about Lyim's words, his shaved head and stance, reminded Guerrand so strongly of Belize under the plinths at Stonecliff, Guerrand thought he felt a chill wind play across his face.

"Don't let your anger allow you to lose sight of the goal," Bram whispered in his ear.

"It's only strengthened my resolve," Guerrand snarled back under his breath. "You just worry about doing your part."

"I had hoped to delay this," Lyim said, casually slipping on his abandoned trousers, without any sign of embarrassment. He eased his tunic over his head. "I would be interested to know how you managed to find your way back here so quickly." His words were light enough, but his tone suggested there were servants who would pay dearly for the slip-up that had granted them freedom. Particularly at this moment.

Walking slowly around the bed, Lyim picked up Kirah's discarded tunic. He tossed it to the pale woman casually. "You should probably get dressed, my dear." Kirah wiggled into the shirt and trousers under the protection of the covers.

"First the plague, and now this! You seduced Kirah just to punish me again!" raged Guerrand.

Lyim sat down within reach of Kirah on the bed, tying the strings at the neck of his tunic. "Let me assure you, I never seduce a woman to punish anyone but myself with the inconvenient entanglements that inevitably ensue." He sighed, as if it were a necessary burden he must bear. "Still, you underestimate your sister's attractions, Rand."

"Oh, damnation, both of you!" Kirah wailed. "Why did you have to burst in here now, Rand? You would have been safe! He promised he would let both of you go afterward. That is . . ." Her voice trailed off awkwardly, having revealed more than she'd intended.

"He told you that? Kirah," Guerrand groaned, "Lyim told you he was giving you the antidote to the plague, too! What made you believe him now?"

There was a brief, pregnant pause, after which Guerrand actually laughed aloud when he realized he was the greater fool here. Kirah had come to Lyim willingly, even if she would never admit the truth of it to herself. She wanted to believe his lies, just as she wanted to be where she was right now, from the moment she had first encountered Lyim's charm.

Guerrand didn't know at whom he was angriest. His hand went to the sword he had thrust through the belt at his waist. He saw Lyim reach for Kirah's arm.

The threat was obvious. Where was Bram with his spells? Guerrand was searching his mind desperately for another answer, when a stream of pink mist swirled out from Lyim's gauntlet and formed itself again into the unimaginable beauty that had led Guerrand through the halls. He shifted his eyes suspiciously between her and the potentate, surprised that Lyim appeared unable to see her. Words, more sharply pointed than any sword, came into Guerrand's mind.

He managed to conquer his rage to say with unexpected calm, "The circumstances *have* changed."

"How so?" Lyim was always willing to play the cat-and-mouse game, at least briefly.

"Your gauntlet led me here. She protected us so that no sentries or servants stopped us along the way. Even the two outside your door were oblivious, and still are. They probably can't even hear you."

Lyim's eyes narrowed, and his composure finally shattered. "Guards!" he howled. When the door remained closed, Lyim looked as if he meant to charge toward it.

But Guerrand and Bram stood shoulder-to-shoulder to block his escape. "*She's* preventing them from hearing you, and you know it," Guerrand said, his tone ripe with meaning. "You're on your own now, Lyim."

Never losing his sneer, Lyim renewed his grasp on Kirah's arm. "Not entirely." He glared at Bram. "Try casting a spell, and she suffers with me."

Guerrand shrugged with feigned indifference, feeling a positive surge of power course through him. "None of us, not Kirah, not Bram, not me, is as important as stopping you from destroying magic. Bram and I vowed this before we left; Kirah will have to suffer the consequences of her rash behavior." Guerrand meant the words for himself, but he knew Bram would hold back. The lord of Thonvil simply wasn't capable of casting a spell that would harm Kirah. At least not yet.

"I *know* you, Rand," Lyim said smoothly. "You couldn't watch while anything happened to her."

"I've come to terms with the fact that Kirah has chosen sides here, and it isn't with me."

"That's not true, Rand!" Kirah cried. "I—"

"Shut up!" Lyim hissed, clamping a hand over her mouth. Above his fingers, Kirah's eyes went wide with horror at witnessing this side of Lyim. She struggled to break free, but he only tightened his grip on her. Kirah thrashed defiantly until her energy was spent and she fell limp against his side.

"You're lying about the gauntlet," Lyim challenged Guerrand, Kirah forgotten. "You're just making a guess based on your knowledge of artifacts."

"Tell me," Guerrand said, "did your head throb so badly you could scarcely think when she first called upon the magic in you?" He could tell from the subtle, wary shift in Lyim's eyes that his remark had hit home. His guess about the mist woman being a manifestation of the gauntlet was correct.

Kill him, a voice as musical as warm wind said inside his head. Guerrand looked to the mist woman. Her lips didn't move in speech, though she smiled seductively. *That's why you came here. I can't attack him directly while he wears the gauntlet, but I've left him vulnerable for you. Do it quickly!*

But why have you turned on him? he asked the voice in his head.

Because I sense great magical power in you, more than in

226

this one. Her red head jerked toward Lyim, who sat looking at Guerrand's distraction with wary puzzlement. *There is no hatred for magic in you, only . . . urgency.*

Kill him and become potentate, she prompted again when she saw him hesitate. *Touch me, and you will understand everything.*

The woman didn't wait for him to respond. She slid her fingers into his hand. Guerrand tried to pull away, but he felt . . . nothing. Only air touched the flesh of his hand, yet it was as if his whole body were enveloped by her soft fingertips. He knew he was under a spell, but he was powerless to stop it. As promised, every question he had ever asked seemed answered by a new, unswerving confidence in himself. He felt raw and energized at the same time.

Suddenly the woman withdrew her vaporous hand from Guerrand's. He gasped as if all the breath had been drawn from his lungs in one vicious burst. He fell to his knees, gulping for air.

At his side in a blink, Bram yanked him back to his feet. "Rand! What's the matter with you?"

"You *have* seen Ventyr," Lyim accused with a gasp, watching Guerrand's face closely.

"Lyim," blurted Guerrand, his eyes earnest, "it's as I feared. The gauntlet has a grip on you, not the other way around! It's controlling you just as much as magic ever did, only you can't see it."

Lyim laughed. "You're such a fool, Rand. Always looking for the good in people. Well, some people don't have any in them. I'm proud to say I'm one of them.

"I vowed to destroy magic long ago," he continued bitterly, "years before I seized the opportunity Ventyr offered. I'm using her to further *my* ends."

"The gauntlet is an artifact of magic, a sentient thing," Guerrand said. "You don't own it. No one can."

"No, but as long as I'm potentate, I control it."

"Then why can't you stop Ventyr from appearing to me?"

Lyim's eyes blazed. "Because everything I've ever wanted or had eventually turns to you." He held the glove up reverently, its gems catching and reflecting the lamplight. "But I'll see us both dead before I let you take this from me!"

With his teeth bared like a snarling dog, Lyim flung Kirah's wrist aside and sprang at Guerrand. The curved sword sliced the air, but Lyim batted it away with his gauntleted right hand. Sparks flew as the steel rang against the magical glove. Guerrand slashed with all the ferociousness of his hatred for Lyim, but every attack was met by the impenetrable fist or palm. Lyim parried the blows effortlessly, regardless of how much force Guerrand put into them. He was laughing, and the more Guerrand's anger grew, the more Lyim howled.

But Lyim stopped laughing when he noticed Bram crouched by the door. The spellcaster's eyes were closed in concentration, left hand gripping his carved staff, a crushed red rose visible in his right. The enraged potentate cast about, looking for something; his eyes settled on the round table. With a hand on each side, Lyim snatched up the table, dumping the soiled dishes to the floor. Jerking it over his head, he tossed the massive weight across the room toward the spellcaster.

"Bram!" cried Guerrand as the heavy table sailed toward his unsuspecting nephew.

Bram cracked an eye, saw the table coming, but looked unconcerned. When the table came within arms' reach of Bram, it smashed in midair as if it had hit a wall. It crashed to the ground without harming Bram, who closed his eyes and returned to his casting.

Relieved, Guerrand looked back toward his enemy just in time to see that Lyim had snatched up a soot-covered poker from the fireplace and flung it toward him javelin-style. Guerrand dodged to his left, but the filthy missile caught the outer muscle of Guerrand's right thigh. The mage felt nothing at first, except disbelief at the sight of the sharp, black poker sagging halfway through his leg.

The pain, however, followed instantly.

Guerrand fell over with a shriek, clutching the shaft of the poker. He was only vaguely aware of Lyim sprinting for the door to the studio.

"Rand!" Kirah cried, rushing to his side. She touched her hand to the wound; her pale palm came away red with her brother's blood. "Do you want me to pull it out?" she asked, her eyes streaming.

Guerrand didn't answer. If he removed the weapon, he feared the pain and loss of blood would drive him to unconsciousness. But he had no choice. Biting his lip, the mage wrenched the metal rod out himself with a pain-racked grunt. Without asking, he reached out and ripped a square of cloth from the hem of Kirah's tunic. He wadded the cloth into a ball that fit into his palm. Steeling himself again, he was about to press the cloth into the ragged hole when Bram grabbed his wrist and pulled it back. The younger man examined the wound briefly, then placed both his hands over it.

"I don't have time to heal this completely, and even what I can do will take several moments," he said.

Guerrand struggled to regain his feet, but was met by a commanding glare from Bram. The mage protested, "We haven't time for this. Lyim is getting away!"

Bram's hands felt warm and soothing against the wound as he replied. "I've prepared something to keep Lyim occupied. He'll have more than enough distractions to keep him busy."

Gradually, the gash in Guerrand's leg closed up and the pain receded. When Bram withdrew his hands, he revealed a jagged pink scar. It was still surrounded by a bruise and swelling, but the wound was closed. Guerrand found that he could stand and walk without difficulty, though not without pain. With the sword thrust before him, the mage nodded his approval, then ran after Lyim through the door to the studio.

Lyim attacked immediately as Guerrand entered the room. The gauntlet smashed Guerrand's sword to the side, never letting the razor edge past its defense. Where the fist crashed into a wall it obliterated tiles and plaster as if it were a spiked mace. Guerrand found himself backed against a wall, dodging and slashing to evade the mighty blows.

With the quickness of lightning, Lyim's hand slammed Guerrand against the wall. The hand in the gauntlet clutched and squeezed at Guerrand's windpipe. Gagging, the mage clawed at Lyim's hand and swung wildly at his head. Guerrand felt cartilage popping in his neck. His lungs burned, and his vision swirled. With clinical detachment Guerrand realized he was suffocating.

This was not how their quest was supposed to end! Guerrand's mind cried in protest. He swung his fist again, roundhouse style, at Lyim's head and almost connected. Lyim squeezed his throat harder, but Guerrand was too far gone for it to matter. As the light faded, he found it odd that his last thought was to wonder what was moving behind Lyim.

The squeezing stopped so abruptly Guerrand fell to the floor, clutching his bruised windpipe. He coughed until at last he could swallow again. Gasping, tears streaming from his eyes, Guerrand's first thought was to look for Lyim. But the potentate was nowhere nearby.

Guerrand's head jerked around at the sound of Lyim's anguished screams coming from the bedchamber. Guerrand scrambled to the door in time to see Lyim, a dun-colored blur, running the length of the chamber, followed by a black cloud.

"Bees!" Guerrand rasped aloud. Bram was crouched by the door, a smile of triumph on his face, while Lyim dashed about like a madman, trying to escape the swarm of bees, hornets, and wasps summoned by Bram's magic.

"It took some time to gather a swarm of sufficient size," Bram explained. "They will harry him unmercifully, and by the time they disperse, he may well be helpless."

With blind fury Lyim grasped and swatted at the stinging insects. Each blow killed several, but there were hundreds, all bent on just one thing: stinging Lyim to death. The potentate smashed into walls, rolled on the floor, yet there was no escape. Anger and pain were indistinguishable in his screams.

Guerrand's eyes searched the floor for his sword. He spotted it near the bed, where Lyim had dashed it with the gauntlet. He took a step and nearly toppled over from dizziness. Recalling the tile exercise from his days as Justarius's apprentice, he focused past the pain to reach for the sword. He limped toward the weapon until it rested in his hand. Guerrand held it aloft, intending to run it through Lyim.

Stepping up alongside Guerrand, Bram touched the sword. A bright red flame, so hot it made Guerrand's face tingle, extended from Bram's finger and raced along the curving blade. It swirled and hissed along the whole length of the sword, forcing Guerrand to extend the weapon farther in front of himself.

Bram placed his hand over Guerrand's on the sword's grip. "Plunge that through Lyim's chest," he said gravely.

The potentate, his face splotched with a hundred stings and welts, howled like a wild animal. He flailed his way through one of the blue velvet-covered archways that Guerrand assumed led outside to a balcony, like the one from which Lyim had addressed the citizens of Qindaras.

Guerrand exchanged looks with his nephew before charging after Lyim. The mage crashed through the heavy velvet curtain, sword firmly in hand, ready for whatever lay beyond. Outside, a wind raged so fiercely that Guerrand was nearly knocked from his feet. He held fast to the curtains and blinked against the wind that dried his eyes in a heartbeat. The flames on the sword snapped tautly in the wind but continued burning.

Lyim stood facing Guerrand across a wide balcony. He clung to the railing with his gloveless hand for support, his face red and swollen from insect bites. His tunic flapped like a white sail against the backdrop of black, whirling storm clouds. The potentate's gauntleted hand was held high above his head, as if he threatened the sky itself.

Guerrand realized in a flash that Lyim, in fact, did. The stinging bees were gone now, driven off by the wind Lyim had summoned with the gauntlet.

Guerrand gripped his sword, finding reassurance in the solid feel of it. Gritting back the pain in his throat, he charged Lyim before his fear had time to find voice.

But as he lunged, Lyim also sprang and grabbed the flaming sword with his gauntleted hand. There was a sizzle and a burning smell, but Lyim's grip held firm. Yanking hard, he sent Guerrand sprawling forward off balance, then released the sword. The mage crashed into the railing at the edge of the balcony, and his momentum carried him over. His left hand locked onto the railing while his right held doggedly to the sword.

Lyim watched Guerrand cruelly for a number of heartbeats, obviously enjoying the sight of his enemy kicking and struggling for a better handhold on the rail. The mage refused to cry out, but his grip was slipping. He couldn't hold on long. He clung tenaciously, refusing to give in even as his fingers burned when the flesh tore away from the muscle.

Lyim's gauntleted hand flashed out and grabbed Guerrand by the left wrist. His grip was unbearably strong, his grin unbearably malignant, as he pried Guerrand's hand from the railing. Still grinning, he held his arm straight out, suspending Guerrand over the edge of the balcony.

Feeling strangely weightless, the mage risked a glance

over his shoulder. He dangled at least three stories above the flagstone courtyard where Lyim had addressed his subjects. Startled citizens of Qindaras began to gather and look up in bewilderment.

The view was not entirely new to him, Guerrand realized with neither surprise nor fear. He had been witness to a similar scene in the darkness of the Dream, when the citizens of Palanthas watched a mage give his life for his Art.

"Both of you stay back, or I drop your beloved Rand," Lyim threatened above the gale that still raged.

But Guerrand could see that behind Lyim, Bram was already preparing another spell. They had agreed beforehand that if Lyim could be maneuvered outside, Bram would unleash one of his most powerful spells. By Bram's description, the balcony and everyone on it would be incinerated. Until this point, Guerrand had doubted that Bram could go through with it. Clearly there was no escape from this situation for Guerrand, but he knew the anguish Bram would feel over being the instrument of his uncle's death.

"Do it, Bram," Guerrand rasped from over the edge. He recalled with great comfort the vial Dagamier had prepared on his request, hidden inside his tunic since leaving his study in Thonvil. Now he only hoped it would survive long enough to fulfill its purpose.

The wind died abruptly. "Drop the sword, Rand, and I'll pull you up," Lyim offered, his tone cool, slick even. Still he kept his back turned to Bram, standing near the curtained doorway.

Before Guerrand could respond, he heard Kirah shout. She had grasped Bram's staff and was trying to wrestle it from his grip. "You'll kill Guerrand, too!"

"Which one of them are you really trying to save?" With a mighty tug, Bram wrenched his staff free, then grabbed Kirah and pinned her arms to her sides. He tried to hold her, but she broke free and tumbled to the floor near the railing of the balcony. Guerrand saw the look on Bram's face and knew that the spell was now hopelessly ruined, impossible to cast.

Kirah looked upward at the stony-faced potentate. "Please, Lyim. You promised to release them. Nothing that's happened here has to change that. I'll stay as long as you want if you'll just do as you promised and let them go!"

Lyim didn't respond, just looked at the elaborate gauntlet on his hand with an odd mixture of loathing and lust. Guerrand knew as well as Lyim that everything *had* changed. Lyim had been betrayed in spirit by Ventyr. Guerrand considered the sizable crowd below. There was no turning back for any of them.

Lyim's silence brought Kirah's pale, tear-streaked face to the rail. "Please, Guerrand, do whatever he asks. Is this really worth giving your life for?"

Through the haze of pain and unreality, Guerrand realized that stopping Lyim *was* worth his life.

It's still not too late for both of us to benefit from this unfortunate situation, the soft voice of Ventyr said. *Agree to his terms, and another opportunity to slay him will arise. I will help you.*

Her words rang so familiar to the mage. *At what cost?* he asked the voice in his mind.

Only that you remember the help I have given you to achieve your goal.

Guerrand felt a rare flash of crystal clarity; he knew where he had heard such words before. The mage could almost feel the heat of Nuitari's thumbprint on the hem of his tunic. If he listened to the gauntlet and killed Lyim to become potentate, he would be repaying Nuitari by increasing the influence of evil on Krynn. It would mean the prophesy of the Dream had come true—he would have taken the final step toward evil.

At last Guerrand understood the purpose of the Dream.

"You don't have a choice, if you want to live!" cried Kirah.

Guerrand looked straight up into Lyim's eyes as he said, "Everything in life is a choice." With that, Guerrand summoned strength born of righteous purpose and slashed upward with the hot-bladed sword.

It sliced clean through Lyim's wrist above the gauntlet.

The potentate howled with rage and pain, but Guerrand had moved beyond hearing. Weight returned to the mage instantly. He tumbled downward, still clutching the stump of Lyim's hand in the gauntlet.

For the brief flight toward the cobblestones, Guerrand felt freer than he had since his youth, before magic, before the Dream, since before he'd been marked by Nuitari's thumb. Today he had settled every question and thwarted every enemy. He finally understood the mind of Rannoch, the mage who had thrown himself from the Tower of High Sorcery for love of the Art.

All in all, as the barbarians said, it was a good day to die.

The horrified citizens of Qindaras who witnessed Guerrand's plunge to his death were undoubtedly puzzled by the smile that lit his face to the last.

Chapter Sixteen

As if in a dream, Bram saw Lyim's gauntleted hand fly away against a faint spattering of stars over the city. He watched as the severed stump of Lyim's arm gushed with every beat of his black heart. For a blackguard, Lyim screamed like a woman.

Bram staggered to the rail of the parapet and gasped. His uncle had already hit the ground. The gathered crowd was swarmed around Guerrand's crumpled body, obscuring Bram's view. He closed his eyes. There was no way a man could have survived such a fall to hard flagstone.

Bram's heart filled with rage. He spun around for the man responsible, but Lyim was gone from the parapet. Bram dashed through billowing curtains. The bed-chamber beyond was empty; bloody footprints were everywhere. Lyim had taken Kirah with him as a hostage. Bram recalled the palace's endless corridors and chambers, and his heart constricted. It could take him days to find them.

His mind leaped to an image of Guerrand out on the flagstones. Perhaps there was something he could do for him first. The least he could do was to keep the crowd from desecrating his uncle's body.

Yanking down the curtains, Bram quickly stripped away the coils of decorative sash cord. He knotted one end to the railing and tossed the rest over, noting that it reached within easy dropping distance of the ground. The crowd noted it, too, and closed in.

Bram waved his staff across the plaza. A ball of light formed at the staff's tip and raced away from the balcony. Above the crowd the light split into dozens of tiny lights. Each streaked toward a different person, surrounding its target in shimmering, soft fire. Bram knew that the simple faerie light was harmless, but it was more than the magic-wary citizens of Qindaras were willing to risk. All those immediately near Guerrand fled in panic. Bram stepped over the railing and slid down the sash cord to the courtyard.

Guerrand lay on his back in a splash of red blood that was slowly spreading along the narrow canals between flagstones. Both of his legs were clearly twisted and broken, as was his sword.

Bram expected to see his uncle holding the gauntlet, but Guerrand's hands were empty. Several small bits of broken glass spilled out from beneath his tangled cloak; something he carried there must have smashed upon impact.

"I vowed to stay until the job was done, with or without you, and that's what I intend to do," Bram said solemnly, his throat thick. He reached out a trembling hand and gently closed his uncle's eyes for the last time.

Find the gauntlet, he told himself, trying desperately to focus his thoughts. He scanned the nearby area, but saw nothing. Enough time had passed that someone in the crowd could have already grabbed the glove containing the potentate's severed hand. Perhaps it bounced farther afield than Bram anticipated. Or it could have landed under Guerrand's body.

Bending down again, Bram reached out tentatively to move his uncle's broken body. Suddenly, the ground started to rumble gently beneath his feet. He glanced up toward where people had been fleeing the courtyard, but those who remained, at a safe distance, seemed in no hurry to leave.

That would change drastically in a heartbeat, when the crowd would clear like smoke on a windy day.

The quaking continued, growing to the point where it couldn't be ignored. Bram clambered to his feet and spun around in time to see jagged slabs of rock sliding down from the upper floors of the palace. He was too stunned to flee with the few remaining citizens who ran screaming from the courtyard as the palace began collapsing in upon itself.

The unbelievable scene reminded Bram of Guerrand's description of the destruction of Bastion. His uncle had described in vivid detail how the magical mortar that held the great nave together had vaporized, only to coalesce as living vapors. Those monstrosities streaked through the air, shrieking and wailing and attacking whatever they encountered. In a short time they had torn the building down until no two stones were stacked on top of each other.

Were the gods of magic destroying the Palace of Qindaras, just as they had their own stronghold? Or had Lyim gone completely mad and was killing himself, taking everything nearby with him? Including Kirah.

Then Bram remembered Justarius's admonition: the palace would not survive if the gauntlet were removed from it without the potentate. Guerrand had found a way to make that happen.

If he hoped to find the gauntlet, Bram would have to search fast, before the courtyard was covered with rubble. Rocks were tumbling dangerously close. With an eye toward the crumbling palace, Bram frantically hauled up on Guerrand's shoulders and groped beneath his body. There was nothing but blood under the dead mage.

Bram's gaze was caught by a small plume of strange, purple smoke rising slowly from his uncle's cloak. Bram watched as the smoke spewed out faster, accumulating above Guerrand. The swirling smoke took shape and became solid. It was a winged creature, larger than Bram, with massive arms and red, glowing eyes. Its skin was dark and rough, its hands large and clawed. Tusks protruded between thick, cracked lips.

The creature glanced down at Guerrand's shattered form and grunted. Its red eyes fell next on Bram; the creature snatched him up in its hot, scratchy arms. Bram barely managed to hang on to his staff as the hideous beast's wings spread wide and it raced across the courtyard, away from the disintegrating palace.

Bram struggled against the creature's hold, but his strength was like a child's next to the massive sinews of the animal. It ran several paces, then hopped into the air with its wings spread. Gusts of air from the beating wings rushed past Bram's face. He kicked and punched against the unyielding hide until his knuckles bled. He strained to grasp his staff and cast a spell, but the creature seemed to realize the staff's importance; the wooden rod was wrested from Bram's grip. Then the creature balled up its melon-sized fist and, with a small rap, knocked its cargo unconscious.

* * * * *

Bram awoke with a start, instantly aware that he was no longer being carried. He sat up and looked around, surprised when he recognized his surroundings. The creature had unceremoniously deposited him at the doorstop to Bastion. Bram saw no sign of the winged beast against the breathtaking panorama of pine trees and majestic rock cliffs. The magical creature had obviously flown with its unconscious burden a great distance at someone's behest.

He had a growing notion who was responsible for his premature departure from Qindaras.

Bram's guess was confirmed when the great mirrored door behind him opened. A leg clad in black silk robes stepped out, followed by the rest of the woman. "Hello, Bram," Dagamier said calmly.

"Hello?" he repeated, his head pounding. "What am I doing here, Dagamier? That creature dragged me away before I could kill Lyim!"

"Lyim's not dead?" she asked, startled.

"No," he rasped, "but Guerrand is!" Dagamier showed no surprise at Bram's revelation. He explained the situation that existed when he was dragged from the courtyard beneath Lyim's palace by the winged creature.

The wizardess pressed slim fingers to her lips and turned away briefly. "Guerrand must have fallen on the vial I prepared for him," she muttered.

"What vial?" Bram demanded. He recalled the broken glass he had seen on the flagstones by Guerrand's body.

Dagamier paused to form her thoughts. "Guerrand pulled me aside just before you both left when you agreed to the Council's request. He asked if I could think of a way to draw you safely from Qindaras, something he could activate himself when he deemed the moment right. I suggested a crystal vial, stoppered with lead, containing a creature with instructions to bring you here, much like a homing pigeon delivering a message."

"But Kirah was there, too!" exclaimed Bram. "She climbed into the mirror before we left Thonvil. That damned creature snatched me up before I could find her, and now Lyim's got her."

Dagamier looked insulted. "I had no way of anticipating your aunt's uninvited presence when I created the vial."

"But why would you agree to create such an item when you knew I had vowed to stay until the job was done?"

"Guerrand asked me to," she said without guile. "He knew I was proficient at summoning monsters. Your uncle told me he wouldn't activate it until Lyim was dead. He wasn't supposed to crush the vial prematurely by falling on it."

"He wasn't supposed to die, either!"

"Yes, he was," she countered grimly. "Did you understand your uncle so little you didn't recognize the fatalism that prompted him to accept this mission? I believe that from the moment he received the summons to Bastion, Guerrand believed he would soon die."

"But why?"

Dagamier's rigid shoulders lifted in a shrug. "He just knew. I don't understand how, exactly—he didn't confide in me. It was one of the reasons he was so set against your going with him. He didn't want you to prevent what he saw as his duty. His fate, if you will. That's what I believe, anyway."

Bram turned away to ponder that. In hindsight he recalled phrases, worried glances, attempts to persuade him to save himself first.

"I didn't get the chance to avenge Guerrand, or even bring him back for a decent burial," he said to himself in a ragged, mournful whisper. "He must still be in the courtyard under tons of rubble."

"You knew of the Dream?" she asked. "The one where he repeated Rannoch's leap from the Tower of High Sorcery at Palanthas."

"Of course!" Bram returned. "He was more than my uncle and mentor, he was my closest friend."

Dagamier looked reflective. "Guerrand was a bit obsessed, I think, about the minor nuances between the philosophies of the Orders, at least as far as they concerned him. He was haunted by the fear that he might ever feel compelled to turn to the black robes."

Dagamier's words were less than complimentary, yet Bram did not take offense. There was no condemnation in her tone, only a stoic observation. "Mourn him if you will, Bram, but also take heart in the knowledge that he conquered his fear at the last."

Nodding gently, Bram closed his eyes and called upon the strength of Chislev to heal his aching heart. Even before training with Primula, he had believed in the natural cycle of life, birth, growth, death—even reincarnation. But never had it touched him so closely. Not with Nahamkin, good friend that he'd been. Not even with his own father, Cormac, whose pyre he'd lit to send his spirit skyward. That seemed so long ago now.

With a faint trace of a smile, Bram looked up at Dagamier. "Maybe Guerrand will be reincarnated as a sea gull. He would like that, I think." Dagamier actually gave a gentle smile in return, and her pale face was transformed in the cold breeze.

"Are you always so insightful, Dagamier?" he asked suddenly. "I would not have guessed it from Guerrand's descriptions of you."

Dagamier raised a brow in bemusement at his gaff, though he could see she was not really insulted. "Guerrand and I had an . . . interesting acquaintance," she murmured thoughtfully. "We seldom agreed, but I always respected him. Well," she amended with a memorable smirk, "at least after a time."

"I know he felt the same," Bram said solemnly. An awkward silence descended.

"What are you going to do next?" Dagamier asked at length.

Bram's face took on a determined look. "Go back to Qindaras to kill Lyim and get Kirah back."

Dagamier stepped up to the railing that ran along the top of the steep drop-off in front of Bastion. She folded her hands before her with a primness that defied her sensual dress. The wind blew the skirt of her black robe open to briefly reveal well-shaped, milky-white legs. "How long has it been since you've slept or eaten?"

He ran a hand through his tangled hair. "Too long, I'm sure. Strangely, I don't feel hungry, but I suppose it would help me to think more clearly."

"Exactly." She sniffed the air with good-humored disdain. "A bath probably wouldn't hurt either. Come on." She motioned toward the door leading into Bastion. He followed her into the observation area.

Inside, she gave Bram directions to a small but comfortable guest chamber. "I'll have water and other amenities for bathing sent to your room, along with a tray and wine. Send your bearer to notify me when you're ready to talk again. We'll need to discuss our strategy against Lyim before the Council of Three arrives."

"They're coming?" Bram dreaded having to report failure on all accounts.

Dagamier nodded. Her look was almost sympathetic. "LaDonna sent a missive. We have until tomorrow morning to prepare."

Weary and heartsick, Bram trudged off to follow Dagamier's directions. The reminder of Guerrand's death brought on a new and unrelenting funk. When the bearer at last finished filling the copper bathtub and left, Bram turned to the meditation that always helped steady his nerves. But today, two passes through the mantra did not bring the relief that one typically did.

Shucking his clothing, Bram moved the food tray to the side of the tub and sank into the hot, sudsy water. He poured himself a glass of the green Ergothian wine and sipped pensively, recalling in vivid detail the events in the palace courtyard. He would have to have his wits about him when he spoke to the Council of Three.

But hot water and cool wine on an empty stomach

began to relax him in a way the mantra had not. Bram hefted the bottle of wine, surprised to find he had drunk it all. The water in the copper bath had grown stone cold. He had completely lost track of time. Somewhere in Bastion, the black-robed wizardess must be anxiously waiting for his call.

Dagamier has been surprisingly kind, Bram thought to himself in the warm way wine induces. And not as hard on the eyes as he remembered. Unexpected thoughts of her flooded his foggy head. Bram squinted through bleary eyes, looking for the bell left by the bearer. Spying it at last next to his right arm, he managed to direct his hand to snatch it up. He just succeeded in giving it a ragged jangle before he lost sight of everything altogether.

The exhausted and inebriated lord of Thonvil had passed out in his bath.

* * * * *

Lyim sat slumped on a divan in the back room of the temple to Misal-Lasim. He had scarcely moved from it in the last several days. His severed right arm was bound in a clean rag. He felt like he had stepped back more than five years, to when he had a snake head for a hand. Aside from the initial agony of the conversion, the snake hand had been more inconvenient than painful. This wound, however, still throbbed. He was weak from blood loss.

But he had lost so much more than blood in the days since the palace's collapse, which Salimshad had helped him to escape.

Lyim could hear the worshipers in the temple and knew without looking that the numbers in attendance had dwindled dramatically. Just then Salimshad pushed through the curtained archway that separated the back room from the temple proper. He lifted up the condor mask. Sweat glistened on his fine elven features in the torchlight.

"Did you hear the questions of your followers, master?" Salim demanded softly. He could tell from Lyim's expression that the potentate had not. "The destruction of the palace and the loss of your hand before their eyes has caused many to lose faith in our cause. You must do something immediately, unless you intend to abandon your goal of destroying magic. You must rekindle the fire in their hearts, master, and reclaim their loyalty, or all is for naught!"

"They're lucky all they lost was their faith," Lyim said tonelessly.

"But you can regain everything!" protested Salimshad. "I scoured the ruins of the courtyard until I found the gauntlet. You can use it to rebuild, if that's your desire."

Lyim stirred from his self-pity to exclaim angrily, "Don't you see? I'm handless again!" Lyim waved his stump, the new bandage showing spots of blood already. "I can't wear the gauntlet without a right hand. Even if I could forget that Ventyr betrayed me to Guerrand."

"She can no longer betray you to him."

Lyim actually smiled, though it lacked conviction. "Thank you for finding the one bright spot in this whole disaster, Salim. Guerrand can no longer steal what is mine. In that context, his death may actually have been worth the loss of my hand."

"You recovered your hand once before under much more trying circumstances," Salim said.

"You're talking about me using my magical skills," Lyim accused him.

Salim shrugged. "As you yourself have said: 'only a diamond can cut a diamond'. If you do nothing but sit in the back room of this temple until you die, you will have given victory to those who tried to destroy you. You might as well have fallen from the parapet yourself, instead of that mage sent to assassinate you."

Lyim paused, considering. "Tell me again why you think Guerrand's nephew Bram may no longer be a threat to me in the city."

Salimshad nodded. "When I was searching the courtyard for the gauntlet and your hand, I saw him being carried away by a fearsome-looking winged creature. I don't know where it came from or why, but Bram was struggling to escape it. I have doubts that he would even have survived the creature's entrapment."

Salim removed the mask and set it on a shelf. "And what of his relation?" he asked cautiously. "Are you sure you can trust her?"

"Kirah?" Lyim snorted with a visible jerk of his shoulders. "You know better than to ask that, Salim. I trust no one. Besides, if she meant to kill me, she would have tried while we were pleasantly engaged."

"She doesn't blame you for her brother's death?"

"Kirah is still in shock, I think. But I have reminded her that I was willing to save Guerrand, and he declined my offer. Kirah cannot deny the truth of that. She was there. She saw."

The elf squinted into the shadows. "Where is she now?"

"She went to the marketplace for food."

"Is that why you have kept her around when you can no longer torture her brother with the sight? Any of the novitiates would be happy to bring you food."

Lyim shrugged again dismissively. "Kirah serves me in many ways. She comes in handy now that I can no longer wear Ventyr. I have no one else to wait on me since all the servants not killed in the destruction of the palace have fled. I have no power to draw them back, nor am I likely to ever again."

Salimshad looked at him questioningly. "So you *have* given up."

Lyim scowled at the elf's critical tone. "It would take a miracle to persuade the citizens of Qindaras I am god-touched after they witnessed my vulnerability on the parapet, not to mention the destruction of the palace. A damned miracle . . ."

Suddenly Lyim's dark eyes squinted with a new, evil light. "I think I may just know where to find such a miracle." He stood and raced for the door, insight and energy coming all in a burst. "Meet me at the palace with a work detail of fifty diggers. I need some of the things from the storage rooms. And arrange to have someone put up notices and inform the priests to announce another rally at high sun in the ruins of the palace courtyard. Yes," he said, "that should give me enough time."

"What if the people won't come?"

Lyim scowled. "Not everyone has turned against me so quickly. Enough will appear out of curiosity, and the rest will hear by word-of-mouth of the miracle Misal-Lasim will grant me at high sun tomorrow!"

* * * * *

For the third time in a week, the citizens of Qindaras were gathered in the courtyard of their potentate's ruined palace. Bells rang all over the city, announcing the call to hear the potentate's words. Priests at daily worship had been ordering the faithful to attend.

Kirah shivered in her borrowed cloak. Winter had returned to Qindaras with a vengeance after the destruction of the palace. She was waiting with the faithful and feckless alike for the potentate to address his people. Though Lyim had made it clear he expected her to stay close, Kirah had slipped away easily enough today. Salimshad had been preoccupied with preparations and preaching at temples since Lyim had given the order to assemble the citizens.

Kirah had been busy herself. She had to learn if Bram was safe. Someone had to have seen him in the city. Kirah was determined to keep looking on the sly until she found him. Yesterday's trip to the market stalls had given her an opportunity. After collecting a few apples, she'd spent the rest of her time trying to find anyone who knew anything about Bram's disappearance. No one she spoke to had remembered much detail about the mayhem in the courtyard that night. But she'd overheard Lyim's elf say that he'd seen Bram being carried away by some hideous, magical monster. Kirah couldn't credit that, though. Bram would not have used his own magic to run away from anything.

Kirah was less certain about herself. Everything had got so tangled since she'd been forced from the mirror in Lyim's sculpting studio. Guerrand had been so angry. She'd never had a chance to explain. Now he was dead. Kirah squeezed her eyes shut. She couldn't think about that. It hurt too much to contemplate that she'd finally got one person she loved, only to lose another.

Kirah opened her eyes again, determined to focus on the event at hand. Stalwart or stupid, citizens had obviously taken to looting, for even the ruins of the five hundred thirty-four domes had been scraped for their metal, however little the metal might be worth. Kirah could imagine nothing more desolate than the heaps of rubble: shattered masonry, broken rafters jutting up like great ribs, tumbled doors with hinges creaking in the cold wind.

The bells had stopped pealing, but the echo over Qindaras continued for many moments. When it finally ceased, the potentate scrambled like a common chimney sweep to the highest point on the rubble that a man with one hand could reach. Even at this distance, Kirah could clearly see that the stump of Lyim's right arm was still wrapped with a rag.

Kirah noticed with the eyes of a lover that Lyim looked exhausted. She knew his was a soul completing a long march into madness. She was powerless to stop him—or stop herself from wanting to stay with him.

"Citizens of Qindaras!" Lyim cried. He managed to silence the whispers and cries from the crowd. "We are standing in these ruins today, a reminder of our transgressions. I have spent the two days since the palace's destruction in fasting and prayer to Misal-Lasim. He has revealed to me that our lack of faith brought down this centuries-old palace just as surely as if we'd torn it down with our hands!"

The wind whipped at Lyim's loose clothing as he paused, letting the crowd absorb his words. "We were chosen by Misal-Lasim from all the people of the world to fulfill a mission. But we grew complacent, lazy, from the evidence of Misal-Lasim's goodwill in restoring Qindaras, and we failed! Misal-Lasim destroyed the palace and recalled the harsh weather to show us the error of our sinful ways!

"But the news is not all bad! Misal-Lasim has given us a second chance, a new lease. We must recommit ourselves to the destruction of magic, as so many of you did just days ago, in this very place. To that end, we will march on the greatest storehouse of magic in this world, the Tower of High Sorcery! United, we can destroy it. Misal-Lasim's favor will be ours once more!"

The potentate's cry to arms was met with a mixture of cheers from those who had never lost faith, and the jeers of those who had.

From somewhere in the crowd, a man shouted, "How do we know this quest is blessed by Misal-Lasim? Our homes were not destroyed, only yours!" Guards posted throughout the crowd heard the speaker, however, and surged forward with raised poleaxes to punish the man for his insolence.

"Let the man speak!" Lyim decreed. The guards dropped the man's arms, but remained by his side. Lyim asked him to repeat his question; the man nervously complied.

Lyim considered only briefly. "I, too, have asked such questions. But I have faith. Faith enough to prove the power of the god we serve. Behold!"

Lyim closed his eyes for many moments in concentration, then raised the stump of his arm high. "I wish for the restoration of my hand so that I may better serve the will of Misal-Lasim!"

With his left hand Lyim stripped away the bandages. His face twisted in pain, and he grabbed his wrist with his left hand. Fresh blood spurted from the stump, then stopped. The skin at the wrist, shriveled and crusted, started to stretch. Nubs of finger bones appeared and grew, then raw red muscle and exposed veins crept across the bones, finally forming into the shape of a hand. The agony on Lyim's face receded as flesh spread over the new bones. With gritted teeth, Lyim flexed the newborn fingers, formed a fist, and held it aloft.

A hush fell over the crowd. Slowly, the crowd began to chant. The sound was a rolling, gathering thing, until the courtyard vibrated. There was not one dry eye in the ever-growing crowd. "Aniirin! Aniirin! Aniirin!"

Kirah, though moist eyed like the rest, had seen enough magic to recognize a wizard's wish spell. But the good citizens of Qindaras were certain they had witnessed a miracle. Perhaps they had, Kirah mused. Lyim had reestablished their faith in the beat of a charismatic heart. He might march to the Abyss to further his goal of destroying the Art, but after today's demonstration, it was clear the citizens of Qindaras would follow him there.

Chapter Seventeen

Bram knew that something was wrong the moment he opened his eyes. Different, anyway. He was tucked up in a warm bed in dry clothes. The last thing he remembered, he'd been bathing, drinking a bottle of green wine. Recalling the taste of the drink, he shivered, causing his head to throb. A knock rang out on his door.

"Come."

Dagamier strode in, her face an unreadable mask.

"You're awake," she said. "I was afraid you would sleep through the Council of Three's arrival."

Wincing, Bram put a hand gingerly to a throbbing temple. "I-I'm sorry," he muttered. "I'm having a hard time recalling how I got here. Into bed, not Bastion," he added hastily. "I was in the bath, and the last thing I remember was—" He stopped, blushing furiously.

"Don't worry," she said. "The bearer found you asleep. He removed you from the bath and put you to bed."

Dagamier's words were comforting, but something about the way her eyes regarded him made him wonder if she could read his mind. Or perhaps the bearer had not been alone in putting him to bed. Either possibility made him decidedly uncomfortable. He sat up, tucking the sheets around himself while he searched for his clothing.

"Are these what you're looking for?" she held out his tunic and trousers, newly washed and neatly folded.

Bram took them with a grateful if pained flash of white teeth. The black-robed wizardess turned her back, the hem of her silken robe brushing his bare feet.

Bram wasted no time jerking the borrowed night-shirt over his head, then replacing it with his own well-worn garments. "We were going to talk last night about the meeting with the Council. How long before they're scheduled to arrive?"

The young woman turned around, graceful and silent as black smoke. "Any time now. Par-Salian is predictably punctual. Justarius is always a hair late and a touch harried. LaDonna likes to make a grand entrance after them both whenever possible."

"I have to leave for Qindaras to retrieve Kirah the moment the meeting is concluded," he said. "Lyim is as helpless as we could ever hope for. His protective palace is destroyed; he has no place to hide; he's lost his hand, and along with it the gauntlet. Come to think of it, he may even have bled to death. At the very least, he can't wear a right-handed gauntlet without a right hand. He can't use Ventyr to absorb magic anymore."

"I wouldn't count on any of that," Dagamier said softly. "There are any number of ways a mage could reattach or regenerate a severed hand in less than a day."

"Maybe so, but there's a good chance he doesn't have the gauntlet anymore," said Bram. "Guerrand was holding it when he fell, and it flew into the crowd. Why don't we suggest the Council send an army of mages or even monsters into Qindaras before Lyim can restore his hand or find the gauntlet? If we move quickly—"

"I'm afraid it's already too late," Dagamier said grimly.

"What do you mean?" he demanded.

"Your sense of time was thrown off when you were being carried back here by the winged servant," she explained. "It's been longer than you think since Lyim lost his hand—nearly a week."

"That doesn't prove he's had time to find the gauntlet, or even to recover his hand," challenged Bram.

"No," she agreed. "However, I've been experimenting with spells this morning; not one of them has worked."

Bram stared at her. "So after all we went through to stop him, Lyim's still in control. Magic is still susceptible."

"We all feel vulnerable while Lyim has the gauntlet," Dagamier confessed. "For as long as I can remember, the Art has been my whole life, my only companion. And now I can't use it, for fear of strengthening someone who intends to destroy the thing that sustains me." She gave Bram an envious look. "At least you can still cast your kind of magic. I wonder if our two disciplines are very different," she mused.

"Watching Guerrand for so long, I've noticed more similarities than differences between his kind of magic and mine. My uncle and I even discussed the subject on cold winter days before the fire. He'd promised to mentor me in wizard magic to broaden my abilities, but we never got around to it. We thought we had plenty of time. . . ."

"I wish I possessed your magical skills now," said Dagamier fiercely. "Then, at least, I'd be more useful."

"Perhaps, when Lyim is safely disposed of," Bram ventured, "we could share knowledge of our disciplines." He suggested it, as much to persuade them both that there would be a day when this nightmare was over.

Dagamier smiled. "I will look forward to that." But her spine visibly stiffened with the next thought. "Until then, we must deal with the Council of Three."

"So now we are something to be dealt with?" said a voice from the doorway, making both of them jump. The speaker's voice was good-natured.

Bram saw the white-haired Head of the Conclave first over Dagamier's shoulder. Par-Salian shuffled into the smallish chamber without knocking.

Dagamier whirled around. "Of course not, Par-Salian," she said a bit breathlessly, though without apology. "Are LaDonna and Justarius waiting in the hallway?"

"No, they have been delayed by some disturbing news we received from our spies still in Qindaras. I came ahead to report them to you."

Bram looked flustered. "I can explain—"

"We already know of Guerrand's death," Par-Salian interrupted, "and your unwilling flight from that city. We were greatly saddened by his loss, of course, but Guerrand died as he wished—defending the Art. Now we must prepare for the repercussions of that defeat."

"What have your spies reported?" Dagamier asked anxiously. "It's as I feared, isn't it? Lyim's got the gauntlet and his hand back."

Par-Salian's face looked more careworn than usual. "Worse still, I'm afraid. Lyim has assembled an army of extremely powerful magical creatures. He's leading them toward Wayreth even as we speak. If he gets inside the Tower of High Sorcery wearing that gauntlet—"

There was no need to finish the thought.

"We had anticipated the possibility of an assault on a tower, of course, but we had hoped to eliminate Lyim before that became a real threat. I'm afraid that, without the retrieval of the gauntlet, the destruction of his protective palace merely hastened the inevitable.

"We'll just have to stop him before he gets to Wayreth then," Bram said with a conviction he didn't entirely feel.

"Exactly," said Par-Salian. "Now all we have to do is figure out how."

Neither Bram nor Dagamier were reassured to see that even the most powerful mage on Krynn looked frightened.

* * * * *

Bram stepped from the faerie road and into the seclusion of his topiary garden at Castle DiThon. The lord of Thonvil shivered in his thin tunic. Night and day had begun to blur during the seemingly endless meetings with the Council of Three in the isolation of Bastion. Days and weeks were muddled in his mind by the speed of travel on the faerie road, not to mention his unexpected flight from Qindaras. He had completely lost track of time, of place, and didn't recall that it would now be the dead of winter in Thonvil. By Bram's closest reckoning, less than a fortnight had passed since he'd left with Guerrand for the distant city on the Plains of Dust. So much had happened. So much of it tragic beyond anything he had considered when last he'd stood here.

The Council had been reluctant to let him leave, even briefly, at such a time, until Bram explained, "Circumstances have left my holdings in the hands of a gnome." They waved him off after exacting a promise to return within the cycle of one day.

Strangely, Bram hoped to see regret in the eyes of the black-robed wizardess when he announced his temporary leave. Instead, he'd found support, and that was almost as good. She seemed very different than he remembered her from his unexpected trip to the first Bastion. Smarter, softer . . . Considering the changes he'd undergone since their first meeting, Bram had to ask himself if she was so different, or if he just saw things differently now. He supposed a little of both was closer to the truth.

In little more than a week Bram had come to rely on Dagamier's practical counsel. In an odd way, she seemed to fill a tiny corner of the void his uncle had left.

Secretly, Bram had feared returning to Thonvil, a place fraught with images of his uncle. At Bastion, he'd occasionally been able to forget, or at least pretend for just a moment, that Guerrand was not gone. Bram mumbled aloud his goals like a mantra, so he would not be distracted by memories of times that would never be again. "Get in quietly. Summon Maladorigar. Turn things over to Hingham as regent. Then get back to Bastion."

Determined to see, and be seen, by no one who would ask about Guerrand and Kirah, Bram invoked one of the first tuatha skills his mother had taught him. He seldom used it, since it required of him a level of concentration that made other spellcasting impossible.

The tuatha never referred to the skill as invisibility. For them, visibility while among humans was a rare occurrence, invisibility the norm. He thought of it as shrouding himself. During his first weeks with Primula, she had struggled to reach through the mire of "Bram's overdeveloped, stubborn human side" to speak to his latent tuatha skills. She'd promised he would one day perform the skill without thought; he would just "be" tuatha. Bram had scoffed, then. It wasn't that he had intentionally resisted her, but as if Primula spoke another language, one that didn't even use the same symbols.

The analogy proved almost too apt. The innate tuatha magic did not require prayer or study, used no physical symbols at all. It sprang from mental images conjured from nature. Once Bram had truly grasped that, his studies progressed rapidly, though the bulk of his two-year absence had been spent learning to control and maintain focus, which were essential to tuatha magic.

There were many images from nature Bram could have used to shroud himself, but he concentrated on thoughts of the wind, of being one with the slight breeze that ruffled the hair at the nape of his neck. Today he had need of speed as well as concealment. He shook his arms, rattled the tense muscles of his broad shoulders and neck until he felt himself lighten. It was a feeling similar to the weightlessness of levitation, and yet dissimilar; it was an indescribable feeling, one of . . . transparency.

When he was certain he was as invisible as the wind, Bram slipped into the castle. His steps slowed when he crossed into the foretower and noticed sentries wearing livery he hadn't seen since he'd become Lord DiThon. The tall, circular entry hall and the stairway were alive with servants and soldiers. Stubbornly maintaining his focus, Bram hastened up the curving stairway, slipping through the hustle and press of bodies. His curiosity quickly turned to concern. Had some disaster struck while he was gone? Was someone ill? Bram took the stairs two at a time as he raced for his study, where he could gather his thoughts and contact Maladorigar.

Bram burst through the door, literally, since he didn't need to open it in his airy state. What he saw inside made him instantly lose his focus. The feeling of opacity flooded back into his body like an adrenalin rush.

Emperor Mercadior Redic V sat at the dusty desk Bram had shared with his ancestors, indulging in a glass of ruby port. One of the robust emperor's bejeweled hands was wrapped around the delicate stem of the snifter glass; the other was riffling the drawers of Bram's desk.

Mercadior looked up just as Bram's focus dissolved and his form materialized.

"What's going on?" Bram demanded, bowing to his emperor only as an afterthought.

"What, indeed?" The emperor arched an ironic brow at the young lord. "Strange that my guards didn't announce your arrival, DiThon."

Bram ducked the pointed observation. "What has brought the emperor of Northern Ergoth back to Castle DiThon?" he asked as pleasantly as concern would allow.

"The mysterious disappearance of all the DiThons," Mercadior responded cagily. "Your gnome, that fast-talking little fellow whose name I can never remember, sent me a reluctant missive, seeking direction in your absence."

"Maladorigar contacted you?" Bram asked, surprised at the gnome's temerity.

"He feared the whole lot of you DiThons had been kidnapped . . . or worse."

"A little of both, I'm afraid," Bram said ruefully.

Mercadior regarded Bram's serious, haggard face. "Your uncle?"

Bram's words caught as he revealed as much as he could about Guerrand's accidental death and Kirah's abduction without revealing Council secrets.

Mercadior's chest rose and fell in a silent sigh, though he did not look surprised. "That begins to explain a great deal that I suspected, but Astinus would not reveal to me."

Everyone had heard of the mysterious and mercurial sage of Palanthas. Astinus recorded everything said or done as it occurred on Krynn. "You went to Astinus to find out what happened to us?"

"No," Mercadior said with a tinge of impatience, "I knew nothing of your disappearance before I left to ask Astinus what he knew about the difficulties my mages had been experiencing. Thalmus had questioned the Council of Three about the occurrences, but they were characteristically close-lipped about the matter."

Bram squirmed uneasily. "What did Astinus tell you, exactly?"

"Only that the source of the magical flux was an artifact in the Plains of Dust. He said the Council of Three had sent assassins after the renegade who was controlling the artifact."

Bram was careful to not respond, aware that Mercadior was watching him closely.

"I began to piece events together," the emperor continued, "only after I returned to Gwynned and received your gnome's frantic missive." Bram could feel the press of Mercadior's intelligent gaze. "You and your uncle were the assassins sent by the Council of Three, weren't you?"

Whatever the consequences with the Council, Bram knew he could not lie outright to his emperor. "Yes," he admitted in a tremulous whisper.

"I knew it, yet I could not understand why. I was not aware you and your uncle were assassins."

"That is likely part of the reason we failed," he confessed. "The Council asked Guerrand because he was once a friend of the ex-mage who controls the artifact."

Mercadior nodded slowly. "That explains Guerrand's part, but what about you? Why would they send a farmer to confront an evil maniac with an artifact?"

"Because I have magical skills that are impervious to the artifact's power," Bram blurted. "I learned this just after my father's death, after your first visit here."

The emperor sipped from his glass of port and considered Bram thoughtfully. "What does the Council plan to do next to stop this threat?"

"They've learned through spies and surveillance that the renegade is leading a vast army of citizens across the plains. They believe he is headed for the Tower of High Sorcery at Wayreth, where his ability to drain magic would be almost unstoppable. The Council is preparing to mount an ambush far from Wayreth, outside the dwarven stronghold of Thorbardin, which lies directly in Lyim's path to the tower. The hill dwarves who occupy the lands outside the city have agreed to join the fight. The noble Hylar dwarves, who reside in Thorbardin, have also signed on, with the promise of the return of the dangerous artifact that their ancestors created, then foolishly traded away. Par-Salian has even enlisted the aid of the Qualinesti elves, whose forests surround the tower at Wayreth. I've agreed to use my magic in the ambush."

"Then sign me up, and two hundred of my best cavaliers!" Mercadior announced boldly, as if the battle were but a draught game. He saw Bram's eyes open in helpless amazement. "I have as much an interest as anyone in seeing magic thrive, DiThon," Mercadior explained reasonably. "More, perhaps.

"Besides," the emperor added without shame, "fighting shoulder-to-shoulder with the Qualinesti won't hurt me in my quest for a treaty with Solostaran, the Speaker of the Suns. Just think, DiThon, we may accomplish in one battle what I've struggled for years to gain through diplomacy! Once that treaty is signed, there'll be no question that Northern Ergoth has again outflanked Southern Ergoth both militarily and economically." The emperor seemed more than pleased at the prospect of achieving his long-held goal. "Make that three hundred cavaliers!"

Bram was overwhelmed by this unexpected turn of events. "I'll have to speak with the Council, of course, but I'm sure they'll welcome the aid." The appearance of three hundred armed knights would be quite a coup.

"You'd better move fast, then," said Mercadior, his thoughts speeding forward. "It'll take the better part of a fortnight to get such a vast contingent to Thorbardin, even if I commandeer every one of Anton Berwick's ships for the cause. Still, I think it can be done."

Bram stood. "I just have to speak with Maladorigar and assign a regent in my absence."

"Never mind that," Mercadior said, leading Bram to the door. "I'll leave one or two of my top lieutenants here to help the gnome run things. Just get yourself back to wherever you were and clear it with these mages. I'll be gathering my forces and waiting for your missive. We may not be able to use magic against this Lyim, but a few good cavaliers from Northern Ergoth can still stave his skull in with maces!"

Bram dug his heels in, despite the pressure of Mercadior's optimistic hands. "I should warn you, Sire, that this battle will likely be the bloodiest you've ever seen. In addition to his army, Lyim also has some incredible creatures under his control, which he seems to use as bodyguards. Refugees have described them only as vicious and terrifying. We believe they're extraplanar . . . and almost indestructible."

But Mercadior wasn't cowed. He shook his fist skyward. "We'll see how indestructible they are against a Northern Ergothian sword!"

* * * * *

"Watch your step here, my lord."

Lyim ignored the soldier's warning. He could see for himself that the ground was tangled with corpses. "They tried to defend this?" he asked with contempt, sweeping his hand over the low stone wall that lined the street.

Isk, wearing a spattered suit of mail, kicked aside a broken spear. "I don't believe they ever hoped or intended to stop us. These men just wanted to slow us down, to give the others time to retreat into the manor house."

Lyim scanned the bodies more carefully, squinting to see through the drifting smoke. He noticed the telltale signs of a suicide stand: clusters of bodies where small groups of defenders, standing back-to-back, had fought until overwhelmed; defenders and attackers fallen into the same heap, sometimes with their arms still locked about each other.

Lyim surveyed the scene, unmoved. He turned back to Isk. "Show me the manor."

The assassin pointed down the street, farther into the heart of the town. As they moved down the broad avenue, shapes could be seen moving through the smoke: Qindarans, looting whatever was left in the devastated buildings. He could hear the sound of doors being broken, furniture smashed, screams from fugitive citizens discovered in their hiding places.

The village had the misfortune to lie along Lyim's route of advance at the eastern foot of the Kharolis Mountains. Behind his army stretched the flat, cold, seemingly endless Plains of Dust. Ahead, the land rose into a mighty mountain range that cut across the continent from Newsea in the north to Ice Mountain Bay in the south. To cross from west to east involved a trip of more than thirty leagues over a series of high, rugged mountain ridges. This land was home to mountain and hill dwarves, living both below ground in the huge, subterranean fortress of Thorbardin, and in countless villages scattered through unmapped hidden valleys.

The Kharolis Mountains were an unbreachable barrier to an army, if not for one pass. Lyim intended to march straight across that opening, because on the far side lay the great elven forest of Qualinesti—and the Tower of High Sorcery at Wayreth.

Towns such as this one provided Lyim's force with much-needed experience in attacking. His army, which had begun as nothing more than a rabble of civilians, was now at least a rabble flushed with victory. Dozens of similar villages and settlements in their wake had been reduced to scorch marks on the ground. With each battle, the Qindarans became more convinced of their own invincibility and the righteousness of Lyim's cause. And with the land stripped of all forage and shelter behind them, the force had little choice but to go forward.

Lyim's thoughts were cut short as he and Isk approached an imposing structure dominating the center of the town. Its walls were thick, built of closely fitted, mortared stone, and its heavy wooden doors were bound in iron. The building was not a castle, but clearly it had been built with some consideration toward defense. Against normal attackers, it would have been a substantial redoubt.

Lyim stepped up to the stone wall and examined a breach that had been torn through it. The hole was taller than he was, and almost a full arm-span wide. Enormous stones that had been ripped from the wall were scattered up to forty paces away. Around the edges of the hole, clearly visible, were deep, parallel grooves—claw marks. Lyim ran his finger along one of the gashes and marveled again at the strength that could have gouged out such a mark.

Isk was watching his master as he studied the breach. "Most of the people have overcome their fear of the nabassu. Having them lead the attack creates tremendous confidence."

"I don't want the nabassu at the forefront of the army from here on out," Lyim ordered. "They will be kept back, as a surprise reserve." He stepped into the gloom beyond the torn stone wall.

Isk followed Lyim through, but the potentate's attention was focused on the interior. His eyes adjusted to the dim light, and he slowly took in more details of the building. They were standing in a great hall with a high, vaulted ceiling. Most of the building appeared to be one large room, a common architectural feature of the region. The windows, which were high above the floor, were small to begin with. They were still tightly shuttered against the attack. Lyim motioned upward to Isk, who in turn shouted an order to a group of soldiers. Moments later, shutters banged open and beams of light streamed in, forming gray shafts in the smoky air.

The light revealed that the stone floor of the room was covered with blood. Spatters and splotches marked where injured persons had fallen, pools stood where corpses had lain, and long smears showed the tracks where bodies had been dragged to the heaps that now filled the corners. Men and women, children and elders, all were piled haphazardly against the cold walls. Most were humans, though many dwarves were also evident. "There must have been hundreds of them in here," Isk remarked.

Lyim made no immediate response. He studied the scene for several moments more, then turned back toward Isk. "Continue searching the town. Every cellar and haystack should be turned inside out. Kill everyone who is found. I want no prisoners.

"Also, if you see Salimshad, tell him that I want his report in my tent immediately."

Isk nodded. "I'll see to it, Sire."

Satisfied, Lyim strode toward the front door. Several soldiers raced ahead and raised the bar, still in place where the defenders had put it, and opened the door for their potentate. Lyim stopped and examined the outside of the door. It was covered with scorch marks where flaming arrows had been fired into it, but the wood had never really ignited.

All of the arrows were burned away, but the arrowheads were still embedded in the wood. Lyim reached up with his gauntleted right hand and grasped the edge of one that barely protruded from the surface. Pinching it between his thumb and forefinger, he wrenched it free. Any normal man using blacksmith's tongs would have struggled with it, but it had been easy with the strength of the gauntlet.

You see, Ventyr, how easily we can work together, Lyim thought. *Nothing has changed, really. We've lost the palace, but gained our freedom.*

The sultry voice of Ventyr responded, coldly and as if from a great distance. *I never desired freedom. I have told you, as long as you are Potentate of Qindaras, I must and will serve you.*

Lyim smiled. *Just as I have told you, my servant, that if you ever betray me again, as you tried to do with Guerrand, I will see you thrown into the hottest volcanic inferno in Neraka. You are still useful to me, but I will not tolerate betrayal from any servant.*

There was no answer. It seemed to Lyim that Ventyr's will had weakened considerably since the destruction of the palace. She acted almost like a human who had suffered a tremendous shock. The gauntlet was withdrawn where it used to be vibrant, dull and apathetic where it used to be clever and imaginative. He realized that he had come to think of Ventyr as a completely free entity in Qindaras. Now he understood how closely the gauntlet was tied to the palace. Without that focus and outlet for the absorbed energy, Ventyr seemed to feel almost purposeless. Most of her efforts went into maintaining control over the nabassu. Lyim was not certain whether Ventyr's current attitude toward him was petulance over the palace's destruction, or an actual weakening. He didn't care, as long as she did as she was commanded and absorbed the energy of the tower when he entered it.

This close to his goal, with Kirah to distract him otherwise, he cared only that his power continue unabated.

Now Lyim returned to his camp outside the town to celebrate another victory and await the arrival of Salimshad.

* * * * *

Kirah sat hunched over the brazier inside Lyim's tent. She tried hard not to hear the tormented groans from the dying men outside, but it was an impossible feat. Sons called for mothers, husbands for wives. The howls and barks of village dogs were cut off in mid-voice; she knew why, could see their heads being severed by Lyim's troops just for the sport of it.

The tent flap flew back suddenly with a loud cracking sound. Kirah, her nerves as tightly strung as lute strings, jumped back from the brazier at the unexpected noise. Lyim burst through the sunny opening, face bloody and scratched above his broad smile. The flap slapped closed behind him, cutting off the burst of light.

"They tumbled like ninepins," he said happily, though a bit out of breath. Lyim kicked a camp stool into position by the brazier and settled himself upon it with a contented sigh. "I'll have to wait for Salimshad's report, but it looks like we lost less than two score of our troops." Lyim unbuckled his heavy breastplate and let it slide to the floor, then unlaced the thick, padded shirt he wore beneath the armor. He held out a leg toward Kirah expectantly.

She knelt before him and slipped the boot from one foot, then the other. "I'm glad you weren't hurt." She looked to the cuts on his face. "At least not terribly. Let me clean those wounds," she offered, raising a slender hand to his face tenderly.

Lyim pushed her hand away to lean into the warming brazier. "They're just scratches." He grinned at her, almost a scornful look. "Your concern touches me."

She had gotten accustomed to his cynical need for her. Theirs was a cat-and-mouse relationship. Still, Kirah looked at him oddly. "You know I'm concerned, Lyim. I didn't want you to set off on this crusade of yours to begin with." She got on her knees and took his left hand, the one without the gauntlet, into her smaller ones. "It's not too late, you know. Let's go back to Qindaras and begin rebuilding," she pleaded. "Right now. Right away."

Lyim snatched his hand back and stood up, hands jammed onto his hips. "Why would I give up the battle when I'm so near reaching my goal? I'm winning!" He pointed through the tent flap. "I've just decimated an entire village, losing less than two score of my troops."

"You're butchering surprised villages full of farmers and merchants." Kirah looked into his dark eyes intently. "The Council of Three won't try to stop you with a handful of frightened village militiamen. They are going to challenge you with a real army long before we reach the Tower of High Sorcery, and all your people will die for nothing."

Lyim threw his head back and laughed. "The Council? They couldn't stop a stampede of rabbits! I have Ventyr back under control; I have my nabassu! They can't stop me, Kirah. Not anymore."

"They also have Bram."

Lyim snorted. "His magic had little effect against me. It was Guerrand whose suicide caused the destruction of the palace."

Kirah's heart lurched at the reminder. "But that's just my point! I've already lost Rand! Must I lose you and Bram as well?"

Lyim looked at her slyly. "That's what this is about. You're not afraid for me, but for your nephew."

She shook her head. "I'm afraid for you both. For all of us."

Lyim shrugged. "You made your choice back in Qindaras, Kirah. So did Bram. Unfortunately for him, he chose to side with the losers. You were much more far-sighted."

Kirah cocked her head, listened to the groans of dying men outside. "Was I?" she asked rashly, knowing she risked his wrath. "Slaying innocent men, women, and children hardly seems like the winning side to me."

"Shut up!" Lyim's hand curled into a fist, and he raised it to strike her. Kirah stood defiantly. His hand dropped back slowly, and his face took on that bemused smile he wore of late. "I'd forgotten what a little hypocrite you can be," he said instead. "You're bold enough to enjoy warming my bed, yet the sounds of a few men dying prick your conscience. You disappoint me, Kirah. You used to be tougher."

Kirah's eyes narrowed angrily. "I'll admit that I want you," she said, stiffening her back, "but I *hate* what you're doing."

"What is it the bards say?" Lyim posed, then snapped his fingers as if the answer had just come to him. "Love me, love my flaws." He shrugged again. "In any event, you made your choice, my dear. It's too late to turn back now."

Kirah scowled at him fiercely, though she shrank inside. "My conscience wrestles with that every moment."

Lyim snatched at her arm, pulling her into his embrace. "Every moment, except those spent right here." Lyim wound his hand through her pale hair and tugged her head back for his kiss.

Refusing to be distracted, Kirah pushed with all her strength against his chest. "Why can't you be content with being the most powerful man in the Plains of Dust?"

"Do you think I'm looking for contentment?" Lyim asked incredulously. "The Orders of Magic and all their unthinking dogma nearly ruined my life. I would be dead now, or worse, if I hadn't been smarter than they are. I can't let that go unavenged.

"You're growing tiresome, Kirah," he said sourly, pushing her away. "I came in here to share my victory with you, but all you're doing is putting a damper on my joy." Scowling, Lyim spied a wine flask on a small table near the brazier. He snatched it up, yanked out the stopper, and sniffed the contents. Satisfied, he threw back a mouthful of the rosy liquid and settled himself again onto the small chair by the brazier.

"Never mind," he grumbled. "Salimshad will celebrate with me. Where is he, anyway? He should have reported by now."

Kirah sat quietly, aware that she had already overstepped the limits of safe restraint.

The tent flap flew back again, startling both Lyim and Kirah. "What the—?" muttered Lyim. He turned his shoulders to look behind him toward the door. "That better be you, Salim," he growled, shielding his eyes against the burst of sunlight. "I hope you have two good excuses prepared, one for why you're so late, and the other for why you didn't see fit to knock."

"Please forgive this humble servant for intruding, Sire," trembled a voice unfamiliar to both Kirah and Lyim. "Master Isk sent me here with an urgent message, and I—"

"What is it, man?" Lyim demanded harshly, screening his eyes. "Damn it, come away from that blinding light so that I can see you!"

The man hastened to do as he was told. His face was

streaked with sweat, and his clothes were spattered with mud. Away from the light, Lyim saw that he was little more than a boy.

"Give your message!"

"Salimshad is dead, Sire." The boy spoke the words in a burst and stepped back, his head bowed.

Lyim shook his head once, quickly, as if he'd heard wrong. Kirah could see the light of understanding dawn slowly in his eyes. He held very still. "How?"

"He was overseeing the execution of captives, as you ordered," the boy explained. "One of them had apparently concealed a knife, and—"

"Are you saying he was careless?" Lyim had the wired tenseness of a tiger watching prey. Kirah recognized the pose, and she grew frightened for the boy.

The boy's mouth opened and closed wordlessly. "I don't know that, Sire. I only know what I was told."

Lyim's eyes locked, unseeing, on the boy's. "And who told you this?" His gauntleted hand flexed around the flask until it burst.

Leave! Kirah hissed to the trembling boy inwardly. *Run while you still can!*

It was already too late.

Lyim's gauntleted hand sprang forth like a snake and closed about the boy's throat. He lifted him off the ground, the boy's feet kicking helplessly.

"Lyim, let him go!" Kirah cried, trying desperately to break through his trance of anger. "He didn't kill Salim; he only delivered the message!"

With a last, desperate gurgle, the boy stopped struggling and his eyes rolled shut in death. His toes slowly drooped like wilting petals.

Still holding the dead boy high by the throat, Lyim burst out of the tent. "Isk!" he bellowed.

Looking through the open flap, Kirah could see the nearby troops moving away. They were accustomed to scenes of horror and brutality, but greatly feared the anger of their potentate.

The assassin hustled through the dead bodies to Lyim's side, his expression grim.

"Next time, deliver your own message."

Looking at the boy's crumbled windpipe, Isk must have realized he'd made the right decision sending the boy in.

"I'm sorry about—"

Lyim cut off the assassin's words, whether apology or condolences. "You're second in command, now."

Isk barely suppressed a smile. "Yes, sir—"

"We're continuing on immediately," Lyim interrupted again tersely. "The Council of Three must know we're coming by now. Undoubtedly they've prepared some sort of ambush for us between here and Wayreth. It's time they learned what they're really up against. Gather the troops and prepare to leave at once."

"But, Sire," Isk began hesitantly. "The troops have fought since dawn. They're tired—"

"They're lucky they're not dead!" Lyim snapped. "Which is what will happen to anyone who is not ready to head out at high sun!" Lyim spun around to glare at Kirah, whose pale face poked through the tent flap. "And you, my dear, had better develop a taste for this battle. You'll be riding behind me from now on."

With that, Lyim dropped the boy carelessly and stepped over his lifeless body on the way to see about readying the nabassu for flight.

* * * * *

Before returning to Bastion and the preparations for war, Bram stopped in his uncle's sunny study in the gallery. Memories of Guerrand were ripe here, inspired by the familiar, heady scent of the herbs Rand gathered for his spells.

Bram stepped behind the desk made neat for the first time before their departure for Qindaras, settling himself in Rand's chair. He sat silent and unmoving for many moments, hands cupped over his mouth in a pensive pose. When he was ready, he slid open the drawer where Rand had slipped a wax-sealed letter on the day of their departure.

"Read this if something happens to me and I don't return," Rand had said.

Bram traced a finger over his name on the envelope. He turned it over quickly, broke the wax seal with a flick of his thumbnail, and pulled the folded parchment forth:

My dearest friend Bram:

It occurs to me now, as I write this, that you are my dearest friend. I feel like my last words to you should be ripe with inspiration. Yet the only thought that comes to mind is something I said to you once before, on the stairs of the keep as I stole away to follow my dream: "Remember to always do what you know in your heart is right."

This comes to me now, I think, because it is good advice. If you are reading this, I have followed it myself. I knew from the day you returned from Primula's realm that I would soon learn the meaning of the Dream. After so many years of wondering, I welcome it, whatever the outcome. I did, after all, promise myself to the Art.

Be of good faith, Bram. And remember, a man with nothing to die for has even less for which to live.

Yours, Rand

Chapter Eighteen

"There you are!" exclaimed Bram as he spied Dagamier. "Par-Salian said I'd find you here." He stepped through the doorway and into the small tower that formed the western point of the equilateral triangle surrounding Wayreth's tower complex. "I've always wondered why the first wizards named this complex the *Tower* of High Sorcery, when in fact there are no less than five towers here, not to mention two foretowers."

"Tradition," the black-robed wizardess grunted. Dagamier was shoveling damp sand one-handed into a burlap sack that she held open with the other. The shovel was defying her attempts to jab it through the small mouth in the sack. She flung the tool aside with a disgruntled snort and wiped her sweaty, gritty brow with the back of a slender hand. "I was overseeing the workers digging the trenches out front, but apparently the elves the Speaker of the Suns had sent from Qualinesti took exception to my direction," she explained without insult.

Dagamier spoke of the small army of dwarves and Qualinesti elves who had pledged to help defend the Tower of High Sorcery. For several days now they had been occupied with digging ditches and putting up sharpened stakes and ramparts to protect the tower against conventional assault, since the tower's magical defenses were not operating properly, thanks to Lyim's gauntlet. Spies working for the Council of Three placed Lyim's own forces several days' march east of Thorbardin, so the defenders at Wayreth were working faster than ever in their fortifying efforts.

"Par-Salian assigned me to this task to cool my heels, I believe. I'm supposed to fill up as many of these sacks as I can, so we can drop them on invaders from the tower's walls." She looked with a mixture of longing and irritation at the results of her labors. "I've managed to fill exactly two of them. At this rate we'll just have to hope Lyim and his troops are stopped at Thorbardin."

"We can't count on that," Bram said, though he knew Dagamier was just being cynical. "Here, let me help." He hastened over to take up the shovel. "I'm used to hard labor, or at least I was when I had to plow the fields around Thonvil by myself."

Dagamier squatted down and held the sack open to Bram's loaded shovel. "I always thought lords had tenants, or at least oxen, for that."

Bram laughed at the memory of the reality. "I do now, but I didn't back before we met at the first Bastion."

"A lot has changed since then, hasn't it?" Dagamier observed.

Bram nodded thoughtfully. He shoveled and Dagamier sacked sand for some time in silence.

Between conferences with the Council of Three in the last weeks, they had shared many of the details of their lives since their first meeting at Bastion. Most of the revelations sprang naturally from discussions about their differing magical disciplines. Bram realized in the silence of their labors that, though she knew about his life in Thonvil, he knew nothing about Dagamier before her first appointment as one of Bastion's guardians.

"I found some of Guerrand's letters during my brief return to Castle DiThon," he remarked. "Among them was one he wrote from Bastion to a gnome friend of his, though I don't think Rand ever posted it. He mentioned you."

"Oh?"

"Rand wrote that he was ever on eggshells with you, that he wasn't sure if even a lifetime of study would help him to figure you out."

Dagamier looked up, with an odd mixture of amusement and annoyance, from the bag she was holding. "Is that so?"

"I brought it up because of how it made me feel," Bram said quickly. "I don't know very much about you, except that, unlike Rand, I feel entirely at ease with you."

She refused to look up and meet his eyes, but Bram could see a faint blush in the alabaster skin of her cheeks. "So what more would you know?"

He stopped his labors and leaned against the wooden handle of the shovel. "I'm not sure, exactly. Where do you come from? Have you any family? What makes you happy?"

Dagamier brought herself up from her knees, brushed the sand from them, and moved to sit on a nearby bench. "Those questions are easy enough to answer." She folded her hands on her lap with a primness that contrasted with the way her black robe parted sensuously at the knees. "I don't know, I don't know, and magic."

Bram's arm nearly slid from the handle of the shovel. "You don't know where you're from? But how can that be?"

"That's an odd question from a man who only recently discovered his true heritage," Dagamier remarked, though not unkindly.

The mage continued. "In my case, the explanation is simple enough: I was the only survivor of a shipwreck in the Straits of Algoni, off Southern Ergoth. I simply washed ashore on a piece of driftwood one day in Pontigoth. I don't remember this, of course, since I was just a babe, but was told it by Lomas, the fisherman who found me and took me into his family. The last of his kin died of the pox when I was nearing eleven. I lived on the streets after that, not a bad place in Pontigoth, fairly safe as port cities go. I met a mage, fell in love with the Art, and eventually made my way here to take the Test. End of story. Or the beginning, as I like to think of it."

"So you assume your parents went down with the ship?" When Dagamier nodded, Bram added, "Then you have no idea who they were, and you have no family to turn to now."

Dagamier shrugged her lack of concern. "That's never seemed important to me. First I had Lomas's family, then the mage briefly, then LaDonna, who recognized my talent during my Test and has championed me ever since."

Bram squinted at her. "In an odd sort of way, you've always reminded me of what LaDonna might have looked like when she was young."

Dagamier chuckled. "Don't tell LaDonna that. She goes to great lengths to make people believe she still is young. Besides, it's not so odd that I should unconsciously imitate my mentor. You look a great deal like your uncle."

"Rand and I were related," Bram countered, "but I see what you mean." He looked at the determined, self-made woman with a new appreciation. "You've had a hard life, haven't you?"

"Hasn't everyone?" she returned. "It's a hard world." Dagamier frowned her discomfort at the turn the conversation had taken toward her. "It's even harder without the use of magic, a situation that might become

permanent if we don't get the rest of these sacks filled."
She returned with a resigned sigh to the pile of sand
and held open a sack.

"Why don't you let me cast a spell that will dry up
this sand and make it lighter to shovel?" he suggested.

"Be my guest."

Bram took his staff firmly in hand and concentrated
on the sand. Instead of the dark, moist pile, he pictured
a hot wind blowing across it, carrying away the mois-
ture. As he exerted himself, the sand gradually light-
ened in color. Soon, flecks were tumbling down the dry
outer surface.

Dagamier winked in delight at Bram. She scraped
away the thin outer layer of dry sand to reveal the
dark, wet mass underneath. The wizardess squeezed
his shoulder encouragingly.

A thin vapor began rising from the mound of sand,
until the entire pile was as dry as dust.

Dagamier regarded with satisfaction the fruit of
Bram's efforts. "That ought to satisfy Par-Salian," she
said. "Thank you."

"For what?"

"For bringing magic back into my life. I've felt so
helpless without it, just waiting for Lyim's next move."

Bram flushed his pleasure. "It was a minor spell,
believe me."

Dagamier looked down at the warm, brown hand
still resting lightly on her shoulder. "It seemed tremendous to me."

Bram's hand flew back to his side. "We won't have to
wait much longer," he said quickly to cover his embarrassment. "We've worked hard to prepare. We can hold
Lyim off."

"Yes, I think so too." With an expectant smile,
Dagamier visibly shook off her usual negative mood.
"When you first came into the foretower, you said,
'There you are,' " she reminded him. "Were you coming
to bag sand, or was there something else you wanted?"

"What? Oh, yes." Bram's thoughts and heart were racing so that he could scarcely think straight. "Yes, I came to say good-bye before I leave for Thorbardin."

Alarm darkened Dagamier's expression again. "I thought you were to stay here with . . . the rest of the mages, in case Lyim broke through and made it to Wayreth."

"The Council of Three decided this morning to send me to bolster the defenses outside the dwarven city with my magic." Bram smiled ruefully. "I think what they really want is for me to keep the mountain and hill dwarves from fighting each other, and to prevent the strong-willed Mercadior from attempting to take over the whole lot. In any event, I can travel the faerie road and return here if I'm needed."

Dagamier struggled to lighten her tone. "Then we should be saying 'see you later', not 'good-bye'."

"Good-bye is more traditional," Bram said, his eyes smiling warmly into hers. Turning to leave, he reached out and impulsively touched her cheek. To his greater surprise, Dagamier's hand flew up and briefly held his there.

"See you later," she said in a soft voice, dropping her hand from his with obvious reluctance.

"Of course," Bram responded, his throat tight. "You owe me lessons in magic, and I intend to collect!"

Laughing, Dagamier pushed him roughly toward the door. "Go save Thorbardin, so the rest of us can remain idle here."

Bram smiled encouragingly at the black-robed wizardess as he slid through the door.

* * * * *

A chilly wind plucked at the corners of Bram's cloak and forced its way underneath to prickle his skin. He wasn't concerned about the weather, though; the wind that made his body shiver was blowing out of the east, and carried with it the sounds of an army on the march. It was still faint, just a distant rumble and clatter that faded in and out, and even then only when he listened carefully.

Several of the dwarven scouts who had been posted far to the east had already reported back. When Bram had arrived from Wayreth and joined the forces assembled, he had first been surprised to see that dwarves were used as outposts. With their short legs how could they carry a message back to the main army quickly enough for it to be useful? But their great endurance enabled them to run almost all day without stopping for rest. Indeed, just that morning Bram saw two dwarves arrive who had been running ahead of Lyim's advancing army since the evening before, and they were still able to give a precise account of what they had seen. Bram was beginning to believe the amazing legends of dwarven strength that were spread as tall tales in Northern Ergoth.

The dwarven scouts reported that the forces from Qindaras had marched north out of the Plains of Dust, then followed the foothills along the southwest coast of Newsea. There the army joined up with the Hillhome highway, which led directly toward the mountains and fertile lands to the west. And Wayreth.

If any of them had harbored a hope otherwise, there could be no doubt now that Lyim's target was the Tower of High Sorcery. Thorbardin would hold no threat or interest for an ex-mage who was bent on destroying magic. The tower beyond the dwarven city was the only logical choice, since it contained the greatest concentration of magical energy and knowledge outside the Lost Citadel itself. If the tower were destroyed, the cause of magic would be irreparably harmed.

There was one stumbling block to Lyim's progress: the Kharolis Mountain range. Just outside the hill dwarf settlement of Hillhome, some twenty leagues north of Thorbardin, was an opening in the northeast-

ern Kharolis Mountains known only as the Pass. It was
not a true pass, but a break in the mountains, as if some
gigantic hand had scooped a valley right across the
range. The Pass was the only place an army could cross
the mountain range. It connected a swamp on the
south edge of the Plains of Dergoth with the western
coastline of Newsea. The Pass was less than a league
wide, but an army could not ask for a better passage
through the mountains. If Lyim's army made it through
there, they might just be unstoppable.

The forces determined to stop Lyim's progress
included Mercadior's three hundred cavaliers and a
dwarven host comprised of just under five hundred
feuding hill and Hylar mountain dwarves. The
dwarves had put aside their differences, temporarily at
least, to do battle with Lyim's legion.

Far to the west, Bram could just make out the round
contours of Skullcap. He had heard the legends of the
ancient structure of the mages. Originally known as
Zhaman, the spires of the magical fortress had soared
above the Plains of Dergoth, but an explosion loosed
by the notorious mage Fistandantilus during the
Dwarfgate Wars had caused the structure to collapse
into the hideous mound it now was. The eerie, skull-
shaped remains rose solitary against the bleak flatness
of the Bog, an enormous stretch of tangled, stinking
swampland.

Bram looked around at the rocky face of the mountain that formed the southern flank of the Pass. Hundreds of sturdy Hylar dwarves from Thorbardin would
soon be concealed in those rocks, ready to set off an
avalanche against the unsuspecting army that
approached. An equal number would be similarly
positioned on the northern flank.

"Remind all of your lieutenants to wait until the
army is halfway through before setting off the rock
slides." The speaker was Thane Hothjor, the leader of
the contingent from within Thorbardin. He was tall for

a dwarf, only about a head shorter than Bram, and massively built. The great, blackened axe that Hothjor swings about as easily as a stick probably weighs half as much as I do, Bram thought incredulously.

Hothjor was addressing the representative from Hillhome, a stocky, unsmiling dwarf named Tybalt Fireforge, who served as head constable in the village. Even now he wore a constable's uniform—shiny leather breastplate and shoulder protectors hardened in boiling oil and dyed blue, gray tunic beneath to his knees, gray leg wraps, and thick-soled leather boots. The rest of his Neidar forces, waiting in the hills now, were not so nattily dressed; most were hardworking, hard-muscled farmers who wore mismatched armor that was no less effective for wear. Hillhome had a mayor, one Holden, but rumor had it he was too comfortably entrenched in a warm cottage to fight here himself. Besides, he couldn't have held a candle to the vitriolic Fireforge.

"Don't you worry about my men following orders, Hylar," Tybalt Fireforge snapped. "You just keep your diggers from running like cowards when they see the enemy."

Thane Hothjor's face turned purple. "Look, you—"

"Gentlemen," Bram interjected, a hand lowered to a thick shoulder of each dwarf. "I understand your people have a history of bitterness, but—"

"You call the Great Betrayal 'bitterness'?" bellowed young Fireforge. "Reorx's Beard, man, his people sealed the gates of Thorbardin against my ancestors during the Cataclysm. They left the hill dwarves to starve, to suffer the full force of the gods' punishment!"

"Nevertheless," Bram cut in again before Hothjor burst a blood vessel defending his people. "You both agreed to put aside your differences to help stave off this newest threat. Please, save your anger for the enemy."

"We agreed to help only to save Hillhome," grumbled Fireforge.

"And the Hylar came from Thorbardin to fight," said Hothjor, "only under the condition that we would recover the Gauntlet of Ventyr, which never should have left our vaults in the first place."

Fireforge arched an accusing brow. "Someone less charitable might suggest this whole crisis could be laid squarely at the ugly feet of the Hylar."

"It happened centuries ago!"

"My dear dwarves," Emperor Mercadior interrupted, thumping his battle gauntlets against a palm impatiently, "we will all be to blame for the destruction of magic if we do not get on with reviewing our plans for defense. Hothjor?" The emperor waved a peevish hand for the Hylar thane to continue.

Hothjor's eyes narrowed to sparkling slits in his bearded and scarred face as he gave Fireforge a superior smirk. "The Pass is too wide to inflict serious casualties with an avalanche," he resumed in his booming voice, "unless the army is a great deal more spread out than we expect. We're not trying to crush them with boulders. We want to cause a panic that will separate the tail end of the column from the van. Once the army is split, the hill dwarves and Mercadior's cavaliers on the plain will charge into those that run toward the west. Our job, at that point, is to move down and keep the two halves of the army apart so we can destroy it a piece at a time."

Hothjor ran his fingers through his long beard. "We're going to be badly outnumbered, even though we'll be facing only half of the invaders' army. And we can expect that, once the course of things becomes clear, some portion of those trapped to our west will turn and try to fight their way back through us. When that happens we'll be pinned smack in the middle of an army that outnumbers us eight to one. When every Hylar stands his ground without flinching, we will be the anvil against which these invaders are smashed by Mercadior's hammer. It will be a day filled with glory!"

At that, the assembled Hylar officers banged their axes and hammers against their shields and clomped their thick, booted feet, an annoying tendency Bram had come to see both Neidar and Hylar shared. Nevertheless, the Hylar were a fearsome sight in their heavy armor and long beards and braids, wielding their rune-etched weapons. Their cheer raised such a din that Bram feared the carefully planned avalanches would be triggered. But at a wave of Hothjor's axe, the Hylar fell immediately silent. At a glance from the surly Fireforge, the Neidar officers from Hillhome quieted as well.

Hothjor barked a single command, "Go!" and the Hylar turned and disappeared into the rocks as easily as mountain goats. Bram watched in amazement as the fluttering plumes on their helmets bobbed momentarily above the boulders, then were gone.

Mercadior turned to Bram. "Of course, you're the pivotal element here, Bram. Our ambush is designed not just to destroy the invader's army, but to give you a chance to attack Lyim with your tuatha magic. With any luck, he is still unaware of our forces, so he will not expect your presence here." Mercadior lowered his voice, though Hothjor and Fireforge were otherwise engaged with their lieutenants and no longer listening. "I'd feel best if you worked within the protection of my cavaliers."

"With all due respect, Sire," Bram replied as diplomatically as possible, "I'll need the vantage that I gain from the mountainside. I may not be able to spot Lyim from down on the plain with your horsemen."

"I don't like it," Mercadior said, frowning, "but then I haven't your magical perspective. Very well, DiThon, in this I will defer to your judgment. Just remember, you are here only to engage Rhistadt directly. His forces are the concern of the warriors."

Pursing his lips, the emperor squinted to the east, as if he thought to see Lyim's army approaching. "I'll be rejoining my troops as well," announced Mercadior, intentionally drawing both Fireforge and Hothjor back into the discussion.

The plan for the attack had been Emperor Mercadior's. The dwarven contingents had agreed to it largely because it kept their forces completely separate; neither the Hylar nor the Neidar would have agreed to fight alongside one another. With his massive helmet tucked under his left arm, the emperor of Northern Ergoth extended his right hand first to Hothjor, then Fireforge. "May we meet again after the battle," he declared, gripping each dwarf's mighty hand. The warriors seemed to share a bond that went beyond their short acquaintance.

Bram was startled when Mercadior next extended the same warrior's blessing toward him before he turned and scrambled back down the steep slope to where his war-horse waited with several of his cavaliers. The emperor mounted and rode westward. Eventually Mercadior disappeared into the long, wide depression that sheltered the Ergothian cavaliers, along with the hill dwarves. From atop the rocks Bram could see their lance tips and scattered helmet plumes, but he knew that they were completely hidden by the rolling ground from anyone marching through the Pass.

Bram realized it was time to invoke the skill most used by all tuatha, one he could employ only because of his half-tuatha heritage. After a moment's concentration, picturing himself as the wind, he shrouded himself from normal view.

Next, Bram began a complicated series of gestures and intonations that would, in time, turn the gray sky above the battlefield to a dark and stormy cauldron. He would not bring rain—not yet, at least—but with storm clouds to work with, his tuatha magic could accomplish much. The spell took some time to complete, and it would be even longer before the storm clouds were entirely gathered.

By the time Bram finished the spell, the sound of the

approaching host was distinct and could not be denied. Heart hammering, Bram scanned the horizon to the east. The ground fell away gradually, with numerous folds and rises. Before long he could see tiny black specks appearing and disappearing over the crests. There were only a few at first; advance scouts, he assumed. But shortly the few became too many dots to count. Together they flowed like a river across each small slope. The specks grew larger and more distinct, until Bram could make out individuals among the mass.

Panicky thoughts began racing through Bram's mind. The scouts were too far ahead of the main body; they would see the Ergothian warriors and hill dwarves before the trap could be sprung. Once the scouts saw the danger, their shouts would alert the rest of Lyim's army. Not only would the ambush be ruined, but the entire contingent would be in grave danger.

Bram held his breath as the scouts marched onward. When he thought they must be nearly on top of Mercadior's army, they descended into a nearly imperceptible dip in the ground. In the blink of an eye, more than half tumbled to the ground. They were pierced by bolts fired from the powerful, heavy crossbows of Hillhome's dwarves who were concealed in the tall grass. Within moments, the survivors were overwhelmed by other dwarves who sprang up as if from beneath the ground. Bram could scarcely believe how quickly and silently the dwarves had accomplished their task. Someone—perhaps Mercadior—had foreseen the need to guard against such an advance element.

By now the forward element of the main body was entering the Pass. Confident that their scouts would alert them to any danger, these marchers were oblivious to their surroundings. They walked in an extended mob. Many carried their spears and halberds thrown over their shoulders, others gripped them just below the heads and dragged the tail ends of the poles along the ground. Some wore armor, but many did not.

Besides men hoisting weapons, there were countless wagons, carts, horses, donkeys, fancy carriages, even women and children marching along with the mass.

Bram scanned the field for any sign of Lyim. He had hoped the potentate would be easy to spot. Perhaps Lyim is riding in one of the closed carriages, Bram thought. Was Kirah with him? Or had she stayed behind in Qindaras?

His thoughts were cut short by the sound of a boulder tearing loose from the side of the mountain and tumbling earthward. The attack had begun. The air was filled with the clamor of cracking rock. Hundreds of Hylar threw their weight against the great levers wedged beneath key stones on the side of the Pass. The cracking turned to rumbling, and then to a tremendous roar. Stones of every size, from fist-sized rocks to boulders as big as houses, tumbled and smashed down the slope. The mountainside that had been silent and peaceful moments ago was now transformed into a churning torrent of stones, trees, and earth. Bram could feel the mountain shuddering beneath his feet.

Below him, the Hylar had already cast aside their levers and grabbed up their weapons: the massive axes, hammers, maces, picks, and heavy swords favored by their race. Like the dwarves themselves, many of the weapons were centuries old. But Bram knew that even those blades predating the Cataclysm were keen as razors and as solid as these mountains.

Bellowing their battle-cry of "Thorbardin!" the Hylar rushed down the mountainside, now scoured clean and covered only with soft dirt. On the plain below, the huge mass of boulders and earth was still surging forward under its tremendous momentum. The mob of people in the Pass was collapsing in on itself. Those on the flanks of the army of Qindaras ran in panic toward the center, directly away from the avalanche. The army of Qindaras was being pinched in the middle, resembling an enormous hourglass laid on its side.

But as the rock slide petered out, a second wave of terror burst out from the swirling dust to crash into the compacted mass of Qindarans. This new force of dwarves rushed across the churned and broken ground as easily as if it were a drill field. Bram could almost feel the crunch as the forward edge of that onrushing pack crashed into the clustered and dazed enemy.

The deep, rumbling war cry of the dwarves mingled with the screams of dying humans and the shouts of men. The incessant clash of steel ringing against steel rose above it all. From Bram's position above the fight, there were no distinct sounds. There was only a constant roar, like a waterfall of steel. He could see that the dwarves from both sides of the Pass were easily cutting their way through the panicked ranks of Lyim's militia. They seemed impeded as much by the fallen bodies, laid out like trampled rye, as by the armed resistance of their foes. It would be very short work for the two prongs of dwarves to link in the middle. Then, all they had to do was maintain their positions, until Lyim's army fell.

Away from the paralyzing press of bodies at the waist of the Pass, Lyim's officers were already sorting out their troops and organizing the inevitable counter-attacks. Mercadior's plan was working beautifully. The humans seemed unconcerned about the possibility of a threat from any other direction.

Bram looked for some sign of Lyim Rhistadt or the deadly extraplanar creatures the Council of Three's spies had reported. He saw neither, but was reassured by the dark, brooding sky that had answered his summons.

Mercadior struck. His cavaliers emerged from beyond the Pass in three long, unbroken lines. They formed ribbons of color, each cavalier in his family crest, each horse draped in the same hues. Their lances pointed skyward with pennants fluttering.

Flanking them on foot were the dwarves of Hill-home. Next to the Ergothian cavaliers, they looked drab in their simple, earthy tones. But they advanced with their powerful crossbows cocked and loaded, and there was no questioning their deadly intent.

The cavaliers and dwarves advanced forty paces as a body, then stopped. By now, the Qindaran forces had noticed them and were running in great alarm back into the mass of people in the Pass. Ranking enemy soldiers struggled to form whatever spearmen they could find into a hasty line to oppose the horsemen. They shoved and kicked and even threatened with their swords to stop their soldiers from fleeing in panic and to form them into close ranks. Only a solid, unwavering wall of spear points had any chance to withstand the coming armored charge. Bram watched anxiously, thinking that if Mercadior did not order the charge soon, the opportunity might be lost.

The dwarves raised their crossbows and fired. Bram judged the distance to be no more than one hundred twenty paces. The dwarves could hardly miss such a massive body of targets at that range. Bram twitched as the front rank of humans collapsed backward like a swath of wheat cut off at the base by a scythe. The second rank of dwarves stepped through the first and fired another volley, with the same effect.

Fear rippled visibly through the throng of Qindarans. Wounded and dying spearmen toppled back into the men behind them, tangling their weapons and clutching at comrades for help. Gaps opened in the thin line. Men were looking over their shoulders while officers screamed at them to stand their ground.

The dwarves dropped their crossbows and unslung their heavy hand weapons. Mercadior, in the middle of the front rank of cavaliers, was easily identifiable by the imperial crest on his tunic. At a wave of his lance, the lines of chargers began trotting forward. Lance tips lowered. Then the mighty horses were charging ahead, clods of earth churning beneath their hooves and dust rising in their wake.

Rather than face that onslaught, the Qindarans

dropped their spears and fled. The undisciplined citizens of Qindaras, eager enough to butcher a huddled group of village militia on the plains, were not prepared to stand firm before a thundering line of armored horsemen. Men who might have survived even in small groups by turning aside the onrushing enemy instead turned their backs and tried to escape. But there was nowhere to go in the compacted mass west of the Pass, no way to outrun a horse, no place to hide.

The cavaliers crashed into the panicking humans without slowing down. They stabbed with lances, slashed with swords, smashed with maces; every stroke felled an enemy. The vicious war-horses kicked and trampled. Wherever the horsemen plunged in, Lyim's army melted away. Where the horsemen passed over, the ground was carpeted with bodies and stained red.

A few Qindaran soldiers tried to break past the cavaliers and flee westward or climb up the flanking slopes. These the hill dwarves either shot down with crossbows or cornered and offered a choice: surrender or die.

Still, Lyim did not appear.

Watching the battle unfold from high above, Bram could scarcely believe that all was going so well. The badly outnumbered dwarves and cavaliers were slaughtering their enemies. The humans west of the Pass were all but defenseless. Only those to the east, where a concerted counterattack was mounting against Hothjor's dwarves, seemed capable of resisting.

But Bram did not feel the thrill of victory. He was too aware that the primary reason for fighting this battle in the first place had been to kill Lyim. Even if the army of Qindaras was completely destroyed, little would be gained if Lyim escaped with the gauntlet. Bram continually scanned the plain east of the Pass, looking for any sign of the former mage.

An odd noise from the western end of the battlefield grabbed Bram's attention. A piercing shriek, high-pitched and dissonant, cut through the din and seemed to scrape the nerves inside Bram's ears. His heart skipped when he looked back to the west. Dark shapes raced on leathery wings through the sky. There appeared to be several dozen of them flying in a loose mass. Each was much larger than a man. Their limbs were gaunt and skeletal, ending in oversize hands and feet equipped with long, sharp claws. Even at a distance, he could see enormous tusks protruding from their dark mouths. Their eyes burned like embers.

Bram had heard of the terrifying, enormous creatures under Lyim's command. But preliminary reports said nothing about their flying. That one, crucial fact could change the face of the battle, or at least the viability of Hothjor's plan.

Dwarves scrambled for their crossbows almost too late as, in twos and threes, the otherworldly creatures wheeled and dived toward Mercadior's cavaliers. Filthy, snaggled claws raked the unprepared warriors. Armor, helmets, heads, and limbs were torn away by unearthly talons. Horses with their faces slashed, blinded by blood and terror, stumbled and crashed to the ground. The monsters' shrieks of bloodlust rose above the din of the battle.

Bram could tell by the sounds that the tide of battle was turning, that these flying beasts from outside Krynn were slaughtering his friends and allies as easily as the cavaliers and dwarves had earlier slaughtered the Qindarans.

The surprise appearance of the flying monsters made Bram doubly glad he had summoned the storm clouds before the battle began. Now he removed a pinch of dust from his robe and sprinkled it into his left palm. Raising the open hand, he blew the dust away, then swept the head of his staff through the tiny cloud. The dust scattered, but swirled back together, then spiraled upward in a tiny whirlwind. As it rose, the wind around Bram increased. The wind spread down the mountainside, picking up momentum as it descended, until it was whipping up dust and twigs with considerable force. Soon it would sweep across the entire Pass, and eventually grow to such power that nothing would be able to fly in it.

As the wind intensified, the creatures strafed Bram's position on the mountainside. He knew they could not see him, since he was magically concealed. Still, his heart skipped a beat when their nearness revealed the man whose greed and ambition had brought this disaster about. Crouching low across the back of one of the enormous, gargoylelike flying creatures was Lyim Rhistadt. Dagamier was right—Lyim's right hand had been magically restored, the gleaming gauntlet evident as he held to his creature's hideous neck. Bram could well make out the feral gleam in the potentate's eyes.

Before Bram could fashion a spell, Lyim's mount banked abruptly away, fighting against the wind. The spellcaster spotted something that he had been both afraid and hopeful to see. Kirah rode behind Lyim, her armored arms wrapped tightly around his waist. Fear and excitement mingled in the eyes he knew so well. Bram couldn't tell if his wayward aunt was captive or captivated by the force of Lyim's personality. Either way, he couldn't let her presence change his plan of action, or the hoped-for outcome.

Kneeling in the soft earth left behind by the avalanche, Bram clutched his staff in one hand. With the fingers of his other hand he dug into the ground and squeezed together a lump of soil. Head bowed, Bram hastened the elemental spell, chanting over and over the mantra his mother had taught him, all the while tracing patterns in the dirt with his fingers. New patterns were scratched over the old ones, glowing briefly, only to be replaced by yet another tracing. Soon Bram was surrounded by the complex sigils. They completely covered the ground from the hem of his brown robe to as far as his arms could stretch. They began shifting by themselves behind his tracing finger, flowing together into even more complex patterns and interwoven knots.

Slowly the slope below Bram swelled, then pushed upward in a slight hump. Cracks appeared around the mound. Again it heaved upward, then again, when suddenly the ground burst up in a spray of dirt and rocks. Part rock, part dirt and clay, the pile towered above the lord to twice his height.

At Bram's final order, the earth elemental's sunken, stony eyes opened and stared at him. Bram had only to speak his command, and the elemental set about carrying it out. Like a wave it rolled down the mountainside, absorbing whatever lay in its path and leaving a rippling earth wake behind. The elemental plowed straight through to where the cavaliers fought a valiant battle against the winged fiends. Aware now of the threat, the mounted warriors defended themselves bravely with sword and shield. The dwarves with their crossbows kept up a steady fire, although the usually lethal bolts had little effect against these monsters. All the while, the fiends hovered and swooped just out of reach, occasionally diving to rake at a cavalier or dwarf.

The elemental planted itself in the midst of the cavaliers. As one of the flying creatures swooped low to claw at the mound of earth, the elemental flung an enormous earthen limb upward. Lyim's creature smashed into the elemental, then was enveloped by it. It was obvious that the winged creature thrashed and tore at the suffocating mound, but it could not break free from its prison. The struggling stopped abruptly and the great paw opened, dumping out the fiend's limp corpse.

When two more of Lyim's winged monstrosities ventured too close to Bram's elemental and were mashed to pulp, the rest withdrew to higher altitude, circling and considering carefully this new opponent. Remaining in flight was an effort for them now, as Bram's wind buffeted them harshly.

Bram's gaze, however, was locked on Lyim, clinging with Kirah to the back of his flying fiend. The potentate was shouting commands to the creatures, who seemed to be forming for a renewed attack. Lyim looked flushed with victory. The appearance of the monsters had altered the course of the battle enormously. Now that the cavaliers were reduced to defending themselves against attacks from the air and the Neidar bolts were being fired skyward, the human army on the ground was renewing its attacks vigorously. A wedge had been driven through the Hylar in the center; not yet large enough for reinforcements to move through, but it would continue to widen unless the cavaliers returned to the battle.

The wind and the storm had at last reached their peak. Bram scrambled atop a boulder that had survived the avalanche. There he gripped his staff with both hands and thrust it skyward as if trying to pierce the clouds. When he snapped the rod suddenly downward, a bolt of lightning arced from the churning storm to transfix one of the flying creatures. A scream pierced the air, rising above the clash of the battle and the rush of wind. The monster crumpled and plummeted toward the ground, limp and smoking.

Bram steadied himself on the boulder. The wind threatened to blow him to the ground just as surely as it grasped at the flyers. Standing firmly, he extended his staff and prepared to draw forth another lightning bolt.

Overhead, Lyim turned his flying monster away from the battle. Before Bram could strike a second time, one after another the creatures wheeled and flew from the field. Within moments they were nothing but specks disappearing against the churning, blue-black sky.

Stunned combatants on both sides seemed to pause as all eyes watched the monsters depart. Could they be retreating to regroup and attack anew? A cry arose from the Hylar, who were taking full advantage of the distraction to pinch off the waist of the battlefield once again. Shouting Mercadior's name, the cavaliers charged anew into the churning mass of Qindarans. The invaders appeared dispirited by the flight of their champions. For the first time since the fight began, whole groups were tearing themselves away from the army and fleeing back toward the east. Many of those trapped west of the Pass, facing the combined onslaught of Mercadior's cavaliers and Bram's elemental, laid down their weapons and begged for quarter.

Above the battle, Bram shook his head. How could Lyim have turned what looked like disaster into victory, and then so abruptly abandoned the field, consigning his army to complete destruction? All blackguards were cowards on some level, but was Lyim so fainthearted as to flee during victory?

Bram watched the last of the flying creatures disappear into the western sky, and suddenly knew the answer. His heart turned cold.

The score of monsters were flying at top speed for an unsuspecting Wayreth.

Chapter Nineteen

Fanned by the news of Salimshad's death, the fire that had long burned inside Lyim grew with each league that he drew closer to the great Tower of High Sorcery at Wayreth. The ultimate target of his obsession was nearly in his grasp. The loss of his Qindaras stronghold had forced him to take bold action that was about to pay off.

Damn Salimshad for his carelessness! Lyim thought to himself. The elf's ignominious demise was the only thing marring an otherwise perfect campaign.

Despite Salim's annoying death, events north of Thorbardin had played into Lyim's hands. He had anticipated the Council would launch a preemptive attack during the weeks that his army marched; it was just a question of where. He was not surprised to find Guerrand's nephew on the battlefield in the Pass, since Bram was the only spellcaster on Ansalon with the potential to thwart him. In fact, Lyim had counted on his being there because it meant the spellcaster would not be waiting at the Tower of High Sorcery.

The moment Lyim recognized Bram's handiwork in the form of the earth elemental, he knew it was time to abandon his army to whatever fate awaited it. He wouldn't need that ragtag bunch for what lay ahead, but he did need Bram out of his way. Lyim was confident his nabassu could slash through whatever fortifications the mages at Wayreth had fashioned. Without Bram's magic to offset the creatures' supernatural powers, no soldiers would withstand their terrifying onslaught.

Now Bram was more than thirty leagues away, mopping up the remains of Lyim's discarded army. On the back of a flying nabassu with Kirah behind him, Lyim had the Towers of Wayreth in his sight.

In normal times, as the Council was proud of saying, Wayreth "could be found only by those invited to seek it." Ancient enchantments necessitated by the persecution of wizards just prior to the Cataclysm hid the site from all eyes. Lyim knew that those enchantments drew from the magical fabric as did all wizard spells, and thus would be weakened as Ventyr drew closer to the tower.

The end is near, Aniirin.

Lyim was mildly surprised to hear Ventyr's voice in his head. The gauntlet rarely communicated anymore, unless Lyim opened the discussion. *Soon we will return home in triumph*, he responded.

Return home to what? Ventyr asked. *The palace is destroyed and the citizens are dead. Qindaras is no more.*

Lyim found this exchange with Ventyr mildly annoying. It had never been so negative before. *We'll rebuild, Ventyr. Just do what you're supposed to do here, and you'll have all the power you need to restore the palace.*

With a wave of his hand, Lyim directed the nabassu's attention to the two black edifices rising from an opening in the canopy of the great Forest of Wayreth. They dived, and the fire in Lyim burned ever hotter.

As they approached, Lyim could see the Council was obviously expecting the towers to be attacked. Nearby trees had been cleared away to deny an attacking force protective cover. A wide ditch had been dug outside the triangular wall encircling the towers, and the excavated earth used to construct a rampart behind the ditch. The felled trees were embedded in the rampart and in front of the ditch like giant spikes to impede charges.

Elves armed with bows stood guard on the rampart. They looked up in response to the screeches of the diving nabassu, and with only moments to react, most dived for cover. Some of the more valiant defended themselves with spears and arrows; they died where they stood.

Lyim circled the tower once, staying above the fight. He had seen something in the rear courtyard that caught his interest. As his nabassu came round again to the back of the towers, he saw it once more: a group of mages, gathered in the open and looking desperately toward the sounds of slaughter that came from outside the rampart beyond their wall.

Lyim pulled away the cloth he had wrapped around his face to protect himself against the cold blast of wind during the flight. He leaned back to speak to Kirah. "We're going down." A brief command to the nabassu turned the creature downward. Lyim and Kirah flattened themselves across the monster's back just moments before it touched ground and skidded on its taloned feet across the smoothly paved courtyard.

A group of more than a dozen mages, who had been desperately working to transport the many valuable magical tomes in the towers to a vault beneath a guard tower, tumbled across the flagstones toward the blockhouse. Lyim laughed at the sight of these men and women, once the most powerful wizards in the world, fleeing in terror at his arrival. One unfortunate mage in a white robe was pinned beneath the ghastly foot of the nabassu. The monster split the mage open with a single swipe of its razor-sharp claw. The armload of scrolls slowly turned red as the pooling blood soaked into them.

Lyim jumped to the flagstones from the monster's

back as it turned to pursue the other wizards and trap them against the wall. The creature stopped when a woman in black robes stepped purposefully before the group. Lyim peered at her, amused by her futile bravery. Then he recognized her as Dagamier—she had been one of the defenders of Bastion years before when Lyim had sought to use that fortress to gain access to the Lost Citadel. He thought she had died after being pierced through the midsection by a naga's tail spike.

"You failed to stop me once before, Dagamier. Do you think you can succeed now, without your precious magic to aid you?" Lyim taunted. But the woman, apparently unfazed, strode forward, all the while appearing to be casting a spell. Lyim calmly extended the gauntlet before him to trap whatever energy she could muster.

Suddenly the woman lunged, striking Lyim's forearm with a concealed dagger. Pain burst in his arm, searing and hideous like Guerrand's sword cut. Lyim stumbled backward and saw that his sleeve was soaked with blood. She hadn't been casting a spell at all, but simply trying to distract him until she got close enough to use her knife.

"Get her!" Lyim bellowed. The nabassu sprang, faster than any human could react. Curved and dripping teeth sank into Dagamier's shoulder. Kirah, still strapped to the fiend's back, cried aloud when the wizard's blood spattered against her arms and legs.

A clatter of hooves rang like dwarven hammers against the stones of the courtyard. Dagamier forgotten, Lyim's head jerked upward. Centaurs simply began appearing from thin air! The centaurs carried powerful bows in their hands and had long swords strapped across their backs.

Where did they come from? Lyim hissed to Ventyr.

They have opened a pathway from the faerie realm directly into the courtyard of the towers. I cannot see farther.

The centaurs immediately opened fire with their

long, painted arrows at the nabassu circling overhead and diving to attack. At Thorbardin the dwarves' crossbow bolts had bounced off the nabassu's thick, stony hide, but the biting arrows of the centaurs sank in. Nabassu shrieked with rage as the shafts pierced their wings and cut their flesh. Several tumbled to the ground thrashing wildly, too badly wounded to fly but too strong to die.

Lyim turned back to his nabassu mount, but it was already streaking skyward with Kirah on its back, escaping from the storm of lethal arrows. When one of the missiles narrowly missed Lyim, he knew it was time to leave the fight to the creatures from the Abyss.

Lyim tugged up the gauntlet, turned, and dashed toward the southernmost of the two towers. The path was clear for him to reach his goal.

* * * * *

Bram burst through the faerie road portal, directly into the courtyard at the front of the Tower of High Sorcery. Behind him came Mercadior and thirty of the emperor's most experienced cavaliers, now on foot, led by none other than King Weador himself.

The king had watched the battle outside Thorbardin, had witnessed Lyim's sudden departure. He, too, knew where the renegade was headed at flying speed. Concerned for the future of all magic, Weador had materialized in Thorbardin. Bram was already preparing to leave for the tower, and though the tuatha themselves could not fight, Weador offered to lead Mercadior and his human warriors through the faerie realm to surprise Lyim at Wayreth. Mercadior, glad for the opportunity to meet the object of his curiosity, had instantly agreed to continue his part in the battle.

Bram noted the cavaliers had a dazed look about them after their trip through the faerie realm, but they snapped back immediately when dumped in the midst of the fray. The warriors from Northern Ergoth raced across the courtyard and streamed up onto the sand-bagged scaffold erected around the tower's outer wall. There they joined the Qualinesti, who had formed into clusters of archers. Around each group was an outer ring of elves whose gleaming long swords slashed at any monsters that ventured too close.

Overhead, the hideous fiends circled and dived, uttering their horrid shrieks. Weador watched them for several moments, then turned to Bram. "I see now why the tide of battle almost turned against you at the Pass. Those are nabassu, voracious and evil fiends from the Abyss. They come to your world rarely, and then only to kill."

Another familiar voice startled Bram. "Once again, I am forced to save you, foolish human. This time I had to bring a hundred of my friends just to extricate you, but Habakkuk will surely reward me for my sacrifice."

Bram spun around and found himself facing a horseman. "Aurestes!" He was stunned, but glad to see the cantankerous centaur who had guided him to Primula's realm. Unfortunately, there was no time for pleasantries. "Tell me, how badly pressed are the defenders here?"

Aurestes pawed the ground. "The battle is new enough that there is more panic than real damage yet. I saw two mages in the rear courtyard, one slain, the other badly wounded."

"Who?" Bram demanded, then realized the centaur knew no one at Wayreth. "Can you describe them?"

The horseman's face scrunched in thought. "One wore a white robe."

Bram let out a sigh of relief.

"The other was a young woman, a brave Black Robe who stood up to the enemy leader. She wounded him with a dagger before his mount struck her down."

Bram's breath caught, became ragged. He couldn't think; he couldn't hope. He just knew. Only Dagamier would stand against Lyim, armed with only a knife. At least there was hope she was still alive.

Aurestes's urgent voice penetrated his stupor. "Bram! I fear I saw the man who was wounded by the mage enter the tower. I was pursuing when you arrived."

Bram's eyes snapped wide. "A bald man? Was he wearing an unusual gauntlet?"

Aurestes considered only briefly. "Yes, he was bald. I don't recall if there was a gauntlet or not; his arm was bloody from the woman's attack."

Without another word, Bram raced for the foretower. He bent to scoop up a fallen sword from a slain elf and tucked it through his belt. He paused inside momentarily and listened. Where would Lyim go? He didn't need to ponder long, for just then an eerie blue light shot through the doorway to the Hall of Mages. Squinting against the glare, he dashed into the chamber.

Despite the light, he had no trouble spotting Lyim atop the dais, where the empty seats of the Council of Three rose above the other eighteen.

Gauntlet held high, Lyim's whole body shook as if raw bolts of electricity coursed through it, sending sparks into the cold shadows at the edges of the circular room. He was facing toward Bram, but he saw nothing. His head was tipped backward and his back was arched sharply, almost as if he were held in the grip of some monstrous, invisible fist. Lyim no longer stood on the dais, but was somehow suspended a hand's-breadth above it, twisting slowly in the crackling, surging air. Lyim's garments whipped around him, though Bram could feel no breeze. And all the while, bright, purplish bolts of energy surged from the walls and the air into the bloodstained gauntlet on Lyim's right hand. The tower acted as a conduit to whatever magical energy remained in the world, funneling it directly to the man who would destroy it all.

Bram's fingers tightened about the staff that he carried always to power his spells. He felt like a straw through which the magic traveled, a pipeline for the effect he envisioned. Eyes closed, he swayed slightly when the energy suddenly surged, alerting him that he had marshaled enough to send the spell forth.

A familiar, startled cry robbed him of his concentration. Bram's eyes snapped open and locked with horror upon the too-thin form of his aunt bursting through the door. Oblivious to Bram's presence, Kirah launched herself at Lyim's charged form. A halo of energy seemed to form around her as she approached.

"Kirah, no!" Bram cried. "For the gods' sake, don't come between us again! I won't hesitate a second time!"

But either it was too late to stop her momentum, or Kirah didn't care to try. She stumbled forward like a wraith and reached out to her lover with arms held wide.

The power flowing into Lyim flooded through Kirah's arms, saturating her. Without the gauntlet to protect her, she was exposed to the energy's full force. A flash of light blinded Bram for an instant, then he saw Kirah tumbling backward across the hard floor. Lyim appeared unaware that anything had happened.

Holding his staff before him with renewed determination, Bram channeled the power of Chislev through it.

Lyim's body spasmed, as if struck a physical blow. But the potentate of Qindaras was oblivious to anything but whatever was happening inside his twisted mind. Bram concentrated on the elemental nature of wood, the strength of oak and vallenwood. In his mind, flesh and blood mingled with the essence of the tree's heart. Across the room, where vibrant light danced around Lyim's spread-eagled form, the mage's body was already changing. His legs were joined into a solid mass, rooted to the floor. Jittering bolts of light danced across Lyim's fingertips as his arms grew rigid, his flesh turned to bark, his clothing to leaves and vines.

Then the display of light stopped. The elaborate gauntlet of ivory, jade, and silver interlocking plates fell away from the tree like any ordinary glove to the cold, stone floor of the audience hall. Bram scarcely saw it land. He was on his way to Kirah's side.

She lay in a tangle against the wall. Her exposed flesh was blistered and bruised, her eyes swollen nearly shut. Bram lifted his aunt up onto his lap and cradled her pale head. "Just rest, Kirah, and I'll heal you," he said, trying to sound more soothing than desperate.

She shook her pale head weakly. "Don't."

"But you'll die!"

Kirah managed a weak smile. "I've been dead before, at least in my heart. I can't imagine the real thing is any worse."

"Don't go, Kirah," Bram pleaded. "I've lost too many people already."

Kirah looked faintly toward where Lyim stood as a tree. "I couldn't go back to the way things were after I've been with him."

"But Lyim's not dead!" Bram pleaded. "I've just contained him in the form of a tree, so he can stand trial before the Conclave for his crimes."

"They'll find him guilty and have him killed," she managed, though her voice was growing weaker by the word. "As they should."

Bram couldn't deny the truth of Lyim's probable fate. Still, he had to try. "It's not *your* time yet, Kirah. You can choose to stay!"

Kirah smiled, a faint trembling of the lips. "I made my choice long ago." With that, her eyes sank shut. Kirah's thin face took on the most peaceful countenance Bram had ever seen.

Studying Kirah's silent, pale face, he saw the little girl he'd grown up with, so near in age were they. He recalled when he had seen her close to death before, relived in a flash the anguished fight he and Guerrand had waged to save Kirah from the medusa plague. Lyim had tried to kill her then, but this time, when by all rights she should have been safe, Lyim had succeeded.

Just when he thought his grief would choke him, a gentle hand came down upon his shoulder. Bram's breath was coming in great, shuddering gasps, and his chest and shoulders ached from the strain. Startled, he spun around and saw Par-Salian.

"It's done, Bram," the white-haired wizard said softly. He stooped to retrieve the Gauntlet of Ventyr. Holding it up to the light of a torch, Par-Salian said, "So many lives lost because of an ornate glove." He sighed. "At least magic is safe again, thanks to your efforts."

"Perhaps magic is secure, but that's no comfort to me!"

Par-Salian regarded him gravely. "You've lost a great deal—"

"A great deal?" Bram repeated dully. "I feel like I've lost everything. First Guerrand, then Kirah!"

"Magic requires that level of commitment from those who practice it. Guerrand knew that and accepted it."

Bram frowned. "I begin to think he was the lucky one. I would rather he had taken me with him. That much I was willing to give."

Par-Salian pursed his lips. "Apparently the gods had more need of you on this plane. I would venture it's because they gave you more than most here and here," he suggested, gently tapping Bram's chest and temple.

Bram's anger was slowly slipping into numb acceptance. "But why Kirah? She had no commitment to magic."

"No, but your aunt had her own commitment to Lyim that had nothing to do with magic. Devotion to a cause or a person—" Par-Salian shrugged helplessly. "They're equally strong.

"By the way," he continued in a lighter tone, "Dagamier has been asking about you. We carried her to my study after she was wounded in the courtyard. Justarius is tending her."

Bram perked up visibly. "She'll live, then?"

Par-Salian gave a gentle smile. "LaDonna's convinced Dagamier's too stubborn to die."

"May I go to her?"

Someone cleared his throat behind Bram and the venerable mage. Turning, Bram spotted King Weador. "Mercadior sent me in to discover the cause for the nabassu's hasty departure. They just fled to the four winds, abruptly and without explanation, almost as if chased." Weador glanced from Lyim's tree form to the gleaming gauntlet in Par-Salian's hand and nodded somberly. "I thought I detected a difference in the magical fabric."

"They're gone?" Bram repeated dully, but he already understood why the nabassu had fled. Lyim had brought the creatures from the Abyss; his death had released them from their servitude. It had delivered them all.

Bram sighed and looked up at Par-Salian. "It really *is* over, isn't it? We're finally free of Lyim Rhistadt."

The head of the Orders of Magic saw the spark of hope in Bram's aching heart and smiled his agreement. "We're free of his threat, Bram." Par-Salian looked admiringly at the twisted trunk that looked so incongruous in the charred council chamber. "We still must deal with the man, but that will come in due time.

"For now, Justarius and LaDonna are already organizing the tower's return to normal. Spellbooks and equipment are being brought out of hiding and placed back into the libraries and laboratories even as we speak. Before they join us, Bram, I would speak to you about something that has occupied my mind since your return from Qindaras."

The white-robe's tone concerned Bram anew. "What is it, Par-Salian? Is something else wrong?"

"No, Bram. I was wondering, however, if you've given thought to what you would do next."

Bram blinked. "I haven't had much time to consider, but I suppose I'll return to Thonvil after I see Dagamier. Why?"

"You have defended magic as if you were one of Bastion's guardians. I believe it was Dagamier who pointed out you were, in effect, its seventh sentinel." The venerable mage seemed almost to blush. "Would you consider making your bond to the Orders in word as well by accepting a magical apprenticeship?"

Bram started even further. "With you?"

"I have not taken a student in many decades," Par-Salian confessed, "but I have not seen one with such aptitude, not even Guerrand. Magic is, quite literally, in your blood. I observed you with Dagamier these last weeks. You would be ready for the Test in record time, I'm sure. The Orders could use such a mage as you would become, one who had command of both wizard and tuatha magic."

Though stunned, Bram was certainly flattered. And interested. But not just yet. He told Par-Salian so. "First, I must bury my aunt."

Par-Salian's white head bowed respectfully. "Of course. There are many dead to bury and wounded to tend." Turning to the Lyim-tree, the master wizard swept his hand across the scene, then balled it into a fist. The tree with its many tendrils and sagging branches shimmered slightly, then faded from view, gone to a place of safekeeping that only Par-Salian knew.

He glanced at his hand briefly, then turned back to Bram. "That felt good again, after so long. Thank you."

Turning away, the master of the White Order strode toward the door leading to the foretower. "As for that other matter, you know where to find me when you're ready, Bram. Wayreth will always be open to you."

"Thank you," Bram said with true warmth. "If there's nothing else the Council requires of me, I'll make preparations to transport Kirah back to Thonvil. I'd like the therapy of traveling overland, but I'm afraid I couldn't manage that alone. I'll have to take her on the faerie road."

"Gods' speed," said the mage, holding a blue-veined hand up in farewell.

Bram looked at Kirah. He felt more at peace with her peace now.

"Take your journey of healing, and let us bring your aunt back on the faerie road for you," Weador offered at Bram's shoulder, so softly the young man was not startled, though he'd forgotten the king of the tuatha was still present. "You know she will be as safe with Thistledown and the others as if she were in the hands of Chislev himself."

Bram was touched by the offer. "You've done so much to help already, King Weador."

The tuatha smiled wryly. "Remember, we tuatha thrive on the positive energy of humans. Even half-humans." He turned abruptly serious. "I would see you study with Par-Salian, Bram. I believe it is your destiny."

The king rightly interpreted Bram's pensive silence as approval. Despite his royal status and his diminutive stature, Weador gathered Kirah's slight form up in his arms with the tenderness of a father. With an encouraging nod, the king of the tuatha and his silent charge disappeared from view.

Seeing Dagamier would be a tonic for his mood. Bram retrieved his beloved staff as he left the Hall of Mages. Through the door of the foretower, he could see that mages were already busy magically removing the bodies, the defensive spikes, and filling in the trenches. Work that had taken weeks to do by hand would be magically undone in less than a day. Mercadior and his cavaliers, Aurestes and his centaurs appeared to have already gone, unlikely ever to return. Bram would have liked to say thanks, or at least good-bye . . .

Bram knew that when *he* stepped from the tower after seeing Dagamier, he would not be saying good-bye. Spring on the moors of Northern Ergoth would heal his spirit. Time would heal his heart.

And then he would return and let magic fill his soul.

DRAGONS
OF
SUMMER FLAME

An Excerpt

**by Margaret Weis
and Tracy Hickman**

Chapter One

Be Warned . . .

It was hot that morning, damnably hot.

Far too hot for late spring on Ansalon. Almost as hot as midsummer. The two knights in the boat's stern were sweaty and miserable in their heavy steel armor; they looked with envy at the nearly naked men plying the boat's oars. When the boat neared shore, the knights were first out, jumping into the shallow water, laving the water onto their reddening faces and sunburned necks. But the water was not particularly refreshing.

"Like wading in hot soup," one of the knights grumbled, splashing ashore. Even as he spoke, he scrutinized the shoreline carefully, eyeing bush and tree and dune for signs of life.

"More like blood," said his comrade. "Think of it as wading in the blood of our enemies, the enemies of our Queen. Do you see anything?"

"No," the other replied. He waved his hand without looking back, heard the sound of men leaping into the water, their harsh laughter and conversation in their uncouth, guttural language.

One of the knights turned around. "Bring that boat to shore," he said, unnecessarily, for the men had already picked up the heavy boat and were running with it through the shallow water. Grinning, they dumped the boat on the sand beach and looked to the knight for further orders.

He mopped his forehead, marveled at their strength, and—not for the first time—thanked Queen Takhisis that these barbarians were on their side. The brutes, they were known as. Not the true name of their race. The name, their name for themselves, was unpronounceable, so the knights had begun calling them by the shortened version: brute.

The name suited the barbarians well. They came from the east, from a continent few people on Ansalon knew existed. All the men stood well over six feet, some over seven. Their bodies were as bulky and muscular as humans, their movements as swift and graceful as elves. Their ears were pointed like those of the elves, but their faces were heavily bearded like humans or dwarves. They were as strong as dwarves and loved battle just as well. They fought fiercely, were loyal to those who commanded them, and, outside of a few grotesque customs such as cutting off various parts of the body of a dead enemy to keep as trophies, the brutes were ideal foot soldiers.

"Let the captain know we've arrived safely and that we've encountered no resistance," said the knight to his comrade. "We'll leave a few men here with the boat and move inland."

The other knight nodded. Taking a red silk pennant from his belt, he unfurled it, held it above his head, and waved it slowly three times. An answering flutter of red came from the enormous black, dragon-prowed ship anchored some distance away. This was a scouting mission, not an invasion. Orders had been quite clear on that point.

The knights sent out their patrols, dispatching some to range up and down the beach, sending others farther inland. This done, the two knights moved thankfully to the meager shadow cast by a squat and misshapen tree. Two of the brutes stood guard. The knights remained wary and watchful, even as they rested. Seating themselves, they drank sparingly of the fresh water they'd brought with them. One of them grimaced.

"The damn stuff's hot."

"You left the waterskin sitting in the sun. Of course it's hot."

"Where the devil was I supposed to put it? There was no shade on that cursed boat. I don't think there's any shade left in the whole blasted world. I don't like this place at all. I get a queer feeling about this island, like it's magicked or something."

"I know what you mean," agreed his comrade somberly. He kept glancing about, back into the trees, up and down the beach. All that could be seen were the brutes, and they certainly weren't bothered by any ominous feelings. But then they were barbarians. "We were warned not to come here, you know."

"What?" The other knight looked astonished. "I didn't know. Who told you that?"

"Brightblade. He had it from Lord Ariakan himself."

"Brightblade should know. He's on Ariakan's staff. The lord's his sponsor." The knight appeared nervous and asked softly, "Such information's not secret, is it?"

The other knight appeared amused. "You don't know Steel Brightblade very well if you think he would break any oath or pass along any information he was told to keep to himself. He'd sooner let his tongue be ripped out by red-hot tongs. No, Lord Ariakan discussed this openly with all the regimental commanders before deciding to proceed."

The knight shrugged. Picking up a handful of small rocks, he began tossing them idly into the water. "The Gray Robes started it all. Some sort of augury revealed the location of this island and that it was inhabited by large numbers of people."

"So who warned us not to come?"

"The Gray Robes. The same augury that told them of this island also warned them not to come near it. They tried to persuade Ariakan to leave well enough alone. Said that this place could mean disaster."

The other knight frowned, then glanced around with growing unease. "Then why were we sent?"

"The upcoming invasion of Ansalon. Lord Ariakan felt this move was necessary to protect his flanks. The Gray Robes couldn't say exactly what sort of threat this island represented. Nor could they say specifically that the disaster would be caused by our landing on the island. As Lord Ariakan pointed out, perhaps disaster would come even if we didn't do anything. And so he decided to follow the old dwarven dictum, 'It is better to go looking for the dragon than have the dragon come looking for you.' "

"Good thinking," his companion agreed. "If there is an army of elves on this island, it's better that we deal with them now. Not that it seems likely."

He gestured at the wide stretches of sand beach, at the dunes covered with some sort of grayish-green grass, and, farther inland, a forest of the ugly, misshapen trees. "Elves wouldn't live in a place like this."

"Neither would dwarves. Minotaurs would have attacked us by now. Kender would have walked off with the boat *and* our armor. Gnomes would have met us with some sort of fiend-driven fish-catching machine. Humans like us are the only race foolish enough to live in such a wretched place," the knight concluded cheerfully. He picked up another handful of rocks.

"It could be a rogue band of draconians or hobgoblins. Ogres even. Escaped twenty-some years ago, after the War of the Lance. Fled north, across the sea, to avoid capture by the Solamnic Knights."

"Yes, but they'd be on our side," his companion answered. "And our wizards wouldn't have their robes in a knot over it. . . . Ah, here come our scouts, back to report. Now we'll find out."

The knights rose to their feet. The brutes who had been sent into the island's interior hurried forward to meet their leaders. The barbarians were grinning hugely. Their nearly naked bodies glistened with sweat. The blue paint with which they covered themselves, and which was supposed to possess some sort of magical properties said to cause arrows to bounce right off them, ran down their muscular bodies in rivulets. Long scalp locks, decorated with colorful feathers, bounced on their backs as they loped easily over the sand dunes.

The two knights exchanged glances, relaxed.

"What did you find?" the knight asked the leader, a gigantic red-haired fellow who towered over both knights and could have probably picked up each of them and held them over his head. He regarded both knights with unbounded reverence and respect.

"Men," answered the brute. They were quick to learn and had adapted easily to Common, spoken by most of the various races of Krynn. Unfortunately, to the brutes, all people not of their race were known as "men."

The brute lowered his hand near the ground to indicate small men, which might mean dwarves but was more probably children. He moved it to waist height, which most likely indicated women. This the brute confirmed by cupping two hands over his own breast and wiggling his hips. His own men laughed and nudged each other.

"Men, women, and children," said the knight. "Many men? Lots of men? Big buildings? Walls? Cities?"

The brutes apparently thought this was hilarious, for they all burst into raucous laughter.

"What did you find?" said the knight sharply, scowling. "Stop the nonsense."

The brutes sobered rapidly.

"Many men," said the leader, "but no walls. Houses." He made a face, shrugged, shook his head, and added something in his own language."

"What does that mean?" asked the knight of his comrade.

"Something to do with dogs," said the other, who had led brutes before and learned some of their language. "I think he means these men live in houses only dogs would live in."

Several of the brutes now began walking about stoop-shouldered, swinging their arms around their knees and grunting. Then they all straightened up, looked at each other, and laughed again.

"What in the name of our Dark Majesty are they doing now?" the knight demanded.

"Beats me," said his comrade. "I think we should go have a look for ourselves." He drew his sword partway out of its black leather scabbard. "Danger?" he asked the brute. "We need steel?"

The brute laughed again. Taking his own short sword—the brutes fought with two, long and short, as well as bow and arrows—he thrust it into the tree and turned his back on it.

The knight, reassured, returned his sword to its scabbard. The two followed their guides deeper into the forest.

They did not go far before they came to the village. They entered a cleared area among the trees.

Despite the antics of the brutes, the knights were completely unprepared for what they saw.

"By Hiddukel," one said in a low voice to the other. " 'Men' is too strong a term. *Are* these men? Or are they beasts?"

"They're men," said the other, staring around slowly, amazed. "But such men as we're told walked Krynn during the Age of Twilight. Look! Their tools are made of wood. They carry wooden spears, and crude ones at that."

"Wooden-tipped, not stone," said the other. "Mud huts for houses. Clay cooking pots. Not a piece of steel or iron in sight. What a pitiable lot! I can't see how they could be much danger, unless it's from filth. By the smell, they haven't bathed since the Age of Twilight either."

"Ugly bunch. More like apes than men. Don't laugh. Look stern and threatening."

Several of the male humans—if human they were; it was difficult to tell beneath the animal hides they wore—crept up to the knights. The "man-beasts" walked bent over, their arms swinging at their sides, knuckles almost dragging on the ground. Their heads were covered with long, shaggy hair; unkempt beards almost completely hid their faces. They bobbed and shuffled and gazed at the knights in openmouthed awe. One of the man-beasts actually drew near enough to reach out a grimy hand to touch the black, shining armor.

A brute moved to interpose his own massive body in front of the knight.

The knight waved the brute off and drew his sword. The steel flashed in the sunlight. Turning to one of the trees, which, with their twisted limbs and gnarled trunks, resembled the people who lived beneath them, the knight raised his sword and sliced off a limb with one swift stroke.

The man-beast dropped to his knees and groveled in the dirt, making piteous blubbering sounds.

"I think I'm going to vomit," said the knight to his comrade. "Gully dwarves wouldn't associate with this lot."

"You're right there." The knight looked around. "Between us, you and I could wipe out the entire tribe."

"We'd never be able to clean the stench off our swords," said the other.

"What should we do? Kill them?"

"Small honor in it. These wretches obviously aren't any threat to us. Our orders were to find out who or what was inhabiting the island, then return. For all we know, these people may be the favorites of some god, who might be angered if we harmed them. Perhaps that is what the Gray Robes meant by disaster."

"I don't know," said the other knight dubiously. "I can't imagine any god treating his favorites like this."

"Morgion, perhaps," said the other with a wry grin.

The knight grunted. "Well, we've certainly done no harm just by looking. The Gray Robes can't fault us for that. Send out the brutes to scout the rest of the island. According to the reports from the dragons, it's not very big. Let's go back to the shore. I need some fresh air."

The two knights sat in the shade of the tree, talking of the upcoming invasion of Ansalon, discussing the vast armada of black dragon-prowed ships, manned by minotaurs, that was speeding its way across the Courrain Ocean, bearing thousands and thousands more barbarian warriors. All was nearly ready for the invasion, which would take place on Summer's Eve.

The knights of Takhisis did not know precisely where they were attacking; such information was kept secret. But they had no doubt of victory. This time the Dark Queen would succeed. This time her armies would be victorious. This time she knew the secret to victory.

The brutes returned within a few hours and made their report. The isle was not large. They had found no other people. The tribe of man-beasts had all slunk off fearfully and were hiding, cowering in their mud huts until the strange beings left.

The knights returned to their shore boat. The brutes pushed it off the sand, leaped in, and grabbed the oars. The boat skimmed across the surface of the water, heading for the black ship that flew the multicolored flag of the five-headed dragon.

They left behind an empty, deserted beach. Or so it appeared.

But their leaving was noted, as their coming had been.